WHEN THE MUSIC FADES TO MURDER

THE SINGER MUST DIE

WHEN THE MUSIC FADES TO MURDER

THE SINGER MUST DIE

By

Brent Kroetch

www.penmorepress.com

WHEN THE MUSIC FADES

When the Music Fades to Murder The Singer Must Die
By Brent Kroetch
Copyright © 2016 Brent Kroetch

ISBN-13: 978-1-942756-76-7(Paperback)
ISBN :-978-1-942756-77-4(e-book)

BISAC Subject Headings:
FIC008000 Fiction / General
FIC031010 Fiction/ Thrillers / Crime
FIC022000 Fiction / Mystery & Detective / General

Edited by C Wozny
Cover Illustration by Christine Horner

Address all correspondence to:

Penmore Press LLC
920 N Javelina Pl
Tucson AZ 85748

BRENT KROETCH

Dedication

For Ann Rogers and Cooper Dale Bolden
With Love

Table of Contents

CHAPTER ONE

ONE BAD MORNING

Kyle "Ham" McCalister muttered every profanity he'd ever heard, from way back in the dim past to the newer and bluer ones acquired courtesy of those grizzled detectives so adept at colorful cop speak. Then, and just for the sake of originality, he spat a few more that he dreamt up on the spot. The fact that none made a mite's speck of sense mattered not a whit. It was a pride thing.

And a sanity thing. For nearly half an hour he'd navigated what should have been a five-minute stretch of The Strip, burning, both figuratively and literally, through the traffic, heat and humanity of downtown Las Vegas. The traffic, bumper to bumper and temper to temper, absorbed his curses indifferently. The masses seemed to be poking a stiff, deliberate, obscene finger to his eye while they crawled and stalled along at their whim, and no amount of cursing modified that whim in any way, shape or form.

And what worsened his mood over and above the miserable traffic was the fact that his partner had ditched him. Drew Thornton, damn her hide, was here, somewhere in the city, yet she'd managed to go MIA. That both exasperated and concerned him, for the one agreement he and Drew had, the only absolute of their new firm,

McCalister and Thornton, mandated they be available to one another, always and without delay. Night, day, weekends, whatever. Never out of touch. Now Drew had broken that implacable rule. Ham's ire was such that he'd like to break her pretty little face, though he knew that would be an impossibility. The lady was a weapon in heels.

At that, she was likely at the gym, pummeling some wannabe he-man into a sobbing, wimpy pile of self-pity. It was her way. She enjoyed toying with the tough.

The sudden and ferocious beeps from behind focused his attention on the now moving backlog of cars ahead. Traffic surged forward, with him the only roadblock. As he sped out of range of the raging hordes, he saw the cause of the delays and the abrupt reprieve: an accident off to the side, replete with ambulance, cops, flashing lights, gawking tourists and assorted hangers-on. Rubber-freaking-neckers had caused the whole thing.

"Why in hell do people do that?" he ranted as he slowed to ogle the scene.

Chastened somewhat by a niggling consciousness of hypocrisy, he downshifted, hit the gas and nearly spun out on the looming curve before he slowed to a more appropriate and legal city speed. Damn that Drew. She'd violated the faith. If she'd answered her phone he wouldn't be in this mess. A plane to catch, a partner to find and a case on hold.

Still incensed, about as happy as a crab in a hot pot of water, he wheeled into Drew's drive and, as always when he did, his jaw involuntarily dropped. His anger dissipated, replaced with a tinge of awe. Drew had done well for herself, he half laughingly, half enviously thought. Truth be his witness, much more than well.

Her perfect commercial for upper class acclaim stood on nearly one-third of an acre, landscaped to emphasize the desert rising to the mountains behind, as well as the two-story splendor of brick and the oversized picture window façade. Palm trees that only slightly hid the bend in the drive pulled him along to the turnabout that fronted the porch and the oversized garage. The interior, he knew, was no less imposing, especially her great room, so large as to turn the grand piano into a dollhouse adornment.

The piano, in particular, was an affectation which greatly amused him, as her legendary tin ear made his own set appear gold by comparison. He'd once heard her "sing", back when they were relatively new recruits to the Las Vegas Police Department, at an off-site Christmas party where she'd been feeling way too much holiday cheer. She'd grabbed the microphone from the band's singer, demanded they strike up "Yesterday," and proceeded to butcher not only the tune but the words as well. Not that she'd been hooted off the stage, but she did have to pull her gun and threaten to shoot the next son of a bitch who heckled her.

Needless to say, that was the last she'd sung in public. And the onset of office rules that prohibited firearms at social gatherings.

He shook off the memory and, as he did, he caught a brief glimpse of the smallish cottage in the back. Her pool house, as she called it, was more of an undersized living area, complete with shower, fireplace and extra bedroom. It was there that he sometimes crashed after enjoying too little sense and too much beer. It was, in fact, his favorite part of the house, for as hospitable as the grounds were, as enticing as the front entrance was, nothing compared to the backyard opulence, where the pièce de résistance dwelled: the pool, surrounded by fountains, outdoor kitchen and a variety of luxury seating, free formed and tiled in slate, the lights of which invited the watching mountains into the warmth of its embrace.

The full effect of the house and grounds could, in comparison with his humble abode, be described as a testament to taste and planning. But then, why shouldn't it be? Although she'd never confirmed it, rumor had it that Drew had grossed slightly more than one-million dollars in her three years with the private detective firm of Allen, Samuels and Thornton. A sum that, despite his own recent success at staving off foreclosure, loomed as unattainable as any mirage a thirsty man might dream up in his fevered imagination. An ultimate reminder that, prior to the Truckee River case, living off a medical pension and securing cheap paying jobs from time to time, he would have had to borrow a nickel to rub the two of them together.

Not that he couldn't have scored something like this himself. But his unwanted sense of ethics had been too cruel, too resistant, too monotonously cantankerous about righteousness—as he defined it. Still, Drew offered—more than offered, she'd begged him to join her—had used every trick in her devious book to get him to become Allen, Samuels, Thornton and McAlester. But with those two sleaze-balls, Samuels and Allen involved, he'd refused. He would never be able to shave again, he'd told her, nor get a haircut. Who could look at the devil in a mirror? He would have ended up with hair to his waist, a beard the size of Arkansas, wandering the Nevada desert in search of redemption. Not his thing.

His mind snapped back to business and anger when, as he pulled further into the drive, he saw it. There, parked in the drive, not in the garage, sat her Mercedes M-Class SUV. The only car she owned; the one, she argued, seeing as silver color was a sight so common along The Strip that she'd be even less conspicuous than he in his cheaper and less comfortable white follow-mobile. Which he admitted was probably right. Still, why spend that kind of money for a work car? To which she replied that he had no class, let alone M-Class.

So she was here. Concerned now, he checked his weapon and warily approached the door, using the palms for cover. If she was there and failed to respond to his summons, she'd have a damn good reason. And a pissed off former perp was as likely that reason as not. She'd left a long trail of angry "customers" in her career. This would not be the first time one had returned with a vengeance.

He noiselessly sidled up the porch, approached the window-patterned door and, careful to present no target, peeked through. That quick interior view confirmed his fear. Her ordinarily impeccable neatness was replaced with total disarray, clothes scattered around, empty bottles upturned on tables, and other debris he didn't take time to detail. He flipped the safety off the Browning 9 millimeter he routinely carried, both for its firepower and its aim, and slowly, silently, tried the knob.

Locked.

Off the porch, around the garage and out to the back, skirting the large pool and attached Jacuzzi. Onto the patio, toward the French doors, again keeping his frame as small as his 6 foot 3 inches allowed. He reached across, used the siding as a shield and twisted the glass knob.

Unlocked.

Quickly, soundlessly, he charged through the door, not bothering to close it behind him. He took a shooter's crouch and swung the pistol side to side, ready and willing to let loose at whatever.

Nothing.

A noise, off to the side, from off the living room, maybe toward her bedroom. A door from the sound of it, but soft, more a click than a slam. The shower door, maybe. A killer cleaning up his mess? Careful, eyes and ears alert to the smallest disturbance, he half-walked, half-crouched his way around the spacious kitchen, along the protective wall of the debris-strewn great room he'd spied from the porch, and on towards the long hall, at the end of which he'd find the master bedroom. Before that, along that curved hallway, lay all sorts of possible traps, whether behind closed doors or otherwise.

Tense, legs stinging from the effort, knees protesting his prolonged crab-walk, he eased to his full height just before the great room took its left turn to the wide, and now very silent, hall. He stuck his neck out, just enough to peek, not enough to present a target, for a first quick glance. Only shadows, nothing more. No lights, no discernable movement, no sound. No life.

Still cautious, heart annoying his ears, he swept into full view, gun up and ready, before he inched down the hall, eyes striving to see beyond the curve ahead. A spot where he'd again bend and peek before rounding. Caution, far more than manliness, was the buzzword here.

Ham reached the first room, a bedroom on the left, and silently twisted the knob. The door opened on well-oiled hinges, and he rushed in and through the dimness, knees only inches from the floor. Not only was the nothingness deafening, but so too was the cursing in his head. That had been stupid, he remonstrated. Barge into the unknown, chance a stumble, a noise, give away his position, helpless to fend off any intruder at his back who lurked outside the room.

Just get on with it, he told himself. Forget the other rooms. The danger was almost certainly down the hall. So be ready. Go for it, face it directly, get it done before it's too late. If it's not already.

He slipped back into the aisle, left the door as is, and sidled along the edge of the hall. He achieved his objective and chanced a peek around the curved divider. Movement. Slight, almost unseen, but movement nonetheless.

Ham backed up, made himself small and waited. Let the threat come to him. Now that Ham knew the danger lay ahead, now that he could anticipate the man's charge, the tables were turned. Because he, suddenly, had become the threat, the one with the edge. Which meant that perp would hit the floor before he turned the corner, by damn and to hell with him.

Then he'd go find Drew. And hope he was in time.

Anxious, slow-moving seconds passed before a soft swish sounded. Feet against carpet, he suspected. A slight shuffle, no more. The perp was good. He'd give him that.

But he was better. The moment the shadow paused, just shy of revealing itself, he got ready. Gun up, aimed, arms outstretched, both hands on the grip, finger twitching in anticipation. He was eager, but he'd been here before. He knew to wait, to not tense. A tense finger pulled the gun, sent the shot wide, leaving him defenseless while he sought to re-aim. No more than a split second, but more than enough time for him to hit the floor, some assassin's bullet caressing his heart.

The seconds crawled into a minute, a minute to a minute and a half. Unsure, suspicious, Ham questioned his own senses. Perhaps the movement he thought he'd detected was no more than a deeper shadow among a shroud of dimmer ones. Perhaps there had been no real difference at all, merely a chance figment of an all too rattled nerve.

Ham rose up, still prepared, rocking gently on the balls of his feet, set to dash. If the perp wouldn't come to him—if there even was a perp—he'd initiate the visit. Keeping the gun front and center, he followed its aim and lifted his foot, leaning forward, ready to rush. The perp rounded the corner, in full dim view, bearing straight down on him.

Only a half second to size it up: an impression of one shorter than he by a good half foot, easy to slam into the ground, like the linebacker he used to be. Something from his subconscious, a scream of *Wait, wait, wait! Don't shoot! Don't even tackle!*

Drew lowered her weapon, her eyes flaming redder than her wild mane of hair. And there she stood, lips drawn tight, with hot eyes that burned a hole through his head, in all her charming nakedness. Charm only slightly offset by the gun in her hand. He didn't need to see it to know she grasped her Glock 22 G4, a 15-round piece of death that she called her bedside stash, the one she liked to introduce as Ms. Advantage.

All Ham could think to say was, "You're naked."

"I do that when I have sex. Unless I'm in the car."

Ham shook the thought, if not the image, from his mind and snapped, "What the hell were you thinking, charging me like that? I could have shot you. Should have shot you, for Pete's sake."

"I could say the same to you. You're lucky I took a split second to glance at your face. You're not looking at my face, Ham."

"How did you know I was here? Am I losing my touch?"

"What, you don't think I have this place alarmed to hell and back? You set it off when you broke in through the patio door."

Trying to slow his breathing, biting out the words, he complained, "I called a bunch of times, Drew. You're supposed to answer my calls no matter what. Or have you forgotten that, along with your pants?"

Her smile revealed more pity than humor. "I know you don't get much, but come on, try to remember. Would *you* stop to answer the phone?"

"Just get dressed," he snapped, "then come on out to the kitchen. I'm going to make some coffee. We've got business to discuss."

Ham holstered his pistol, swung on his heels and deliberately stomped his way to the kitchen. Just a little gibe, a physical manifestation of his frustration, nerves, anger— and a great deal of embarrassment.

He reached into a corner cabinet and blindly, unerringly pulled out a filter and the small can of grounds she kept, mostly for him. As for Drew, she might have a cup now and then, upon rare occasion even two, but she stocked his brand because she herself lacked any interest in the subtleties of varieties. Coffee was simply not important to her. She was so heedless of it that she could actually start her day without that jolt. He'd seen her do it, though it disgusted and sickened him. To Ham, no emergency, no provocation, no time constraint was that imperative. Work without coffee, what a sin. A complete, total abomination before and to the Almighty. Senseless masochism to boot.

Inevitably, as the elixir brewed to aromatic excellence, his visual memory kicked in and, as he mentally replayed the recent encounter with his friend and partner, his breath came quicker, thinner. In all their time together, in and out of trouble, professional or personal, he had never thought about it, her being naked, or what she might look like in the buff. But now that he'd seen it, my god, he had to question his own manhood that he had not exhibited even idle curiosity. To discover that even a Da Vinci lacked the necessary talent to capture her essence shook him to his heretofore brotherly core.

Drew sauntered in with a curt, "Pour me a cup," and plopped herself at the table. Ham, eyed her over; she was sporting bicycle shorts, tennis shoes with no socks, and a tight half tee. Deliberately, he turned his eyes away from her and busied himself with preparation.

"Here you go," he announced.

"Have a seat, Ham," she ordered, "and quit acting like a schoolboy. So you caught me with my pants down. So what?"

Ham chose to ignore the comment. "What in hell went on here? There's garbage all over your living room. You have a party and didn't invite me?"

"It was a party for two. What's going on?"

"We got a case."

"Must be a doozy for you to come crashing into my house and all. You changing your style? No longer attempting staid and steady?"

"Don't start on me, Drew." He waited for the response he knew he'd regret. But she surprised him and let it go, her eyes brimming with curiosity. "Yeah, it's a beaut, all right," he nodded. "Intriguing. And guess what? We're back in the music game."

The curiosity in her eyes was replaced with wonder. "Well now, that's a coincidence."

Ham's chose to ask the question with raised eyebrows.

Drew's lopsided grin twisted into a full blown, self-satisfied smirk as Ham nearly spit his coffee on the table and jumped out of his chair so fast it slammed backward to the floor. "I take it your answer just walked in," she laughed.

The walking answer appeared out of nowhere, clad only in boxer shorts, shaking his long frizzy mane of still-blond hair. Russ Porter, one-half of the Big Two of the legendary Truckee River band. The singer-songwriter, rock and roll hall of fame inductee, a living, walking, boxer-clad legend. One of the greats, a colossus across the worldwide stage of fame. Part of the band that for nearly thirty years had ruled the charts, much as The Beatles had in their prime. Until, as it must, age and ennui slowed them down, though never really shutting them out.

Shock at seeing Russ' face gave way to a warm spread inside his chest, tenderness he reserved for few. When he'd first met Russ in Hawaii, it had been anything but pleasant. Intimidating, of course, challenging, yes, but over the course of the case, getting to know Russ and his colossus partner, Blake, he'd learned to overlook the image and see the man. Even now, probably pushing mid-sixties, his somewhat craggy face drew Ham in, especially those impossibly light blue eyes and the frizzy, ash-blond hair that draped across his shoulders, sort of a cross between Phil Spector at his unnatural worst and Art Garfunkel at his natural best.

Before Ham could close his mouth and attempt to speak, Drew broke the silence. "So let me ask you again," she drawled, "would *you* have stopped to answer the damn phone?"

Ham shook his head in self-mockery. "Well, hopefully, I wouldn't have been in that position with Russ in the first place. But I get your point." Accepting the hand Russ proffered, he shook it warmly. "It's great to see you, Russ. How are you? How've you been since...?"

"Since," Russ sighed. "Yeah, 'since'." He shook his head, regret leading the way. "Okay, I guess. Nothing's the same."

"How about a cup?" Ham offered, as he retrieved the toppled chair he'd formerly occupied. "I make a mean pot of coffee, for which I, myself, do compliment me."

Russ plopped into a chair next to Drew while Ham tossed a question over his shoulder. "What brings you to Vegas?" His face flamed to the shade of Drew's hair and he had to force himself not to bite his own offending tongue. "Never mind, I guess I walked into that one."

"I know what you mean," Russ chortled. "But besides the obvious, I'm repaying a debt to an old buddy who called in a favor. There's this piano man, a singer who works a lounge at a casino, a guy Vick Martin wanted me to see, which I did last night. Vick's a recording engineer, one of the best, and he did me some favors back in the day. The kid singer did him a more recent favor of some sort—or at least that's what I'm figuring—and in turn is calling in Vick's chit. You know how it goes." He shrugged.

"When it comes to the music business, nope, I don't," Ham reminded him. "But whatever." Turning to Drew, he demanded, "Why didn't you tell me he was coming?"

"I love you, Ham, but not enough to invite you to our alone time."

"Is that what they call it now? Alone time? I didn't even know you guys were having 'alone time'. When did this start?"

"Let's just move on," Drew said loftily. "So what's this big music emergency? Clue me in, Ham man."

"I'll fill you in on the way. Thanks to your morning gymnastics, time's passing us by. We've got a plane to catch." Glancing at his watch, he amended, "Or at least we did. I need to reschedule, I guess. By the time you pack and we get out to McCarran, it's not going to work."

"Where are you headed?" Russ inquired. "Maybe I can help."

"Santa Cruz, California. We were supposed to meet our client at three o'clock this afternoon. With the layover in Phoenix, it'll take us five hours to get there, counting travel time from San Jose to Santa Cruz. That's why I had us on the morning flight."

"First class?" Drew demanded.

"Of course," Ham pretended to be affronted. "I'm not a barbarian."

Their grins reflected a shared memory of those flights over the course of the Truckee River case, flights that included first class service to Hawaii out of the dead of winter, and flights back into winter that exceeded first class. Private jets with catered service would never be their norm, but it would always be their preference. Spoiled, Ham asserted, that's what they were. No small thanks to Russ.

"Santa Cruz?" Russ exclaimed. "Well, hell, man, no problem. We can leave when you're ready, take my plane. I'll drop you off on my way to Tahoe. In fact, you can stay at my cottage. I'll have the caretaker let you in."

"Cottage?" Ham asked, surprised. "You have a place in Santa Cruz? You never told me that."

"And I should have, why?"

"I've never heard cottage and caretaker used in the same sentence," Drew laughed. "What rock and roll royalty call a cottage is something I'll never experience."

"Is it as big as this?" Ham wickedly, innocently inquired. "I don't want to stay in a hovel."

Russ' elaborate shrug presaged the answer. "About two of these would fit inside is my guess. Like I said, a cabin, smallish, intimate." Russ grinned lewdly at Drew. "I take my dates there."

Drew puffed out what Ham now knew to be well proportioned breasts and snapped, "I'm not the type you should cheat on, honey. Lorena Bobbitt had nothing on me. And I won't even need a knife."

That last rattled Ham's jaw, a jab upside the head with a brass knuckle glove. Obviously, much, much more had transpired between them since Ham had last seen Russ than he had previously imagined. More, even, than this morning's events revealed in all their weird particulars.

Drew had some explaining to do. Whether she fought it or not, he would not be denied. Given their long shared lives, she owed it to him, and he was going to cash that chit, one way or another.

But that would have to wait. "How soon can we get going? I'll have to let them know our new schedule."

"First things first," Drew insisted. "Who is this guy, why are you excited, and why should we bother? We don't need to go to California to drum up money. There's more than enough right here."

"It's a $225,000 retainer against fees. I told him that covers three months' fees, expenses extra, should it end up taking that long. Or, in the alternative, if there's nothing we can do, consider it payment in full." Drew's soft whistle confirmed that he'd caught her full attention. "That answers two of your questions right there. As for who he is, I've not heard of him personally, but I take it he casts a shadow in the music industry. His name is Ronny Damon, he owns a studio, is a producer, and releases on what I take it is a mid-size indie label."

"Jeezus," Drew spit, "where did a lightweight twit like that get that kind of money? Are you sure he can pay?"

"He's not that lightweight," Russ informed her.

"You know him?" Ham was amazed to hear the surprise in his own voice. Because he definitely should not have been. This was Russ Porter. If the man was any kind of player, Russ would know about it.

"I know of him. Haven't met him. Different circles." He rose, sauntered to the fridge and helped himself to a bottle of milk and another of orange juice. "He's B-List, but that's enough to run to seven figures. Albeit on the low end of that scale," he informed them between alternate swigs of white and orange drink.

Drew rose, pushed away her unfinished cup. "We'd better get started, I guess. Russ and I need a quick shower, then we'll pack and get on our way. Okay with you? Ham and Russ responded in tandem. "Absolutely, let's do it."

Ham suspected that though he and Russ agreed on the answer, they disagreed on the meaning of the question. And that his wait might be a bit longer than a quickie.

CHAPTER TWO

A MINOR CASE OF MURDER

Unhappily, Ham was right on the mark. Nearly an hour elapsed before a refreshed looking Drew and a lasciviously smirking Russ reappeared, each more rosy-cheeked than should have been the case from a simple wholesome shower. Still, and in the end, it mattered not, since Russ' private jet waved the tarmac goodbye a mere minute past noon. They'd reach San Jose in an hour and a half, meaning plenty of time to rent a car and make their three o'clock in Santa Cruz. No need to reschedule.

Such is the life of a superstar, Ham mused. Deadlines were for little people. Like B players, opening acts forced to lay out a couple of grand for hired help, and that only if they could find any. Unlike superstars such as Super Russ, who had more volunteer labor than the man could possibly count.

Ham shook the thought off, stretched away his worries, and delighted in reclining further into the captain's chair in which he sprawled. Though competition for space was nonexistent, he nevertheless felt privileged to dwell in that kind of opulence and nervously reserved a small sense of protectiveness just in case somebody more important claimed ownership—like maybe the megastar owner. Though with Russ happily ensconced next to Drew, the likelihood of that probably sat on the other side of never.

He forced a deep, calming breath and glanced around, admiring the interior, the obvious luxury. Because of the tables and stunning leg room afforded each seat, the plane, despite its size, would only accommodate sixteen passengers, fifteen if an attendant occupied the rear seat, as was now the case.

As he breathed it all in, a sense of wonder enveloped him. In his heart, and in his mind, the lavishness of the décor and the comfort of the seating nearly rivaled the incomparable splendor of a full moon over the endless desert, a phenomenon he'd supposed impossible. The seat he lazed in was not merely huge and hugely comfortable; it was soft beyond any leather accommodation in first class seating that any airline proffered. Looking around, he saw that each of the eight swivel captain's chairs was equally plush, and each couch as well.

This wealth, such unimaginable self-indulgence lived as a life style, something taken so for granted as to become so routinely normal that it warranted neither thought nor comment, spun his mind to the point of vertigo. He'd known such people existed—he'd lived in Vegas far too long not to know in an intellectual sense—but to witness it yet again, to see it up close and personal one more unexpected and heart-racing time, threatened to burst one of the chambers charged with supporting his circulation.

Forcing and feigning a calmness beyond his ability to feel, Ham heaved himself from the contours of his greedy seat and wandered over to the wet bar. He perused a selection of wines and beers revealed through a tinted refrigerator window, rows that sat snuggled below a well-stocked rack of harder stuff. Spying real bottled orange soda—he wasn't even aware that still existed—he grabbed one, popped the top with an old fashioned bottle opener that swung from the bar, and returned to the comfort and vast expanse of his private seating area. Sipping contentedly, he noticed a magazine rack nearby, snatched up a *Sports Illustrated* and leaned back with a contented sigh.

If this presaged how this newest case would unfold, he'd be living it, Ham mused. Anything that starts with heaven can't end in hell, right?

Remembering the actual onset, the traffic and terror, he shrugged away the chill crawling up his back, firmly and forcefully. Some things presaged, some did not.

While pretending to skim the magazine, he studied the puzzle of Drew and Russ. There had been a noticeable spark between them back at Tahoe, toward the end of the Truckee River case, but he'd never thought about it igniting. What he felt about it, he couldn't figure. But why it was his business, he could.

Maybe not really his business, he sighed, but regardless, he would be watching. Watching and judging. Judging and watching. And remembering that image of... *no. Toss it. She's like your sister, you freaking perv.*

To Ham's scarlet-cheeked relief, the steward chose that moment to arrive with his cart, upon which sat silverware, crystal glasses sparkling with water, china cups for tea or coffee "as you might wish," and several dishes of eye-popping entrees, each on its own china plate. The attendant reached across Ham with a "May I?" and unfolded, not a tiny, flimsy tray, but a huge wooden table, then arranged the setting. Before a groveling Ham could get out a "Thank you so very much," the steward did the same for both Russ and Drew, leaving the passengers with their excess.

Ham busied himself with scarfing as much as possible before his stomach could alert his brain that it was overtaxed. He noted that Drew and Russ ate at a more leisurely pace, though just as eagerly.

Despite his best efforts, most of the plates on the table stayed covered, as neither his stomach nor mind would be so easily duped. He beckoned to the ever-alert steward who, clearing away the debris, inquired, without apparent irony, "Will there be anything else, sir?"

Ham waited, heels gently bouncing the carpeted floor, fingers noiselessly tapping the leather armrests, until the others blotted the remains from their lips and sent the dishes away.

"Are you ready?" He congratulated himself that his voice held not one note of pleading.

"Sure," Drew affirmed. "I fed my face, I'm satisfied, and I admit to a bit of curiosity. It's been a while since I've seen you in such a state."

"Oh, you'll be in a state, too," Ham assured her. "Take a look at these pictures." He withdrew six large glossies from a manila folder and stretched across the aisle to plop them in Drew's lap. "They're killer."

Drew studied them closely, idly handed them to Russ. "In more ways than one," was all she said aloud, but the widening of her eyes shrieked, "Jeezus!"

"Our good Mr. Damon is under suspicion for those murders, though not under indictment, at least not yet."

"Where did you get these?" Drew demanded. "They look like official crime scene photos. Please don't tell me you stole them. My license and I don't want to hear that."

"No problem," Ham said. "Remember my buddy in Reno, the one from the Nevada State Police?"

"Your old football pal from university days? Yeah, I remember. Never liked him much, but what about him?"

"A few phony questions about a 'similar murder' in Reno got the California cops to fax those to him, and him on to me. No stealing about it. Just lying. And another favor I'll regret later, no doubt."

Drew's cheeks flamed with dander and her jaw twitched. "How long has this been in the works? And why didn't you let me in on it until now? This isn't any way to work."

Ham put up his hands, less in surrender than in supplication. "I got the call this morning, just before 6 o'clock. I had this stuff put together and on the way to your house by 8 a.m. That's hardly keeping you out of the loop. Not to mention," he couldn't resist adding, "there was a delay in looping you in that can't be laid at my doorstep."

Russ' voice sounded thoughtful as he asked, "What exactly am I looking at here?"

When he looked up, glancing from Drew to Ham, his eyes narrowed to slits of concentration. "I'm not just curious, I have a reason for asking."

Ham's voice rose a note and his eyes lit as he exclaimed, "That's the thing, see? I've never even heard of anything like this, let alone seen it. It's why I had to have the case. I mean, it's so cool I can't believe it."

"Three dead bodies are cool?" Russ asked wryly. "My, my; you are one majorly jaded man, aren't you, my friend?"

"I don't mean it that way, Russ." If offense could color the walls, the plane would be black. "That's not even fair."

Russ' grin was Cheshire in its subtlety. "It was a joke, Ham."

"Oh." Ham's face relaxed as he lamely feigned awareness. "I knew that. I was just messing you back."

Drew's snort negated that attempt, so Ham gamely forged on. "Anyway, you see what I mean. Those are the initials of the victims' names that you're seeing in the photos, initials neatly carved into the cheeks, first name on the left side, last on the right. In order of victims, we have C on the left cheek, D on the right, a guy named Charlie Davis. The second victim, we have E and b, for Evin Boyd, and finally, F and G for Fran Gallaugher. From the lack of blood, the initials were carved postmortem. And as you can see from the frontal shots, there are three neat and closely packed bullets, right in the heart, identical for each victim. Which means the killer knows how to use a gun. I don't care how close you are to a target, you can't put three bullets on a dime unless you're one hell of a shot."

"Last time I was at the range," Drew agreed, "I was at ten yards, putting fourteen rounds on a quarter, but I'm better than most."

"Charlie Davis, Evan Boyd and Fran Gallaugher, all from Ronny's stable," Russ murmured, still studying the pictures. "Interesting coincidence."

"You've heard of them?"

"Not a lot, but they made the charts. And don't look so surprised," Russ admonished. "I'm only in semi-retirement, I didn't quit completely. I keep an eye on the charts, make a point to listen to them, even though most of it's crap these days, not like the old times when there were real melodies, backbeats, true rhythm, poetic lyrics and—"

"Russ," Drew gently prodded. "About the people?"

"Oh, right. There's money there, but again, nothing whopping, a bit of pocket change. The best was the one by Fran Gallaugher. That one hit the Top 20. It was a nice little tune. I liked it. Blake did, too."

The wistful melody of Russ' sigh probably caught even Drew's tin ear; but she, like Ham, refrained from responding. The man was entitled to his private grief.

"So why did he call us?" Drew wondered. "There's a bunch of local investigative talent that would be far more connected. Doesn't sound right, if you catch my drift."

"Yeah, that was my thought. When I asked, all he said was that he'd heard things."

Russ' head snapped up. "What, that you worked for me and Blake?"

"I sincerely doubt it," Ham shrugged, "and for a couple of reasons. Number one, it's been closely held. If there was even a rumor that detectives were working for Truckee River it would have hit the rags big time, given the circumstances. And besides that, Damon would have just come out with it, wouldn't he? I mean, why not? It's the perfect entrée."

"No, it isn't," Russ replied. "It's not like I know him personally, but from what I do know, I wouldn't touch him."

"So tell me what you know about Ronny Damon," Ham requested. "I researched him. There was a lot of pap there; nothing specific that tells me what kind of guy he is."

"He's got a bit of a shady reputation. From what I hear, he won't sign new talent unless they agree to go through his song publishing firm; and the terms, as I understand it, are not so good. Plus, he ties them up for too long, which is why the A players won't work with him."

"Well, that doesn't sound good," Drew sighed. "So why are we doing this?" Without pause she added, "I mean besides $225,000 and a particularly weird and interesting case. So never mind. Asked and answered. But I will check his ass out three ways from Wednesday, you can count on that. And if I don't like him, if I don't want to work for him, we take the money and run."

As Ham nodded agreement, Russ waived the photos before them. "Have you noticed anything odd here?"

Ham and Drew exchanged curious glances and shrugged. "It's all curious" Drew replied. "What exactly are you asking?"

"Look," Russ exclaimed, "lay the photos in order. See what we have? Moving left to right, from victim one to victim three, we have C D E b F G. Get the idea?"

Ham's puzzlement colored his voice as he answered, "Charlie Davis, Evan Boyd, Fran Gallagher. So what?"

"You're not looking, Ham. Why all capitals except b?"

"I don't know. I hadn't really noticed, but I expect...."

"What?" Russ prompted. "What do you expect?"

Ham shrugged, his mental haze reflected in glazed eyes. "Maybe the killer ran out of time, or maybe carving the capital b is too difficult. I mean, it is harder than the others, wouldn't be easy to do on someone's cheek. Or maybe he just forgot?"

"Maybe," Russ agreed, "or maybe it was deliberate. Lower case b is a musical symbol for flat, so Eb is E flat. Now I know this may be a crazy theory, I know I don't know squat about investigating crimes, but I do know my own business. So let's think about it from that standpoint for a moment, from the angle of the music business."

"Please do," Drew invited. "I'd love to hear it."

"We've got three singer-songwriters, albeit of small stature, victims out of the same studio, the same publishing firm. Let's assume for a moment that the killer is in the business; motive, whatever. Whoever is doing it is murdering in the scale of C minor, whether they know it or not. And I'm guessing they do. It's simply too coincidental otherwise."

Ham rubbed his brow, staring at and not seeing Russ. He heard Drew clear her throat, her habit just before tearing apart a suspect. Instead, to his surprise and interest, her voice carried amusement.

"Russ, my sweet, sweet dear, I do not have one solitary clue, of any sort, in any manner whatever, about what you are trying to say. And if I had to guess, seeing Ham's lost look, neither does he. Would you care to elaborate, remembering you're talking to musical dunces? What, for instance, is a scale of C minor, and what could that possibly have to do with anything in the real world of murder?"

Russ sighed and rubbed his chin before answering. "Okay," he finally said, "trying this again. We don't have to go deeply into it, and it wouldn't be helpful if we did. But my theory is that, assuming a musician is behind this, he's deliberate in choosing his victims, and very, very deliberate in choosing the order thereof."

"All right," Ham shrugged, "I understand your point and it's fascinating, to massively understate the case. And he's doing this according to some kind of a musical thingy?"

"Key, yeah. All music is in some key or another, the whys, hows and wherefores of which you don't need to bother yourself with. But you should consider that if there's another murder, and there could be if Ronny's not the killer, you should look for your victim to have the initials AB. If I were you, I'd check out who in his circle has those initials and then... well, you know... do your thing. And by the way, if that does happen, if my theory holds and the next victim is AB, you'll again find the b carved in the cheek to be lower case because the next note in the scale is A flat."

Before he or Drew could comment, a crackle announced the pilot's intention. "Mr. Porter, if you and your guests will prepare for landing, we'll be touching down in 10 minutes."

That was all, no demand for seat backs upright, no insistence that we stow carry-ons—no nothing. The privileged class did as it pleased. *As I please. The perks of thumbing a ride with The Great One.*

Ham glanced out the window, more a reflex to the pilot's declaration than an act of curiosity. His eyes saw but his brain barely registered a misty coast with inlets and cays, and bright blue sky caressed by wispy white clouds, the ceiling for a mass of humanity that stretched to the haze-engulfed mountains beyond.

What did register was that Russ' theory made some kind of lunatic sense. It was definitely a place to start. A fascinating, unique and mind-boggling step one.

It also meant a relatively easy payday, if true. Because another murder meant that Ronny would be off the hook—if his claim of police harassment and constant surveillance was more fact than paranoia—and they would be done, could wash their hands of the rest. Collect the check, tip the hat, say thanks a lot and goodbye and good luck.

It would be a hell of a shame, though, to miss out on the end of a case like this. He'd trade his beloved Mustang to get the chance to chase this one down. What a rush. The adrenaline charge would probably burst a few vessels, but that would be small cost for a large thrill. Some cop was going to have the case of his career. Or any cop's career. If he'd grabbed a case like this when he was on the force, he'd still be on it, hip be damned.

He pulled himself away from the unseen vista and back to business. "Okay, Russ," he nodded, "maybe I'm buying it. What's the full key? How many victims before it's complete?"

"That's the strange part," Russ started.

"*That's* the strange part?" Drew inquired. "Okay."

Russ turning a serious face toward Ham. "I mean it. The key is C, D, Eb, F, G, Ab, Bb and C. You've already got C, D, Eb, F and G, three victims. So the next is Ab, then Bb, with C left over."

Drew was one of those rare and fortunate people that could figure odds and fractions on the fly. For her, an easy one. "So we have a potential for five victims. Three dead already, with two more to go, the Ab victim, followed by a Bb target. So what's with the extra C?"

Russ' shrug indicated he thought it obvious. "Look for somebody he's got, or used to have, that is known by one name. You know, like Enya, Beyoncé, Bono, Madonna, Pink, like that. It'll be a C, like Cher." Pursed lips issued apologies when he added, "At least that's my best guess."

"Okay," Ham nodded, "six possible victims, which would make this guy a real player in the wacko serial murder game. And if that's the case," he added to Drew, "we should be able to profile the bastard."

"With Russ' help and assuming it's not Ronny."

"Assuming that."

"I can't help you profile," Russ stated flatly. "Not my area of expertise. Music, remember?"

"That's exactly why you can in this case," Ham replied. "What you do, maybe while you're wandering your various properties or partying in the sky, is you jot some notes about the ins and outs of the business that could create jealousy and hate and a motive for revenge."

"I cannot think of one single thing that could provoke somebody to murder, let alone go on a serial rampage. There is nothing that justifies or explains it."

"You said that Ronny has a shady reputation, that he signs and cheats his talent," Drew pointed out. "Just give us a few notes on how that works, down to and including the scoop on songwriting royalties, or anything else your remarkable mind thinks might be beneficial to ignorant outsiders like me and Ham."

The plane hit the tarmac with a barely felt thump, much smaller than the jolt to his conscious when he realized he'd spent his time on everything except the victims. While seeking the thrill of the hunt, fantasizing an easy 200 grand plus, and playing Superstar in The Sky, where the hell had been his heart?

Shrouded in greed, selfishness and ego, that's where. A heart beating for one.

The flash of humiliation that coursed through him could have melted the steel frame in which he flew, should have sucked him through its melting carcass and pitched him into the mountain of denial where history buries its shame.

He shook off the vision, but not the self-castigation. That was a prize of reckoning he had not just won but fully earned. He'd been guilty, his offense heartless indifference. Never once had he thought ahead, never once considered that if three people were needlessly slaughtered, more might follow. Only what was in it for him. Harrison's "I, Me, Mine" could have been written with him in mind, Ham mused. Not to mention "You're So Vain," a clear shot at his ever-present ego.

Right, there you go. Back to it's all about you. Jackass.

"All right," he spat, "no more of this crap. Just stop it." Surprised he'd said it aloud, and in reaction to the curious looks shot his way, he recovered with, "Find out who is next and put an end to it. Because I promise you now, nobody else dies on our watch."

As he packed up bits and pieces of paperwork, he mentally crossed fingers and toes. Determination, even bravado, were fine and good for a seasoned detective, he reminded himself. But luck was better. And they were going to need a boat-load if this killer had the skill to slip in under the cop's radar, seemingly at will. Anybody that good either had a resumé full of murders to his credit, or the killer had a great deal more in the brain department that Ham could ever hope to enjoy. Maybe both, and if that were the case, they'd be chasing shadows in the dark.

Russ caught his attention long enough to proffer a warm handshake and an even stronger grip on the shoulder. After a tender kiss to Drew's cheek—a kiss, Ham thought, that revealed maybe more than he intended—Russ addressed them both. "You take care of yourselves; and Drew, you call every day to let me know what's going on and that you're okay. Whether I'm right or wrong about a killer key, it doesn't change the fact that there's a murderer out there. When you two pop up and stick your investigative noses into his business you become irritants. And when you become irritants...."

"We become targets," Drew finished. "And so be it." Turning to Ham, jaw set, eyes hard, she declared, "You're right. Not on our watch. Let's go disrupt some plans."

CHAPTER THREE

AN ODD LITTLE MAN

The more Ham considered Russ' theory, the greater substance it had. No half-witted killer would bother to carve his victim's initials onto lifeless forms. Even for a madman, whose reasoning was unfathomable to most, there could be no motive. Though many of that class enjoyed tweaking their pursuers—and sometimes the public—it was generally to gain publicity, the lure and siren of that peculiar set of psychos. And so far, this one had not. Different motives, different plans.

He glanced over at Drew, who had not spoken since they'd left the airport, and even now was staring absently out the window. He guessed that she, too, was worrying it through, anticipating, preparing, and perhaps formulating questions she intended to throw at their reputedly sleazy client.

Or maybe just daydreaming about Russ.

Without preamble, he asked, "So are you going to marry him?"

"Don't be an ass."

"It's what I do best."

Her icy silence would have frosted the windows if not for the heat.

The tone of Ham's voice indicated a brotherly concern when he asked, "When did this start, Drew?"

"It started out at Tahoe, the night you and Charlie spent chastely necking by the fire," she snapped.

At the mention of Charlie, his heart threatened fibrillation but was vetoed by the abrupt warmth of his loins. Charlie, Blake's daughter, Russ' adopted goddaughter, the one woman in his life, ever, who melted the steel in his chest while at the same time turning his tongue to paste. Even in the first blush of young love, entering a doomed marriage on a cloud of hope, he had not suffered such selfless devotion, such total dedication. Though he had not spoken to Charlie in weeks, only seconds passed between memories of her hair, her hands, her... well, her aura, for lack of a better word. And her independence. Though it often kept them apart, sometimes months at a time, he loved that too. She wouldn't be Charlie without that endearing streak.

He shrugged off the image and turned serious eyes to Drew. "Why didn't you tell me? It's not like we've ever kept secrets."

Drew turned fully to face him. "Let me ask you this. Have you seen Charlie since Tahoe?" Ham's flaming face confirmed the truth. "I thought so. But you never said a word, did you?"

"It's not the same," Ham stuttered. "I mean, well, you know."

"It is the same," she insisted. "Because it's real. For both of us. And I didn't want the interference just yet, with you playing big brother, asking Russ stupid things like what his intentions are, saying 'Don't break Drew's heart', nonsensical and unwanted crap like that. Because you'd do it, you know you would."

Ham's shame-faced grin pleaded guilt. "Yeah, I guess so. Still, he is twenty years your senior."

"See? There you go, and right after I warned you off. Anyway, twenty-three. So what?"

"Well, I mean, what is this, a money thing? It can't be his body."

For the first time since they left the airplane, Drew's smile was real, even if mischievous. "Oh yeah? How do you know? You haven't seen his body. I have."

"Not true. I've seen all but what the boxer shorts cover, remember? Or are you forgetting that little scene in your kitchen?"

"Take your mind out of your shorts and back on the road. We're finished here." Though her words struck him as curt, the tone conveyed a different intent. Call it a gentle order.

He suspected she courted heartbreak, but he let it go. Orders were orders. "What's the GPS say we've got left?"

Drew checked the readout and announced, "About ten miles. According to the route, you'll be turning in eight, and then it's only a couple of miles to Russ' house. I can't wait to see it," she beamed.

"Me, too," Ham agreed. "Are we going to poke around, maybe find evidence of who else he's boinking?"

"Ham," she snarled, "I am warning you"

"Okay, okay. Just having a little fun. I'm done now."

"Why, thank you so much," she drawled, then sat well back in her seat, arms crossed against her chest, and pointedly studied the scenery from her side window.

Ham received the silent treatment, interrupted only by directions from the sweet-voiced GPS, until they arrived at Russ' "cottage", at which point gasps echoed throughout the car. Though he could not be sure, he suspected the GPS may have joined them in a group puff.

Ham's hands shook as they pulled up the short drive to what were obvious bluffs below. Visions of blacking out, awaking in a burnt out car, bathing-suited gawkers pointing at the desert buffoon, caused him to hit the brakes harder than intended. He was braced, but Drew plunged forward, saved from mashing her face by a seat belt that bit into her chest and forced the air from protesting lungs.

Nevertheless, she managed a strangled yell. "You idiot! What the hell are you trying to do, kill me? Christ, Ham, what in the name of God is the matter with you?"

"Sorry. Not familiar with this car."

"You're familiar with brakes and gas, aren't you? Next time I'll drive, thank you very much."

The caretaker saved him the embarrassment of a reply by opening Drew's door and ushering her out with a welcoming bow. "I am so very glad to meet you, Ms. Thornton. I'm Gardner Jennings. Russ informed me that you and a guest would be arriving. I am very clearly instructed to see to it that you enjoy your stay, so anything you need you just let me know."

Ham almost laughed at Drew's blush and little girl giggle. Instead, he whispered, "If you don't marry him, I will."

"I didn't know you were that flexible," she murmured back.

"For this," he said, waving his arm in emphasis, "I'm willing to learn."

Gardner picked up their bags and led them up the stairs to a landing, leaving behind the mature palms that lined the drive and the carefully manicured shrubs, the varieties and types of which were a mystery to Ham.

Uneducated his eyes might be, but they did respond to beauty and this picture postcard of a house held him captive.

The caretaker urged them through the entry and into a scene that rivaled Hawaii. He thought of that site as God's masterpiece, but this had to be a close competitor. The blue Pacific lay exposed in its naked beauty as far as the eye could see, welcomed into the house by those huge glass windows that led through the hall, past a sitting room and on to the magnificent and expansive patio beyond. All of this sat atop the bluffs that had spooked his imagination.

Drew whistled softly. When she spoke her voice spoke wonder. "This is the most beautiful, relaxing view I've ever seen. How could he ever leave here? God knows I wouldn't."

"Shall I show you to your rooms?" Gardner inquired. "And lunch. Are you hungry? I could whip you up pretty much whatever you want."

"Yes to the rooms, no to lunch," Ham replied. "Unless you want some, Drew? That pit of a stomach still got room?"

"You'll have to excuse Ham," Drew advised Gardner. "He's never mastered English. His native language is Boorish."

Much to Ham's amusement, Gardner's large brown eyes reflected a mixture of fright and confusion. The man looked as though he wanted to bolt from the room but couldn't get his legs to work. He stood as rooted to the spot as any of the shrubs he nursed. A six-foot statue in blue jeans.

Ham rescued the lost man-child with a friendly hand to the shoulder and a gentle verbal nudge. "The rooms, Gardner?"

Gardner's relief was comical in effect. A confident swagger replaced the uncertain grin as he hefted their luggage and nodded to the staircase. "The guest rooms are just up these stairs. Ms. Thornton, you'll take the one at the end, and you, sir, the one on the left." As he led the way he tossed back over his shoulder, "They both have master baths and pretty much anything you need, like toiletries, bathrobes, swimming trunks if you're so inclined, and a variety of sweaters and windbreakers. It can get cool at night, what with the ocean breeze and all."

Gardner deposited Ham's suitcase in his suite before escorting Drew further down the hall. As anticipated, the view was as wondrous as throughout the main floor, and the bathroom expansive and fully supplied. He quickly unpacked his few belongings, just a few shirts, an extra pair of chinos, and underwear, socks and toiletries. Not knowing how long they'd be in town, he chose to travel light, figuring on buying whatever else he might need, should such need arise.

A sudden urge to wash up overtook him and he found himself at the sink, water running, soap in hands. No matter how decadently opulent the ride, airplane air made him feel sweaty and crusty, like an old salt mine. Scrubbing vigorously, eyes stung by wandering soap, he splashed his face with ice cold water, swabbing away the lye and grime. He toweled his face, wiped dripping water from his hairline and ears, and checked the offending sting in his eyes.

Though large and still piercingly green, the whites were blurred to pink. He looked like he'd been on a three-day bender. Ham applied drops to both eyes, blinked away the resulting tears, and checked again. Better.

With a stab of regret, the now clear reflection of his eyes brought back that old memory, back when his ex-wife was still his date, when she used to croon that he had eyes women swam in and men perceived danger in. By the end she'd claimed otherwise, that women perceived danger and men got bored.

That always made Charlie laugh, so what the hell. Screw the old bat ex.

He stepped back from the mirror, not entirely displeased with what he saw. At six-foot three, around 190 pounds, he wasn't his old football physique, but days at the gym kept him close enough. He was especially pleased that his hair, shorter than in his youth, was nevertheless firmly on the brown side, only slightly flawed by graying temples.

His reflection presented a sweat-stained shirt that so contrasted with his now dry face that it stood out like virtue on The Las Vegas Strip. Ham stripped it off, wadded it up and tossed it into a convenient corner before picking a freshly laundered shirt from his reserves. He was tucking in the tails when Drew's voice floated up from behind.

"If you're through primping, we better move along."

Ham nodded, finished his chore and walked toward her, keys dangling from his fist. Before he could object, she yanked the keys from his hand and dashed for the stairs. She clearly intended to make good on her earlier threat to take the wheel, and with the visual image of ruination on the beach still fresh in mind, he decided to let it go, even agreed with her.

By the time he caught up she had the car started and the air conditioning running at full blast. Referencing his ever present notepad, he punched the address of Ronny's studio into the GPS, then waited interminable minutes for that mechanical misfit to locate itself.

The robotic voice finally announced its awareness. "Turn right at the indicated spot and the guidance system will start."

It took less than twenty minutes to maneuver through surprisingly sparse traffic. Or maybe it only looked sparse to him, Ham thought. All the cars together, moving or parked, could have fit into a single lot at the Bellagio.

As they pulled up to the property, they passed an obvious undercover cop car parked just outside the entrance. Two men, both in suits, probably sweating through a tedious assignment, glanced at them when they slowed to pull around and head up a short driveway that led to a single-story brick enclosure. If he had expected something sexy, neon signs with music motifs celebrating the enticing and exciting world within, he was to be disappointed. And he was. It could have been a car repair shop, for all the romance the building exuded.

Drew aimed a thumb over her shoulder, indicating the cop car so noticeably staked out in front. "Looks like our client was right. They want him to know he's marked."

"Trying to prevent another murder is my guess. No reason to be so blatant about it otherwise," Ham agreed.

"They'll have us identified before we leave, you know."

"I know," Ham nodded grimly. "I suspect we'll be having a little chat with them; not one of our choosing."

They pulled next to the only car parked in the six-car lot. "Okay," Drew announced, "let's go see what kind of scumbag you've got us involved with now."

"A scumbag with almost a quarter of a million dollars to spare," Ham reminded her.

"Not from the looks of this. I'd guess a quarter of a hundred."

They entered the low-slung building through a glass door, the only opening in the unappealing structure. A narrow hall littered with plaques and pictures of various acts led to the studio control booth, similarly adorned with memorabilia. Inside the booth squatted a long white leather couch, a smallish engineering panel, a computer, and mysterious equipment Ham could not identify. The lone swivel chair sat unoccupied.

Beyond the window that ran the length of the booth was a large, rectangular and empty recording space. He recognized the singer's booth, glassed in with a microphone and stool. Off to the right, glass walls set off a larger sound room, where a full set of drums sat eerily silent, like the rest of the studio.

Where was the music, Ham wondered? Where, for that matter and more importantly, the music maker?

Drew threw up her arms, silently demanding the same. Ham shrugged before he noticed motion on the other side of the glass, a short man rushing across the cavernous space, although the "rush" was more of a walrus' waddle.

Ronny was still drying his hands when he finally made it to the booth, winded and sweating an apology. "I was in the bathroom. I hope I didn't keep you waiting too long." He tossed the crumpled, damp paper towel into the trash before reaching for Ham's hand. "Ronny Damon. Pleased to meet you. You must be Ham."

Ham shook the man's meaty and limp hand, clamping his jaw against the temptation to chortle at this little bowling pin of a dude. With a sunken chest leading to hips that would test any doorway and a rotund little face, Ham visualized Ronny as the one pin, neatly lined up in the alley, cheerily waving at the next bowler in line.

He might have got past that, might not have let loose a snort of mirth, were it not for the crowning touch, Damon's hair: parted an inch above his left ear, oily in its attempt to stay coiffed, and for all that, thin and wispy. Most of his real hair resided in his ears.

Ronny looked genuinely confused. "I'm sorry, is something funny?"

"It's just the situation," Ham covered. "I get to meet a record executive and I find out he goes to the bathroom just like regular people."

"I understand," Ronny beamed. "I get that a lot."

I bet you do, Ham deliberately did not say. Aloud, he announced, "This is my partner, Drew Thornton."

"Pleased to meet you, Drew. May I call you Drew?"

"Yes. May I see your check?"

Ham coughed, spewing shock from his lungs. "Drew gets pretty much straight to the point, which is also why she's damn good. What she means is, let's get the business part over with first, shall we?"

"Oh, sure, of course, how silly of me." He reached behind him, picked a folder from among the many tossed on a lower shelf, and withdrew a check. "Certified, $225,000 as we agreed." His eyes wavered with confusion as he glanced between the two of them, clearly uncertain who was boss.

"I'll take that." Drew deftly plucked the piece of paper from Ronny's hand, glanced at the writing and, apparently satisfied, folded it twice and stuffed it in her purse. "Good. Let's get on with it. You know there are cops outside watching you?"

"Yeah. I told you they were. They follow me everywhere, do everything but tuck me in at night. Christ, it feels like somebody's breathing on me all the time."

Ham gritted his teeth, biting back exasperation at the man's speech. Ronny was one of those conversational stylists that ended almost every declarative statement as a question. It forced Ham to push past that irritating habit and focus on the meaning. In other words, an exhausting exchange.

"Is it always so quiet here?" Drew asked. "Where're all your people?"

"It's just me. I'm the owner, producer, engineer and music arranger," he replied, his sunken chest swelling a quarter of an inch. "I do it all."

"Can't you afford to hire help?"

"I don't need to. I'm the best."

"Ooo-kay," Drew drawled.

Ham loved how her innocent face showed not the slightest trace of disbelief. "You said you heard some things. Before we cash the check, I want to know what they were. Otherwise, no deal."

"You mean why I chose you guys instead of more local talent."

"That's the one," Ham affirmed.

Ronny's shrug was so casual, so natural, that it rang truth. "Pure serendipity. There's a lounge act out where you are, a kid by the name of Kyle Grady, he plays piano, mostly old standards, at one of the smaller venues."

Drew and Ham exchanged curious looks, wariness the watchword. "Yeah, I'm familiar with him," Drew replied. "What about him?"

"I know you're familiar with him," Ronny grinned. "It's why you're here."

"Cryptic, obscure," Ham sighed. "Please do explain. I'm all agog."

Ronny turned to face Drew. "It's simple," he told her. "Kyle called me during a set break, all excited, wound up to the point where he was almost breathless and could barely speak. He recognized Russ Porter as soon as he walked in with you, and he knew who you were because you'd busted him as a teenager. Some minor thing, he said, shoplifting maybe? He wanted to know if I'd set it up as a way to... well, he asked if I had set it up. Anyway," he rushed on, "I checked up on you, found your website for McCalister and Thornton, couldn't get ahold of you, called Ham and here you are. Simple," he shrugged.

"Not simple, more like devious," Drew replied. "Is this a move to get to Russ? Is that your game?"

The fire in Drew's eyes forced Ham to jump in. "I think that's obvious. The question is why he thinks Russ can help him."

Ronny had the good grace to blush, his rounded face lighting like fire. "Well, you know, I figured, what the hell, it's a good angle. If I can get Russ Porter behind me, character me up, I'd have some pull, you know?"

"Which is why you were so willing to pay the outrageous total I quoted you," Ham accused. "You figure to buy your way into Russ' circle."

"Well, are you going to help me or not?"

"Any truth to the rumor that you cheat your talent?"

Ronny's eyes darted left, right, anywhere but straight at Ham. "Where did you come across that? Who's been shooting off his mouth?"

Ham tossed it off. "I'm an investigator. It's what I do. What you're paying me to do."

"I'm not paying you to pry into my private business affairs," Ronny snapped. "And I consider your insinuation an insult."

"Just answer the question," Drew ordered.

"I'm a well-respected man," Ronny asserted. His sudden and forced smile intimated an intention that Ham at first did not catch. "But where are my manners? Please, sit down, make yourselves comfortable. I'll fetch us some coffee. Got some freshly brewed in the back room." Before either could answer him he rush-waddled out.

Ham held a finger to his lips, for now he understood. On his way out the door Ronnie had surreptitiously flipped a switch, trying without success to hide his effort behind his rolling, bowling pin of a butt.

He waited until Ronny disappeared from view and then, in response to Drew's arched eyebrows pointed to the control panel. He further clued her in with pure inanity.

"Seems like a nice guy. Pretty impressive. A real heavyweight. What do you think?"

Drew's vicious grin and dancing eyes belied her answer. "I think so, too. There's no way he'd get involved in anything shady. He doesn't need to. Like he says, he's the best, and the best don't wander far from the path of rectitude. They're just too righteous and firm of character."

Ham covered his barking laugh with racking coughs. "Damn," he muttered when he got himself under control, "I hope to hell I'm not catching Russ' cold."

They spoke no further until Ronny returned with a silver tray littered with sugar, cream, spoons and steaming cups. "I forgot to ask what you wanted in your coffee, so I just brought a little of everything." His beaming face confirmed he had indeed heard The Compliment. And just as obviously accepted it as Off the Cuff Truth.

Drew took a demure sip before setting the cup on the table before her and staring directly into Ronny's eyes. "Do you know anybody with the initials AB?"

Ronny's eyebrows rose. "Why do you ask that?"

"It's just something we're looking into," Ham informed him. "A theory."

Ronny's jaw dropped, whether in amazement or admiration he couldn't tell. "You've made that much progress already? Since this morning? Before you even got here?"

"It's what you're paying for," Drew said. "We're expensive, but there's a reason for that. We're the best. Like you claim, only we have—"

"A different business," Ham finished before shooting a warning look Drew's way. No need to antagonize a high paying client, his eyes reminded her.

Her grin flashed so quickly Ham was uncertain he'd seen it. "Yes, a different line of work. Exactly what I was going to say."

"What we need is a list of the people you've worked with," Ham explained. "Especially anybody with the initials AB."

Ronny's eyes narrowed. "All of the people I've ever worked with? Why?"

"So we can investigate your associates," Drew snapped. "Duh."

Ronny's rotund face swelled with rosy indignation. "I see no reason to be rude. I was just asking."

"Just asking is waste of our time. And your money," Drew replied. "How about if I stop you in the middle of a recording session and ask why you're putting a bass line on a pop song? How would that help?"

Ham shot her a look, a mental reminder. *We're not grilling a suspected perp, here. Back off.*

Her square jaw and marble eyes told him she'd heard and her very clear reply was *Screw you*. Nevertheless, she supplied a brief nod, reclaimed her coffee and sat back into the sofa. Her tone softened when she told Ronny, "That's my way of reminding you there are cops on your tail and we may not have much time."

As if to prove her prescient, two men appeared from nowhere, blocking the entrance to the control booth. Both were dressed to the dime store hilt, replete with matching wingtips, which either proved they shared an ironic sense of humor or that they combined to shape a fashion moron. The effect might have been slightly less ridiculous if they weren't the quintessential Mutt and Jeff, not to mention that the smaller man, were it not for his broader shoulders and obvious man-breasts, could have offered Ronny a run for his money at any singles bar anywhere.

"Hello, Damon," the little Jeff drawled. "It's always a pleasure."

Ronny rose to his full five-foot five-inch height, possibly in deference, possibly in defiance, Ham thought, until Ronny's voice dripped acid as he introduced his unwelcome company, then his intent became clear. "Ham, Drew, may I introduce you to our esteemed comedy team of Santa Cruz cops." Waving a hand toward the short man, who stood nose to nose with Drew, he introduced, "This is Detective Wilson," and pointing to a man tall enough to look down on Ham, added, "and, of course, Detective Cassel. They specialize in making a mockery of crime. What a pair."

"You're a funny man," Mutt informed him. "I wonder if you'll be this funny on death row, hmm?"

"You got a warrant?" Ham asked.

"We're not here to arrest anybody," Jeff replied. "Yet."

"We're here for you," Mutt explained. Reading from his notebook, he recited, "Ham McCalister and Drew Thornton, lately of the Las Vegas P.D., now high priced talent out of Nevada. I'd like to know why you're messing around with a small time punk like him?" he asked, pointing an accusing finger at their client. "How much are you clipping him for?"

"You got a warrant?" Ham repeated.

"Are you carrying?" Mutt parried.

"Yes."

"Licensed in California to do so?"

"Yes, both of us," Drew assured them. "Now if there's nothing else we can do for you, it's been a pleasure and goodbye."

Tall Man ignored the comment. Instead, he held his hand out, palm up, fingers wriggling. "Let's see them," he demanded.

Ham, knowing this to be an argument they could not win, signified assent by reaching for his wallet and pulling out the card. Drew hesitated but a few seconds, then did the same.

The detective made a show of inspecting their permits, then handed them off to his partner. "We'll need to verify this, make sure they're legitimate. You'd be surprised how often people try to fake this stuff."

Drew jumped to her feet, face and hair merging in color. "What the hell is this? You can't do that, you ass. I know what you're setting us up for here. The minute you leave with those, we're carrying without license, giving you cause to arrest—and me cause to sue the living hell out you and this entire goddam city. So you might want to rethink it before you go stepping on toes larger than your dick."

"There. Now you know how they work," Ronny snarled. "Law and facts be damned, they do whatever they want. Be careful they don't plant something on you."

"All right, hang on here a second," the larger detective pleaded. "We're not here to start a fight." Nodding at Ronny, he added, "Not even with scumbag here." Turning to Ham and Drew, he shrugged. "The Chief asked us to bring you in, that's all. She wants to talk to you. And yes, the paperwork is a pretense that we'll use if we have to. We can drop all this if you'll just agree to come down and talk with her."

"Make an appointment," Drew growled. "A week from leap year would probably fit my schedule."

The tall man shrugged. "Easy way or hard way. It really is your choice."

"We'll be there," Ham sighed. "Can you give us maybe an hour?" At the shake of the detective's head and the sight of his arms spread wide in helplessness, Ham nodded. "Don't lose us at a stoplight. We haven't learned the town yet."

He almost laughed at the look of sheer relief on the big man's face. "Don't worry about it," the cop said. "You just stay close on my tail and I'll clear the way."

Preparing to leave, Ham paused to whisper to Ronny. "Get me that list we talked about."

"It'll take me some time," Ronny whispered back. "But I'll try."

"That's not what I want to hear, Ronny. Remember what Drew said about time. I want to hear from you today. Focus, first, on anyone and everyone with the initials AB. Go back as far as you can on that. Then start the rest."

CHAPTER FOUR

A MAD DOG KILLER EXPOSED

That Mutt of a cop lived up to his word. He didn't just clear the way, he absolutely battered it. Sirens blared and lights flashed as he flew across the little town, up, down, around and through what traffic lined the beach-front streets. Drew, expert as she was, struggled to control the unfamiliar rental. Ham gripped the armrest as he silently prayed she'd hold on through the sharp swerves and the weaving in and out, entreating more so once he observed the fine sheen of sweat adorning her forehead.

"For heaven's sake," he barked, "just let them go. If they want to kill themselves, that's their own personal business. We don't need to join them in a freaking suicide pact."

Drew grinned tightly, her jaw an echo of her resolve. "And let these small town, small time, small dick hicks show me up? Ain't happening."

Professional pride. Drew, he knew, didn't just have it, she owned it, loved it, nurtured it. It was her baby; the baby she'd never had, but would nevertheless raise.

With ruthlessness, not tenderness.

Ham gnashed his teeth and held his tongue firmly idle rather than goad her competitive rage. Instead, he spent the next three panic inducing minutes praying as fervently as his dimly remembered pious rites allowed.

Hi, God, this is Ham. Well, not really 'Ham', it's Kyle. Kyle McCalister by birth and baptism. You may not remember me, but I remember you. Especially now that I may be making an unexpected and unwelcome appearance before you. Forgive me for my life. It was all accidental. Every bit of it. I didn't mean to do it.

A blessed second later, as they took wing over the speed bump fronting the sheriff's department parking lot, Ham's head battered the too short car roof. Drew ignored his shriek, added more speed and flew toward the braking cop car ahead. At the last impossible second she slammed her own brakes, wrenched the wheel as far and as fast as that mechanical steerage would allow, slewed the car 180 degrees, and, with her own rear bumper, gently tapped the rear end of the now abandoned police undercover cruiser.

For ditched it was. Ham, once he caught his breath, noted with amusement that the cop car stood empty, doors wide open, lights and siren still blaring. They'd abandoned the vehicle with the alacrity born of panic. Both men now lay prone, faces planted firmly into ground, hands protectively over heads.

Drew, he reasoned, was in for one rough new ride. She seemed unconcerned, merely muttering, "Wussies."

Mutt and Jeff remained frozen in place as Ham and Drew exited their vehicle and approached the intersected bumpers. Big Man recovered first, pushing himself up to a more dignified position. He ostentatiously brushed unseen dirt from his suit jacket and, to Ham's amazement, grinned at Drew. "I ought to lock up and kick your ass for that little stunt."

Drew's returning smile was prim, proper, more lady-like, Ham knew, than she'd ever exhibit were it real. "That would take a much bigger man than you. But you can always try."

Ham waited for her to coyly blink her lashes at the oversized cop. There. Perfect. Slow, deliberate, provocative. Drew at her demon best.

Only anticipation of her demure little woman act kept him from guffawing. Thus forewarned, he obliged himself to examine his feet, even as he shoved shaking hands deep into pockets and sucked in air that threatened to explode like thunder from his lungs.

He heard but did not see Jeff snarl, "Get up, you damn fool. What's the matter with you?" Ham assumed he must be speaking to the still grounded cop, since he continued, "You trying to embarrass me in front of this lady?"

Ham wasn't sure but thought he might have heard a snarled, "Screw you, Wilson," Answered by, "I'm going to kill you, jackass." Whatever.

He and Drew followed a sauntering Wilson and a still fuming Cassel through the front entrance, around and through a smallish booking area straight to the chief's office. Wilson rapped on a glass door adorned with gold lettering which read "Valerie Simpson, Chief of Police. Knock Before Entering."

Without waiting for a reply, Wilson popped his head in just enough to announce, "They're here."

Ham heard a muffled "show them in" and felt a firm and very insistent push from the still steaming little bitty bit of a detective. With a glance over his shoulder, Ham assured the guy, "You push me again, little man, you'll wish to hell you hadn't."

"That a threat?" The man's smile turned grim, his eyes set. "Against a cop? You sure you want that kind of trouble?"

"Right, fine, that will do," the chief told Wilson. "Thank you for bringing them in, I'll take it from here. You two get back out on the streets."

The chief turned toward them, proffered her hand, shaking Ham's first, then Drew's, before inviting them to take the school-like chairs fronting her desk. She reclaimed her own chair and swiveled back and studied them as if they were specimens of curiosity, some extraterrestrial freaks of nature.

Drew let the silence crawl on for a while, and then stood up. "Well, if that's all, we'll be on our way."

"Sit down, Ms. Thornton. I'm not trying to be impolite, nor am I trying to intimidate you. It's just that with your reputation I expected someone of a... well, bigger stature." She may as well have made the comparison out loud, for she brushed her own bigger body. Though she could only stand nose to nose with Drew, her hips and chest dwarfed Drew's own. Drew, much to Ham's relief, only responded with a polite nod, not a blistering comment.

"And as for you," she told Ham, "you're much better looking than that faxed photo from your personnel file. Must have been a bad day."

Ham reddened but offered up a friendly smile. "Yeah, well, I guess, thanks. Anyway," he rushed on, "you wanted to see us?"

"Yeah, I did, I do, and thank you for your cooperation." Even as Drew snorted in reply, she offered, "How about coffee? Or soda, we have that, too, if you prefer."

"Bourbon would be good," Drew commented, rounded eyes all innocence.

The chief grinned, reached into a bottom drawer and lifted a half used bottle of Jim Beam up and onto the desk. "Neat or with ice?"

Drew laughed, caught and, as Ham could tell, delighted to be so. "You know, Chief, I think I'm going to like you."

"The name's Valerie Simpson," she offered, putting the bottle back from whence it came. "You can call me 'Val', everyone does, civilian and otherwise. Hearing 'Chief' is foreign to my ear. Makes me wonder who you're talking to."

'Okay, Val, so why are we here? Your clown corps already checked our weapon permits. You plan to warn us off, or what?"

Val shook her head, her short black hair barely ruffled by the waggle.

Apropos of nothing, she asked, "What kind of name is 'Ham' by the way? I take it that's a nickname since your records all say 'Kyle'."

"Yeah, it goes to my youth. I was bigger than most; they started calling me Big Mac, which led to Hamburger, which finally led to just plain old Ham. You know how kids are. The name stuck and I got used to it. Like it, even."

Val nodded. "I see," was all she said.

Drew cleared her throat. "Val? About why we're here?"

Val actually started. "Oh, of course, I'm sorry. It's just nice to have visitors. We don't get many here, you know. Small beach town and all that. So how can I help you?"

Ham sighed, weary of her mental wanderings. "Isn't it the other way around?"

"No, not at all," she replied. "I meant exactly what I said. How can I help you? Is there anything you need, information on the cases, whatever? We're a small department and I don't mind telling you, murder is uncommon here. Very, very rare, in fact, and yet all of a sudden we've got three in the last month. About every ten days, almost like clockwork. And so here we are, invaded by two big-timers from Sin City, out to check the case. I'd be a fool not to let you help us, don't you think?"

Ham and Drew exchanged startled glances before Ham leaned forward on the desk, hands clasped, elbows splayed. "You do know we've been hired to protect your suspect, right?"

Val's shrug indicated a moot point. "If he's guilty, there's not a damn thing you're going to be able to do to protect him. We'll get his ass. But, if he's not, better I should know sooner than later. Gives us a chance to get the real perp, rather than let the case go cold."

"You know, Val," Drew said, "this is great to hear. I wish more chiefs were like you, more interested in justice than wiping a case load under the rug. I'm in and I think I can speak for Ham to say he is, too."

Ham's smile was unforced, wide and accepting. "Fine, then, cutting to the chase here, how about you let us see your case files for these murders? That will help kick start our investigation. And if you'll do that," he promised, "and we do discover that Ronny's the perp, we won't tell you—there's privilege there—but we will leave town immediately. You could probably take that as a clue."

"In our rush we'll have forgotten our notes," Drew put in. "Ham's rather addle-minded these days, what with his dick thinking about Charlie all the time."

Val's eyebrows arched, as if to say, "Oh. I had no idea," but otherwise made no reply.

"Charlie's my lady friend," Ham explained. "And I'm not half as addled as Drew, what with her doing—"

"Nothing and nobody," Drew snapped.

Ham had the decency to look abashed, for he had almost let Russ' name out of their carefully protected bag. God, if he'd let that one fall, it would, no matter how determined Val might be, slip out from someone, since she'd have to let her detectives know. And then the damned press would be all over their asses. Goodbye investigation. And hello, very pissed off Russ.

"I was going to say," Ham ad-libbed, "with Drew doing her memoirs and all."

Shock and delight lit Val's face and energized her eyes. "Really?" she exclaimed. "You're writing a book about your Las Vegas adventures? God," she breathed, "I'd love to read it. I'd love to live it!"

Drew's eyes threw darts at Ham as she responded, "It's in the early stages yet. But I'd be glad to send you a copy once it's done. You can give me feedback before I send it to my editor."

Val reacted with a quick, delighted clap of her hands. "I think we got a deal all around," she affirmed. "Let me get somebody started on making copies of our files." As she headed out the door, she threw back over her shoulder, "I'll just be a minute."

Drew's jaw jutted displeasure, disgust emphasized by her glacial stare. "My memoirs? What, are you trying to make me look like a total freaking loon in front of her?"

Ham leaned back in his chair, folded his hands primly across his belly and flashed his best crocodile grin. "What, as versus me thinking with my dick, is that what you mean?"

"I was saving you from yourself," Drew admonished, "and keeping you chaste for Charlie. Who, by the way, would string what was left of your balls from the roof if you so much as blink at Val."

Ham's shortened breath, lowered voice and studied refusal to look Drew in the eyes belied his denial when he muttered, "I never even noticed."

"Oh come on, Ham. Be honest with yourself, if not with me. I saw you staring a hole through her breasts. More than that, I was afraid that the drool pooling in your lap would splatter onto the floor and give you away."

"She is a nice looking lady," Ham admitted.

"Nice looking!" Drew exclaimed. "Jeez, with those breasts, those hips that make mine look like yours, her perfectly unblemished chocolate skin and those big round eyes, Christ, even I was getting a woody."

Someday, Ham vowed silently and with a prayer, I'm going to be faster than Drew. In the meantime, all he could come up with was, "I didn't get a woody, and you can't, so let's drop it."

Drew's evil grin alerted him that his prayer would never be answered, not in this life, and that this would haunt him for a long, long time. Unless he threatened to tell Russ about her woody, he thought. That might get him off the hook.

Ham spent the next seven minutes studying the ceiling, the walls, the view out the window, the chief's awards wall, anything but Drew, until Val returned with a folder that she ostentatiously waved before them. "Here it is, people. Everything we've got, including notes from the detectives, coroner reports, crime scene photos, the whole enchilada."

"This is really great of you, Val. I can't tell you how much I appreciate it. And how unusual this is, in a good way."

"Just one thing," Ham added to Drew's thanks, "regarding Wilson and Cassel. If you could kind of call them off us, that would help, too." At the glare from her narrowed eyes, he rushed on, "Not that we'll be doing anything you can't know about, and in fact will know about when we have anything useful to impart; it's just that we'll need freedom of movement without having to worry about looking over our shoulders all the time. You understand what I'm saying?"

Val's smile was tight. "Oh yeah, I understand completely. You should know, however, that I have faith in all my people, and especially Detectives Wilson and Cassel. They can come across a bit off-putting, but they, the both of them, are extremely bright, very quick on the uptake. That goes especially for Pete, although he's also the one who's got a monopoly on temper between the two of them. But it's really not bad, you get used to it. I like him, actually. I like both of them. They're good guys."

"That's funny, because Ham likes your—"

"Style!" he shouted. "I was telling Drew I like your style."

Drew's laugh rang as hollow as Ham figured she intended it to. "If you say so. That aside, I can tell you this, Pete wouldn't last three minutes in Vegas. We'd take him out, beat the shit out of his little punk ass, and leave him on the Strip to be picked over by the tourists."

Val's shrug indicated relenting agreement. "I'll have a talk with them, ask them to go a bit gentle and remember that you're helping us." She took a second to glance at both before adding, "You won't betray my trust, will you?"

"Won't happen," Drew smiled. "You're the first chief I've actually been able to identify with, let alone like. I'd be pleased if you'd consider me an ally."

"I'll do that, Drew, and you, too, Ham." She stood up, came around the desk and shook both their hands warmly. "Come back anytime for that bourbon."

"Count on it. And again, thank you. We'll keep in touch."

Val escorted them out, waving as they disappeared down the drive. Ham, watching her through the rearview mirror, mumbled, "This isn't right, you know."

Drew waited until she'd pulled out of the lot and turned out of sight. "What's not right?" she finally inquired. "That we're screwing her or that she's trying to screw us right back?"

"Exactly," Ham affirmed. "No cop, no matter how nice, is going to give out official work product, especially to some private investigators."

"It's a trap," Drew agreed. "But it's a good one. We can use it to our own advantage as long as she thinks we don't know the full score."

'Yeah, well, that's the thing. I find it hard to believe that she thinks we're that naïve. Which means—"

"It's a trap without subterfuge. You saw her eyes when you asked her to get Mutt and Jeff off our tails. She recovered well, I'll give her that, but that puts a bit of a crimp in her plans. So my guess is that—"

"She'll tell them to go right on going on. Their part is to play out of control cops who just won't listen to their little chief of police lady because, after all, she's only a woman and what could she possibly know about a man's rough and tumble world of crime."

"Right on the head, Ham. That's why you get the big bucks. Any obvious clue, you eventually pick up on it."

Ham laughed at her old joke, one he often employed himself. "I hate that I have to share those bucks with you when it's always me that has to solve the obvious."

Drew's grin matched his own until her forehead creased in thought. "What do you suppose are the chances they didn't put a GPS on this car?"

"About the same as getting five consecutive royal flushes at the casinos."

"And a bug?"

"No, not without a warrant. The Supreme Court made that one out of bounds. As a matter of fact, same with the GPS if it's to be used long term. They get around that irritant by claiming, with straight face and innocent eyes, that they assumed we were only going to be in town a few days and that they had reasonable suspicion to believe that we'd lead them to a serial killer. Meaning, in their minds, our roly-poly client."

While talking, Ham had been perusing the crime photos, which did indeed appear to be samples from each of the three murder sites. The kill shots were well placed, and the blood was as expected. Though he'd known the victims' initials had been carved on their cheeks, it still jarred to see them. A cold chill ran down his back. This was one psycho sick son of a bitch.

More interesting, at least for now, was Cassel's report on his interviews with various witnesses. One jumped out, grabbed him by the collar and shook him until his head swam.

"Bingo," Ham muttered. "Let's see if we got an address."

"What is it? What have we got?"

"Just a second," Ham replied as he flipped through pages. "Here," he finally announced. "Detectives Wilson and Cassel interviewed one Amber Bailey after the first murder, and again after the second. If they interviewed her after the third, there's no record of it, which is strange given that, according to Cassel's report, they viewed her as a potential suspect."

Drew wasted no time with questions. "Put the address into the GPS," she snapped. "We'll go conduct our own interview. You can tell me what they wrote in their report while I drive."

Ham punched in the address and returned to the file. "She released a CD on Ronny's label, and according to this, she shared songwriting credits with Charlie Davis, the first victim, which was why they talked to her after his murder. Says here that she didn't have an alibi, claims she was home that night, by herself. They haven't as yet followed up on that, haven't talked to the neighbors or anything. Why, I don't know."

"Pretty sloppy work," Drew commented.

"At the least. She was interviewed again after Evan Boyd's body was found, again because of shared songwriting credits, and because all three worked with Ronny. No alibi is listed here and it's not even clear to me that they asked." Ham looked up, staring half at and half through Drew. "Odd. There's something wrong here."

Drew reached blindly into her purse and pulled out her cell phone. She flipped it to Ham and demanded, "See if you can get Russ on the line for me. You'll see him on the speed dial. Maybe he knows who this Amber Bailey is. If so, we can go in forearmed in case she tries to screw us around."

Ham took to the opportunity to stick it in a bit more. "On your speed dial, huh? Wow, this *must* be serious."

"Just dial the phone, Ham, and spare me the high school humor."

Ham completed his chore and handed the phone off to Drew.

"Hello, handsome. Miss me yet?"

Ham rolled his eyes.

"We've got a lead we're following," she continued, "a singer-songwriter out of Ronny's stable by the name of Amber Bailey. Yep, that's right, but she's not a victim, she's a suspect." Ham heard scrambled words emerge from the cell but none intelligible enough to understand. Finally, Drew announced, "We've asked Ronny for that; he should supply us the list sometime today and we'll talk to the AB's first, warn them of what could happen. In the meantime, do you know Amber, know anything about her?"

Ham glanced at the GPS, noticed that they had less than three miles to Amber's house and circled with his finger for Drew to wrap it up.

"Well, that's interesting," he heard Drew exclaim. "That's the first damn thing I'll ask her about."

She shook her head at Ham's inquiring look and continued, "By the way, the reason we were called is because Ronny wants to meet you. The lounge singer called him, that's how he found out the connection. He told him I was there with you. Ronny's hoping to sweet talk you so he can get you, as he put it, to character him up to the cops. He figures even the cops won't cross a star like you." Drew's burst of laughter clued Ham as to Russ' answer. "Yeah, I pretty much told him that, only not so crudely."

Drew's smile warmed. "You are? When? That's fantastic. See you then." Drew clicked off and turned to Ham.

"He says he got home to Tahoe, rambled the empty place for an hour and repacked. He'll be in this evening. Isn't that great?"

Ham took a moment to think it over, decided honesty was best. "Not really, no. We're here on a job. It's going to be difficult with you going off and playing house with Russ."

Drew laughed softy. "You are such a stick in the mud. Two things, Ham, old boy. Number one, I never let anybody interfere with work." In response to Ham's raised eyebrow, she snapped, "I wasn't working last night and I had no idea you got us a case this morning, so back the hell off. Anyway, as I was saying, and point number two is, how was I supposed to tell Russ he couldn't come use his own house? Answer me that one, Oh Great Sage."

"Yeah," Ham sighed. "I can't argue that one. As for the professionalism part, I know that, too, and I never would have questioned it if it hadn't been for you not answering your phone this morning. But," he rushed to say once he saw the flush on her face, "given the circumstance, perfectly understandable. So forget it. I won't question your integrity again. I promise. How's your sex life?"

"Missing Charlie, are you? Must be, otherwise why get salacious about mine?"

"Touché," Ham laughed. "But how about we get back to Amber? What did Russ tell you that got you so excited?"

Drew shook her head, whether in admiration or disgust he couldn't tell. Then she explained, "That is one hooked up little lady. She's managed to sleep her way around the music world, probably even Ronny, an image that makes me want to poke out my mind's eye. She was a groupie with Truckee River. Neither Russ nor Blake gave her a tumble, but apparently the drummer and bass player aren't so picky."

Ham's confusion rang in his voice. "Well, so what? Number one, that happens a lot in the entertainment industry, and number two, what does that have to do with murder?"

"It's not that. What's curious to me is the connections to Russ we're running into. Ronny hears from Kyle Grady—"

"The lounge singer you and Russ went to hear."

"Right. Ronny hears from him and hires you, hires us, to get to Russ. Amber Bailey is a suspect who all but stalked Russ in the past. Coincidence? Or design?"

Ham nodded agreement. "You're right, and you know how I feel about coincidence. We'll ask not only Amber but also Ronny about that as well, see what he has to say about Amber and her past. I can't think Ronny didn't know about that, yet when he talked about Russ he didn't mention it. Nor did he say anything about it, or her, when we asked who he worked with who had Amber's initials. Our Ronny is hiding something, I'm beginning to suspect."

"Which he has to know is not a good idea when you're paying someone to help you. He must either think we're idiots or that we'll look the other way at incriminating evidence."

"Wrong on both counts," Ham replied gruffly. "As he'll soon find out."

"After we deposit that check," Drew added.

"Oh most definitely," Ham averred. "A jewel like Ronny, he wouldn't have it any other way."

The lady voice from the GPS interrupted them with an order to turn left and followed up with mechanical self-smugness. "Then, destination."

"Show time," Drew said. Nodding toward the driveway, she added, "She's home, I'm guessing. Unless she has more than one car or she has a roomie. If it's a roommate, we'll talk to her. Or him, as the case may be."

A two story townhouse, Amber's residence sat amid a rather upscale neighborhood, so well-tended with small green patches of lawn, hibiscus and assorted shrubbery that Ham supposed the association fees must comprise a major chunk of the monthly payments. Almost still; little noise, either traffic or human, moved through the warmth of the late afternoon. With an appreciative nod, Drew remarked, "She must do okay for herself. Nothing low rent about this."

They pulled in beside the Ford Escape that crowded the right side of the two-car drive, forcing Ham to ease his body out without dinging the dark blue paint of the nearly new auto Amber drove. There was, he knew, no worse way to establish trust with a witness than to first destroy their beloved property. A definite investigative no-no.

They approached the small covered porch and, while Drew rang the bell, Ham noticed two empty glasses, ice not yet fully dissolved, perched on a miniature glass-topped table. The glasses were accompanied by an oversized ashtray, half filled with cigarette butts, some stained with red lipstick, others untainted. So she was not alone. Or hadn't been.

His attention reverted back to the door when Drew pounded her fist emphatically. "Maybe the doorbell doesn't work," she speculated. "Because someone's obviously home."

Drew waited a few seconds, pounded again, then after a short wait made one more try. "Well, either she's taking a nap, in the shower or just plain ignoring us. What do you want to do?" Indicating her keychain, she acknowledged, "I've got a bump key for this type of lock. Simple as releasing your own front door. Want me to try?"

"Not unless we have to." Peeking in the window, he saw among the shadows a living area dominated by a sofa, love seat and entertainment system, and on into what must be the kitchen off to the side. Nothing and no one stirred.

He jumped back when a loud crash resounded through the small area, followed almost instantly by an eerie high pitched scream—or howl, maybe. He glanced at Drew, saw that she too had drawn her weapon, and motioned for her to take the front while he took the rear. Ham left Drew poised and ready on the porch and dashed around the end of the block, two houses down, and back to the fence line that enclosed the tiny backyards of each of the adjoining units along that street. At the third break, he hauled himself over the fence and dropped onto a dinner table sized patio, with a Jacuzzi on the left and a swinging two-seater chaise lounge on the right. Three short steps brought him to the sliding glass door, which stood ajar, maybe one-third open, the entrance obscured by drapes billowing in the slight breeze.

Ham cautiously pushed aside the offending drapery and led with his gun as he slowly entered the gloomy darkness within. No lamps brightened the dreary interior, and with the unit's north-south exposure what sunlight remained failed to make more than a dent.

Suddenly, and before he could determine the direction, his opponent flew at him from out of the gloom, a snarl announcing malevolent intent. He swung his gun up to chest level, trying to identify the oncoming threat, only to discover his attacker had gone straight for his leg, just above the knee, with some kind of multi-bladed knife, twisting it into his thigh, all the while snarling and growling.

Ham could see only white shaggy hair. Using his mouth, not a knife, gnawing, gnawing, ripping at his flesh, it was a cannibal straight from hell, frothing at the mouth, gnashing his life's blood from knee to thigh, intent on dismembering him, a maniac out of control and out of his mind. Reflexively, Ham's finger closed on the trigger he'd been caressing and the shot flew across the room, straight into and through a designer lamp he only had time to glimpse before it showered him and his attacker with shards of debris.

At the sound of the blast, Drew burst through the front door, took a shooter's stance, gun at the ready, and screamed a warning, something about "a hole in your ass, mother-loving jackass!"

And then she laughed. A deep cough of pleasure that caused Ham to reassess, to slow down and take stock—of the little shit of a Shih Tzu gripping and ripping his left thigh.

Ham shook his leg, trying to get rid of the imbedded pest, gave up and pointed his pistol at the little dog's head.

"Don't," Drew shrieked. "For heaven's sake, it's just a little dog protecting his fiefdom. You don't have to kill him." Without a further word to Ham, she knelt down, knees kissing the carpeted floor, arms outstretched in welcome, and cooed, "Here boy. Come on, boy, come to mama."

The little dog disengaged from Ham's leg, plopping with its little legs onto the floor and scampered over to Drew, tail wagging and tongue lolling in welcome. Ham cringed and again raised his weapon when the dog leapt at Drew, only to lower it once the fiend's intention became clear. It clung to Drew's chest in apparent relief and love and began to lick her face, her ears and especially her nose.

"Why you sweet little boy," Drew murmured. "Don't you worry about a thing. I won't let anybody hurt you. I promise. You'll be okay now."

"I should have shot the damn mutt," Ham complained. "Jeez, just look at me. The little monster took half my leg."

"Oh quit whining," Drew remonstrated. "For god's sake, he's—" She paused to pick him up and checked underneath. "Yes, a he," she confirmed. "He's just a little bitty thing, maybe twelve or thirteen pounds. How much harm can he do to a big man like you?"

"Enough to require shots and stitches."

"Oh you big baby, let it go. Something made him jump, let's find out what."

Ham followed her, as he limped, bloody and silently cursing, through the living area, into the kitchen and the separate dining room beyond, worries about stealth obviated by the little killer twerp of a dog that continued to nip at Ham's heels.

"You stop that," Drew ordered. Much to Ham's amazement, the dog sat, eyes alert, tail wagging—and as far as Ham could tell, laughing at him.

They checked the half bath and laundry room, all that was left to be explored on the first floor, and headed for the stairs. Ham led the way to the landing, which opened onto a hall that encompassed two closed doors and an open invitation to a full bath. He felt around the wall at usual height for a light fixture, felt it and flicked on the overhead and mirror lights. Nothing.

He motioned for Drew to take the room on the left as he headed for the closed door just down the hall on the right. With a sigh of disgust, he realized how worthless the silence of the motion was. He might as well have screamed the order out loud for all the surprise left to them.

Ham knew that he wouldn't be any more visible in the black shadow than any possible perp would be to him, and knowing that a panicked person would aim for where he assumed the chest would be, he squatted as low as his lanky frame permitted. He turned the knob and eased the door open with his knee.

Or so he had intended. Unfortunately, the damaged leg gave way under him and he fell forward, giving the lightweight door a robust nudge. The door slapped against the adjoining wall and the resulting rebound whacked him in the head.

"Son of a bitch!" Ham shouted, less in pain than in anger and humiliation. "Son of a bitch of a goddam door!"

Anticipating a volley of shots aimed at the sound of his ill-timed voice, Ham flopped onto the floor, face buried in carpet, and waited excruciating seconds for the explosions and whizzing bullets he expected to buffet his ears—until unanticipated pain in his buttocks triggered a yelp of torment.

Drew rushed in from the other room, the smell of fear and worry oozing from her pores, and managed to screech to a halt just before she tripped over his prone form.

Ham felt a rush of relief, even affection, for his savior partner. Right up until she began to laugh. Not just a giggle, not a smothered burst of enjoyment, but guffaws.

"Get him off me," Ham shrieked.

Drew whistled softly and followed up with, "Here, boy, come to mama." The devil mad killer dog let loose of Ham's butt and leapt into Drew's waiting arms, kissing her with an affection—or affectation—that made Ham want to strangle the breath out of that mangy mutt.

"I promise you, I will kill that thing the next time it even glances my way, even as he's mulling over whatever wicked intent his warped little doggy mind conceives."

"Forget it, we've got bigger problems than a little dog that thinks you're dinner. Come on in here," she instructed, pointing to the room she'd so recently abandoned.

"Amber?"

Drew responded with a grim nod. "At least we know she's not the perp." Bitterly, she added, "If we'd skipped that little conference with the chief, we might have been in time to save her."

'If we'd skipped the conference," Ham corrected, "we wouldn't have had her name yet. So let's not blame ourselves."

He followed Drew into the room where Amber lay stretched out on her bed, flat on her back. Etched into her left cheek was an A; the lowercase b decorated her right. The A flat Russ had predicted.

"Well, this is a new twist," Ham muttered. For Amber had exited the world the way she came in. As naked as God made her.

"There's a towel on the other side of the bed," Drew informed him. "Still damp."

"So what do we have here? She was taking a shower, or had just finished her shower, when the killer came in?"

"Or returned. There were two glasses on the porch; maybe she entertained the killer and for some reason, instead of doing her in then, he came back a short while later."

"Maybe," Ham agreed. "Maybe somebody walks by, somebody who knows Amber, and the perp takes advantage of a lucky break. Because he's now got a witness who can testify that when the suspect was there Amber was alive and well and sipping iced tea on the front porch."

"Pretty smart guy if he thought of it on the spot."

"Experienced," Ham shrugged. "That's all. Never assume amorality carries with it any degree of intelligence."

"Better get Val on the phone."

"Yeah." Ham punched in the number on the card she had provided in her office. As he did, he nodded at Drew. "In the meantime, you snoop around a little. I still don't trust that we'll be given the real poop."

"The whole poop, and nothing but the poop."

Ham grinned at her even as Val answered. "We've got another one here. Amber Bailey is the victim. Everything's as expected, except she's naked. Looks like she was taking a shower.... We're not touching anything," he snapped. "On the contrary, we're being useful citizens, reporting a crime to the proper authorities."

Ham listened for a bit, occasionally holding the phone away from his ear in disgust until, nearing the end of his limited patience, he cut in with, "Maybe you'd like to know that we're only steps behind the killer. There's still ice, or there was, in the glasses out front. Given the warmth today, melting wouldn't take long, so I'm estimating we got here within half an hour of her little social. Also, her body shows no postmortem lividity as yet. From that alone, I'd guess maybe an hour or two, certainly no more than that, and maybe less. Put that together with the ice and it says our killer hasn't had much of a head start."

"All right," Val informed him, "Wilson and Cassel are in the area. I'll send them right out. You wait there."

"In the area, huh? Watching us, or watching Ronny?"

"No need to watch you," Val replied. "They're sticking on Ronny who, very interestingly, is at this moment quite near to you. If he stopped at Bailey's house, I haven't been told yet. If he hasn't, Wilson and Cassel can confirm it. That would be a good thing for him, and a good thing for you. Means he couldn't be the killer, right?"

"Well, yeah, there is that," Ham allowed. "Tell Wilson and Cassel we'll be waiting." Watching the Shih Tzu at the door, snarling and snapping at him from a distance, he added a warning. "Tell them to be careful. There's a killer dog here they may have to shoot."

CHAPTER FIVE

THE VANISHING

The rhythmic rise and fall of sirens announced their looming presence long before Mutt and Jeff burst through the door, guns drawn and at the ready, stomping through what might have proved to be real evidence in their rush to be on the scene. No chance of saving that evidence now, Ham thought bitterly.

The guns pointed at his chest unnerved him a lot less than the yowling. "Will you turn off that damn siren, you freaking moron?" Ham demanded of the smaller and more threatening armed intruder. "No need to bring the entire neighborhood running. Idiot."

"My town, my siren, my choice. Up against the wall," Pete Wilson demanded. "And I mean now, Mr. Big City Detective."

"You want me up against the wall, little man, you're going to have to put me there. And I would strongly urge you not to try."

Cassel stepped between them. "Take it easy, Pete. Remember your blood pressure. And you," he snapped at Ham, "I wish you'd quit provoking him. We're all on the same side here, like it or not." Turning back to Pete, he finished with, "At the chief's orders."

Pete shrugged, neither apologetic nor agreeable. "Where's the dog? You got him locked up?"

Ham pointed toward a corner where the now cowed and shivering ball of fur strove for invisibility. Evidently, he found the storm trooper detectives far more intimidating than he did Ham.

Pete's jaw dropped and he regarded Ham as he might the circus misfit. "This is your killer dog? This little ankle biter?" His eyes narrowed and his face reddened. "So what, now you're a comedian? I would have thought that as an ex-cop you'd have sense enough not to broadcast a danger warning to investigators descending on a murder scene. Really funny, man. And really, really stupid," he added disgustedly.

Ham's casual shrug was his only reply. He did, however, have the grace to flush a bit with shame.

"Where's the victim?" Detective Cassel inquired. "You haven't disturbed the scene, have you?"

"I picked up a towel by her bed," Drew admitted, "just to see if it was damp. It was. Looks like the killer caught her coming out of the shower."

"Is she nude?"

"As the proverbial jaybird."

"Any signs of sexual abuse?"

"None that I saw. Cheeks with the Ab as we expected. Other than being nude, it's like the others, on the face of it."

"Well, let's go take a look," Cassel told her. "Lead the way. And you," he chortled at Ham, "maybe you should stay here and keep your gun trained on that killer ankle biter."

Ham's wry expression allowed that Steve had scored a point. "You think you're kidding," he muttered. "But I've got the scars and blood to prove it."

Drew led Steve and Pete up the stairs, Ham trailing behind, and into the master bedroom. "Have you called the coroner?" she asked.

"On his way. Coming with Val, I think," Steve replied.

"For your information, and as I told Val on the phone, the ice in the glasses out on the porch hadn't melted by time we got here, so, whether the perp was her drinking partner or not, he can't have been gone long. We also think he may have been seen." To Pete he suggested, "Maybe this time you ought to be professional and thorough enough to talk to the neighbors."

Before Pete could utter a snarky reply, Steve good-naturedly jibed, "And that's why they pay you the big bucks, right?"

"Right," Ham allowed. "But my point is, why didn't you follow up on her alibis before, when you thought she might be a suspect? Maybe you could have eliminated her and discovered that, on the contrary, she was a potential target."

"And maybe," Drew added, her voice tinged with anger, "she wouldn't be lying there with holes in her heart and her cheeks mutilated."

"Okay, if you two will step out in the hall, Pete and I can get started. Val and the coroner will be here soon and they'll want to talk to you, I'm sure. Until then, just hang loose."

"Just hang loose," Drew laughed. "So what are you, like, from the 1980s?"

They watched from the doorway as Pete took pictures, a thorough and professional documentation of the scene. He got close-ups of the blood-stained sheets, the cheeks and the towel, as well as dirty laundry in the corner, probably her recently shed clothes. They could see in the mirrored bathroom door that he was snapping pics of the shower, honing in on small pools of moisture, marking the time of last use.

Meanwhile, Steve had donned surgical gloves and was neatly and thoroughly searching the bureau drawers, occasionally putting an item on top, presumably material destined for an evidence bag. Not content with the bureau, he went through her closet, item by item, and her nightstand drawers. Neither appeared to interest him much, as the search took a matter of mere minutes.

Pete exited the bathroom and elbowed his way between them, heading for the stairs and the landing below. Soon after, the sirens ceased their ear throbbing rhythm and Ham breathed a frustrated sigh of relief.

He heard voices downstairs and figured that Val must have arrived. He hoped she had a bit more investigative decorum than her subordinates.

Before Ham could bull-rush in, Drew nudged him and he took the clue. He followed her down to the living room, where they found Val talking to Pete and an older gentleman with white hair and matching goatee. A sort of Colonel Sanders, Ham mused. Only heavier, to a considerable degree.

Val waved at them as they entered and politely insisted, "Ham, Drew, tell me what's going on. How'd you stumble onto this? I mean, this must be your first stop from the office, right? Why? Did you know something we don't, something you didn't bother to let me in on?"

Ham and Drew exchanged glances. "We just were curious," Ham explained. "The files list her as a suspect in the first two murders, yet no follow-up was done. We wanted to find out what her story was, maybe figure out why you people dropped the ball."

"There was no ball dropping," Val snapped. "We got a better suspect, that's all. We would have talked more with her later. But," she confessed with a shrug, "our intent would have been to discuss your client's business and what she knew about it." Her deep sigh expressed her regret much better than words would ever have done. "I wish to hell we had."

Ham let her off the hook. Waving toward the corpulent Colonel impostor, he asked, "I take it this is the coroner?"

"Dr. Melville, meet Drew Thornton and Ham McCalister, of the eminent firm of private investigators of the same name. Out of Las Vegas, here to save us from ourselves." Her smile indicated teasing affection, a welcome relief from Pete's resentment.

"How do you do?" he perfunctorily asked, shaking each by the hand. "I'd be happy to chat but I've got work to do. So if you'll excuse me?"

Pete led him to the stairs, explained, "She's up here. Naked, cheeks marked with her initials, same as the others, but nude. We think she'd just got out of the shower when the killer surprised her."

Val watched them leave, then turned squarely to face them. "Okay, tell me why you're here. And try the truth this time."

Ham studied the intricacy of the carpet's weave, glanced up at Drew who answered with an uncertain shrug. "I was showing Drew the crime photos we had and talking about the victims' initials carved into their cheeks, how unique that was to anything I'd ever seen or heard of before. And then Russ—"

"Rushing through his explanation of the case this morning," Drew interrupted firmly, "Ham was messing around on my piano, which he does when he's thinking, kind of a distraction thing that centers him. Anyway, he's halfway through some riff or other when he stops, looks at me with those wide, piercing green eyes of his and says, 'jeez, Drew, that's it!'"

Ham hid his inward smile with a serious and deliberative nod, thinking, *Nice save. And damn quick.*

At Val's blank stare, Drew explained, "Ham's classically trained, runs through various keys and chords when he's deep in thought, like being on autopilot. He says it empties his mind, lets him see beyond the distractions. Anyway, he's tinkling this beautiful little tune while telling me about the cheek thing, and the order of the murders, the initials you know, and he suddenly pounds on the keys and says, 'That's it'! It's gotta goddam be it.' I asked him what and he explained his theory. Why don't you fill her in from here, Ham? It was your guess."

Ham attempted modesty, tried his best to look embarrassed by his own brilliance. "Forget the cheeks, why would the murderer bother to carve the victims' initials on their bodies at all? Serial killers are a loony breed, but their actions always mean something to them, whether it makes any sense in the real world or not. So what is his reason?"

"Well," Val offered, "we were rather assuming that he was either taunting them in death, which would indicate a personal hatred for each, or, and more likely, he's taunting us. Third, of course, is for publicity, though if that's his motive we're not playing. We haven't released that information, and we're not going to."

"Good," Ham nodded, "you're right on the money as far as it goes. But there's a fourth possibility, and I think it's a very real one, given that the victims are all in the music business. He's playing a C minor scale."

Val took a breath, started to say something, apparently changed her mind and instead just shook her head.

"Okay, here's the deal. Put the initials in order and those are the notes of the C minor scale, which of course is the order of the key. See?"

Val plopped down on the couch, stared up at him as if afraid his lunacy might be contagious. "You're serious, aren't you? You really believe this."

Ham spread his hands, indicating the obviousness of what he'd said. "It's the only explanation that makes sense. Or at least the one that makes the most sense. And it damn sure tells us that the killer is also a musician. Or at least has musical knowledge."

Her answering smile was grim when she pointed out, "Well, that would sure apply to your client, wouldn't it? Meantime, what the hell is a key? And a scale? And what notes are what? Does Amber Bailey fit in? How?"

Ham pretended to read off the names of the victims while surreptitiously reading off the C minor scale from notes he'd taken during Russ' explanation. "We have CD—Charlie Davis —followed by E flat. In music notation a flat is indicated by a small b, which is how Evan Boyd's initials were carved, a capital E and a small b. After that comes F and G, which is Fran Gallaugher. Want to guess the next two notes in the scale?"

Val's expression relaxed from uptight confusion to genuine interest. "Would that be AB?"

"That it would," Ham said. "And so here we are."

"Meaning you were looking for somebody in our report who had those initials, you didn't tell us about it and you got Amber killed." She no longer looked amused. "But let's move on. Explain, slowly and completely, musical scales, keys, notes, whatever it is I need to know to catch up to you. And remember I'm not classically trained or trained at all, so keep it simple."

Drew's wide eyes disclosed an inner struggle to suppress the laughter in her belly. Ham ignored her, a matter of self-defense, as he battled to control his own confusion. He made a pretense of contemplation, as if searching for the right words, while fingers probed his forehead as if to force the phrases out and into the open. Finally, he sighed in resignation and with straight face explained to Val, "It really is difficult to clarify this to someone who's not been schooled in music theory. Perhaps what would be best is for me to write a short explanation in sort of a white paper. That way I can be sure I put it simply and completely. Would you like that?" More importantly, he thought, could he get Russ to do it?

"I would like. When will I have it?"

"Oh, say later today, maybe early tomorrow."

"In the meantime, tell me the rest of the key. Or scale or whatever. What initials are we looking for, and how many more murders before the list is done?"

Ham sighed with frustration, knowing the end would be difficult to grasp, because it was for him as well. "That's the thing, see. Next is B flat, meaning B and B for the initials. Then comes C, but that's all. So we're thinking maybe a one-named artist whose name starts with C, you know, like Cher."

"Well, I haven't seen Cher around the community so I doubt she's here. But I see your point. So we look through the file, see if we have someone with the initials BB. And, if not, are you going to ask your client?"

Pete's voice sounded behind them. "If they can find him, you mean."

Val looked at him, the question in her eyes, and he responded with a grim nod. "The son of a bitch ditched us."

Ham noted that Steve's face was as cloudy as Pete's and suddenly understood Pete's foul mood—even for Pete—upon arrival to the scene. Ronny had apparently outwitted his pursuers, or as Ronny thought of it, his tormentors.

Ham might have laughed had he not instantly recognized the obvious. His client had just purchased himself an arrest. And one hell of an interrogation. The question was, would he have one hell of an explanation?

Any impulse to derisive laughter that may have remained died in his throat as they wheeled Amber out, the white sheet announcing her condition.

"How long has she been dead?" Val asked the coroner.

"Less than two hours, I'd say. The body has barely begun to cool. Given the ambient temperature, my best guess at the moment is that it's probably around an hour and a half."

The coroner nodded to the techs and they continued with their task of wheeling the deceased from the premises. None one of them spoke for several minutes after Amber, the coroner and the techs disappeared down the road, siren off. No need for speed now.

Finally, Val sighed, adjusted her uniform jacket and stared a hole through her detectives. "All right, give it to me straight. Did you screw up?"

"Yeah, we screwed up," Steve admitted. "He hadn't tried anything stupid before, in fact he seemed to get perverse enjoyment from yanking our chains. He'd wave to us as he drove off, once even stopped in front of a coffee shop, ambled over and asked us what we'd like. Said coffee and cop food—which we figured was a tweak about the donut stereotype—was on him, so go wild."

"I told him to wildly go to hell," Pete interjected, "which made him laugh as he walked away, head shaking like he'd made a world-class ass of us, rather than himself. The guy's a bigger jerk than most."

"Well, that's not really the point, is it?" Val asked. "The point is, how did you manage to lose him? And at the worst possible time?"

"He went into one of those large department stores, over by the boardwalk. As usual, we pulled in, he waved, shouted he'd be a while and to make ourselves comfortable. Unless we wanted to spend some quality time shopping with him." Pete looked down and mimed spitting on the floor. "The smartass offered to show us ties for the better dressed man."

"It looked like business as usual," Steve added. "We waited and waited, for almost an hour. Finally, we decided we'd best go see what he was up to since even a dilettante like him can't spend all day on narcissism. The upshot is he was gone, out the back and out of there."

"His car is still there, or was when we left, but he's not. He either flagged a cab, which we haven't checked yet but will, or he hot-footed it out of there, or he had another car parked and ready, and that seems unlikely since I don't see how he could have done that without our knowing—"

"Unless an accomplice left it for him," Val pointed out.

"Yeah, unless that. Anyway, you can bet we'll check cabs first thing, as well as the store security tapes. They show the back exit, and there's a camera on the back lot. We'll have his ass in a well-worn sling before we're through."

Val peered at Ham and Drew, both silent and grim, and gave a quick, disapproving shake of her head. "I am dearly hoping that you two know nothing about this. I'm equally hoping the security cameras won't catch you in the back lot of that store. If they do, you'd best tell me now, and tell me why."

"There's nothing to tell," Ham answered for them. "We came here straight from your office, just as we said. We couldn't have gotten here when we did if we'd stopped off to help our client elude you first, now could we?"

"Besides," Drew added, "there's no percentage in it. We're being paid to help him, not to put the spotlight on him. Which," she added disgustedly, "he managed to do well enough without our help. The damned idiot."

Ham opened his mouth to add his perspective, but before he could speak, Val pointed a finger at him and said, "You promised you would keep me informed, and I promised you I'd deliver what we have. You'll get a copy of the notes and photos as soon as they're ready. We'll let you know when we've picked your client up and you can do what you want about that, but in the meantime I know that you and your partner have things to do and people to see, so we won't detain you."

He'd been dismissed before, but rarely so politely. He waved Drew out the door and on their way.

Which, Drew being Drew, she refused to do until she'd taken care of one last detail. "What about the dog?" she asked Val. "We can't just leave him here."

"Don't worry about it, we'll call animal control."

"What," Drew cried, "so they can lock him in a cage, put him to sleep if no one adopts him? Forget it, that's not happening. We'll take him with us."

"No, we won't," Ham snapped. "Number one, we don't have time to take care of the diminutive beast, and number two, he's a vicious, paranoid little asshole. Let animal control deal with him."

Pete's laugh was anything but humorous. "This hulk of a wannabe man is afraid of little bitty dogs. And spiders and flies, I'm guessing."

"Very amusing," Ham replied dryly. "The point is that we don't have time to take care of it, feed it, walk it, clean up after its poop. That's reality."

Drew would have none of it. In a voice that brooked no denial, she shot that down fast and firm. "That's nonsense. Gardner would be happy to watch him while we're gone." Turning to Val, and with her most ingratiating grin, asked, "If that's all right with you?"

Val shrugged, apparently unconcerned either way. "Yeah, I guess, at least until we notify the next of kin. It's their call, but until then, sure. It saves me the trouble of waiting on those lazy asses at animal control to finish their martini lunches and drag themselves out here, grumbling and stumbling all the way, and me having to listen to it and pretend commiseration. So sure, why not?" With that she turned on her heels and very deliberately left them to show themselves out.

Ham climbed into the passenger seat and buckled up. He was just about to slam the door when Drew reached in and delicately delivered the dog to Ham's lap. "What the hell are you doing?" he screeched. "I'm not holding this thing!" As if to reinforce his objections, the mutt snarled and bared its tiny teeth at Ham, drooling as though he craved Ham for lunch.

He jumped out, tossed the dog into Drew's arms and ran around the car before she could balk. To his surprise and relief, she did not. Instead, she slid in beside him, all the while petting and cooing at the diminutive assassin. "Let's take him back to the house," she suggested, "and get him comfortable."

Ham backed out the drive and continued on as his mechanical guide demanded. They'd completed about half the trip to Russ' place before she turned to him, eyes alight with pleasure. "What shall we call him?"

"How about if you open the door at the next stoplight, let him out, and we'll call him lost."

"You're not funny, Ham," she frowned. "Show a little compassion. This poor little guy has lost everything, his mama, his house, his security, everything he's ever known." She suddenly sat upright, slapped Ham on the arm and declared, "That's it, though, you hit it. A home run. What better name for him than 'Lost'?"

"You're going to keep that thing, aren't you?" Ham lamented. "That means I'm going to have to invest in shin guards and several pairs of heavy socks before I set foot back in your house again."

"Oh, don't worry. I'll bring him over to your house so he can get to know you." She scratched the dog's ears and he, in response, curled into a white ball on her lap, making little grunting sounds of contentment. "He'll grow to love his Uncle Ham, won't you, Lost?"

Yeah, Ham thought. Like a favorite food group. Out loud he replied, "Let's forget about your new toy for a minute. Time's not our ally. So what do you think?"

"I think, for starters, you damn near blew it back there."

"Yeah," he admitted, "the explanation, I know. Nice save, though." Laughing softly, he added, "I almost choked on my own shock when you told her I was classically trained. I half expected you to wax poetic, tell her how I caress the keys with feeling, creating symphonies of tears. It was great stuff, and I do mean great."

"Yeah, well, we're partners. It's what we do. You were about to out Russ and I think he would have been more than a little pissed about it. You know how he is about privacy and all."

"Yeah, I know," Ham chuckled. "And again, it was nice work. I owe you one."

"It wasn't bad," Drew admitted, somewhat smugly. "Especially since you can't play a note to save your life."

"Agreed on that. I couldn't tell a C minor from an elephant. To my credit, I recognize a piano when I see it, but I wouldn't know what to actually do with one of those things, not if you held a gun to my head. I mean, what the hell is it with those black and white keys anyway? Why not all white or all black? For that matter, why not green and gold, like a football team? That would make as much sense."

"Yeah, you'll have to tell Russ about your pontifications regarding his instrument. I'm sure he'd have some choice words in reply to that."

"Speaking of responses, I guess we'd better try to get in touch with Ronny, get an explanation and warn him what's coming. If it hasn't already."

Drew pulled out her phone, hushed the dog and punched up the number. "I'll see if he's sent us the list before I begin to grill him. I don't want to give him an excuse to put that off, and knowing arrest is imminent is one hell of an excuse."

Ham drove the last mile to their destination, waiting for Drew to pounce, but she never did. Instead, she clicked off the phone and announced, "They either got him or he's not answering. I hope it's the former, because if he's not answering our call he's in more trouble than we thought."

"We'll drop Lost off and run around to the studio. Maybe he's there. Actually, did you try that number?"

Rather than answer verbally, Drew dialed again, and again time passed before she simply hung up and put the phone back in her purse. No need for explanations of that.

Dusk approached as Ham and Drew pulled into Russ' driveway. This time Ham entered slowly, inching toward the drop-off, and parked outside the garage, just to the side. The sight caused him to suck in a breath of wonder as he gazed at that huge orange blob in the sky, just now kissing the sea, painting the heavens into a mural of inexplicable marvel.

The ocean reflected the celestial splendor above, as if jealous of its fiery brilliance and determined to outdo and outshine its competition. It grabbed the color, spread it across its waves and turned its vast surface into a kaleidoscope of color, enhanced by dancing, glaring dots of blinding white. It was no wonder, Ham mused, that Russ had bought this piece of paradise. The real wonder was that he seldom spent time here. If he had been the fortunate son that claimed this rapture, he'd never let it go.

They got out of the car and on up to the massive entrance, ready to let themselves in. The caretaker, however, had either been watching for them or he had heard them pull up, for as they approached that oversized oak front door, it swung silently open and Gardner bade them welcome.

"What have we here?" he cried with delight upon seeing the ball of fur bundled in Drew's arms, all hair except for a pair of dark, wall-eyed pupils peeking out from beneath shaggy growth. "Why, isn't he cute? Where'd you get him? Can I hold him? Is he going to be staying here?" He did everything except jump up and down and clap his hands with child-like glee.

All this over a pooping, biting machine of death?

An unusual man, Ham decided, one worth keeping a wary eye on. Though he had to assume Russ, being no fool, would have known that. So the man-child was probably harmless, if somewhat bizarre.

Ham pushed past a cooing Gardner, a beaming mama Drew and a tail-wagging, tongue-lapping, face-kissing dog who busied himself slobbering germs all over Gardner's chin. He dashed up the stairs, two at a time, retrieved his laptop, powered it up and opened his email. Sure enough, a message from Ronny waited, with the subject line reading "list."

Damon had attached the list as a file, which Ham clicked on and scrolled through. Without counting, he estimated it must contain at least fifty names. That was a lot of potential suspects to investigate, more than they had the resources to handle. They'd have to parse the list based upon what they knew and what they suspected. Start at the top and work through, as it were.

One thing, one vital thing, caught his eye and his attention. Grimly, he closed the lid, with the list still open, and held the laptop under his arm as he descended back down to the first floor and on into the living room. Drew was waving goodbye to Lost when he walked in, a bit of relief from his perspective.

"We got the list from Ronny," he announced. "Take a look," he urged, handing her the computer. "Tell me what you see. Or don't see."

Drew regarded him curiously but refrained from comment as she sat and opened the machine on her lap. She skimmed all the way through before she scrolled back to the top and read again, more slowly this time. When she looked up in wonder, confusion mixed with anger evident in her face, she simply nodded.

"It takes a moron to bite himself on his own ass."

Drew again nodded, but absently, as she pulled Ronny's check from her purse, unfolded it and smoothed it open. She snapped a picture of the payment with her phone's camera, then busied herself with multiple tasks on the machine.

Ham waited, tried to be patient as he waited for an explanation, finally lost control. "What exactly is it you are doing?

Drew held up a finger, the universal sign urging patience, and continued with her tasks. Soon she looked up and announced, "It's done."

"What's done?" he asked with exasperation.

"The check is deposited and it's cleared. If he's going to jerk us around, I'm going to make sure we get well paid for the pleasure he receives from it."

Ham's eyes widened to impossibly large plates. "How in the name of heaven do you do that?"

"It's an app for the phone. Pretty standard now, and you'd know that if you weren't married to the Stone Age. I mean, your phone is what, five years old? That's ancient technology. You really ought to update to one of these."

"I don't understand those kinds of phones. They're a complete and utter mystery to me and as useless as a sixth toe. Me, I'm content to just use a phone to make a call. What a concept, right?"

"I guess that's so," Drew grinned. "After all, you have trouble figuring out how to use an AM-FM radio. I suppose it is best you leave the high tech stuff to the Thornton side of McCalister and Thornton."

Ham waived her and the conversation aside. "What do you suppose he was thinking? Why would he give us that list —extensive and by the looks of it complete—and leave off the only initials we asked about? Why would he think he could not even mention Amber Bailey and figure we wouldn't find out eventually? He must have known we'd be more pissed than your new mutt on his worst day."

"What was he going to say once we got the list?" Drew agreed. "That there was nobody with the initials AB that he's worked with? How could he claim that when even the cops knew about her?"

Ham plopped onto the sofa and rubbed his face as he tried to massage away sudden fatigue. "Maybe he'd just claim she was so unimportant that he'd merely forgotten. Or maybe he'd say he didn't want her name associated with his for some business reason of his own."

"Biting himself in the butt."

"I'm not sure. He's either more clever than we give him credit for—and a lot smarter than Mutt and Jeff think—or he truly is a few watts shy of a light bulb. If we can find the unctuous bastard, maybe we can get an answer."

CHAPTER SIX

AND THE ARRIVAL

While Drew sat in the living room playing with her furry and foul companion, Ham stretched out on a well-padded lounge chair, out on the deck. His attention was split between the data base Ronny had provided and the huge ball of moon that shone above and lighted the sea below. The silvery stream of light seemed to lead directly to Russ' beach house, as if the moon, a heavenly groupie, resolved to shine its brightness on the Star of all Stars.

Ham sipped at a Mai Tai, courtesy of Gardner's thoughtful attentiveness. The mixed drink, fruity and with a kick that surprised, complete with tiny umbrella, was more appropriate to Russ' Hawaiian digs than it was here in Santa Cruz, but he appreciated it nonetheless. Appreciated to the point of one and only one, he told himself. Beer he could drink. But these, they go down too easily and soon he'd find himself kissing the floor.

He reluctantly pulled his eyes from the night extravaganza and back to the more mundane lists of names and dates. Ronny had not bothered to alphabetize, so going through required book marking his start points.

Like finding names with BB as their initials. According to Russ, B flat was next on the scale, and if more death were to follow those would be potential targets. They would need to be interviewed, warned and, if required, protected. Fortunately, he had time. The killings averaged one per week or more, so at the very least he probably had a few days to prepare the targets for possible danger. And to pick their brains.

His eyes spun—whether from the initial effects of the intoxicating mixture of three types of rum, Curacao, orange juice and syrup, or whether from minute examination of a multitude of data he wasn't sure—as Ham found his first subject, one Barry Braxton. He highlighted the name and moved on.

To a break, he decided. Work was all good and fine, but at the moment he preferred to lounge, staring into the face of nature's perfection, as he sipped the unfamiliar but enticing drink, and wished that Charlie sprawled beside him.

A quick flash of envy tinged his moonlight with green as he thought about Russ' imminent arrival. He didn't begrudge Drew her new relationship—though he held massive doubts about Russ' motives—and he was happy for her that her newfound friendship would get a chance to blossom here in seaside grandeur. Inside, though, it opened up an emptiness, one neither drink nor work could fill.

He grabbed what was left of his Mai Tai and took it with him to the railing that separated the deck from the rocks and surf below. He listened, enthralled, as the surf crashed on and battered those huge boulders, intent on reducing them to pebbles, or sand. The salty spray, wind borne, reached up to him, a misty gift from Poseidon himself.

Visions of Charlie dimmed his view of the moon and surf as her face came into full bloom, surprisingly real and here. From her almond eyes that hinted at some exotic influence, to her astonishing mane of blonde hair that nearly touched her lower back, it emerged, so solid he felt he could reach out, touch it, caress it, along with her slim but elegantly curved physique, perfectly suited her five and a half feet of height. All set off by a face maybe just a touch too round, but provocative nevertheless, and with a smoothness that laughed at her age, which fell only a couple of years south of his own. The vision was so real, his imagination so keen, that he even saw the blossom that adorned her ear: this time a large white flower that might have been a gardenia.

He closed his eyes against the wish, an attempt to flush the poignancy from his soul. Three weeks it had been since he'd seen her, held her, laughed with and at her. Loved her. Three weeks that now felt like three empty years.

Shutting his eyes didn't work, and he wasn't surprised. The image was so powerful there was no way to shake it. So powerful he could smell her hair, the light scent she always wore. It was all there in his mind, too powerful to deny.

With a sigh and a lopsided grin, he shook his head at his own folly. Falling for a free spirit, one of the qualities he most admired in her, did have its downside. She came and went as she pleased. And truth be told, he wouldn't have it any other way, even if he could.

"Well," she said at last. "Are you just going to stand there with your mouth agape, staring at me, or are you going to say hi?"

"Wait, what the?" His eyes widened, his mind swirled more and he reached out to touch the vision. It was a real person. "Drew?"

Charlie chuckled as she pointed to the almost finished drink he cradled. "Exactly how many of those have you had?"

"Charlie! It *is* you," he exclaimed. "What are you doing here?"

She put her hands on her hips and feigned a pout. "You're not glad to see me?"

He gave her a warm kiss, which she returned with heat. Finally, she pushed him lightly, stepped back a touch and laughed, "Wow. Has it been that long? Look out for the fire below."

"For crying out loud, I thought I was staring into the blackness of the ocean and seeing your face floating in the waves. What in hell are you doing here?" He held up a hand to halt her reply. "Not that I'm not happy you are. On the contrary, I was just wishing you were. God, I have missed you."

"If you missed me, you should have called and asked me to come out."

"You hate Vegas."

"True," she conceded. "If I wanted to live in a desert I wouldn't pick a place made of neon and concrete. I'd pitch a tent in the Mojave. I don't see how you do it. But," she added, "we could have met up at Tahoe."

Ham shook his head feeling like an idiot. "Never mind all that. You still haven't told me what's going on."

"Simple," she smiled. "Russ called me, told me about you and Drew being here, about the case, and that he was coming on down. I couldn't resist."

"You made good time from Honolulu. I don't suppose Russ had something to do with that."

"Your split-eared grin tells me you already know the answer to that. Anyway, Hamster, it really is great to see you. I've missed you, too. We might have to think about our living arrangements, if you know what I mean."

Drew and Russ appeared through the glass doors, arm and arm and sporting smiles at least as wide as Ham's and Charlie's. "Surprise, Hamster," Russ laughed. "I figured you'd give Drew less of a hassle about me being here if you were occupied as well."

Ham hung his head, chin on his chest. There it was, the nickname contagiously moving from Charlie to Russ. And Russ knew it. His wicked grin said it all.

Charlie's habit of adding "-ster" to the names of those closest to her included Ham himself. At first teeth-gnashing, he'd grown accustomed to it from her, even secretly found it endearing. But from other people, even from Russ or Drew, it grated, precisely because it was the type of thing that could spiral out of control. Big kids, old adults, it would stick. "Hamster," they would say, "how's it hanging?" And how could he present himself as a professional known as Hamster? He'd be laughed right out of the business.

"I didn't know they were this much of an item," Charlie whispered in his ear. "When did all this happen?"

"I didn't either," Ham muttered. "And to answer your question, I have no idea. Didn't until I found them *in flagrante delicto*. And that only this morning."

Ham drew Charlie close and turned to face Drew, with a look akin to that of a teenager in the first throes of passion. "You knew about this?" he demanded.

She replied with straight face. "I cannot tell a lie. Maybe."

Russ waived Gardner over and asked for a pitcher of Mai Tais. "He makes a superb concoction," he assured Drew. "Better than I get in the islands, I guarantee you that."

Charlie, the one confirmed nondrinker in the group, asked for a ginger ale instead, and Ham, also objecting, said he'd content himself with a beer. "A light one, if you have it. Another one of these would make the flu seem like a vacation, if you know what I mean."

"Don't worry, Hamster, if you get sick, I'll hold your head."

Ham knew she would do exactly that. She was that kind of loving, caring, giving...

Back to business! This is exactly what I warned Drew about. Don't you go crossing that line, dammit.

Charlie claimed one of the half-dozen lounge chairs and patted the one next to her in invitation. "Russ told me about the case and what you discussed on the plane. Fascinating, in a very bizarre sort of way, I must say. So what have you found out since? What's going on?"

For her benefit, and Russ', Ham provided a recitation of their introduction to Ronny, including a hooting description of his unctuousness. From there he filled them in about the two detectives, the Mutt and Jeff partnership, along with meeting Val. Only when he got to the point of discovering Amber's death did the smirks fade into soberness. In the end, Charlie displayed anger, Russ shock.

"So I was right?" he demanded.

"Looks that way," Ham affirmed. "So now we look for his contacts that are BB. I ran across at least one, a guy named Barry Braxton. Ever heard of him?"

Russ thought a second, then nodded sharply and suddenly. "As I recall, he hit the top ten once with a ballad." Russ rubbed his head. "Now that I think about it, I recall it, that tune. Give me a second." He strummed an air-guitar, then looked wide-eyed at Ham. "Right, and here's something odd." He paused dramatically before announcing, "The song is in C minor. Now how about that for some kind of coincidence?"

Drew bolted upright, her face lit with wonder. "What about Amber Bailey? Did she chart, and if so, with what?"

Russ shrugged. "I don't really know. I do know she hit the charts a couple of times, or at least that's my vague memory. Nothing big, though, not top ten, or even top forty as I recall.

As for the particular songs, I can't think of them at the moment."

"Do a search," Drew instructed Ham. "Let's see what we get."

Ham pulled up a search engine on his still open laptop, entered the singer's name in quotes and came up with her website. "She lists three songs as charting." He read them off and asked, "Ring any bells?"

Russ shook his head. "Does she have any links to samples or anything? Maybe that would jog something."

"Yeah," Ham mumbled as he scrawled down the page. "They link to purchase, to samples and to ring tones. Which do you want?"

"Try the samples, let's see if that's enough. I don't want to have to buy them."

Drew jabbed him in the ribs. "I knew you were cheap, but that's a new low. Not even supporting your fellow performers. Wow."

Ham hit the link for the first song and turned up the volume. Russ listened for probably no more than ten seconds before he told Ham to move on. "That's not it." A few seconds into the next one he again shook his head. About five seconds into the final link he snapped his fingers. "Got it. That's in C minor. Does she say how high it charted?"

Ham scrolled back up to the history section, nodded and replied, "It topped out at number forty-two. It was actually her highest charting hit, and her longest lasting one. It stayed on the charts for three months, bounced around between the forties and seventies before it dropped off."

"That leaves our first three victims," Drew reminded them. "Charlie Davis, Evan Boyd and Fran Gallaugher."

"Evan Boyd I can tell you about," Russ said. "He hit in the twenties, I think it was, with a beautiful little song, actually. In C minor."

Ham searched Evan Boyd and Fran Gallaugher, found and played several samples for Russ, and he affirmed the expected. "One each in C minor. Their top hits, too."

"Always the top hits for each victim, all in C minor," Drew mused. "So he's not only killing *in* C minor, he's killing *to* C minor."

"I wish Pop were around," Charlie lamented. "He would have loved this. He loved nothing more than a weird puzzle." The fact that she hadn't used "Popster" told Ham more about her pain than the soft tone of her voice.

"I know," Russ sympathized, his eyes warm and moist. "I miss him, too, every damn day. My partner, my best friend, the closest thing to a brother I'll ever have."

Ham and Drew paused in respectful silence, allowing Russ and Charlie time to cherish the memory before Drew again pointed out, "Killing to and in C minor. What does it mean?"

Russ rubbed his chin, a thoughtful gesture, and in the end shook his head. "You're beyond me now. That's your thing, you and Ham."

"It's something we'll have to ask our esteemed client once he chooses to emerge from hiding," Drew said flatly.

"It'll probably be at the jail," Ham reminded her. "Pete and Steve were one pissed off team of detectives after his little stunt."

"Will they arrest him?" Charlie asked. "Won't that make it harder for you if they do? I mean, will they even let you talk to him?"

"They'll have to charge him or release him," Drew informed her, "and within a certain amount of time. They don't have the evidence to arrest him, so yeah, it may take us a day or two, but we'll get to him."

"Unless…"

"The brilliant idiot theory," Drew finished for Ham.

"Right."

"The brilliant idiot theory? What does that mean?" Russ asked.

"So stupid as to commit a crime where he's the obvious perp," Drew explained. "But brilliant enough to leave no clues."

"You're kidding, right?"

"Unfortunately," Ham sighed, "she is not. There aren't many, but there are a few cops who believe in that crap and therefore…"

"Plant the nonexistent evidence."

"Precisely."

Russ threw up his hands in disgust. "Un-flaming-believable," he muttered. "That's right out of the dark ages."

Charlie's reaction was not nearly as subtle. Her nostrils flared and her face flushed with rage. "That's the kind of crap that pisses me off about this system. It's no longer a criminal justice system, it's a criminal system of justice. And it's why we're the most incarcerated country in the world. One of every four people behind bars in the world resides right here. And we're the only ones who take children, put them in prison and never let them out. It's beyond scandalous, it's heart-breaking."

Charlie's sense of justice was both well developed and well defined, Ham knew. She herself had been the victim of sloppy police work a few years ago, and were it not for Ham's help she might have seen the worst of it. Which he knew was less important to her than just plain old fair play.

Ham nodded, sympathetic to a point. "I know how you feel about it, Charlie, and in many ways I agree with you. But it's not just bad cops, and in truth most cops are truly dedicated to working within the rules, and they do their best to ensure they get the right people put away. It's the damn politicians who pander for votes that have made this country a jail cell. Until and unless we run them out of office, nothing's going to change."

"Yeah that. Land of the free, my big broad ass."

Unable to contain themselves, the rest of them burst into laughter. Charlie's tiny hip size made her hyperbole ridiculous.

Gardner appeared from the gloom and announced a visitor, waiting for the laughter to subside before he intoned in serious voice, "Ms. Valerie Simpson is here to see you," he informed Russ. "Shall I show her in?"

"Please," Russ responded as he unfolded his lanky frame from the chaise lounge, "and see if she'd care for anything to drink."

"You know Val?" Drew asked, clearly surprised and just a touch suspicious. "How so?"

"She stopped by after they appointed her chief, just to introduce herself, and wanted me to know that they'd keep an eye on my place when I was not in town. So," he said, "it's not what you think. Although, if I'd had more time..."

Ham also rose when Gardner ushered Val in, though Charlie and Drew remained seated as etiquette permitted. And as Drew's scowl demanded.

"Nice to see you again, Val," Russ offered, as he warmly grasped her hand in both of his. "It's been a long while."

"Too long, and that's because you're never here, which I must tell you hurts my feelings. It can only mean you lack appreciation for our beauty and culture, which come to think of it is more offensive than hurtful."

"Folks, meet the Chamber of Commerce for the city of Santa Cruz," Russ grinned. "Val, you've already met Drew and Ham, so let me present Charlie Hollister, Ham's inamorata." Val's rapid blinks indicated confusion. "Ham's lady friend," he explained.

Russ examined her empty hands. "Did Gardner offer you something to drink?"

"He did, but this isn't a social visit, I'm afraid. I'm here in my official capacity."

Russ' eyebrows arched but he wouldn't be denied. "Indeed. Well, that doesn't mean you can't relax a bit with an old friend. Officially relax, as it were."

Val laughed, appeared to consider it and finally shook her head. "I'd better not. Can you imagine one of my guys, they stop me and smell alcohol on my breath? Scandal city, to say the least. Suspended police chief, to say the most."

"All right, well, have a seat and tell us what's on your mind."

Val ignored the offer and directed a question at her host. "What brings you to town now, Russ?" She pointed a finger at Ham and Drew. "Would it have something to do with their case?"

"It has to do with me," Drew snapped. "And that is all." She didn't say "so back off" but she might as well have, the way her eyes flashed it.

Val clearly caught the message, and just as obviously found it funny. "No worries. I'd already put that together." At Drew's astonished gape, she nodded, smothering a soft chuckle. "Ah, come on, that story you tried to sell me about Ham the music virtuoso, and his stuttering attempts at explanations. I wasn't buying. So I asked myself why. Why you would make up such a patently absurd tale? When I heard about a new couple staying at Russ Porter's place, it added up. That would be you two, and it would also follow that Russ was the mastermind who presented the music scale murder theory. And so," she announced, "that is why I'm here."

She pulled up a chair rather than claiming a more comfortable and relaxing lounger, and pulled it closer to Ham. "I've come to let you know, officially and for the record, that your client is wanted for questioning in the murder of Amber Bailey."

"So why tell us?"

"This is just a courtesy between professionals. Between colleagues. If you know we're looking for him, and if you know where he is or you help him hide from us, you could be charged with obstruction of justice. And you know Pete would just love to do it." Her smile took the sting out of the tone, but not the statement.

"You got a warrant out on him?" Drew asked.

"It's being processed now. We'll be ready to pick him up before the next twenty-four hours elapse. But that doesn't matter right now. What does matter is we want to talk to him and we don't know where he is."

"And you think we do."

Val shook her head. "I didn't say that and I did not mean to imply that. I take you at your word to exchange information and keep us informed, and I just thought that if you'd heard from him it would make it easier on your professional ethics if I threatened you unless you turn him over to us."

"Nice move," Ham said with admiration, "I like it. But the straight and absolute truth of the matter is that we have no idea where he is. We've been trying to reach him since we left Amber's place."

Val stood, duty done and ready to leave. "I won't take any more of your time then. And I'll look forward to hearing from you."

"Quit with the formality," Russ chided. "You did what you had to do, your point is made and I'm sure Drew and Ham got it. Now relax a bit, why not. Besides, I think you may be interested in hearing what we've discussed."

Val's eyes showed keen interest as she sat back down. "Okay, I accept your invitation with pleasure." Turning to Gardner, she said, "I'll take a soda, whatever you have." To Russ she added, "I meant what I said about my guys nabbing me as a drunk driver."

"We could always call you a cab," Drew laughed.

"That would be fine, except leaving my cop car, a marked one, out front of Russ' house all night might trigger a little more tongue wagging than I want to incite."

"Wouldn't offend me at all," Russ assured her.

Val turned to a frowning Drew, presumably to deflect the implication. "You have something new?"

Drew glanced at Ham, who gave a shrug and a small nod. "It seems our boy has been busy with his music lessons."

She explained that each of the victims' top hits were all in the key of C minor, with Russ jumping in to add detail when she stumbled over the scale. "So it seems that he's focused on people whose initials fit the scale, but beyond that, he's hitting people who not only fit the scale with their names, but with their songs as well. The only thing we've concluded about our loony so far is that this is one fixated animal."

Val threw up her hands, whether in anger or confusion—or both—Ham couldn't tell. "I don't get it. Why bother putting the notes on the cheeks if he's killing to C minor? It seems redundant now that you've found out about the songs."

Charlie spoke into the answering silence. "He couldn't know that you'd have somebody like Russ to help you figure it out."

Ham and Drew exchanged knowing glances, and Ham waived for Drew to go ahead. "I'm not so sure about that. Ronny, it turns out, called us specifically because he wanted to get to Russ. And of course there's that little coincidence of one of the victims being a stalker of the members of Truckee River."

Val stared at Russ as she asked Drew, "So you think Russ might somehow be a key to this insanity?"

"Too many coincidences where even one is too many," Ham agreed. "The thing that really—"

The interruption from his cell caused him to whistle softly. He stood, walked rapidly across to the French doors and left the others behind. "What's up, Ronny?" he asked as soon as the call clicked in. "The cops want you for questioning. They're preparing an arrest warrant. You got your attorney standing by?"

The silence on the other end of the line was deafening in its intensity. Finally, a long, sad sigh emerged. "That's what I thought." The click emphasized the finality of the statement.

Ham returned to the veranda and met their questioning eyes with a nod. "That was him. I told him about the warrant and he hung up on me. You may have to search for him. I'm afraid he may not stick around."

"And flight is evidence of guilt," Val reminded them.

"And flight is evidence of guilt," Drew agreed. "The damn fool."

They fell to silence and allowed the rhythmic crash of the surf take its turn on stage, a star of natural wonder with which no mere mortal could compete. Even a Chopin nocturne, with its short and sweet dreamlike quality, paled in comparison to the music of the ocean, could not vie with the transcendent ease in which it transported troubled souls to calmer waters.

Into the silence walked Gardner, deftly holding a silver tray replete with a pile of finger sandwiches, assorted in variety. With more than a hint of a plea in his voice, and only a quick glance at his watch, he politely invited them to dig in. "I thought you might be getting hungry. It is, after all, growing late."

"Thank you, Gardner, that was kind of you. Why don't you take off for the night, and I'll see you in the morning."

Nothing slow about Russ, Ham thought as Gardner waved a goodbye. He could take a hint, a characteristic that he'd keep in mind and maybe find useful later.

After Gardner disappeared, Drew turned to Russ. "He doesn't live here?" She sounded surprised, as was he. Apparently they'd both surmised Gardner was a live-in.

Which in effect he was. "There's an apartment above the garage where he stays. That way he can pretty much come and go as he pleases without disturbing me when I'm here, plus it gives him a private life, if you know what I'm saying."

"A babe magnet?"

"You've seen him," Russ grinned at Ham. "What do you think?"

"That and the fact he works for you, yeah, I imagine he's pretty much a player on the local fling scene."

"Hamster, you're always in the gutter," Charlie remonstrated. "Come up for a bath, why don't you."

"I like my living arrangements," Ham laughed. "It suits."

Val abruptly stood and announced her departure. "It's been fun," she informed them, "and I'd really like to stay, but I do have work in the morning. So if you'll excuse me."

But Charlie stopped her, and the rest of them, dead in her tracks when she announced, "It's not the people, you know. It's the songs. He's targeting the songs, period. Figure out that connection, the connection between him and the songs, and you got him."

Russ leaned around Drew and stared Charlie in the eyes. "So the people are irrelevant? How can that be?"

"Victims are never irrelevant," Charlie apologized. "Ever. And that's not what I mean to say. What I do mean is that just like a serial killer who randomly seeks out victims, this one seeks victims who might as well be random—except that his victims have to have the right names to fit within his game."

Val plopped back down, thoughts of a good night's rest seemingly gone in a flash. "If this is all correct—and I'm still having headaches trying to wrap my mind around it—then the upshot is that these people have been picked, not randomly, but with great care. He's done his research. He may or may not know his victims, may or may not be trying to pin it on Ronny Damon, and may or may not even know Damon. But one thing is clear, he's got a systematic plan. He has chosen to victimize people within one recording company, singers who have the required attributes, which are names and songs."

A distinct ping pierced the air and Ham flipped open his laptop. "And here's something," he murmured.

Ham's screen attracted attention with its red letter warning of an urgent message in his inbox. He pulled it up, scanned it quickly, and slowly read it again. And again.

"Well," he announced, "we have a development here." Looking at each, his eyes etched with acid, he continued, "Our roly-poly client may not be on the run. He may be intent on suicide, if I'm reading this right."

Drew straightened, leaning around Russ to get a closer look at Ham's face. "You serious? What's happening?"

"I probably shouldn't do this with Val here, but what the hell. It's information we should turn over anyway, I guess. I'm not sure this fits under client privilege, at least not as it pertains to withholding evidence."

Ham read the note that was sent from Ronny's email address.

Dear Mr. McCalister and Ms. Thornton,

I am sorry I got you involved in this. As for me, I just can't go on with it. I can't go on like this. I wish to return all rights to songs to the original songwriters, and I wish to endow $1,000,000 from my assets to a fund for my publishing roster of clients. It is also my hope that Russ Porter will help any he is able to with respect to recovering their careers, as I believe many have deserving style and talent, talent that I now admit I stole from them. What I did to them I am too ashamed to put down here and will wait to explain myself to—and apologize to—God. May he and the victims forgive me.

You may consider this my last will and testament, dated this date at this time as stamped on the mailing. I do not expect I will see you in the future, not with where I am headed, though I pray I be wrong.

I remain your client, I should also point out, at
least for the time being. So please act accordingly.
I wish you both all the best.

Ronny Damon

If there was anything to say, no one said it. Silence hung in the air like fog teasing the ground, shock and dismay its lonely companions.

Val finally stood, the first to move, and quickly adjusted her jacket. She nodded a curt goodbye and offered an opinion. "We're looking for a body, I'm guessing." The last thing she added as she trudged out was her muttered, "This is going to be a really long night."

"We never did tell her about Barry Braxton," Drew offered. "Shouldn't we have let her in on that as well?"

Ham's answer was a shake of the head. "That may be moot, or it may not. What we're going to do is go find Braxton's ass, then we'll see. This note sounds a bit off to me, so let's just bide our time a bit."

"We're not going to tell them?"

"Nope."

"Well, we better pray Barry Braxton's not dead when we get there. You do know we'll be arrested on the spot if he is, don't you?"

"That's why I'm calling Gary Thomas," Ham announced as he pulled out his cell. "I think it behooves us to have him on standby."

At Russ' curious look, Drew provided the background. "Our attorney, one of the best in Nevada, also licensed in California and Colorado, and an old classmate of Ham's at the University of Nevada Las Vegas. He'll be able to arrange the bail."

Russ' flaming face added heat to the night. "They'll arrest you over my dead body," he snapped. "By the time I'm through with Val they'll wish they'd never heard of you."

Drew patted his arm, an affectionate afterthought. "You're sweet, my dear, and you are very much a heavyweight. But you're out of your league here. I don't think it'll be Val, it's Pete and Steve, our little Mutt and Jeff team of hotheads. I doubt you'd carry much credence with them. Hell, they might even enjoy getting into it with you. Imagine the press they'd get if they arrested you for interfering with a police investigation."

"They'll be patrolling outhouses in Los Gatos if they try," he huffed.

"Probably," Drew agreed, "in the end. But in the beginning they'd enjoy themselves. If they even know who the hell you are," she added.

"I doubt there's a human being alive in this or most other towns who don't know who I am, even if they don't recognize me on sight anymore." Russ' agreeable manner offset the vain-sounding statement.

"True. But wait until you meet them, you'll see. My guess is the only music they've ever heard is the theme to *Dragnet*. It's probably their wedding song."

Ham, who had been studying his computer, looked up, a bit of exasperation on his face. "If you two are through, so am I. I've found two other names on Ronny's list with the initials BB. Besides Barry Braxton, there's Barbara Bessler and Bodie Briggs."

"I take it," Charlie drawled, "you don't think your client is the killer. Otherwise you wouldn't still be looking for victims. Am I right?"

"You, my dear, are exactly right. Nor am I going to accept that Ronny's looking to blow his brains out, or however people end it. Not that man."

"He loves himself too much for that," Drew agreed. "So back to the key issue. Where the hell is he?"

"And why the red herring?" Ham muttered.

"That," Drew agreed, "is the $225,000 question, isn't it?"

CHAPTER SEVEN

INTO THE FRAY LIGHTLY

Ham padded down the stairs, wearing shorts, t-shirt and running shoes. If luck held, he'd have time to log a few miles around the neighborhood before the others joined him in the kitchen.

Though an avid jogger, he ran not for exercise, but because it was the one activity that completely emptied his mind. As for exercise, that was a descriptive misnomer. Because of his injured hip—from that damn car that ran him down and ended his career almost three years gone by—for him jogging was run one, drag two, limp three.

As he fixed his eyes on the road ahead, looking more down than out, the rhythmic pounding of his feet against concrete pushed aside all conscious thought and let his mind go where it would. And invariably, when on a case, that 'where' led to insights that he did not believe he had the deliberate mental acuity to evoke. He'd sprain his brain trying, which would be embarrassing enough, but the sling around his head would represent a badge of dishonor.

Smiling at the mental image, he refocused on his feet, letting the yards and sounds fall away. As he approached a crossroads, he noted the street signs, retaining just enough consciousness to store away his route, and headed left. The area through which he ran sported some exquisite seaside housing, along with perfectly groomed grounds, yet none of this registered.

Nor did the fact that a car slowly followed him down his route.

Ham's red and flaming face had nothing to do with the morning sun and his quickening pace. It had everything to do with a thought, a realization that slammed him with a slug of shame. Hell, he should have recognized it the second he read it, should have felt the slap across his face. A face that had been too distracted by, and too intent on, the ever lovely Charlie. And by his awe of Russ, to be honest. And to the Mai Tai, and the surf, the moon. Oh, hell, on the fact that he'd been treating the time as vacation, little more than an interesting lark. For money.

And so there it was again, that same damn bugaboo that had haunted him ever since he'd become involved with the world's most famous band.

Drew had even challenged him, as the night grew late, after Ronny's email, and long after Ham had grown weary. She'd leaned into his ear, whispering as if the words could not be spoken aloud in decent company. "Ham, I'm a little confused here."

"Yeah, me too. It's pretty strange."

"No, not that. I'm talking about you."

"Me? What about me?"

"Since we were kids, I kinda always looked to you for moral guidance, you know? You were always the one, your innate cynicism aside, that I could count on to ultimately do the right thing. And you're kind of throwing me now," she softly declared.

"When I was partnered with those rats Allen and Samuels, even though I was making a boatload of money, I wasn't happy. I knew I was in bed with scum, but I figured what the hell, I'm a single woman and I've got to make a living for myself. Although I didn't get involved in any of their less than upstanding antics, I felt dirty just being around them. Then with the fee from Truckee River, I could put that behind me, join up with you and feel moral again. Now you get me involved and in bed with a piece of scum like Ronny. And for what? For the money? Is this where I'm headed again? Is this where you're going to take me?"

Ham had fumbled for words, an explanation, a counterargument, but settled for a weary shrug and a promise to talk about it on the morrow.

Well, it was tomorrow, and what could he say? That it was another chance to hang around the famous, the rich, the in-crowd. The royalty of the music world. Like Blake Garrett and Russ Porter, two giants of the industry. Then taking their money—and for what purpose? To perform mindless tasks that they themselves could hire out to better and more able help? Or get for free from the authorities, who would never dare deny them a favor.

That didn't really fit in this case, he decided. Ronny was hardly a heavyweight, and Ham had not had any idea of Russ' involvement when he accepted the retainer.

"The obscene retainer," his devil conscious reminded him.

"Forget it," his angel advised. "Honest fees for honest services."

His angel lies, he realized. The fact remained that he would have done this case for far less, would have charged his usual $10,000 plus expenses. Maybe even less in this case, because of the cheek thing. Instead, he'd demanded and received $225,000 and maybe expenses. And who needed expenses when the trip, room and board were all on rock and roll's richest and most generous man?

Ham stopped abruptly, slapping his hand against his head. "Out," he demanded. "Out, damn spot!"

He rested his hands on his knees and slowed the breath that he hadn't been aware he'd been panting. Though fatigue was not really an issue, his rambling mind was. This time, this routine, had betrayed him. Instead of wandering toward revelation, his mind had cornered itself with guilt, an old argument he knew from experience he could never win. The futility of that contest aggravated his already tortured mind.

He clamped his jaw and set off, determined to recapture the fleeting realization rather than waste emotional and mental effort on the insoluble. And it worked, for less than a quarter mile further down the road the thought came floating back. "Mr. McCalister and Ms. Thornton."

"Mr. McCalister and Ms. Thornton." Ronny was nothing if not an arrogant and self-important nit. It had taken all of seconds to confirm that fact. And it was clear that this insufferable little roly-poly man would never be so obsequious as to address hired help—and he would consider two private dicks on his payroll as little more than that—with such formality, thereby conferring equal status. Ronny considered nobody his equal, maybe not even Russ, whom he just naturally assumed would be eager to deliver him a favor.

And there was something else. Something in the wording, the strained pleading "I can't go on with this, I can't go on *like* this,"

With this, like this. With murder, as a killer? What, he decides he's going to off a bunch of lowly protégés, comes up with a plan to kill them by scale, spends a fortune for hired help to keep the cops off his tail, then decides to end it all with a confession and suicide? No matter how he looked at it, no matter from what angle, that wouldn't fly. Why spend the money? Why bring the heat down on himself and then kill the only person of real interest to Ronny—which was Ronny himself.

No. If Ronny were the killer, he'd enjoy the game too much to put a premature end to it. Maybe if there were no other out, if the game had gone to conclusion and that conclusion was death row at San Quentin, then yeah. Ronny would likely prefer death, especially on his own terms, to some lesser beings owning his body, his days, his remaining years. But that possibility was not even close to breaking the horizon.

And the upshot of that was suspicion, a nagging, almost to the surface inspiration. His client, he suspected, had meant something else entirely with that email. It was another game to play, but one without invitation, one with hidden rules. Or no rules, maybe.

What those rules might have been got lost in the roar of a passing car. Just as Ham turned another corner, this time into an alley that he supposed would lead to a street directing him back to Russ' residence, the growl of a hungry engine and the odor of greedy exhaust tickled his consciousness, brought him back to the here and now of suburbia. He turned to face the intruder and continued to jog in place, not wanting to lose his momentum, as he hugged the fence and waived the offending vehicle by.

The car sat, threatening and angry. Ham, irritated by the idiot behind the wheel, squinted his eyes in an attempt to identify the driver within. He realized it was useless, for the blinding sun beat down on and was deflected off the windshield, effectively shielding the driver from view.

He was about to jog up to the vehicle and reason with the moron when, without preamble, the car revved itself to action and bolted forward as if shot from a cannon.

And he was the target.

Ham's reacted solely on instinct. He gripped the top of the fence and leapt upward, pulling his legs as high as his hips could bend. He felt but ignored the shards of wood that dug into his knees as he scraped them up the side.

The driver—Chucky in a drag car—raced at him, an evil grin, Ham imagined, splitting his face. Without regard to his own safety, the occupant slewed forward, seemingly intent on doing a 180 in the cramped confines of the alley. Ham waited, and hung, body tensed, for the inevitable crash now microseconds away. He jumped just as the car approached, just as it tore out part of the fence, just as it sent wooden stakes of lethal proportions scattering throughout the air.

Ham's anticipated landing place, the roof of that oversized and obscenely gas guzzling monster, proved more elusive than he'd hoped. For, just as he leapt, as he was mid-air and grasping nothingness, the car swerved left, out and away from his flailing limbs. He landed head first, forehead mugging the ground, followed by the marriage of his hands and knees to asphalt.

So much for your imitation of Spider Man, his subconscious mocked him. *Bite me*, his conscious mind retorted.

Ham picked himself up from the turf, bleeding from all points of contact, but mindless of that, such was his anger at himself. To be so wrapped in the ethereal that he ignored reality was a self-inflicted death penalty. Plain truth, he'd forgotten his professionalism, had set himself up like any mark at the carny.

The homicidal vehicle spun out of range, raced out the alley and onto the intersecting boulevard without slowing.

His mind's eye snapped only a bad and out of focus photo of the killer's weapon: something big, black and angry. Whether a Ford Expedition, a Cadillac Escalade, a Lincoln Navigator—or the Secret Service—was blurred into background. As was a California license plate of shadowy design.

Shaken, and very much stirred, he reversed course and limped his way back to the street upon which he'd encountered the damnable alley. To his relief, the vehicle and its Chuckie impersonator were nowhere in sight. Dragging his more injured leg behind him, he half walked, half scuttled his way back to Russ' manse, where a white tornado rushed him the moment he opened the door.

The little freaking Shih Tzu, a flash of fang, snarl and drool.

Ham kicked out, groaning with the effort his scraped and bruised knee exerted, and hoped against hope that the little mutt would back away. No chance.

It perched on its haunches, ready to leap, to inflict pain and ruination on Ham's face or neck, and Ham knew he was the lion's prey. No chance of escape. Fear welled through him, sweat ran down his neck and a quick plea to Mother Mary escaped his lips just as he caught Drew's sharp command, "Lost! No! You bad boy, come to Momma."

The dog immediately turned and raced to his new mistress, tail wagging, mewling with joy, as Ham's heart hit the limit. Only Herculean strength kept him from collapsing in a sobbing heap, such was his relief. He'd actually felt less terrified by that murderous automobile than he did of this little ankle biting spawn of Satan.

Drew swept him up in her arms and the mutt took the opportunity to turn its head back in Ham's direction. Although he refused to give the little Shih Tzu-head credit for the intelligence necessary to form such intent, it seemed to him as if the smug mutt stuck his tongue out at him. And gave him a dog laugh to boot.

Drew cooed at the little dog, petting and fussing over him even as she examined Ham, looking him up and down, from head to knees, from bloody abrasions to raw open wounds. "If this is what happens when you jog, you might want to think about sticking to a treadmill."

"I need coffee."

Drew tossed her head in the general direction of the dining area. "In there. Russ and Charlie are up and drooling at the bounty Gardner's whipping up. Quite a spread."

"Oh, and you're not?" Ham teased. Since they were little, she'd been a source of amazement to him. At any one sitting, if she were hungry, she stuffed more food into that flat and narrow stomach of hers than he could put away in a day.

Ham limped into the kitchen, the aroma of apple-smoked bacon kissing the air, determined to outperform its competition from eggs, waffles and onion-flavored hash browns. Charlie and Russ glanced up and started to wave a brief hello before Charlie's eyes flew wide.

"What in the name of all that is holy happened to you?"

Ham plopped into the chair opposite and waited as Gardner poured and delivered a cup of brew. "A little accident. How come you guys are so wet? You been out there swimming already?"

"I did some laps in the pool. Russ, the macho man, braved the surf. I wouldn't go in there but Russ believes that the great whites that populate the area will leave him alone. They're too in awe of him."

"There are great white sharks in these waters?"

"Full of them," Russ allowed. "According to the Santa Cruz Sentinel, there are more than 200 of them around here. We're in a feeding ground known as The Red Triangle."

"And guess what the 'red' means," Charlie added. "It's for the blood in the water after one of those beasts attacks."

"Makes for lively swimming," Russ mumbled. "So what kind of accident?"

Drew returned, still holding her pet, just in time to hear the question. "What the hell did you do? Man, I can't leave you alone for a second, can I?"

Ham provided a brief description of the alley incident and shook his head with self-mocking humor. "Either he's a road hog who really hates joggers or it was something personal."

"Jeez, you think? That's great detective work, Hamster," Charlie said.

"Are you sure it was a guy?" Drew asked. "Could it have been female?"

Ham considered the question for all of a microsecond. "No, I'm not sure at all. It could have been an extraterrestrial jerk intent on taking me back to the mother SUV for all I could tell."

"Well, let's get you cleaned up," Charlie decided. "Russ, where's the medicine cabinet? Do you have iodine, swabs and such?"

"Upstairs, in my bath, in the cabinet under the sink. You'll find a box with all the normal and necessary first aid goodies in it. You can't miss it."

While Charlie left to fetch the kit, Ham sipped at his coffee and filled Drew in on his subconscious insights. She nodded approval when he mentioned how unlikely Ronny would be to address them so formally in his note, and most especially again when he offered his opinion on the impossibility of Ronny quitting the game before the end was nigh.

"'I can't go on with this, like this.' Can't go on with murder, can't live with being a killer? Then why start? Why murder the people who he gets rich off of, why spend money to hire us to keep from getting caught—if that was indeed his thought—and then give up before we really even start?"

Charlie returned with the kit, pulled a chair up before Ham and began her ministrations. Ham watched idly as she dabbed at various wounds, preparatory to application of salves and bandages.

"Anyway," he continued, "I just don't see Ronny quitting. He's too arrogant, thinks he's smarter than the rest of us, especially the Santa Cruz cops. So Ronny had something else in mind when he sent that 'urgent' message. I'm thinking it was maybe intended to get to Val after all. And that somehow we played right into his hands."

"Hold still," Charlie ordered. "You can talk without your hands, can't you?"

"You're working on my forehead. How can that be a problem?"

"Because you're waiving them in front of my face. I can't see what I'm doing. Now stop it."

Ham obediently clasped his hands in his lap. "So you see what I'm saying here. We're going at this blind."

"The key to this is likely to be the driver in the alley. Someone followed you, waited for the right moment and a secluded location and went for it. Aside from indicating this place is being watched, it suggests that you're a threat to whoever is doing this. And that wouldn't be Ronny. On the contrary, actually."

Ham snapped his head back, pointing accusing eyes at Charlie. "Damn! Take it easy, will you? You're supposed to be nursing me, not sending me through the roof."

"Oh, don't be such a baby." Turning to Drew she innocently inquired, "Is he always like this?"

"He's afraid of ointments, bandages and pint-sized dogs. You just gotta learn to live with it."

"I'm glad you're amused," Ham growled. "Meanwhile, the point is that our killer is getting desperate. And I don't know why, unless he thinks we're closer than we actually are."

Drew shook her head. "The interesting point is that if this was done by the killer—or at the direction of the killer—he's broken out of his C minor scale in order to go after you. The why is the answer. What is it that the killer thinks you know that you obviously don't?"

"I don't know," Ham shrugged. "Maybe my little adventure in the alley isn't connected at all. Maybe it's a rare and true coincidence."

"I'd rethink that, Ham," Russ argued. "You might listen more to what Drew has to say. You'll forgive me, and I mean no offense, but in my opinion Drew is sometimes a little faster on the uptake than you. This might be one of those times."

As he flashed back to Drew's rescue of his near running off at the mouth with Val, Ham could only sigh and say, "Offense taken. And truth recognized."

"Because what we have here," Russ continued, "is somebody targeting people on a musical scale, a killer who is at the same time targeting songs on that very same scale. The murderer thinks Ham knows something vital and has therefore stepped outside the scale to go after him because of it. And you have a client, who is also a suspect, gone missing, but not before he sends a will and a suicide note. Now how does this all fit together?" He glanced back and forth between Drew and Ham. "Well? You're the detectives. Clue in this musical fool."

Into the answering silence, Gardner appeared, laden with platters of scrambled eggs, waffles, hash browns and the saliva-inducing apple-smoked bacon. He ladled out two scoops of eggs to Ham and Russ, acquiesced to Drew's demand for a third, and stopped at a protesting Charlie's insistence on one. Drew immediately set the little mutt she'd been cradling down to the floor and stabbed at a slab of bacon. The unhappy fellow whined its insistence on joining the feast, but a steadfast Drew ignored him. At least, Ham thought, there was somewhere she'd draw the line with that little creep of a cur.

Charlie took a dainty sip of her coffee, staring at Ham over the rim. "You do lead an interesting life," she opined. "Makes me jealous."

"Oh, sure, you should talk," he laughed, "born into rock and royalty and all. Blake Garrett's daughter, Russ Porter's adopted niece. Fly in a private jet, flit here, there and anywhere and everywhere on a whim, now that's an interesting life. And I'm the jealous one."

"It sounds like Charlie's wealth intimidates," Russ pointed out as he wolfed down bacon. "Is that why you haven't asked my adopted niece to marry you yet?"

Ham's jaw dropped, tongue tripping over his mouth. He picked uncomfortably at his eggs, eyes fixed on the plate before him.

"Oh look, he's turned all red," Drew chortled. "Poor old Hamster."

Christ, Ham thought, *I'm doomed to have that moniker, aren't I?* It will be known far and wide that Hamster McCalister is available, for a fee and expenses, to perform tricks on his rodent wheel. If the old gang in LVPD homicide ever got wind of that he'd have no choice. He'd have to move.

And change his name. Witness protection for dummies.

Charlie patted him on the knee, turning twinkling eyes on the others. "Maybe we better let him off the hook. My poor little Hammie."

Ham kept chewing because there was no other choice. His mouth was much too dry to swallow.

Oh good god, how bad is this going to get? Well, it serves you right for hanging out with Mensa material when you're the village moron studying to be the town idiot.

Or is that an idiot studying to be a moron, he wondered.

See? You don't even know that.

Ham was saved by Gardner's announcement. "There's a Mr. Gary Larsen here to see Mr. McCalister. Shall I show him in?"

"By all means, please."

Gardner returned with a dapper little man sporting short dark hair, graying slightly at the temples. He kept it closely trimmed and neatly coiffed, and set it off with a thin mustache that gave him the appearance of a throwback to the 1940's. His pinstripe suit and pocket watch, replete with the requisite gold chain and neatly tucked in the fob pocket of his waistcoat, and the red bow tie added to the effect.

The effect in full, along with the fact that he stood a tad under five-foot-four, created nothing so much as the image of a farcified penguin.

Ham stood, offered his hand, and said to Russ, "Don't let his appearance fool you. He's still trying to live down his old university days when he was the resident grass-head. Back then he wore tie-dyed shirts, bell-bottoms and sandals. He also sported an afro, but of course he had more hair to work with back then."

"Thank you for your gracious introduction." Gary offered a warm nod to Drew and turned to stare at his host. "So you're Russ Porter. You don't look like the pictures on your old album covers."

"How kind of you to notice," Russ drawled.

A flush tinged Gary's cheeks. "Clumsily put, I fear. I meant that I'm a huge fan, had all of the Truckee River albums. Still do, as a matter of fact."

Ham waived toward Charlie, who stood, hand outstretched. "This is Charlie Hollister. She's Blake Garrett's daughter, and a sort of niece to Russ."

Gary's eyes widened. "Wow," he told Ham, "you travel in pretty exotic circles. Makes me wish I were your friend."

Ham shrugged. "I don't advertise this, Gary. No offense intended, I just didn't see any reason to blast it around."

"He's trying to protect our privacy," Charlie informed him. "It's why we let him hang with us."

Gary looked as though he'd been caught with his pants down and couldn't figure out how to pull them back up. "Forgive my discomfort. I find myself in awe. Like I said," he told Russ, "I grew up on your music."

Drew arched her brows at Ham and mouthed, "Just barely."

Ham smothered the laugh that threatened to burst forth, rubbing his mouth with his palm until the urge waned. "Anyway, thanks for coming, Gary. We may find ourselves in a spot here and I'd as soon have you in ready reserve."

"How could I resist?"

"Sit down and I'll fill you in on the case, what we think might happen and some developments that occurred since I talked to you last night."

"Perhaps we should do this elsewhere."

Ham's surprise was evident in his voice. "There's no need for that. Charlie and Russ know everything I'm about to tell you. And they can sure as hell be trusted."

Gary had the good sense to look slightly abashed. "That's not what I meant. I'm sure they can, but if I get questioned by the District Attorney or the cops I want to claim client privilege. I can't do that if there are witnesses to the interview."

Russ pushed his chair back from the table, grabbed his plate, a glass of orange juice and silverware. "What say you, Charlie? Want to have breakfast on the veranda? It's a beautiful time of day to sit and watch the surf."

They paused as Charlie and Russ withdrew. Once they'd disappeared through the French doors, Ham leaned across the table and stared Gary in the eyes. "Okay, Gare, what's the real reason you wanted them out of here?"

Gary ignored the question for one of his own. "What in the hell happened to you? You look like you were in a dog fight and the dog won."

"You're not far off," Drew giggled.

"You've been here this long and only now noticing? I'm genuinely touched by your concern."

Gary snorted the obvious. "I meet a living legend and I'm going to waste time noticing you? You aren't serious, I'm guessing."

"He's Charlie's love slave," Drew unhelpfully informed him.

Ham spat his mouthful of scrambled eggs onto his plate and shoved the platter to the side. He'd lost his appetite.

Gary put hands to his undersized stomach, laughter bouncing his waistcoat and fob watch from side to side. "Ham, I am really impressed. How did you, of all people, score with somebody like that?"

"Getting back to business here. Again, why'd you want them gone, really? I've never known you to cave to any D.A., or to any cop, for that matter. On the contrary, you tend to make them cry. So what's the deal?"

Gary's stare was direct and unashamed. "Who's paying my fee?"

"I am," Ham replied immediately. He swept a hand toward Drew and corrected himself. "Rather, we are. There's no double-dipping here, Gare."

"Are you getting your fee from Russ?"

"Gary, get off the pig-o-wagon," Drew snapped. "Number one, we're not getting paid by Russ, Russ has absolutely nothing to do with this, and number two, it wouldn't matter if we were anyway. We're your clients and we're paying you. Period."

Gary spread his hands wide, less in supplication than in explanation. "You can't blame a guy for trying, can you? He's got to be what, a billionaire? My fees would of course adjust accordingly. Especially," he glared at Ham, "because all you'll pay me is what I used to charge way back from when I graduated law school."

"That's the price of having buddies, buddy."

"And it's not like you need the money anyway," Drew added. "From what I've read you rake in billions yourself from your famous bad boy clients, for Christ's sake."

Gary grabbed a piece of the aromatic bacon from the platter and munched on it as he turned dancing eyes to Drew. "A man's got to eat. And a guilty conscious is the best way to make a living, you know?"

"There's no bonanza," Ham repeated. "It's just me."

"Fine. I'll just put up on my blog that I'm working on a case while I'm staying at Russ Porter's house. That ought to be worth a few million." He held up a hand like a traffic cop demanding attention. "Just kidding. But I am not kidding about this. I don't believe for a single second that Russ Porter isn't involved. If that's the case, why are you here?"

Drew clamped lips tight while Ham considered his answer. Finally, he turned to Drew and shrugged. "It's confidential, he is our attorney, and he really does need to know the whole story."

"I guess," Drew agreed. "Just don't hold out for a bigger fee," she reminded Gary. "We're the clients."

"There is some coincidental crossover," Ham admitted. "I don't know that it's more than that."

"You're the one who's always told me that a coincidence is just an unplanned consequence," Gary responded.

Ham related the case as they knew it so far, starting with their client calling them because of their connection to Russ, how Russ discovered that the murders were systematic and done per a minor musical scale. He provided details of the Amber Bailey murder scene, revealed that one of the victims was a former groupie, and that it was Russ who discovered that each victim had a hit song that was written in the key of C minor. "So yeah, a lot of coincidence there, but it's damn hard to see how any of that fits in with Russ personally."

"So let me get this straight," an obviously unhappy Gary summed up. "You discover a dead body, the cops drag you in and basically threaten you—no matter how nicely and no matter how much acting in the form of cooperation. It was, I assure you a damn threat. And you don't call me right away, at that time? What in heaven's name were you thinking?"

"We were thinking we're detectives used to dealing with cops, from the inside and the outside," Drew reminded him. "A threat from a small town force isn't going to bother us a lot. The thought of finding another body is a different matter altogether, though. It could get rough."

"Rough is an apt description," Gary agreed. "Okay, I tell you what. I'll ring my secretary and get one of my associates to get the lowdown on the D.A. here. That way we'll be prepared in case the worst happens. Secondly, any chance your famous friend will let me bunk here for the duration? If not, I've got to locate a hotel and get settled in while you two do your thing."

"Grab some more bacon or whatever you want and let's go join them on the veranda. I'll let Drew put the request to him, but I can't see why not. Russ, once you get past the stars in your eyes, is a normal and good guy. And there's plenty of room."

Gary loaded up a platter of bacon. "Bacon is a weakness, but this is beyond temptation. I've never tasted such pure pleasure. Apple-smoked you say? My cardiologist is going to hate me."

They found Charlie and Russ lounging by the pool, plates in laps, engaged in quiet conversation. "Our friend needs a place to flop," Drew informed them as she pulled a chair up next to the rock star. "Is that okay with you?"

"Sure," Russ shrugged, "why not? Welcome aboard, Gary."

Gary's blush could have driven bats from a cave it was so bright. "I'm a little out of my league here. Forgive me if I stutter but, lord, this is beyond beautiful."

The attorney gaped, platter in hand and probably forgotten, as he took in the scene before him. Especially the infinity pool that invited the ocean in, making it appear as if each embraced the other. "I should have gone into music."

"You have no talent," Ham reminded him.

"Don't let Hamster needle you," Charlie told him. "It's just a bad habit he picked up as a bad kid."

"Hamster?" he mouthed to Drew, who responded with a nod and what Ham could only describe as a vicious grin. He groaned inwardly, understanding he'd never lose that moniker, not while Gary was around.

"Settle in, take a swim, enjoy," Russ offered.

The attorney's sad eyes and drooping lips revealed not just genuine regret but lost lust. "I didn't bring my swim trunks. I didn't know I'd need them."

"Oh, the hell with that," Russ said. "Just swim in the raw. Nobody around here is going to care."

"Unless you're packed, you don't have anything I haven't seen before," Charlie agreed.

"Or," Drew offered, eyes wide and innocent, "you could borrow the bottom part of my bikini. That should fit you."

"You could just swim in your undies, unless of course they've got little hearts or bears on them," Ham suggested.

"Thank you, all of you, for your excellent and creative ideas. If it's all the same to the lot of you, I'll just sit by the pool and study my briefs."

Ham knew his friend. The snickering normally would have brought out the acid side of Gary's tongue: quick, sharp and deadly—that same quality that made him a star in court. Russ' presence no doubt had curbed the impulse, a fact that tickled Ham's wicked side.

Gary covered his apparent embarrassment by shoving a thick slice of bacon into this mouth and pretending to be occupied with the task of chewing. Ham had every intention of saying something to add to his misery—and with the real hope of making him spit the mouthful out—but he never got the chance.

Because sirens shattered the morning air, a rising and falling crescendo of madness that drew louder and nearer by the second. Though they still wailed their unwelcome arrival, a screeching of vehicles could be heard over the cacophony, along with the slam of doors and the pounding of feet at the front of this formerly peaceful property.

All thoughts of swimming, nude or otherwise, withered away. Gary stood and swallowed his mouthful of bacon, throat distending around the meat still more whole than chewed. Nevertheless, he looked the soul of calmness as he dabbed a napkin at his lips and announced, "Okay, people. Here's where I earn my money. What little of it there will be."

CHAPTER EIGHT

WASHED UP AND UNWASHED

The sirens mercifully died away. No doubt the thought of riling a Rock God made the drivers a bit more circumspect than had been the case at Amber Bailey's house, Ham reflected. Being a jackass was one thing, being unemployed quite another.

Ham waited along with the rest, muscles tensed, jaw clenched. Whatever the purposes of the visit, pleasantry was not among them, not with that approach. It was old school, but he followed the dictum that outside of a true emergency, one acted with circumspection. Obviously, that particular theory of law enforcement was not in effect in Santa Cruz.

Peremptory knuckles pounded the door. Russ nodded to Gardner, who stood rooted with wide, nervous eyes. His feet finally crossed to the front door and shaking hands turned the knob. He had not yet fully pulled the door back before Steve and Pete burst through, followed by a slower moving but equally grim-faced Val.

After a questioning glance at Russ, they turned to stare speculatively at Ham. Something in their eyes revealed that Ham had a target on his chest. Why, he couldn't fathom.

"What happened to you?" Pete demanded.

In a more accusatory tone, Steve finished the thought. "Have you perchance been in a fight recently?"

"Never mind me. What's this all about?"

Val opened her mouth but before she began Gary strolled into view, cleared his throat and in a soft and deceptively friendly voice introduced himself. "My name is Gary Larsen and I'm an attorney at law. May I have your names please? And see identification?"

"We'll ask the questions here," Pete snapped.

Gary's eyes turned slate. "Not unless I get mine answered first."

Val nodded, a clear message to Pete. "I'm Valerie Simpson, chief of police here in Santa Cruz. And these are Detectives Wilson and Cassel. Show him your badges, guys."

Gary made of show of studying their identifications and nodded as if finally satisfied with the truth of it all. "And to what do we owe the pleasure of your company, Officers?"

Val ignored the dapper littler man and instead addressed herself to Ham. "Seriously, Ham, I must insist you explain your wounds. Either here or downtown will do."

"Mr. McCalister is my client," Gary responded, "and he will do as I say and when I say it. And right now I am instructing him to say absolutely nothing until you explain to me—in great and minute detail—exactly why you are here, what it is you want, and why you screeched to the world your intention to raid this house. Either here or downtown will do," he mocked.

Val's sighed resignation. "Okay, fine. We're here because we want to question you—all of you—about your client, Ronny Damon."

"We did this last night," Drew reminded her. "Everything we had to say we said then. What else is there?"

Gary shot a warning glance to Drew. "I am also representing Ms. Thornton. She is to say nothing more at this point."

Val's lopsided smile admitted he'd scored his point. "Ronny Damon is dead. His body was pulled from the ocean this morning. He was missing his left arm and half his organs, but the remainder of the body was intact."

Ham's eyes clouded with doubt. "You're saying he drowned? Or that, what, he was dinner for a great white?"

"He neither drowned nor was he dinner before he died. There was a single gunshot wound to the temple. Beyond that, his face is so battered identification is impossible. Interesting in light of the supposed last will and suicide note he sent you last night, wouldn't you say?"

"Then what the hell makes you think it's Ronny?" Drew demanded. "For heaven's sake, Val, quit screwing around and tell us what the crap is going on."

"I did. All that's left to say is that his wallet was still on him. License and credit cards in his name say it's him, alright. And how about that? Right after I tell you he's wanted and we're going for arrest. Coincidence? I think not."

"So the email was right. It was a suicide note. He really did kill himself," Ham whispered in wonder. "I never would have believed it."

"Not unless he tied his own hands behind his back before he did it," Val snapped.

"What? What the hell do you mean? How could you know he did that if his left arm was gone?"

"Because there's a rope tied to his right arm, which is still there, and a rope burn across his back," Pete snarled. "The coroner believes he chafed himself near raw trying to work those ties loose. It doesn't take a famous Las Vegas detective to figure out that the fact that, if so, he could not have then shot himself in the temple. It equally follows that he didn't kill himself and then tie his hands behind his back. See what we're driving at here?"

Ham turned to Gary, who nodded permission. "So you want to know if I had a fight with my client, got pissed, shot him in the head, tied him up and dropped his body into the ocean." Ham paused, rubbing his chin, eyes revealing deliberation. "Hmm. I guess I'll go with 'no'."

Pete appeared ready to snap, while Steve looked like he wanted to laugh but dare not. Val waded into the breach, once again taking charge. "Very funny, Ham. Now, how did you get those bruises?"

Ham explained the morning, how he'd gone for a jog and ended up chased by a murderous black SUV up and down some back alley.

"Did you get the license plate?"

He shrugged. "I was kind of busy. It was a California plate, that's all I know for sure. It had a minor break in the left side brake light, and a small dent by the right one. Other than that, I can't add anything."

"Pretty convenient," Pete remarked. "Big, black, no plate. Nice detective work."

"If that's going to be your attitude," Gary informed the detective, "this interview is over and I invite you to leave."

Val ignored both the attorney's comment and her own investigator. She turned squarely to Russ. "Tell me, do you perchance own a kayak?"

"Yeah, sure, I keep it out in the shed. Why?"

"Any chance it has 'Truckee River 1' on the side, lettered in gold?"

Russ's head snapped up and his back rammed to attention. "And how do you know that? That's a joke between me and Blake. Have you been going through my property?"

"I'd like you to open the shed for us, if you will."

"I don't believe he will," Gary interrupted. "I think you have what you need, and certainly all you're going to get at this time without a warrant."

Val regarded him curiously, a bug on the windshield. "Does this mean you're also Mr. Porter's lawyer?"

Gary arched questioning eyebrows at Russ who responded with a curt nod. "That's exactly what it means. You talk to me, not to him." He quickly glanced at Charlie who also nodded. "I represent everybody in this household. And I say we're through here."

Val stared at Gary, sizing up a new adversary. "We'll be back with a warrant, if that's what you want."

Gary got right into Val's face, eyes looking up only slightly to meet hers, his reflecting ice. It was a Gary that Ham knew from court, the bulldog with only one attitude. Bad and biting.

"Yeah, you do exactly that. And you tell the D.A. to come with you, and feel free to say that I demand it. As for me, I'll bring the press. We'll see what they have to say about you harassing an American institution. My guess is that after that neither you nor the D.A. could get elected greenhorn on a crab boat in Ketchikan. But yes, Chief, you do that. We'll all be all over the news and I can use the advertising."

Pete's temper got the better of him. His face turned crimson and he growled, "Let's arrest the son of a bitch and haul his ass off to jail. Obstruction of justice comes to mind."

"What little mind there must be," Gary laughed. "You can certainly try it. I can't wait to hear what the judge will have to say about that." He rubbed his hands together in anticipation. "This is going to be a really interesting day."

Val's voice commanded instant obedience. "Pete, that's enough. Wait for me outside. And I do mean wait. You get anywhere near that shed, or go anywhere other than straight to the car, and I'll have your badge. You understand me?"

Pete bit his lip with such ferocity that Ham expected it to gush blood and flood Russ' tiled foyer. Face flushed, he stomped from the room, obedient but maliciously so. Not a good idea, Ham mused, for a man who might hope for advancement one day.

Val turned apologetic eyes to Gary. "I am really sorry for the rude behavior. I do want you to know that I consider it unacceptable in my department, and I assure you that neither Detective Wilson nor any other member of my department will treat either you or anybody else with such boorish behavior again."

Ham squelched a grin at the wording. "Detective Wilson," not "Pete." This was a man in line for a dressing down that he'd give half his fee to see. If Damon's estate didn't come after it, he sighed.

"As for you," she said to Russ, "again, I apologize, but this time out of necessity of the situation. You can see why we needed to talk to you. A man, a suspect in a series of murders, is dead, and not of his own accord. Your kayak is found floating nearby. It's something we'd be remiss if we didn't explore."

Russ nodded understanding if not forgiveness. His jaw told a story of anger at the mere thought.

Heaving a deep sigh, Val turned to Drew and threw her arms up and wide, exasperation at its source. "And you and Ham, what can I say? I thought we were on a wavelength here, that we'd made an agreement, and it's one I trusted. Why won't you tell me what's going on, what it is that you're thinking?"

Gary stepped in as he held a forestalling hand to his clients. "Give us a little time to digest the information you came here to impart and maybe to kick it around a little. You've got to understand that this comes as quite a shock to all of us. My clients had no idea that Mr. Damon was dead. I think I can assure you that we would have so informed you, had we known. But let me think it over and maybe we'll have a statement for you later. Will that do?"

"It'll have to, won't it?"

Gary made no reply to the obvious, merely led the way to the door, opened it for their benefit and waved them through. "We'll be in touch."

No one spoke as they watched the exit and the meeting at the cars. Val's face was visibly red and angry, jaw jutting out as she spat unheard words at her offending detective. Pete responded only with nods as he stood with shoulders slumped and his eyes fixed firmly on his shoes. Finally, after what must have seemed half an eternity to Pete, Val spun on her heels, jumped in her car and—perhaps aware of her audience and making a point—slowly pulled away. Neither sirens nor lights breeched the calm of the morning air.

Ham clapped Gary on the shoulder, his smile wide and true. "Gary, you've done some good work, but that was one of your better performances. Well done, my dramatic friend."

"Now can I clip your famous rock friend for fees?" Gary exuded smug self-satisfaction.

"Nope. Still just me and Drew and our scandalous discount."

"We may have to pay it from our own funds," Drew pointed out. She directed her question to Gary. "That little matter of our fee. We made the deposit last night. Do we still have it?"

"Absolutely, though it's probably a very good thing that you did deposit it last night instead of now when you know he's dead. Somebody, his executor, can maybe try to stake a claim if they determine he died before the deposit, but it won't fly given that the check will clearly show to be his signature and there's no agreement that says the work must be performed to receive the compensation. So yes," he summed up, "there shouldn't be a problem. I think you can just go ahead and proceed on that assumption."

"Maybe I should ante up some money here," Russ said. "It looks like I'm neck deep, and it'll take you and Ham and Gary here to protect my interests."

Drew would have none of it. "Forget it. Number one, Ronny Damon paid us to investigate and it doesn't matter that he's gone. Though Gary tells us we get the fee regardless, I know I can speak for both of us when I say that we don't work that way. Ronny wanted it investigated, he paid for it and by god, we'll finish it; if for no other reason than to try to posthumously clear his name. Second, and just as important, Gary works for me and Ham and we've directed him to include all of you in his service, a service for which we pay an agreed upon amount. Which, as I recall, is somewhere south of ten bucks an hour, right, Gary?"

"That would be a raise," Gary mumbled with a smile.

"First thing we do," Ham ordered, "is check out that shed. And we'd best get to it before they come back, if we don't want surprises to slap us upside the head."

Russ grabbed a key off a hook in the kitchen and led the way. "It's quicker to go out front and use the path to the north side."

Gardner hustled to open the door they marched through, out onto the porch and down the few steps to the manicured lawn. Off to the side lay a sandy path that wound its way through various shrubbery and on down to the pier and shed.

Russ stopped so abruptly at that intersection of lawn and path that Ham nearly crashed into him. Only by inches did he manage not to knock the rock legend face first into sand, turf and gardenias.

Before he could ask, Russ silently pointed out to the street. When Ham followed the accusatory finger he saw Steve sitting attentively in his sedan, parked across the entrance to the grounds. A position from which he observed the access to the shed.

"Well, well," Ham muttered. "Somebody's on the ball. I've got to remember not to underestimate him again."

"What'll we do?" Russ asked. The concern in his voice indicated exasperation as well as nervousness.

"We go to the shed," Gary replied. "It does, however, mean that they will in fact be back with that warrant, and that we can expect them to appear sooner rather than later. Nevertheless, there's not a damn thing they can do about you looking through your own property. The cop is for show, nothing more than an attempt to intimidate you. Just ignore him."

Russ shrugged his shoulders, then impishly threw a friendly wave to the watchful and waiting detective before he continued down the path. When they got to the shed, Russ' sharp intake of breath alerted the rest to what they soon saw. The shed had been pried open, the lock picked back. The door stood ajar by a few inches.

"What the hell is this?"

In answer to Russ' question, Ham gently shoved him aside, pulled the pistol from its holster and cautiously drew the door wide.

Drew, her own weapon in hand, reached inside, searching the wall. "Left side," Russ told her, "shoulder height."

Drew fumbled around for several seconds, the sound of hand hitting metal wall echoing within. Finally, a light came on, illuminating the interior. Russ laughed when Drew grumbled, "I should have known you meant *your* shoulder, big man."

The shed, though full of various equipment, both recreational and landscape related, was neatly arranged, the neatness within almost obsessive. "Gardner's doing," Russ shrugged. "I'm not nearly that organized."

A large space of wall was occupied only by oversized hooks and freshly painted white wallboard. A grim-faced Russ nodded the obvious. "That's where I hang the kayak so it doesn't get beat up by the other stuff. They found mine, all right."

"Okay," Gary ordered, "everybody out. Don't touch anything. Don't even turn off the light or close the door. This is a crime scene and we'll let them do their thing once they come back with the warrant." When they just stood there, he shooed them out like a mother hen. "Get. Go, go, go!"

Outside, Russ' dark face, black with anger, turned on Ham. "What the hell is going on here, dammit? How the hell did they get my boat, and more importantly, why? Is somebody trying to somehow involve me in all this crap?" He threw his arms wide, nearly knocking a hovering Gary over with a blow. "Somebody tell me what the hell this is all about, and I mean right freaking now or by god I will have the lot of you thrown off my property." At Drew's surprised and widened eyes, he snapped, "And don't think I won't."

Drew's response was instantaneous and loud. Not with what she said but how she did it. She spun on her heels, stomped her way about five feet up the path and stood there, ramrod rigid, her back to Russ. Ham knew her as well as he knew his own mother and he didn't need his years on the homicide squad to detect that Russ had a whole lot of backpedaling to do with his fiery redheaded lady love. He wondered if Russ had seen this side of her yet, if he even knew what kind of trouble he had just purchased. Let alone the long term cost and how to pay it off over time.

Ham wanted to warn Russ, nudge him toward redemption, but found himself at his inarticulate best. When he tried to grunt a warning it only sounded a discordant and ineffective clearing of the throat. It took Charlie, Russ' adopted niece and the one person here that knew him the best, to calm the Superstar Tantrum. And deliver a rebuke in the process.

"Uncle Russ," she cooed—Ham had never heard her call him that before, but leave it to Charlie, her timing was impeccable—"there's no need to play the prima donna. These people are here to help and you're damn lucky they are. Take a deep breath. And apologize."

Russ' shoulders sagged and his cheeks tinged red. "Yeah. She's right. I am sorry. Too many years of getting whatever I want whenever I want. It's one of the curses of fame, I suppose. Though your father seldom indulged, bless his soul."

Charlie's tender smile let him off the hook. Partially. "I think I'd quickly explain that to Drew, if I were you. And try to make it more chastened and authentic. Uncle Russ."

Ham shook his head, admiration coloring his smile, as he watched Russ humble himself with Drew. He approached her tentatively, tapped her lightly on the shoulder, and when she refused to turn around, he actually got in front of her. His hands waved apology as he whispered unheard words, but Ham noticed that Drew's back began to relax. Unexpectedly, she lightly slapped Russ' cheek and quickly followed that with a laugh and a kiss. All forgiven, apparently. If not forgotten. Knowing Drew, it should probably be deemed probation.

Ham pulled Charlie close, wrapped her shoulders with his arm. "You are one special lady. I don't know how you do it. I was afraid if I'd said anything, he might have killed me with those words of his. Or Drew would have, with her gun."

Charlie's soft laugh tinkled, pure music to his uneducated ears. "Sometimes Russ has to be reminded he's a person, not a legend. As for Drew, she's a woman no one should mess with too often. Russ is getting off easy this time. And I will make sure he knows that."

Ham glanced up and caught Steve's eye. The detective had exited the car, was leaning back against the driver's side door, arms folded across his chest. His face revealed disappointment more than anger at their presumed deceit.

Ham admired the man's restraint. Back in the day, when he wore a badge, had that happened on his case he would have broken a few department rules—along with a few heads. "I think," he announced, "a little fence mending is in order. Gary, if you have no objections?"

"Be my guest. Just make sure it's only the shed."

Ham sauntered to Steve's station and held his hand out in greeting. "No need for the warrant, Steve. Come and have a look if you'd like."

Steve regarded him like a bug under the microscope before he pursed his lips and slowly shook his head. "Thanks, I guess, but I'll wait."

"Okay, as you wish. But you might want to consider that you're in a hornet's nest here. You bring a needless warrant and a search team, you ought to know that though Russ is outwardly a nice guy, gentle and genial even, he does possess a superstar's temper. Take care not to get caught in a crossfire you don't need."

"Is that a threat?"

Steve's slow grin took the sting out of the challenge, but not enough for Ham to reply in kind. "Not a threat, Steve, a warning. To the presumably wise. Why do it the hard way when you can do it the easy way, right?"

"Want to tell me what you were doing in there? What you changed, moved, hid or obscured? Or should I wait?"

"Wrong on all counts. We found what we suspected, which is loss of the boat. The door had been pried open. Someone stole it."

"Or staged a scene."

Ham laughed, dryly, not at all amused. "Whatever. Have a good one, enjoy the wait; or if you're bored and of a mind to, you can follow me. Drew and I are going places."

"Where to? Why?"

Ham answered by grinning widely and turning on his heel. He rejoined his team outside the shed and, to Drew, nodded toward the car. "I think we'd better get over to Barry Braxton's place before we get boxed in. They're not going to quash the warrant and they may want to hold us while they search. So let's get out of here, now, before they can do something stupid."

"You don't have to worry about that," Gary retorted. "They try something like that and I'll have their balls hanging from a tree."

Ham turned serious eyes on the attorney. "I know you're the best. Hell, I've seen it too many times to doubt. But this is a smaller, less gentrified system. They know, or at least I suspect they do, that they'll lose. But they might enjoy the game and I don't want to lose the time. So we'll go, you stay here and protect the place, be the pit bull you are and keep them away from Charlie and Russ. Drew and I can take care of ourselves."

"My gallant hero," Charlie swooned. "I'm overcome with womanly gratitude."

Ham chuckled and ostentatiously wrapped a protective arm around her shoulder. "You are so lucky. Damn but I wish I were as lucky as you."

"I'm feeling kind of a third wheel here," Gary lamented, less regret in his voice than humor.

"Fifth, if you're counting," Charlie corrected.

"Six, if you count Gardner," Ham pointed out.

"Enough," Drew demanded. "Let's do this thing. Russ, you listen to Gary and do exactly what he tells you to do. I know you're used to being in charge, but this is one time you're going to do it my way."

Without further word, she jumped into the driver's seat, put the car in motion and waved at Steve as she passed his frowning face. Ham did not look up as he busied himself with punching their destination into the GPS. He noted with surprise that the address was seventeen miles inland, a distance of some consequence in a town half that size.

They wound their way through small streets and up into the more mountainous interior, darkness increasing with the overgrown trees and smaller lanes. A scenic route that reminded Ham more of *Deliverance* than sunny California.

Barry's "house" proved to be a low-slung bungalow, with an oddly out of place tin roof. Since the driveway was nonexistent, they pulled into a space two doors down and walked back along the broken cement that purported to be a sidewalk. Although a patch of grass graced the entry, the sagging porch and uncontrolled weeds decreased the curb appeal of what must have been at least a fifty year-old relic. Sad to think that someone, at a distant point in time, must have taken pride in this little piece of earth they would have called home, Ham mused. A home that someone would now call a nightmare on a rotting foundation.

Draperies blocked an outsider's view, if draperies they could be called. First glance suggested bed sheets applied to walls, and a second glance confirmed that the sheets themselves had seen better days years before.

"Maybe we should have called," Ham murmured. "It sure as hell looks deserted. Didn't Russ say this guy had a hit record?"

"If he did," Drew conceded, "he long ago spent the proceeds. Well, let's at least try. Bang on the door until your fist is blue. We'll irritate him to the door if he's home."

Ham followed orders, pounding on the door with the side of his fist for a full sixty seconds. His hand feeling the effects, he was about to admit defeat when the door flew open and a tall, cadaverous form filled the frame. "What the hell is it with you people," Barry demanded. "What do want? Can't you take a hint and leave a man in peace? What's the matter with you?"

Ham stared, dumbstruck, at the long-haired throwback to the 1960s. His hair hung in dirty disorder almost to his waist and his eyes shone somewhere behind a psychedelic set of shades. The multi-colored shirt, worn and in desperate need of washing, hung loosely over thin hips, groin and legs barely concealed by the few areas that were not ripped from the bell bottom jeans.

And the stench. The blast of body odor overwhelmed the smell of marijuana that colored the air from within. Ham struggled with reflex to keep the bile inside rather than spew it out, as his body strongly insisted must be the response.

Ham noted that although Drew shared his inner struggle she recovered almost instantaneously. "We're looking for Barry Braxton. Are you he?" she said.

"Who wants to know?

Ham snapped. With the assault on his senses and that pithy and pedestrian line from whatever old gangster movie the guy must have memorized, he'd had more than enough.

Erase that. Make it more than way too much.

"Who we are is none of your damn business. Get your ass out here, we're going to talk. Either willingly or after a beating, your choice."

Ham felt relief and amusement, rather than anger, when Drew jumped in, good cop to his bad. "Actually, though we do have a few questions, our main purpose here is to help you. We think you might be in danger."

Barry eyed them warily, or at least Ham assumed he did from behind those dark glasses. His mouth formed a pout and his words were a stutter. "Um... so you're, um... what is it... who are you again?" A lone bulb must have gone on in his darkened upstairs, for he straightened into a long-limbed tallness that had Ham staring inches up into his nose. "Let me see your credentials."

Barry examined the licenses Drew and Ham proffered him, and though Ham wasn't sure the man had enough mental acuity to recognize the words, he smirked and said, "So you're rent-a-cops, you're not even real. I could just tell you to leave."

"You could, Mr. Braxton," Drew agreed, "it's your property and your call. But I really do think it's advisable that you hear us out. Your life may depend on it."

Barry heaved a sigh of what? Resignation? Relief? Ham's radar beeped warning.

"Sure," Barry said. "Come on in. It's not much but I call it home."

False bravado. That's it. A relieved man who thinks he has the upper hand. Radar reporting, sir. Total ass in target.

The interior, darkened and smelling of smoke, of both the legal and illegal variety, swallowed them as they followed the musician into his digs. And they were complete digs, Ham thought, shaking his head at what he might be catching. He'd need a sterilized shovel just to find a place to sit down.

Ashtrays overflowed with excess of a kind Ham would have busted just years before. Now he had less interest in law than in survival. Preferably with brain intact. "You know, my eyes are a bit sensitive to dark. I don't see so well. Maybe we'd be better off on the porch, if that's okay."

"Don't mind him," Drew said. "This is more than fine. If he needs to see something, I'll be his seeing-eye dog. Mind if we have a seat?"

Ham kept the sigh of disgust buried inside, but he was hating Drew, even though he knew she was dead on the mark, especially because she had put them at risk of catching more diseases than all of Las Vegas' doctors acting en masse could cure in a career.

Barry swept newspaper and other debris of questionable origin off a divan. "Sure, absolutely, sure, sure, sure."

"Okay, he's mastered one word," Ham inwardly sighed. "Let's see if he's got a few more that are relevant to reality."

Drew threw him a warning, eyes small and hard. *Gotcha,* Ham thought. *Ham backs off, Drew takes it away.*

"Thank you, Mr. Braxton. By the way, may I call you Barry? I find 'mister' kind of awkward, like talking to my dad's bosses."

He might have mumbled "whatever," but neither could be sure, since Barry was busy picking at nonexistent scabs that only he could see—ones that he constantly and absently worked at, like a habit from hell—to bother himself with pronunciation.

Drew approached cautiously and reached a tentative hand out, maybe to lightly touch Barry's shoulder with the hope of increasing his concentration. She snapped back her hand inches from the guy's body, as though suddenly concerned the invisible scabs might be contagious.

Drew used her inside voice rather than her cop timbre. "Can you listen to us for a minute, Barry? We fear you may be in danger and we'd like to help."

He tore off his sunglasses, warily stared her in the eyes, perhaps sizing her up. He continued to pick at a phantom scab as he shrugged, "Why? Why would you want to help me?"

"Because we admire you," Ham snapped. "Flaming twit."

"It's our job, Barry," Drew soothed with a sideward glance at Ham. "We're representing a client, a client who is also a suspect. To represent him we need to anticipate events. And you popped up on the list."

Barry's dull eyes shone for a brief second then reverted to his "nobody home" vacuity. "So talk already but hurry it up. I got things to do, man."

Another fix, no doubt.

Ham explained, simply, as to a child bored by the lesson. "There have been a series of murders here in Santa Cruz, all involving people that worked with Ronny Damon. The order of victims has been anything but random. According to our theory of the case, you are a potential victim because of your initials."

A smile briefly touched Barry's lips, which he quickly covered by tugging at those same lips, making a show of working an invisible scab. And the eyes again died.

"That a fact, man? I hadn't heard. I been busy."

Ham's own eyes narrowed and he heard that ping of suspicion. "That's a lot of busy. It's been all over the news."

"What do I care about news? What's it to me?"

"The fact remains," Drew interjected, "you may be the next victim to be targeted. The killer is murdering to C minor."

Barry turned from them, his face obscured by shadows and distance. "Say, listen, where are my manners? Would you like something, maybe water? I got that. I could wipe out a couple of glasses."

Ham and Drew followed his gaze to what passed for a kitchen sink. Had it been fourfold larger it still could not have contained the overflow of moldy dishes with caked on detritus of groceries past.

Ham stuck his hands deep in his pockets, a firm and obvious denial, while Drew murmured a polite "No, thank you."

"Okay, well what should I do? I mean if this lunatic comes after me, do I call you, or what?"

"It would be a little late for that," Drew advised. "But we can probably get the Santa Cruz police to give you protection."

"Protection," he spat. "Hell, they'd pay the mother to finish the job, more likely."

"I take it you've been busted a few times."

"Huh," he snarled, "a few is an underestimate. You sell a little weed down on the pier and they act like you just offed the queen."

"You do know we're in the United States, right?" Drew asked sweetly.

Barry waved away her comment. "You know what I mean, dude. You don't have to be so patronizing."

"Barry, I mean no disrespect by this," Ham said slowly—more not to confuse the man than to soften the accusation —"but I have to ask. I know you had several hits, one even in, what was it, the top thirty?" Barry nodded and Ham continued, "Where did all that money go? I would have thought you'd be living in a nice place, maybe an upscale bungalow like Amber did."

Barry laughed, angrily, loudly and absolutely devoid of humor. "Money. Right. What little I got for my work I spent long ago."

I can guess where, Ham thought, but contented himself with, "I have some inkling of what you rock stars consider "little" and it's probably poles apart from my definition of the term."

"Not unless you consider 'lots' to be less than a few thousand bucks." Barry eyed him up and down, noting the clothes, shoes and probably the neatly cut hair. "And I doubt that by the looks of you. Or you," he added to Drew. "Anyway, Ronny stole it all. Stole my song, the freaking mother, stole it right out from under me."

"Why didn't you sue him?"

That won a grimace of true amusement from Barry. "That takes money, man. And Ronny made damn sure I never had enough at any one time to do it."

"Haven't you released anything else, maybe through another producer and record company?"

"I'm passé, dude. Yesteryear's news, you know? Nobody will touch me now."

I doubt it's for the reason you think, Ham mused. *Try taking a look around.* Out loud he inquired, "Do you want us to get you protection?"

Barry's face drooped, resignation written in his eyes. "Naw. Forget it, man. This guy would probably be doing me a favor anyway. I'll take my chances."

Ham flipped his business card onto the littered coffee table. "If you change your mind, even and especially at the last minute, give me a call. I'll do my best."

Barry nodded and escorted them the few feet to the door. "Hey, listen, man, I do appreciate you letting me know. It's been a while since anybody took the time to care what might happen to me."

Without shaking hands, they waved, over the shoulder style, nearly jogging to the car in their haste to quit the drug house.

"God," Ham muttered. "If that isn't one of the saddest falls I've seen. Dreams to ashes in the split of a life's second."

Drew turned the ignition, let the car idle a bit to bring the air conditioner to speed, then pulled out and into what little traffic traversed the small road. With a quick laugh, she revealed her opinion in turn. "Well we know one thing. He may be a potential victim but he's no killer. The guy doesn't have enough brain cells left to pick his nose, let alone meticulously plan a series of murders."

Ham paused, chin to hand, eyes focused on nothing outside the window. What sense of pity he had experienced had been usurped by a memory.

"I'm not so sure," he drawled. "I mean, you're probably right but I could swear, a couple of times there, I saw something come alive in his eyes. For the briefest of microseconds there was a look of cunning, is the best way I can put it, like he was there, like this was some kind of game. I can't help but wonder if he was in fact playing us."

"Oh, come on," Drew snorted. "Maybe there's a brain cell or two left, maybe not, but if he was playing us it sure wasn't with that pigsty he lives in. I mean, what, he trashed his place waiting for us to arrive? How did he even know we would?"

"I don't know," Ham admitted, "and maybe I'm way off base here. But there's something."

Drew shrugged. "I've worked with you far too long not to trust your instinct. Let's say for a minute you're right. If so, maybe he wasn't waiting on us. Maybe he didn't even know about us. Who does that leave?"

Ham snapped fingers he'd been unaware were previously clenched in a fist. "The cops. They're the ones he expected."

"The cops," Drew affirmed. "But then that takes him off our potential victim list and puts him squarely on the bad guy roster."

"Yet the guy's only a musician. Or at least was. If he was acting he ought to be winning Oscars in Hollywood, not living a flophouse existence."

"Maybe this is his screen test," Drew joked. "And we get to be supporting cast in it."

Ham sounded almost pensive as he added, "Maybe that's what he's got in mind. Maybe we're inadvertent players in a play we don't want produced."

CHAPTER NINE

SEND IN THE CLOWNS

Havoc greeted their return to Russ' oceanfront villa. A helicopter whooped its outlandish presence overhead, at least five news vans cluttered the street in front, and more than half a dozen police cars, with their silent lights flashing like strobes, clogged the scene.

"We may have to give Gary a raise," Drew commented wryly. "It's one thing to act the mouthpiece, quite another to play ringmaster to a gaggle of fools."

Unable to navigate the crowded driveway, Drew parked half on, half off of the property. Nostrils flaring, teeth gnashing, she forced Ham to sprint to keep up as she dashed ahead.

Ham nearly tripped over the debris strewn about the lawn. It looked as though the contents of the shed had been tossed by a hyperactive hurricanes.

In this case, official hurricanes. And all the hurricanes stood lolling, admiring the destruction they had wrought.

Bastards.

Ham halted, half panting, hip screaming abuse. He discovered Gary, off to the side, engaged in hushed but intense conversation with Russ, who gazed off in the distance, his face purple with rage.

Charlie, as he would have predicted, was much more difficult to control. Even above the sounds of the chopper and the news gaggle, she could be heard screaming in Val's face. What those words may have been Ham could not discern, but he would bet a year's worth of his life that they were unprintable in a family newspaper.

While Drew ran to join Russ and Gary, Ham slid up behind Val, catching Charlie's eyes as he came into view. His arched eyebrows were answered with a curt, "She's a damn fool and I decided she ought to know it." She waved toward the house and cried, "Look at those flaming assholes. They're tearing the place apart and they don't give a whit what they destroy in the process as long as they get to show off their tricks for the news pool of leeches." She paused for a gulp of air and when she continued her voice rang with sorrow. "How they could do this to a man like Russ is unimaginable. They're humiliating him."

Val looked up from studying the ground, an intense investigation she'd undertaken when Charlie began her barrage of recrimination. Shame colored her cheeks as she quietly explained. "Your attorney said I should tell the district attorney to come here personally with the warrant. When I told him that, all hell broke loose. He loved the idea, unfortunately, and just as unfortunately, I lost control. This circus," she spat bitterly, "is his show and his alone." She cast a wry look at Charlie. "If you want to repeat your comments to him, I'd be beyond delighted to get his ass out here."

"He's in the house?"

"Yes, Ham, he's in there directing the massacre of a great man's legacy. He corralled a couple of camera crews from the local stations to follow him, so I'm sure he's making a big deal of directing every bit of activity as if he's the kahuna, the all-important prick with the experience and expertise to pull this 'dangerous operation' off, as he put it to the press." Her face darkened as she added, "He's up for re-election, you know."

"Okay, thanks, Val. You sticking around, or have you had enough?"

"I'll be right here, trying to ensure these oafs don't break everything they drag out of that storage shed."

"Good enough." He approached Drew, tapped her on the shoulder and mumbled, "You better come with me. I'm going to break a few heads and I prefer you not stay out here and add to the body count."

Ham stormed up to Gary, Drew dogging his heels, and snapped, "What the hell is the matter with you? Why are you letting them do this?"

Gary turned from Russ and met the accusation in Ham's glare. "Take it easy and lose the lip. There's not a damn thing I can do to stop this; they've got their warrant and they're utilizing it as a campaign piece. But stick around; I will be having a public discussion with Mister District Attorney once he comes back out of that house."

"Why wait?"

Gary's face was inscrutable. "It's my preference. Just be patient. I don't think you'll be displeased."

Ham wanted to argue, would have argued, except that Detective Pete Wilson chose that moment to add his unwelcome presence. "You have no client anymore. You're not needed here," he sneered.

Drew's laugh was long, loud and vicious. "Really! Why don't you ask Russ about that? Or Gary and Charlie. You little tiny prick of an idiot. Is there anything inside there? Anything you use in place of a brain?"

"You keep that wise-ass mouth of yours clamped shut or I'll have you escorted off this property, you understand me?"

Gary placed a calming hand on Drew's shoulder. He strode two steps, going nose to nose with the similarly short man, his smile deceptively inviting. "Two things, Detective. Number one, you don't talk to my client, you talk to me. Violate that order again and I'll have you up on charges so fast you'll never swim to the surface. Secondly, you put a hand on her and it's assault, period, simple, done. That's felony assault, by the way, so it's not just civil, it's criminal. Oh," he added, an apparent afterthought, "let me just go ahead and add one more thing. You direct any of your trained goons to 'escort' her off the property and I'll have you charged with kidnapping."

"Good luck with that," Pete laughed. "Pompous windbag."

Gary looked anything but offended. On the contrary. "Why thank you, my good man. However, luck I don't need. If Val won't do it, you may be assured the Justice Department will. They just love to investigate local police agencies, do it all the time. Shall I call them? It's no problem. They're on my speed dial."

Pete glared, face contorted with rage and hatred. His mouth flew open, snapped shut, opened again, a silent stutter he seemed unable to control. Finally, seemingly worn out with the effort, he spun on his heels and stormed away.

"As soon as his teeny tiny mind resets," Drew advised Ham, "he'll be back to accuse you of Ronny's murder."

"Yeah, he will. Then we'll just have to show him the sad error of his tragic ways, won't we?"

Charlie sidled up to them just in time to overhear the comments. "I wouldn't take it so lightly. He may try to take you in for questioning."

"Not without my attorney, he won't. And I doubt he wants to mess much more with Gary." Ham slapped a hand to the lawyer's back and beamed affection. "You constantly impress me, my friend. Now go sink your fangs into that district attorney. And don't let go until he bleeds."

"Soon," Gary said. "Let him have his fun first. It's likely the last he'll have for a while, I'm guessing."

Val approached, meekly, sorrow and apology indicated by her slumped shoulders and dead eyes. "May I interrupt for a second?"

"No. Why don't you go play with the Press. Surely you want a sound bite, right? Your face featured on the news. Wouldn't that be fun?"

"Ms. Hollister, I know you're pissed. You have every reason in the world to be so, but you're pissing in the wrong direction." She paused, waiting, it seemed, for a reply that was not forthcoming. "Anyway, what I wanted to do was offer you some information and advice. Based on what happened yesterday, I'm guessing it's something of direct interest to you."

Gary's voice was firm and his tone unyielding when he gave his response. "Chief Simpson, you talk to me, not to any of my clients. If I have to tell a single one of you that again I will quit playing nice and we will do this through the courts, and at your peril. Do you understand me?"

"Quite," Val shrugged. With a sideways glance at Charlie, she added, "I'd rather deal with you anyway. You're threatening, but not lethal."

"Fine. As long as you understand, and as long as you make sure your minions follow that order. Now, what is it you want to tell us? Rather, what is it you want to tell *me*?"

"That email Ham received from Ronny Damon. It's evidence now. Particularly the last will and testament stuff."

"That's your news? Hardly a headline."

"The news is that nobody else knows about it yet. But they will. Specifically, you can bet the district attorney will demand a copy of the email once he's finished with the cameras and actually bothers to read my report."

"You're going to have to subpoena it if you want it, which I will fight tooth and nail," Gary snapped. "I'll tie it up in court until you make Methuselah look like a toddler. After this flaming circus, you get nothing for free. And," he held up a hand to forestall comment, "before you plead innocence, I don't give a damn. That's the way it is and the way it is going to be."

"I know that," Val admitted, "but that wasn't my point. I'm actually going out on a limb here because I'm just about as fed up with that ass of a D.A. as you are. There will be a subpoena. So if there's anything that you don't want known, you might want to consider accidentally deleting the message. And losing the hard drive. Though of course I never said that and you didn't hear it from me."

"If you really want to help," Charlie suggested, "you can call those cameras over here and make a formal statement that Russ is in no way a suspect, that on the contrary, he is himself a victim of crime. You can further state that police presence here today is to investigate precisely the facts of the crime against his property and possible threats to his life, and that any police presence in the future will be for protection purposes only."

"I won't do that. I'm not going to take on the district attorney, not that publicly. That's a game I cannot win."

"But the district attorney can make that statement," Gary said. "And I think he might be open to it after I unload the facts of life on him."

Ham grinned at his old friend. Without a word or a tip of the hat he walked off, eyes fixed on the entrance to the overrun house. He walked the few steps up the porch, where two uniformed officers stood blocking his way. Without acknowledging their presence, he pushed past them and was half way through the door before one of them challenged his credentials.

"I'm a private investigator who's been hired to look into this. I need to have a word with the D.A. if you don't mind."

"We have orders to keep everyone out until the search is done. Sorry."

Ham shrugged, feigned indifference. He ambled down the steps, out to the lawn and made a show of looking bored, as if resigned to a long wait. When their attention returned to the commotion inside and around them, Ham made his way around the bougainvillea fronting the side of the yard and up to the cliffs beyond. From there a small path led to the veranda and the French doors in back.

As he'd expected, it had not occurred to anybody to place guards there, since the threat of intrusion would be out front. He eased the door open and stepped into the bright lights of cameras and the buzz of voices and clattering drawers.

At the sight of Gardner and what he was doing, Ham's face lit up. The caretaker was following the District Attorney, who even now busied himself playing detective. Gardner carried a video camera, mic on, missing nothing. Ham caught Gardner's eye, who winked in return and held up a press pass. From where it came, Ham had no clue.

With Gardner documenting the scene downstairs, Ham climbed the steps to the second level, where he found fewer voices and less commotion. He passed his own room, currently empty of prying eyes, and on to Russ', where he expected to find a cluster of searchers.

All he found was a lone searcher. To Ham's relief it was Steve, the more reasonable, even likeable half of the Mutt and Jeff team.

The detective had his hands stuffed in his pockets, not even making a show of searching. Rather, he stood rooted, apparently fascinated, in front of a wall of pictures that documented Truckee River through the years. In addition to platinum and gold albums, the walls boasted covers of each of the sixteen albums the band had released, photos of crowd shots at sold out concerts in various venues, from ballparks to arenas, and most especially pictures of Russ and Blake through the years. Grammy awards littered a bookshelf, along with medals and other rock and roll memorabilia from around the world.

Ham smiled inwardly, aware of what Steve must think and feel as he soaked in the panorama of stardom. The first time he'd seen this—yesterday, he reminded himself with surprise; it seemed so much longer—his breath had deserted him and his mind had fought for comprehension: he really stood there, in the sanctum sanctorum of musical history at its grandest.

"Pretty impressive, isn't it?"

Steve whirled, eyes wide, face flushed, caught in the non-act. Seeing Ham, he slumped in relief and the horror on his face dissolved to humor. "That picture of Truckee River with The Beatles just blows me away. The two greatest bands in the history of music standing together. Or at least two of three, if you put the Rolling Stones up there with them, which I don't, but a lot of people do, I guess."

"What does the warrant cover, Steve? What are you guys actually looking for?"

"Me, I'm looking for nothing. As for the warrant, it covers any and all suspicious documents relating to the recent murders, bloody clothes, weapons, and all that."

"In other words, open-ended. How'd they get that kind of warrant?"

"It was Rob's doing. He's lathering at the mouth over the thought of becoming world famous, the one to bring down the druggie king of rock and roll. He's got one of the local judges in his pocket, probably dirty, if you know what I mean."

"Rob? Is he the D.A.?"

"Yeah, Robert Turner, Definite Asshole. You must have seen him downstairs, beaming, strutting and drooling." Steve regarded him with a mix of humor and curiosity. "How'd you manage to get in here, anyway? Val run interference? I wouldn't have thought she'd be so 'in your face' with Rob."

"It was my own idea. Val doesn't know and I suspect you're right. If I'd asked I'd still be out on the lawn."

Steve's inscrutable smile flashed only briefly. "Maybe not. Val isn't public about it, because she'd like to keep her job, but she does have a tendency to find innocent ways to thwart any case that Rob takes a personal interest in."

"Like this one, for instance?"

"Like this one. Val's embarrassed. She's embarrassed for herself, for the department, and most especially for Santa Cruz. This is going to kill our image as a laid back resort."

"How did somebody like that get elected in the first place?"

"He didn't. He was appointed after our long time D.A. passed away unexpectedly. Six months ago, it was." He shook his head, regret evident in the gesture. "That man was great. He was scrupulously fair, honest, and the best district attorney in the state, as far as I'm concerned. We lost a good man and got stuck with a lemon."

Ham gently brought him back to the present situation. "Have you found anything of interest, bagged any evidence?"

"After an exhaustive ten-second search of each of the other rooms on the floor, I found nothing worth impounding or even noting in a report. I was, of course, highly suspicious of these awards, photographs and memorabilia, so I've been examining them. Nothing so far, though."

Steve's monotone delivery tickled Ham, as did his independent streak. Both sides of the cop that he himself used to play. "So you're in collusion with Val, making sure your esteemed D.A. steps on his own toes. I like that."

Steve's laugh, though soft, somehow echoed around the vast room. "I think Val knew exactly what she was doing when she left Pete outside and sent me in by myself. I didn't actually see her wink but I think I heard it."

"I'm surprised he hasn't gone after me yet, what with my bruises and all. Maybe he's saving that for later."

"Rob didn't bother to read our reports. He was in much too much of a hurry to make an international jerk of himself. When he slows down and starts doing his job he's going to want more information on your bruised and battered countenance. He will, as he always does, jump to the wrong conclusion and assume you got in a fight with your client and killed him. Probably over payment." His expression was more feral than amused. "With him, it always comes down to money."

"You're definitely not a fan."

"I'm not voting for him, if that's what you mean."

"From the way your face clouds up when you say that, I guess my next question is, are you going to kill him?"

"Let's put it this way. I emptied my gun before I escorted him inside." The look on Steve's face suggested the remark was more factual than facetious.

"Careful you don't get yourself suspended. I've run up against people like him in my prior life and often found myself on the precipice."

"You and Drew have your own firm, right?"

"McCalister and Thornton. Why?"

Steve threw his arms wide, encompassing not just the room they were in but the entire spectacle and his dark eyes clouded with disgust. "This is kind of the last straw. The whole thing stinks. There's just something wrong. And I do believe I've had just about as much fun as I can take." He sighed deeply, disappointment thinning his lips. "I'll finish this case, if for no other reason than to make sure that the idiot doesn't put the wrong guy in jail. Then I'm going to resign. I'll need a job." His eyes twinkled as he added, "You need a good detective? I love Vegas, by the way. Not to mention that Drew's kind of hot and I wouldn't mind spending some time around her."

Ham laughed, easily and without embarrassment. Until he noticed the slight flush that colored Steve's cheeks. "My word, you're serious, aren't you? You're really going to quit? What about your pension?"

"Not worth it. Not anymore."

"Maybe you should wait it out until after the election. If Rob loses, problem solved, isn't it?"

"Oh, it's not just that. It's, well, just the whole package." Steve shook his head, maybe to clear cobwebs, maybe to chase away embarrassment. "Anyway, forget it. I'm just in a bit of a funk right now."

Ham regarded him with serious but sympathetic eyes. "Steve, think it over, don't do anything rash. But if you decide you're leaving, do come see me. I could use a good man."

Steve's cheeks flushed a deeper shade of red. "Don't you have to talk to Drew about that? Or are you the boss?"

"If there's a boss," Ham grinned, "it would be her. She's meaner than I am and a whole lot smarter, I guarantee you that. But I know my partner. Don't worry about it."

Steve stared straight into Ham's eyes, a touch of confusion and suspicion in his own. "This isn't a quid pro quo, you know. I'm not going out as a cop on the take."

Ham emphatically shook his head. "If I thought you were I wouldn't even be talking to you. It's not a quid pro quo. We'd both be open to bribery charges, and even that is not the point. I have no use for a crooked cop. No, if your investigation leads you to Ronny Damon, so be it. He's dead and there's nothing much there for me to fight. If it leads you to Russ, however, you can and should expect me to come after you with everything I've got in order to prove you not only wrong but incompetent as well. And then, after it's all over, we still talk, got it?"

Steve's broad grin sealed the deal and they shook warmly on the non-agreement. In Ham's mind, he'd found a jewel, a man to be trusted, a man who could not be bought at any price. Just the kind of expansion for their small firm he hadn't known he'd been needing. The vagaries of chance, he mused. Only in Las Vegas. Or, in this case, Santa Cruz.

He made his way to the door, was nearly out and gone before he turned around, one more point to make. "Steve, thanks for everything, and to show that I'm not ungrateful, here's a tip. Check out a guy, name of Barry Braxton." Ham supplied the address from memory as Steve wrote it down. "He fits the profile for the next victim in C minor. He's also a druggie, so you're going to have to step lightly."

Ham provided a brief recap of their interview, Drew's assessment that a lone brain cell remained to float around his empty skull, and Ham's own suspicion that there may be something more there. "Anyway," he summed up, "he refused protection, so I'm not sure how much you can do. But if you put a watch on him you may get lucky."

He descended the stairs, managed to elude the rampaging search team, and slipped out the way he'd entered. Back in front, though the crowds still swelled, progress had been made. Pete was busy directing uniformed officers as they began restoring items to the shed, apparently having finished tearing it apart.

Drew still wrapped a protective arm around Russ' waist and by the sheer magnitude of her personality kept the crowd at bay. Ham caught her eye and gave a quick shake of the head. He knew from the long years of not just partnership, but friendship, that she'd read it for what it was: "Not now."

Not while Val lurked within earshot. Steve worked for her and it was up to him whether or not he wished to share his conversation with Ham, either in full or in part, about the non-quid pro quo or the information about Barry Braxton. As for Ham, he considered it a confidence that was not his to breach.

Pete, of course, would have no part of that. "What did you find?" he demanded.

"I found that law enforcement in this town needs a shake-up, from top to bottom."

"What's that supposed to mean?"

"Shake-up, it means things need to change."

"You're a funny man, McCalister." His eyes flashed a warning that Ham did not miss. But he also didn't care.

"Thank you, Pete. I'll be here all week."

Pete spun on his heels and stormed away, leaving Val to pick up the pieces. "I don't know why he persists in taking you on," she sighed. "It's such an uneven match."

Ham grinned but otherwise let the statement die. He turned to Charlie, pulled her to him and whispered in her ear. "Take over for Drew, make sure nobody gets near Russ. I'm going to pull Drew and Gary aside for a minute."

The set of her jaw almost caused Ham to lose himself in laughter. He would fork over his entire fee from this case just to watch somebody try to push their way past Charlie and on to Russ. And it would be worth every red cent.

Once he'd led Gary and Drew sufficiently out of earshot, he got them caught up. "Gardner's in there with a press pass and camera, following the DA around Can you believe it? More importantly, there's dissent within the ranks. Steve's not on board with this, not at all, and by his account neither is Val. This is the district attorney's dog and pony show, top to bottom. Apparently he was appointed—"

"After the incumbent died of a heart attack almost six months ago," Gary interrupted. He answered Ham's questioning look with a nod. "I heard from my office. Robert Turner, graduated from Santa Clara law school eleven years ago. He was pretty much a flunky, and from what he's worked on, not likely to become much more than that. The appointment was his reward for being a politician's good little flunky, and this is his big chance, he thinks, to put himself over with the voters. Of course, his thinking and reality don't match."

"Steve is probably going to quit once this is over. I'm thinking we should take him on. He's solid. Meantime, we may have an ally."

"You can't do that," Gary protested. "You'll get us thrown in the hoosegow. And I'm not willing to go."

"Of course not," Drew retorted. "Give us a little credit. I think what Ham means is that we can trust Steve to be straight with us, at least in private." Looking up at Ham, she asked, "That is right, isn't it?"

Ham nodded, opened his mouth to say more, but stopped short when a sudden rush of humanity from behind enveloped them with a cacophony that drowned out the roaring surf.

The district attorney, beaming smugly, led his entourage and the news crew out onto the lawn, clearly intent on staging a news conference right there on Russ' property. Gary's face lit with feral glee as he announced, "You two stay here. I want to have a private word or two with my esteemed colleague."

Drew regarded him suspiciously, then her eyes grew wide with sudden understanding. "You've got something on him. You're going to blackmail him."

"That's so ugly," Gary demurred. "Let's just say I want to reason with him, and I reason so much better without an audience."

They watched Gary saunter over to the smiling D.A. and attempt to gain his attention. The chief prosecutor, in his element with the press, pushed him to the side as he turned to the assembled mics before him. Gary leaned up and appeared to whisper something that stopped the prosecutor cold. He slowly turned to Gary, frowned and began what looked like a frantic and not too friendly conversation.

Even as she watched the exchange, Drew murmured, "Technically, we don't even have a client anymore, so I'm not sure what good this is going to do us."

"The hell you don't," Russ responded, "your client is me. From here on in, I'm the one paying your fees. So don't worry about that, just stay on it."

Drew patted him on the hand, like a proud mother to her precocious child. "Russ, dear, that's very sweet. And of course you are absolutely right, you are the new client. But there will be no fees."

"Of course there will," he said. "I can't ask you guys to suspend your business and not get paid. Where's the equity in that?" To Drew he added, "That would just be taking advantage of our relationship, which is not something I'm willing to do. I'm not in this for the free services I might wangle."

"Drop it, Russ," Ham demanded. "If she hadn't said it, I would have. You're giving us room and board. Let's call it square."

Russ glanced slowly back and forth between them. "If you two don't beat the band." He sighed, the sound of defeat, but his smiling eyes refuted that concession.

Ham's attention was once again seized by the assembled media when he heard an unfamiliar voice intone, "Ladies and gentlemen, may I have your attention please? I have the following announcement to make." Once the assembled crowd quieted, the speaker continued. "There has been much speculation here, and very few facts, so I am going to give you what I can at this time."

The D.A. paused to adjust his mic and set his face in solemn dignity. "We are most fortunate to have in our small town a person of such international acclaim as Mr. Russ Porter. As such, we take very seriously any threat to his property and well-being. That is, in fact, why we are here today.

"Some of you have speculated that this is connected with the body of a local record producer found in the water by the pier."

"That speculation came from you!" one of the reporters hollered.

The attorney's face reddened, but he continued as if unconcerned. "The fact is that Mr. Porter has been the victim of a crime against his property. Because of his high visibility, we are extremely concerned for Mr. Porter's personal safety, as well as for his property per se. And that is why we are here. That, and absolutely nothing more."

"Russ is not under investigation?" another media member shouted.

"Of course not," Rob snapped. "I just told you that. Moreover, because we do have an ongoing investigation, and because of our concerns for his safety, we are asking the assembled media to collect your equipment and depart. This road, as of now, is closed to all traffic save for residents of this street, and we will have patrol cars to enforce this." As grumbles built toward a crescendo, he shouted, "Any further comments we are able to make will come from our office. Thank you and good day." With that, he spun around and retreated to the safety of the front porch.

Gary came back, a gleam of satisfaction lurking in his eyes. "How's that, Charlie? That work for you?" Her delighted relief, revealed in a burst of laughter, caused him to match her laugh for laugh.

"What do you have on him?" Drew demanded.

Gary didn't look like he just swallowed the canary, he appeared to have swallowed the cat that ate it. "Oh nothing, really. There was a case, back when he was a para and an L-One, where he—"

"L-One?" Russ asked. "That means?"

"Sorry," he acknowledged. "It's level one in law school, meaning first year. Anyway, when he was L-One and practicing as a para to pay the bills, he allowed a client to forge a signature on a will. For a little extra cash via kickback. I happen to know this because I know the client. I kept him out of prison. And the D.A.'s name rang a vague bell so I had my office check him out. Once I heard his background I recalled the case. Anyway, he knowingly allowed the forgery and that's misprision of a felony. A very definite no-no. I just wondered if he wanted me to help him remember the details."

"And you threatened to give that to the press."

"Oh, that and the fact that I actually do have the proof." Gary snapped fingers as though the thought just occurred. "Oh, yeah. One more thing. He doesn't know it yet, but he won't be running for re-election. He'll be giving up his law license."

Ham sobered first and accordingly acted as the brake on their mirth. "Not to interrupt here, and it's great that Gary put Charlie's words into the D.A.'s mouth, but we still have a killer out there. Which wouldn't be our problem, except that there's too much connection to Russ."

Charlie turned worried eyes toward him. "You don't think they'll protect Russ? You think they're going to let this drop?"

"I'm afraid so," Ham nodded. "My guess is that they will proclaim Ronny Damon the music scale murderer who, out of remorse, killed himself. Case closed."

"Only Ronny didn't do it," Drew affirmed. "So screw 'em. Let's go find us a killer."

"If you can stay out of jail long enough," Charlie interjected. "That is one pissed off D.A. And while I doubt he'll have the courage to come after Russ, he may consider you an acceptable substitute."

Ham gestured toward the tall cop who was ambling down the porch steps and mumbled out of the side of his mouth. "That may be the key to the cell approaching now." He waved Steve over and quickly made his proposition. "You feel like taking a drive?"

"What do you have in mind?"

"Remember I told you about Barry Braxton?" When Steve nodded, Ham continued, "You'll want to see him, but you might want to have a go at Barbara Bessler first. That's where we're headed right now."

"Sounds promising," Steve said. "We take my car?"

"Only thing is," Ham suggested, "it would be preferable if you leave Pete out of this. Besides not liking his style, I think it's likely we'd get more cooperation without his bluster, if you know what I mean. Can you arrange that?"

Steve shrugged. "Not without a fight, but it's doable. I'll send him back to do the reports and make up a reason why I'll be delayed."

"All right then, let's do it."

"Give me a few minutes, then meet me out at the end of the driveway. After you see Pete leave."

CHAPTER TEN

THE SIREN'S SONG

Ham watched, less amused than nervous, as Steve spoke to an obviously agitated Pete. Though Steve tried to calm his partner, resting a restraining hand on the shorter man's shoulder, Pete would have none of it. He violently shrugged it off, his face red and contorted with anger. When he shook his head in negation, the movement was so rapid and violent that Ham half expected the detective's head to continue in its circle until his neck twisted like a rubber band. It would have been exciting to see it reach its climax and snap back around, he ruminated.

Alas, Val chose that moment to step between Pete and Steve and, with a questioning glance at each, act the referee. After a few words from Steve, and some obviously angry ones from Pete, she nodded and walked away. From the look of Pete's purple cheeks, she'd sided with Steve, a deduction verified when Pete stomped off, heading straight for Ham and the group around him.

Pete, followed close on his heels by Steve, stopped so abruptly in front of Russ that Steve bumped into him from behind. Pete snapped a growl over his shoulder, but otherwise offered no comment. Instead, he pulled himself to his full short height and glared up at Russ. "Don't leave town," he ordered. "Or you'll answer to me."

Gary's soft laugh presaged his reply. "He'll go anywhere he damn well pleases, and if you try to stop him, or arrest him on some bogus charge, I'll have you behind bars for kidnapping, false imprisonment and, oh what the hell, let's add for violating his civil rights." Gary added, softly and without rancor, "You do understand me, don't you, Detective?"

Pete's jaw snapped open, ready with a reply, but he apparently thought better of the idea and clamped his lips shut. He threw a scornful salute to Gary and a defiant, "this isn't over" glare at Russ, turned on his heels and headed toward the street as as fast his half-sized legs could churn.

Steve wandered around, snapping pictures for later use, until Val and Pete pulled out and headed toward the precinct. Even then, he continued the charade for another five minutes in case his partner returned.

Looking relieved that he was minus inquisitive department personnel, he waved Ham and Drew over as he walked toward his car. He had it started and ready by the time they arrived.

Drew picked shotgun, which forced Ham to the backseat. He supplied the address to Steve, and then inquired of Drew, "Did you ask Russ about her?"

"Yeah, same as the others," she nodded, half turned to look over her shoulder at Ham. "Several songs to her credit, a couple that charted, a couple covered by other artists, so she did a bit better than the others we've seen so far. Nothing else noteworthy."

"This is one flaming incredible case," Steve interjected. "I meet Russ Porter, roam his house, look at some of his awards and pictures from around the world... I mean, crap, I'll never have another like this one. It's a hell of a good time to bail, I'd say. Anything else would be anticlimactic."

Drew's gentle laugh floated back to Ham. "I hear you may be interested in a relocation to Sin City. Looking to join the department there? I could give you a reference."

Steve's face colored slightly, a shade of discomfiture. "Well, I hadn't thought about that," he finally replied. "I was sort of thinking, well, I mean I had kind of hoped—"

Ham's snorted laughter rescued the detective. "Forget it, Steve. Drew's just yanking your chain. You'll get used to it in time."

"Ham filled me in," she informed Steve. "If he trusts you, I do, too. I've learned to appreciate his instincts, at least when it comes to men. He's rather hit and miss with women. His ex-wife is an example on the one hand, and Charlie on the other."

"Enough, Drew," Ham sighed. "Let's not let him know what he's getting into before he gets into it. He'll run."

"That reference for the department might be worth a thought," Steve grinned. "You guys always so weirdly fun?"

"Weird, often," Drew told him. "Fun, not so much. Like Ham breaking into your house when you're having sex. That's a specialty of his. Isn't it, Ham?"

"Let it go, dammit. It was your fault."

"Hey," Steve objected. "This is very much and very definitely what they call TMI. How about we get back to Barbara Bessler and the upcoming interview? What do you plan to ask her? Or tell her, maybe is more accurate. I can't see she's still a possible victim, what with Ronny dead. Unless Ronny really was innocent, which I genuinely doubt."

"You're still thinking with old information," Drew reminded him. "Before we got here, before Russ completed the musical picture, before we had the victim list known and anticipated, you might have thought so. But how can you now? What, you believe Ronny was the lunatic killer but then decided to off himself before he completed the scale? And what, he hired someone to tie his hands behind his back after he shot himself, and ordered his accomplice to dump his body in the ocean? Then what? His accomplice threw chum around his body to draw in the sharks?" Before Steve had a chance to respond to the rapid series of questions—or accusations, more like—she turned back to Ham. "We sure we should entertain taking him on? Why not Pete, too? They seem a set to me."

"Jeez, Drew, draw a breath," Ham exclaimed. "Steve, she has all sorts of points here, all of which I agree on. So tell me why you would bet on Ronny as the perpetrator. I, too, had assumed you'd moved beyond that."

Steve drew a deep breath, started to speak, then shook his head. "Call it gut. There's something. Hell, that damn suicide note, that will. Maybe he had a partner and the partner decided he wanted it all."

"Wanted all of what?" Drew asked.

"Well," he stuttered, "all of, of whatever the reason for the murders is in the first place. Money, maybe, and maybe the money is near to hand and only needs some finishing touches to produce. Hell, I don't know. I'm just thinking out loud."

"That's fine. I like that habit," Drew informed him. At Steve's uncertain look, she assured him, "I mean it, it's a good one to get into. Not only does it help you think it through, it provides fresh insight to those of us working the case with you. Some things might be right, some might be wrong, but it should all be considered. So you just keep on with that and we'll work well together. Assuming you don't bail on us for friendlier waters, of course."

"Like begging Russ to hire me on as his private body guard and personal snoop? For a gazillion a year?"

"Yeah, like that," she laughed.

Ham had listened with half an ear as they made their way through meandering roads and lofty pines and journeyed ever higher and further from the coast. "I must say," Ham announced, "this is truly beautiful country. Almost as remarkable, in its own way, as the coast itself."

"The views from where we're going, which is just a few minutes away now, are beyond spectacular," Steve told him. "You can see forever over the valley, into the canyon, and beyond the hills. And the sweet smell of pine is everywhere."

Steve pulled onto a wide, rounded driveway, into a property separate from nosy neighbors and invisible to prying eyes from the road. Lush, landscaped grounds led to a one-story rambler, with a large garage attached at a ninety-degree angle. Clearly, the owner had taken pains to maintain the natural beauty that surrounded the residence, as well as the exterior of the home itself.

Drew whistled softly. "My word, this is really gorgeous. She must have done damn well for herself. I can't imagine how much this must go for."

"About a million and a quarter," Steve informed her. "Actually, that's pretty good for Santa Cruz. It's what you can get when you move off the water and into the hills."

"It's almost as impressive as your place, Drew," Ham said.

"I wish."

Steve cut the motor and talked over it as it pinged its goodbye. "Okay, guys, I'm not really here on an official visit, so I'll follow your lead. You've interviewed the people from Ronny's stable, so I'm assuming you know where you want to lead her. I'll flaunt the credentials if it comes to that and we'll just let her think you're both with the department. Unless she asks directly, in which case we come clean. I don't want to lose my badge before I quit."

"No worries, Steve. Let the lady lead." Ham swung his arm dramatically forward, ushering Drew to the door. "Don't growl and snap," he implored. "Try to sweet talk her."

"Well, golly gee, Ham. I hadn't thought of that. You are so darn intelligent it just plain scares the poop out of me." The roll of her eyes added silent mockery to the declaration.

She rang the bell and they waited it out for perhaps a minute and a half. She tried again, and again they waited, but still there came no response. They were about to leave when Steve whispered, "She's here, or at least someone is. I see a shadow from the side window. Some movement, very little."

"Guess she doesn't want to talk to us," Ham muttered. "And I can't figure why. With Drew here we shouldn't present a threat."

"If it is her," Drew reminded them. "And if it's not, we've got a bigger problem than her snubbing us."

"Call her," Steve suggested. "Do you have the number?" When Drew shook her head, he smiled. "Well, then, let me do my thing." He punched in a number, waited only seconds and announced, "This is Detective Steven Cassel of the Santa Cruz P.D. I need you to locate a number for me. No, I don't need a warrant, it's just a phone number, not recordings or other crap. Let me speak to your supervisor." Seconds later he spoke again. "Yes, hello, this is Detective Cassel, Santa Cruz P.D. I just need... oh, Karly. How are you? Yeah, I want to reach a witness by phone. No, no, not a suspect, just a witness. I want to see if she's home before I go all the way out there. Yeah, okay, ready?" He read off the name and address, nodded as he wrote in his notebook, nodded again as if Karly could see through the phone. "I owe you one, Karly. How about a drink this weekend? Excellent, see you then."

As Drew dialed the number, Ham cocked an eyebrow at Steve. "I'm impressed. Cajole with a sniveling entreaty."

Steve pretended modesty as he agreed, "It's a talent. You're either born to it or you're not."

Drew waved them to quiet and spoke into her cell. "Barbara, my name is Drew Thornton. I'm on your porch with Ham McCalister and Steve Cassel. We're investigators looking into Ronny Damon's studio business. As part of this, we're investigating a series of murders that have occurred and—"

The door inched open to the width of a chain lock, revealing an eye and a bit of hair above. "Let me see your credentials. I've got a gun."

Drew collected Ham's and Steve's identifications, added her own and offered them up. A hand snatched them, and a voice intoned, "Wait a minute." With that the door slammed shut, a deadbolt sounded, and nothing else. No sound, no movement. Just when Ham began to worry that she had, for whatever perverted reason, stolen their documents, the bolt slid back, the chain was removed and the door opened wide.

She was not what their treatment at the door had lead Ham, at least, to expect, and then some. Impeccably dressed in a peach pant suit, adorned with a modest string of pearls, graying hair cut short, she could be anybody's grandmother. On the far side of fifty, he'd bet on it. The first one beyond mid-thirties, except for Ronny himself.

She stood rock still, and a wisp of a smile played on her lips as she waited for Ham to conclude his too obvious inspection. Ham blushed, tried to upend the awkwardness with a lame, "You're not what I thought you'd be. Which is beyond evident."

"I'll forgive you only if you'll forgive me," she smiled, "because neither are you." She quickly turned serious. "Barry called, told me what's happened. He warned me not to answer the door for anybody, for any reason."

"Barry Braxton?" At Barbara's nod, Drew drawled, "I wouldn't of thought he had enough mental juice to dial a phone."

Barbara stared at her, clearly confused and just as plainly deeply annoyed. "What the hell are you talking about, sister? Barry's one of the brightest guys I've ever known. And he's a friend, I might add. Of some years standing."

As still she stood, pointedly not inviting them in, Drew managed to look abashed, as if caught pocketing the silver. It was a look Ham knew well, one that almost always worked to win forgiveness, confidence, even. And this time proved no exception.

"I'm sorry, Barbara, that was uncalled for. I can get a little catty at times, much to my regret."

Barbara waved away the apology and softened. "I should be apologizing to you. Where are my manners? Please do come in. I was just about to make my afternoon tea. Would any of you care to join me?"

Before her boorish partner could chime in and wish for "something a little stronger, like a man might drink"—a hideously infamous *faux pas* from his past that he sometimes unwisely repeated—Drew answered for all. "We very much appreciate the offer. That would be lovely." At Barbara's raised eyebrows, the men responded with, "Please, yes," and "Yes, please."

She led them through a tastefully designed and ornamented living room, past the formal dining room and on into the tile-floored kitchen. A chef's dream, Ham deemed it.

The gleaming chrome appliances boasted state of the art traits and looked to have been removed from crates just yesterday. The oversize refrigerator itself took half a wall, it was that impossibly huge. The center island was approximately the size of his kitchen, Ham noted with an inward sigh, while the wine cooler approached the dimensions of what he had previous to now considered a fairly nice sized fridge. The eat-in area of her kitchen featured a table and seats for eight, which boggled his mind. His entire dining room held room for only six.

I shoulda written songs. Course I can't think of songs. Or music. Or words. I can't play an instrument. Or do anything else you need to write something people might want to pay you for. Damn people.

Ham shoved the thought aside and strode to the table, a lovely piece currently used as a desk; the kitchen probably acted as her center of operations. While the living and formal dining rooms resembled museums, not to be disturbed, the kitchen had papers and notebooks—neat stacks of both—placed upon the table, a few shelves, and even the kitchen island.

He glanced at the open notebooks on the table and spotted a series of musical notes. Not that he knew what they were, but he'd seen sheet music before, and the scores he'd seen looked a lot like the scribbles open before him.

He looked up inquiringly, but Barbara ignored the question. Instead, she snapped closed the tablets, scooped them up and placed them with others atop a shelf. "Please, sit down. Sorry for the mess. I like to record my thoughts in here. It's my favorite place in the house, and close to my beloved tea that I spend most of the day sipping. As for the rest," she said as she swung her arm wide, "it's a bit much for me."

Drew, as was her wont, cut to the chase. "What was it exactly that Barry told you? What is it he thinks he knows?"

Barbara arched a fastidious eyebrow. "Why, Drew, if I may call you Drew, there will be time for that. Perhaps you would be kind enough, in the meantime, to allow me to tend to my tea, take the time to pour and perhaps, just perhaps, to enjoy a sip or two before the taste is lost to neglect."

This time, to Ham's practiced eye and great amusement, Drew's abashed look was genuine. And red. Deep, deep red. "Of course, Barbara. May I help?"

"Thank you, dear, no. You relax. Have a look around if you'd like. I'll let you know when the tea is ready. Proper steeping takes a bit."

Drew nodded, rose from the chair she'd claimed and wandered to the large French doors that opened to the patio beyond. As she studied the expanse, Ham turned to Barbara and nodded toward those same doors. "Mind if we take a look at your yard?" he inquired. "This is very different from what I'm used to and I'd love to get a better look at what I've been missing."

Barbara turned sweet eyes upon him. "Please, be my guest. I'm inordinately proud of it and would enjoy the admiration."

As Ham and Steve approached, Drew began to open the French doors, her obvious intent to follow or even lead the charge. Ham caught her eye, gave an almost imperceptible shake of the head and watched as she backed off. "You guys go on ahead," she announced. "I'm going to stay here and see if I can't learn something about the art of the tea ritual. I'm thinking a lady needs to know at least a few of the finer protocols." Before he poked the bear, she hissed, "Shut up, Ham."

"What's on your mind?" Steve asked when they had moved beyond earshot. "Anything in particular, or are we just scouting it out."

"A little of both. Call it a hunch. I want to get a look at the garden area, the shed, the garage and trash barrel storage space."

Steve stopped, stared into his eyes. "Either you are one hell of a detective, better even than I had imagined, or you have an imagination that plays in another galaxy. Because there's not one damn thing that could have piqued this kind of interest. Is there?"

"There is, and you'd have sensed it as well if you'd been there to talk to Barry. He's either a genius and a world class actor, or he's a complete drug-addled waste of oxygen. Barbara's defense of his brilliance moved the hairs to tingle."

"Do you think Drew got it, too?"

Ham's laugh was soft but sure. "Beyond any doubt. That's why she went to the doors in the first place. Her next step was going to be exactly what we're doing now."

"So why did you tell her to stay?"

"Did I do that?" Ham grinned. "I don't remember saying anything about that, or about anything else at all, for that matter."

"Funny man," Steve intoned. "I, too, sir, am a detective. I, too, sir, pick up on clues. Such as your all but invisible shaking off Drew accompanying us. So, again I ask, why?"

"I really don't know," Ham admitted. "There's nothing to hang my hat on, but I felt uncomfortable leaving Barbara alone."

"Okay," Steve shrugged. "I know that one. So lead on, Your Intuitiveness."

Ham led them toward the tiered garden area on the left and on around the arced path that led to the garage. Just before that structure, he found and opened a gate to the storage area where garbage and recycling cans sat. He checked the bins for oddities. Finding none, he retreated from there, closed and latched the gate and continued toward the driveway.

The three-car garage both surprised and didn't. Surprised because of the overkill for a single, older lady, didn't because of the upscale setting.

There were no handles for opening or shutting the doors, a clear indication that the doors operated with a garage opener. Or, to be more exact, two such devices. Double doors lead to one unit, and a single door provided entrance to the extra, third parking space.

Small glass rectangles decorated the entries at eye level, across the width of the double door and along the breadth of the smaller single unit. Ham peered inside, cupping his hands to ward off as much of the glare as possible. While it was impossible to identify smaller objects, he identified various tools stored on the wall space, probably implements for a gardener. Also discernible was a luxury auto: a Cadillac, number of doors unknown given the dim interior and blinding exterior.

The view through the glass of the single entry door reached out and slapped him upside the head. It spun him around, body slammed him to the turf and stomped all over his chest until he couldn't breathe.

He couldn't breathe, dammit.

Steve must have spotted Ham's distress because he reached out and steadied him with a one-armed hug. "Hey, man, hey, hey, hey. Easy. What is it? What's going on? Whatever it is, don't faint on me, hear? I got no bedside manner. And even less idea of what to do if you freaking keel over."

Breathe, dammit, breathe.

After a whoosh of intake that seared his lungs, Ham bent over and coughed it out. "Well, she may be genteel in the kitchen, but she's hell on the road."

Steve spun him around, and concerned eyes looked into his. "Are you okay? What are you going on about?"

Ham pointed over his shoulder to the garage behind. "That. The black SUV parked in the space on the single side. Guess what? I've seen it before."

Steve's face mirrored confusion until memory washed it away. "The car? In the alley? The one that tried to run you over?" Ham's nod confirmed the accuracy of the guess. "But you didn't see the driver. You didn't get the license plate. How can you be sure? There must be dozens of these around here."

Ham spent precious seconds re-acquainting his lungs with oxygen. "Not with the left tail light cracked and the right back fender wearing a slight dent just off the license plate," he puffed.

Steve appeared stunned, almost mired to the spot, feet and mind unable to move. "So what do we do?" he finally asked. "Do we arrest her? Aggravated assault and battery? Felony status?"

"No. I'm not sure your idiot D.A. would work with us, not after Gary ripped off his balls and proffered them to the assembled media. No," he continued, "what we're going to do is exactly nothing."

Steve shrugged, surrendering to bafflement. "Right, then. Gotcha. A perfect plan. Unassailable."

"Sarcasm becomes you," Ham jibed. "What I mean is, we're going to go back, pretend we saw nothing but the beauty she cultivates, and we'll gush our envy of her botanical brilliance. In other words, get her guard down. And after we do," he announced, "we'll grill her like a fish. We'll find out if she was driving her car that day and, if not, who was."

Ham led the way back to the path and on up toward the house. As he rounded the first corner, he slowed and began to whistle. "Well, well, well." Pointing to the koi pond off to the left, he added, "We just stumbled onto our alibi, my friend."

Steve ranged alongside him. "Perfect. I didn't even notice it before."

"Neither did I. It's concealed by shrubbery coming from that way. A hidden oasis, as it were. We can say we stopped to drink in the magnificent biota, turning in all directions, and were amazed to find this hidden gem. We admired it until we realized it must be time for tea. And we will tell her all this," he affirmed, "first thing upon walking in the door."

Within a short two minute walk they reached the French doors separating the outside from Barbara's Home and Garden kitchen. Drew sat perched across the table from Barbara, both of them sipping from dainty cups as they leaned conspiratorially toward each other. Trust Drew, he thought. Fish caught, netted and ready to gut and grill.

"We were about to send out a search party," Barbara mock scolded.

Drew batted her eyelids, the caricature of a femme fatale. "Just like men," she sighed, "following their dicks to the vast unknown."

"I'm not even going to pretend I know what that means," Steve said, "and I can assure you I'm not near stupid enough to ask."

Barbara looked at Drew, pointed toward Steve. "Is he always that dense? And uninspired, uninterested, and un-self-aware?"

Steve's laugh bounced around the room. "My ex-wife would yell 'Absolutely!', but then she'd rebuke you for belaboring the obvious."

"So what was so interesting out there that you dawdled so long? I would have—"

Ham cut her off before she finished the question he wanted to answer. "Drew, you should have come with us. The landscape is beyond gorgeous. So full, so, hell, I don't know, almost tropical, I guess is what I mean. And then, when you think you're getting used to the lushness, this unbelievable, absolutely incredible koi pond materializes out of nowhere and demands your attention." He turned to Barbara, nearly breathless with his feigned excitement. "Where and how did you get such a piece of perfection? It must have cost a fortune!"

Her eyes narrowed a bit. "I'm surprised you saw it. I've got it tucked away, deliberately, so it's my private sanctuary."

Ham nodded. "Yeah, that I could see. We just happened to stop there to admire the entire scene and I turned a full circle, gazing at everything, every different thing you have out there, to let my eyes wander and enjoy, and this jumped out at me. I wasn't sure what it was at first, went to look and just fell in love. Of course, I've always been fascinated with koi anyway. They're pretty something, if you know what I mean."

Barbara beamed, her frown noticeably relaxed. "I'm glad to hear it. Your description of the pond, I mean. That's what I was going for. Did you notice the small table and single chair just beside the bougainvillea?"

"No," Ham responded with a puzzled frown. "I didn't see anything like that at all. I don't know how but I must have missed it."

"Good," she nodded. "Just checking your story. It's not there."

Ham's shrug suggested his irritation. "Let's not fool around, okay? It's your life we're here to save, after all. And," he snapped as she placed a cup and saucer before him, "forget the damn tea. I'm a man, for god's sake."

Drew smiled, an attempt to take the sting out of Ham's rebuke. "He keeps claiming that. Ever hear of protesting too much?" she asked of no one in particular.

Barbara nodded as she refilled her own cup and Drew's. She arched eyebrows at Steve, who returned a nod. "Notice," he whispered to Ham, "that I gave a really manly nod."

"Very well, tell me what you came here to say," Barbara said quietly.

Drew leaned across the table, laid a gentle hand on her arm. "Your life may be in danger. Did Barry tell you how the murders are occurring? What happens to the victims? What's happened to Ronny?"

Barbara set her cup down, folded hands to her forehead and spoke to the table. "He told me you said Ronny's people are being killed both to and by C minor. I don't know what this has to do with me, at least anymore. I left Ronny's stable many years ago."

Drew and Ham exchanged a surprised glance. "Barbara," Ham prodded, "tell me about that. I can't help but notice that you are living quite, quite well, much better than any of the others we've talked to. How are you affording it? Didn't Ronny screw the money out of you like he did the rest?"

Her sigh sent a shiver of foreboding down Ham's back. "He did, of course he did. That's Ronny. It's the way he works. To his mind, it's not good enough *he* wins. *You've* got to lose. Otherwise he can't prove his brilliance, that he's the best there is and ever was. Which tells you a little something about the size of his head."

"Then how," Drew prompted, waving her arm to encompass the whole, "all this? If you don't mind my asking. And if you do, let me explain my professional reasoning. It's this: I am really damn curious."

Barbara smiled softly and nodded. "Understandable. I wrote a couple of small hits, recorded them with Ronny and gave the rights to his publishing company, as he demanded in order to produce me. After doing three of them, and getting screwed monetarily on them all, I dropped Ronny, got myself a reputable songwriting deal and wrote a dozen songs that charted for other singers. That's where the money is for some of us. Not in recording, I found out."

"You mean," Ham queried, "you made enough money on those dozen songs to live like this, and for the rest of your life?"

She shrugged. "Pretty much, yes. It helped that I got an investment advisor and have done well in that respect. Additionally, I'm an adjunct professor of music for UC Santa Cruz. It's not much, but it does cover my monthly bills, meaning I don't have to pull from investments or savings to live. I do occasionally, for a cruise or something special. Otherwise," she smiled, "I leave it to grow."

"That's smart, all the way around," Ham offered. "But I'm still confused. You're still listed as with Ronny, at least on his site. Why is that?"

"Because it gives him credibility. I asked him to drop me from his advertising and from his web site, but the fact is there's nothing I can do to force the issue. I still have three songs listed as published by his company, and of course the songs I recorded for him as well. So," she shrugged, "he's got me. And, no surprise, he won't let me go."

"You don't need to worry about that anymore," Drew informed her. "You're released. Dead men hold no deeds."

Barbara's eyes flew wide and she nearly dropped the cup she cradled. She caught it just before the crash and gasped as hot liquid splashed her wrist. She jumped up, rushed to the sink and rinsed the area with cold running water. Not until she turned off the tap and wiped her arm did Barbara ask. "What are you implying?"

"That he's dead," Ham announced. "And she's not implying it. She's stating it as a fact. And so am I."

Barbara stood up abruptly, strode over and reached above the refrigerator to the cabinet overhead, and pulled out a half-full bottle of whiskey. "Screw this being a lady shit," she snapped, "time for a drink."

She took a long swig from the bottle before she wiped her mouth with the back of her hand. "God, that's better. Anybody else?" She waited until they, bug-eyed and slack-jawed, managed to stammer 'no', before she clapped her hands together. "Okay, everybody out." At their blank stares, she shooed them to the door, much as a farmer shoos the chickens. "Go on, now, out. Out, out, out."

"What's the hurry," Drew demanded. "We've got more we want to talk about. More to tell you, too."

"Sorry, no time. If Ronny's dead, I got things to do. Now scoot."

"Wait a minute, Barbara. I want to ask you about that black SUV you've got parked in the garage. The one with the dent and the broken light on the back. Any idea why I'm curious about that?"

"I have nothing to say. Except goodbye. Now, move. Go, go, go."

"Let me remind you," Steve declared, "he may be a private detective, but I'm the real deal. And officially, I want to question you. So back off and let's get to it. Unless, of course, you'd prefer to go downtown?"

"Got a warrant?" His silence confirmed her assumption. "Then get out. Right this damn now."

The door slammed behind them, goodbyes left unsaid. "Good god," Steve breathed. "What the hell do you think that was all about?"

"Don't know," Ham replied. "But we're going to find out. Clearly, there's more to our little ladylike Miss Bessler than that whiskey-slugging, genteel tea-slurping musical phenom we were supposed to see. One hell of a lot more. Bet on it."

CHAPTER ELEVEN

THE RETURN

They lingered, not talking. Ham, seething at his missed bet, could tell that his black mood was matched by Drew's, who, he knew from long experience, probably felt one-upped, a mood to put the itch in her trigger finger. Steve, meanwhile, if he felt pissed, hid it better than most. Only an occasional glance at his watch suggested his irritation as they walked towards the vehicle.

The probable cause of his angst announced its approach well before visual confirmation. Pete roared his caterwauling car to a screeching stop just feet from their own car and popped out, sirens still wailing.

"What is going on?" Pete screamed over the clamor. "What the hell do you think you're doing?"

Steve reached into Pete's car, cut the sirens and strode away, hands in pockets. Over his shoulder he tossed an "Ask them" and leaned against the front of his own auto.

"What's the big damn idea?" Pete demanded. "You don't go around *my* town, with *my* partner, investigating *my* cases! I've a mind to arrest you both, haul your asses off to jail."

Ham's grin was as feral as it was false. "Oh, you can try it, little man. You won't walk away from here, but yes, by all means give it a try. I could use the release."

The sight of Ham's bared teeth must have whacked some sense into Pete's hard head, for he backed off a couple of steps, opened his mouth, slammed it shut, rolled his shoulders and turned back to Steve. "What's the deal, *partner*," he spat, making "partner" sound like the worst sort of epithet. "Off playing with the amateurs?"

"Shut up, Pete, before you make a bigger fool of yourself than you must. For your information, she's on Ronny's label, or was, and fits the profile for the next victim. If," he sighed, "there is a next victim."

"Fine, I get that, but why with them? Why did you shut me out?"

Steve regarded his partner with a mixture of pity and anger. "It's that damn temper of yours, Pete, that damnable, uncontrollable anger you wear like some kind of badge of honor. It's going to get you killed someday. And maybe me, too."

Pete's cheeks flamed with color but then, much to Ham's amazement, he sighed deeply and nodded defeat. "So Val tells me, a lot, especially lately. So what did she tell you that got you so worked up that you call, tell me to drop everything and haul my ass up here at Mach speed?"

"Well, you pretty much screwed the pooch on that one. Partner." Steve's pronunciation made the word more than a mere epithet. More like a four letter word.

If Pete noticed, he chose to ignore it. "Yeah, sorry about that. I guess I let my temper get the better of me. I take it you wanted stealth more than speed?"

"My fault," Steve offered, "I should have said so."

"Well, why didn't you?" Pete demanded. "Hell, man, you order me to get my ass up here yesterday, you damn bet I got lights and sirens working. What did you think I'd do?"

Steve shook his head, like an attempt to shake off the mood. "I said it was my fault. That doesn't change you screwing dogs again."

"Okay, let it go. What do you need me to do?"

"I needed you to follow Ms. Barbara Bessler, the occupant of that fine residence. I suspect, or rather we all suspect, she will make tracks to places that we definitely want to know about."

Pete whistled softly. "What did she do?"

"I can answer that," Ham interrupted. "I very much presume she's the one that tried to run me down in that alley. If not, she knows who did. The car that hounded me is in her garage."

"That's not all," Drew added. "When we told her Ronny was dead she tossed us out on a dime. Prior to that, she was all sweetness and light, pure demure, a lady on high. Then, pow! She might as well have announced that she had nefarious work to tend to, the change was so brazen."

"You see the problem," Steve said. "Now she knows another cop is here, and that's for damn sure going to make her a mile beyond cautious."

"Okay," Pete nodded. "I get the idea. But it can still be done. I have a way to introduce myself, and with a legitimate reason for the lights, sirens and speed of approach. Then I can make her think I'm leaving the same way, at the same speed at which I arrived. Because I, too, have nefarious plans to follow."

"Would you mind," Ham sighed, "explaining yourself?"

"I mean, Mr. Used To Be Big City Detective, the guy in the ocean, the one torn apart by sharks? Guess what, asshole, it ain't your client. How about that for a news flash?"

Ham struggled to respond, but with his jaw kissing his chest, the words strangled in his throat. Drew's eyes widened at least as much as Ham's jaw dropped, while Steve just regarded his partner through narrowed eyes. "Go ahead, give us the details," he snapped.

With a smug smile, Pete did just that. "DNA isn't back yet, but the dental records don't match."

"They're sure?" Ham squeaked.

"They are that. No way is it Ronny Damon. Which means your client made an incredibly clumsy and amateurish attempt to close the case against him. All he did was add another murder count. It's already filed and in the D.A.'s office. We're searching for the inept Mr. Damon as we speak. I don't suppose you'll offer him up," he sneered at Ham. "Never mind, it would be the decent thing to do, so of course you won't."

Drew put a restraining hand on Ham's arm and turned stone eyes on Pete. "Alright, you've had your fun. Is that how you are going to explain your presence to Barbara? You're here to tell her Ronny's not dead?"

With a haughty shake of the head, he replied, "Damn right. I'll tell her I'm here to let her know she's not out of danger, that now that the killer walks, she's probably still a target. I'll advise her to lay low and keep us on the speed dial."

"Okay," Ham nodded. "Actually, that's good. You tell her you apprised us of this development and we're on our way back to the precinct to join the search. Tell her we said we'll keep in touch."

"This isn't going to work," Drew objected. "She won't answer the door, remember? Particularly now that she thinks she's got stuff she has to do. And I'd give a year's pay to know what it is."

"She might if you call her like you did before," Steve advised. "Tell her we're on our way out, but Pete is here to offer critical new information. He says he'll only need a couple of minutes of her time."

"I'll try." She punched in the number, let it ring until she reached voicemail. "Barbara, this is Drew Thornton. I know you're busy but it's imperative I speak with you immediately. I'm going to keep calling until you pick up."

She phoned again immediately after hanging up, and again, letting it ring through to voicemail. She dialed three more times without pause until, finally, Barbara picked up and shouted, "What? What's so damn important that you won't leave me alone?"

"Barbara, there's a detective from Santa Cruz P.D. out here with us. He just arrived. You may have heard the sirens. He's in a hurry and needs about two minutes of your time to tell you the latest news. News that definitely affects your safety."

The pause on the other end indicated suspicion, but she responded in a resigned voice. "Alright, send him on up. I won't invite him in but he can talk to me on the porch."

"That'll be fine. And, Barbara, listen to him. It's for your own good. I'll call you later, just to see how you are."

She packed her phone away and nodded to Pete. "Rein in your temper and treat her gently, like she's a lady worthy of respect. She pretty much expects and demands that. FYI, she may even be that from time to time, but she's got her armor on, always."

"Thanks, I can handle it," Pete snarled. He jumped in his car, turned the lights back on but not, thankfully, the sirens, and drove the short distance to the porch. They heard the screech of the tires as he slammed to a halt.

"Oh, hell yeah," Ham mocked. "He can handle it. What a moron."

"She'll eat him for lunch," Drew agreed. "As soon as she learns Ronny's alive she'll boot his ass so far off the property it'll never find its way home."

"Right, let's move it," Steve suggested. "We got to find this creep before he does any more damage." Looking at Ham, almost sneering, almost apologetic, he inquired, "Still think he's innocent?"

Ham just shrugged and jumped in the back, leaving shotgun for Drew. He was not interested in speaking to Steve at the moment, since he really had nothing to say. Drew, being a bit more social, could keep him entertained and away from an aggravated Ham.

Steve turned on the lights but left the siren off as he raced for the precinct. "Drop us back off at Russ' place," Drew instructed.

"You don't want to stick with this?" Steve asked, sounding both surprised and suspicious. "I would have thought you'd want to find your client as much as we do."

"You would have thought right," Drew admitted. "But we're going to do it our way, after we make sure Russ and the rest are safe."

"Okay, I get that. But you are officially warned there's a warrant out. If you hide him, we'll have to take action." His shrug acted as the apology that wasn't in his voice.

"You've been spending too much time with Pete," she said, apprising him. "Don't worry, we'll keep you looped in."

They rode the remainder of the trip in thoughtful silence until, faster than Ham thought possible, Steve cut the lights and drove slowly up the final half mile to Russ' house. Ham and Drew jumped out, waved a quick goodbye to Steve, who had already thrown the car into reverse and begun his exit, and ran up to the porch and inside to the living room. Where they ran headlong into a sledgehammer to the face.

Ronny Damon, in all his roly-poly stout shortness, lounged in one of the big chairs, sipping wine, and appearing for all the world to be very much at home. Russ and Charlie occupied seats nearby, neither appearing nearly as comfortable as the self-assured Ronny.

He looked untroubled by these past hours and days. As he stood, hand outstretched, ready to shake, Ham noted he sported expensive slacks, wingtips and a button down dress shirt. The unbuttoned black leather vest was his only nod to Santa Cruz hipness.

"Good to see you again, Ham, Drew. Just thought I'd drop by, introduce myself to your famous friend and see what's up with the case I'm paying you so much to investigate. Any news? Besides the obvious, I mean."

Ham ignored him for the moment. Instead, he looked to Charlie. "Where's Gary? He's not here?"

"Gary very much did not want to be here at this time. He said to call when you arrived."

"Good enough." Ham turned to Ronny, finally addressed the issue. "You are officially a fugitive from justice. You aware of that?"

"Of course I'm aware of it," Ronny smiled. "I got ears to the ground."

"Ears by the name of Barbara Bessler?" Drew guessed.

"I'm not here to answer questions," Ronny responded. "I'm here to ask them. And to get my money's worth. I didn't do this, not any of it, and I need you to prove it. It's my only hope."

Ham looked over at Russ, who busied himself with a study of the carpet. Charlie sat with arms folded across her chest, a sure sign of discomfort. And Ham didn't blame either one of them. Right at this moment, he, too, would prefer to be elsewhere, with anyone else. But they'd taken the money, they'd gone this far, and morally they had no alternative. He and Drew were obligated to befriend this despicable, oily little creep of a fraud.

"Where have you been, Ronny?" he asked. "Start with that."

"Like I said, I'm not here to answer questions."

"You are exactly here to answer questions. We can't help you if we're in the dark. When I, or when Drew, asks you a question, you are to respond immediately, fully, and truthfully. Otherwise, get out. Now."

Ronny regarded him for long seconds, perhaps seeking appeal, which Ham refused to allow. "Answer it."

"I was at a friend's house."

"Who's the friend, Barbara?" Drew demanded. "And is that how you found out there's a warrant out on you?"

"No on the former, yes on the latter," Ronny admitted. "But I want to keep her out of it. And since I'm paying you, you do it my way. That's an order."

Drew and Ham burst into laughter at the same time. Both tried to speak, both gasped for the necessary breath to do so. Drew found her voice first. "Ronny, you miserable little nit. Do not issue us an order. Next time, I break some bones."

"Don't think she's bluffing," Ham managed. "You'd best take her threat with the seriousness it merits."

A suddenly nervous Ronny ran his hand through what was left of his hair and proffered a stuttered apology. "Look, you got to remember I'm a heavy weight in my field—"

The snort from Russ that interrupted his braggadocio resulted in a redirected argument. "I mean, I'm no Russ Porter, or even anything close to that, but I'm not unknown. I make a decent living and by damn I make some decent music." Again Russ snorted, and again Ronny lost his momentum. "I have a studio."

"Yes, Ronny, you have a studio. Now back to reality. Who did they pull out of the harbor?"

"I have absolutely no idea in the world. No way would I know."

"What?" Drew sneered. "Barbara didn't tell you?"

For once, Ronny sounded rebuked. In a sheepish voice, he replied, "I suppose that's another shot across my bow and I suppose it's not undeserved. But again, I beg you, leave Barbara out of this." He abruptly stood and became a man. "If you can't, keep the fee but get off the case."

Ham and Drew exchanged raised eyebrows and an understanding. Barbara had clearly lied to them about her relationship with Ronny, lies strewn down that primrose path. Sharing a shrug, Drew continued, "How did your wallet get on the corpse?"

"Again, I have no idea. And don't ask me if I don't, because Barb didn't tell me."

They both caught the more affectionate short version of the name. "She goes by 'Barb' most of the time?" Ham asked.

"Well, no, but to some of us, yes. Anyway, I thought I had my wallet with me and intended to buy something at the store the detectives followed me into. I even took the shirt to the cash register, had it rung up, and only then discovered my wallet was gone. I figured I'd left it at the studio, something I've done more times than I'd like to admit. It's an age thing, a forgetfulness I hate. Pisses me off. So that's what I think I probably did and I guess somebody lifted it. Was there money found in the wallet?"

Ham's draw dropped in exasperation. "Jeez, I don't know! And I do not give one good goddam. What is with you? You're charged with murder and you want to know if somebody stole a few bucks from you? Where are your priorities? Do you have any?"

"I had fifteen-hundred dollars in there!"

"That's not nearly enough for bail," Drew answered. "So why worry about it?"

"Who dumped the body, Ronny?" Ham demanded. "I'm guessing you know a lot more than you're giving us. And I'd like to know why. We can't help you if we're blind."

"Again, I have no knowledge of that whatsoever. Whatsoever!"

Ham spread his arms wide, a supplication more than surrender. "Ronny, do you live here?"

His face reflected pure confusion and his voice was soft when he replied. "I don't know what you mean. You mean here? At Russ' house?"

Ham slowly shook his head, pity flooding his response. "No, Ronny, I mean anywhere here on earth." At Ronny's befuddled look, Ham added gently, "Do you have any idea—any idea at all—what you are in for?"

Ronny's eyes reflected genuine fear. "This isn't fair. I didn't do anything. Why would somebody want the cops to think I was dead when it's so damn easy to disprove? Either through dental or through DNA. It's just so stupid."

When Ham answered his voice was unusually placid. "Far from it, Ronny. It's actually a pretty clever ruse. It makes you the murderer."

"How do you figure that?"

"Think about it," Drew answered him. "From their perspective, you faked you own death to avoid arrest and conviction. You killed the songwriters, you killed the man found in the ocean to cover the crimes, and you planted your wallet and planned to waltz away with a bundle of cash, perhaps to live out your days on a beach in Rio."

A Bronx cheer was his response. "What, I'm that stupid? I didn't count on dental? Don't know anything about DNA? I'm such a fool that I thought the wallet was all it would take to fool them? That I have that little regard for their intelligence?"

"That's what the D.A. will claim, yes. And, unfortunately, your reputation doesn't counter that assumption. Given your slimy character, they'll make it stick."

Drew rose from her chair and began her usual pacing routine, developed through years of investigation. "Let's assume for a moment you're telling the truth." She paused to cast suspicious eyes upon him, another trait Ham recognized from the interrogation room. In other words, a silent accusation of bullshit, but what the hell, let's pretend. "Give me one good reason you slipped away from Mutt and Jeff at that department store. What was the purpose of that?"

Ronny looked so confused and lost that Ham, even through his pity, had to laugh. "She means Detectives Cassel and Wilson."

"I don't know," Ronny shrugged. "It was impulse, really. I got tired of their goddam miserable little game, and I got even more tired of their intimidation. I just decided to return the favor, give them something to sweat about."

"Why, you stupid son of a bitch," Ham groaned. "Weren't you aware that the cops were your best alibi? For Christ's sake, man. You choose to lose them on the night that another musician is killed? Do you know what this looks like? What they're going to do with that in front of a jury? God," he exploded, "kiss your ass goodbye and say hello to death row."

Ham punched up Gary's number on his cell. When the attorney answered, he demanded, "Where are you? We need you here." Ham listened a bit, then agreed. "Good. See you then."

He pocketed his phone and nodded to Drew. "He's just around the corner, at some kind of bar."

Russ provided the name, "Flaherty's. Not a bad little hole in the wall. I drop in myself from time to time." His smile was a little abashed as he said, "They start playing a juke box full of Truckee River songs when I do. Always makes me laugh. They're so proud of themselves."

"We'll have to go there," Drew suggested. "Sounds like fun."

"About Gary?" Ham interrupted. "He's finishing off a beer, then he'll be right back. Said to tell our client to cool his heels and not to leave for any reason whatsoever."

"He has no right to order me about," Ronny huffed. "I'll damn well leave if I've a mind to."

"No, you damn well won't," Drew corrected. Her eyes must have convinced Ronny, for he plopped back down, his face flushed and frowning. "You're going to have to turn yourself in, and I want Gary to be with you."

"Why should I do that?" he demurred. "I haven't done one single thing they're accusing me of, so why should I go sit in some shitty little jail cell until they finally discover that truth? Let them find out first, then I'll go see them." His face hardened and he added, "And get my flipping apology. And their resignations."

"Yeah, yeah, yeah. You're a real heavyweight," Russ snorted. "You sit there on that heavy ass of yours, you shut up, and you do what Drew tells you."

Ham paced the room, too keyed up to sit, the mere action of movement, any kind of movement, helped his racing mind. Why, in truth, had Ronny lost the detectives at such a critical time? Which brought on a question he'd yet to ask.

"How did you get away from the store after you lost Pete and Steve?"

"I'd parked a rental out back."

"So you had this planned. It was not a spur of the moment thing, as you claimed before."

Ronny shook his head and quickly added, "That's not what I meant. You're twisting my words. Yes, I had it planned, but it was a spur of the moment plan, a lark. I'd decided that morning to have a little fun with them and drop out of sight. I knew they would catch hell from their chief and it amused me to help them catch it." His gaze shifted between Drew and Ham as he pleaded, "Honestly, that is all I did, and it's what I meant when I said it was a lark."

"Why did you come here?"

"Just to see where the case stood, what you've done." The elaborate show of a shrug instantly raised Ham's suspicions, and his hackles.

"Try again. The real reason."

"Well, why do you think?" Ronny snapped. "I was hoping you had something to keep me out of jail."

Russ jumped in. "He's getting closer to truth. But try this. Did you, perchance, hope to hole up here where you figure the cops won't dare venture again?" Ronny's embarrassment supplied the response, so Russ finished, "That's not going to happen. While I don't really think Val would authorize my arrest for obstruction of justice, I'm not going to have my house used as a hideaway while you're on the lam from the cops."

Ronny looked as though he might dissolve into tears at any second. "Yeah, okay, I understand. Look, just let me leave. I can't go to jail. I'd never make it there. For the love of God," he begged, "have some mercy, won't you?"

Ham shook his head, a firm refusal. "Sorry, Ronny, we can't do it. Russ is probably right that Val won't let anyone arrest him, but they'd damn sure arrest me. Pete would, with total glee. And client or no, I am not willing to go to jail in your place. You'll stay here until they pick you up."

At that moment Gardner escorted Gary into the parlor. "Good evening, all," he cheerily greeted. "What a pleasant day it's been, has it not?" Seeing Ronny's trembling lips, he added, "I mean no disrespect. I'm talking about the incredible weather around here. Beats the hell out of Vegas heat."

He let his smile fade and pulled a chair close to the producer-client and gently leaned in. "Ham has asked me to represent you as well as the rest in this house. That means anything you tell me is strictly confidential. Understand?" At Ronny's nod, Gary rose and waved the others away. "Confidentiality can only be claimed if others are not involved. So out you go, all of you. Move. Go on, get. We don't have a lot of time."

Russ led them around toward the pool. As they sat, he motioned to Gardner. "I don't know about the others, but I could use a drink. A margarita, I think. Anybody else? Anything?"

When no one responded, he tossed a pleading glance to Drew. "You know I hate to drink alone."

"No, you don't," she smiled. "You just like people to think that." His laugh put the period on that truth.

"What do you suppose they're discussing?" Charlie asked. "It's not like that slimy snake is going to give him anything except a disease."

"Gary's nobody's fool," Ham said, thoughtfully. "I imagine he's getting Ronny's side to all this, probably more than we dragged from him. And probably explaining to him what he can and cannot say, to us as well as to the cops."

"But he's your client," Russ objected. "Doesn't that mean you have to know what he said just as much as Gary needs to know?"

"That's different, Russ," Drew interjected. "We're hired to find out who's tried to frame him, if in fact that's the case. Gary's job is to keep him out of prison. He'll pass on whatever he feels he can without jeopardizing the court case, you can bet on that."

"We trust him, Russ," Ham agreed. "He's the best and then some. As honest as the desert is hot."

"That's a ton of honest," he laughed. "Ah, here comes Gardner now with that little something that washes away the stink from this kind of day." To nobody, he toasted, "Here's to it."

They lounged in companionable silence, eyeing the sun's dance with the sea's horizon until, as it ultimately must, it graciously bowed out. Just as the sun dipped out of sight and darkness descended, Ham's phone shattered the stillness.

"It's Pete," he announced when the caller ID came up. "Yeah, Pete, what's up?" He listened for several very long seconds to words which leaked past his ear and on to the wind they were so loud, before cutting Pete off to say, "I can't say I'm all that surprised. And no, I haven't been holding out on you, so get a grip. It was just a hunch, that's all." He listened for several more seconds before saying, "Okay, thanks for letting me know. And I will stay in contact, no worries." As he hung up he muttered, "Flaming asshole."

Ham pocketed his phone and announced, "Barbara waited for about an hour, probably thinking that was enough time for anybody to lose interest in her, the sped over to Barry's house. She's still there. Pete is convinced we're keeping major secrets, or that maybe we're involved in the killings, probably as accessories before and after the fact. Anyway," he sighed, "he's going to stick on her tail, which I applaud."

"This doesn't make a lot of sense," Drew pointed out. "Ronny was at Barbara's, Barbara's at Barry's, and Barry puts on such a convincing act he ought to be on Broadway. He adeptly played us for fools."

She rapidly punched in a number on her cell and within seconds had reached her intended party. "Val, this is Drew. Listen, we've discovered some interesting information and I wonder if you can help me out. I need you to do a complete background on Barry Braxton, one of the singer-songwriters out of Ronny's stable.... Thanks, Val, and yes, I think it's very important. I may have more to give you soon. Yes, you too. Bye."

Just then, Gary led a scared and depressed looking Ronny out to meet them. "We're ready. I'm going to call Val and let her know that we can get our hands on Ronny, but that we want to self-surrender. I don't want that idiot cop back out here letting the world know he's making a bust."

"Hell," Drew responded, "I wish you'd done this about two minutes ago. I just got off the phone with her. She's going to know I held back."

"I'll take the hit. She'll understand I needed to interview him first. She won't like it, but she'll let it pass. She really has no choice." Drew started to say something but he held his hand up to stop her. "I'll reason with her."

Gary walked well away from the group in order to make the call in quiet and privacy. Ronny took a seat near the others and cast longing looks at the drink in Russ' hand, which Russ ignored. Every now and then, Ham saw Gary's hand gestures, expressive of emphasis or persuasion, but the words were drowned out by the breaking waves below. When Gary concluded his business, he called to Ronny, "Time to go."

To Drew he said, "You were right. She thought the timing of our two calls a bit odd, but I explained that you'd been busy looking into Barbara's background and didn't know what was happening—true enough, really." Turning to Ronny, he said, "I want a bodyguard to keep an eye on you. I mean no offense or disrespect, but I know you're scared and I don't want to take a chance on you skipping out on me. Not for what it means to me," he stressed, "but because they'll be so heated about a botched self-surrender they may well shoot you on sight rather than arrest you." Seeing Ronny's panicked mien, he said, "Oh, yeah, I've seen it happen. So you mind yourself. Drew," he nodded toward her, "if you would be so kind as to bodyguard him?"

"My pleasure," she said. She pulled the gun from her purse and waved it casually. "Let me loop you in, Ronny. I don't like surprises. Pisses me off something fierce. And when I get pissed I get an itchy finger. Bottom line, you try to run you won't have to worry about the cops. I'll kill you myself."

Ham watched them leave, then raised a hand to Russ. "Okay, I think now I shall accept your kind invitation and have a margarita. Along with a beer. Or four. Then," glancing at Charlie, "I don't know about you, but it's been a long day for me. A quick bite and off to bed." When Charlie added a nod to her sweet smile, he grinned. "I think Drew can handle things until morning." Looking at Russ, "Assuming she doesn't again find herself *in flagrante delicto*."

Russ' evil leer promised she probably would.

CHAPTER TWELVE

WHERE THE GREAT ONES DWELL

Ham woke to darkness, a cloying emptiness that sucked him into cold, unwelcoming, claustrophobic arms.

Something had touched him. Something he'd heard. A rustle, a hiss, a hum, a whisper.

He lay still as he peered into nothingness, ears attuned. The only noise that disturbed the silence was Charlie's soft breathing, a half whistle, half snore that soothed rather than irritated. It was a sound with which he'd grown familiar and found oddly comforting.

Ham threw back the covers and blindly groped for his shorts and tee-shirt. He tossed them on, not bothering to locate footwear, and padded out. Descending the stairs, he was met by a house as silent and dark as his mood.

The noise that had awakened him, he realized, came from his head. It had been the realization of what he'd done. This damnation of a case that threatened not just him, not just Drew but, and most especially, Russ. The threat that he'd brought on the world's greatest living band. Or what remained of it after he got through messing up their lives.

Growing up he hadn't cared much about music—he'd been too enthralled with sports to bother with the long hairs

—but that had changed since his first encounter with Truckee River and the great Blake Garrett, not just the world's greatest songwriter, along with his partner, Russ Porter, but one of the world's kindest and gentlest men. A man who should still have been around to entertain and bless humanity with his presence.

Unbidden, unwanted, the line from John Lennon's classic "I'm So Tired" jumped into his brain and refused to leave. "I wonder should I get up and fix myself a drink; no, no, no."

Yes, yes, yes.

Ham drank moderately, though if motivated, he could put away his share. Now, tired and more than a little angry at himself, as well as the circumstances, he used the little bit of moonlight playing through the windows to direct himself to the well-appointed bar. Pouring three fingers of bourbon into a tumbler, he added a handful of ice and took the drink out to the veranda.

He leaned against the railing that separated the patio from the seabed a dozen feet below. Mesmerized by the crashing surf and the splash of moonlight toying with the waves, he let his mind roam, knowing it would take him somewhere he needed to go, given enough time. And, taking a swig of bourbon, enough of this.

Ronny's resurrection had changed everything. Not just the unwanted attention on Russ because of that damn kayak with its even more damning Truckee River One markings, but the entire case, because, maybe, just maybe, Russ had been wrong about the music scale motive.

Yet he could not accept that both Russ and his own instincts could be that far off. The murders had been a product of some warped plan. The etched cheeks had been clearly intended to draw attention and to make a statement. The nonrandom order of the victims, likewise, meant something. But what?

It had all seemed so clear. If not the who, if not the why, at least the plan. Somebody, for some reason, a musical killer with a C minor fetish and an agenda, or a vendetta, more like, had swerved from his path of reason—if one could use that term so loosely—and gone after Ronny. And instead of just killing him, he or she had planted evidence that suggested the presumed dead Ronny was himself the killer. At which point the whole theory went to hell. For as Russ had pointed out, there is no R in the music scale, which runs from A to G and starts over again. So Ronny Damon was an outlier. Meaning that something had changed, the killer had deviated from a carefully laid out plan. A not so simple plan, but a plan nonetheless.

But then, perhaps that was the plan all along, the actual point of this entire macabre exercise. To point the finger directly at Ronny. Why? Because Ronny had been the target all along. And maybe the killer hoped to set it up such that the law became the murderer. One final joke on his target.

If that had not been the killer's intent, the question, then, was what could have caused the killer to make such a drastic deviation from his course? Had Ronny become a threat? If so, why? And how? Ronny, to Ham's way of thinking, represented little danger to anyone except himself. He might be oily, he definitely was smug, and he might have been a swindler, but that was not a man who had a chance of joining the Mensa crowd. Or even the sub-Mensa crowd. He'd been a C- player in an A+ game.

Unless the obvious was actually truth, that Ronny had graduated from con man to killer, trying to protect his little fiefdom and his paltry rewards. Rewards, though major to Ham and most other working Joes, were themselves a minor scale in the more major scale of the industry as a whole. Had Ronny, full of self-recrimination and remorse and fear, decided to end the series before he got caught, before he had to pay the ultimate price for his perfidy, by murdering some innocent who became the bait in the harbor?

That, Ham rejected. For one, Ronny was far too self-centered to believe he'd become a victim of his own game. Not to mention that the act would have to be worth Ronny putting out a quarter of a million of his own dollars on the chance that two PIs would find non-existent proof of someone else's guilt.

Unless it was to get to Russ. That would be worth all the money, all the risk, and much, much more to a man like Ronny. But then it got out of hand?

No. That self-same assessment of the producer's personality led him to reject the notion that Ronny would do the killings himself. Period. If anything, if he'd had the brains and the guts to put together such a Machiavellian plan, he would have, if cornered, cashed in and fled like a frightened thief into the night, not stuck around long enough to see if a warrant was forthcoming.

So Ronny had not been the mastermind, and the killer, still out there, had gone off scale. Which brought Ham back to the inescapable fact that Ronny had become a big enough threat that he had to be set up, the plan be damned.

That still didn't eliminate a desire on the part of the unknown perpetrator to ultimately get to Russ. In fact, it not only made perfect sense, it was the one thing in the whole crapola of a mess that did. Russ' former groupie appeared on the victim list, Ronny wanted Russ' help, and it all started with Russ escorting Drew to a club in order to assess the potential of a musician: a request that led them straight to Santa Cruz, where Russ just happened to have a house. And the lure had been a musical notation etched into cheeks, an impossible to resist bait.

So he'd bit, taken the bait without a thought of the hook, and once again escorted a leading figure of Truckee River right into a well-designed trap. God, if he wasn't a moron masquerading as an idiot, there was no danger in the desert.

Ham shook his head, failed to disturb the cobwebs there, and half-finished the drink he'd neglected. If he couldn't clear his mind, then the hell with it. He'd fog it.

A sound, soft and melodic, floated briefly on the breeze. He focused his senses, wondering if that in fact had been what awakened him rather than Charlie's rhythmic snores. But there was nothing more. If in fact he'd heard it at all, it was gone with the wind.

His decided he may as well refresh his drink and maybe review the information he'd stored on his laptop. Something could pop yet. If not, at least he'd provide his subconscious a refresher course, then let it do its thing while he slept.

Returning to the inside, almost to the bar, he heard it again. Low, slow, but more sustained. And for the first time he noticed a light seeping through the frame of a door, one that he'd passed multiple times but had not explored.

Reflexively, he grabbed for the gun tucked in the back of his shorts. Not there. He'd left it upstairs, beside the bed. Briefly, he thought of running up the stairs to fetch it but rejected the idea almost before it formed. No time.

The door was slightly ajar, maybe an inch from closed, and Ham cautiously pulled it wide. He startled at the sight of carpeted stairs that led to a basement he'd had no idea was even there. Apparently, he thought grimly, Russ' tour had been less than complete.

He crept down the stairs, making no sound, senses alive, fully alert. Someone was down there. He could feel it, smell it even.

Almost at the bottom of the stairwell, the cause, the source of what he'd heard became obvious. It could only be Russ.

Ham expelled a breath of relief, though a quiet one. The gentle playing of a master's touch was something he was loath to disrupt.

Ham listened, enraptured, to the beautiful melody playing out, without the distraction of words. Russ' soft fingers drew life from that keyboard, forcing more from it than the instrument could possibly have been designed to produce. Ham closed his eyes, drawn into another world, one which allowed no escape and no other entry.

The sudden silence startled him, though not as much as an unexpected voice. "I take it you like it."

Ham's eyes snapped open as the heat burned his cheeks. "I'm sorry. I didn't mean to intrude."

"No need. You're welcome here. Come join me."

Russ sat at a keyboard, surrounded by recording equipment and at least seven guitars. What the difference might be between them Ham could not fathom, but then he didn't expect to. Russ' world was off planet to him.

"Where's Drew?"

"Upstairs, asleep."

"And you can't?"

Russ shook his head.

"Still too pissed off?"

Russ sighed deeply and gave an elaborate shrug of the shoulders. "It's not really that. I'm just lost, that's all."

"That's a hell of an 'all'."

"You ever wish you could turn the clock back?"

Ham considered that a moment, and seriously. Finally, he shook his head, slowly, as the words formed. "I can't say that I do. What I've lost is not worth seeking. Not like you. I have no past glories to reclaim."

"That's not what I mean at all. The glories, as you put it, those are nice memories, but as time passes they feel almost like someone else's. No," he said slowly, "what I mean is lost in memory. People I loved, people I will always love. Lost in time."

Ham slapped himself mentally upside the head. As always, Russ had been talking above him. "Well, people sure, though not much. I haven't really been that close to anybody."

"So you have no regrets?"

Ham's eyes dimmed as he understood. "Regrets, yes, and more than a few. I've screwed up more in my life than I ever set right."

Russ looked up from his keyboard, staring Ham directly in the eyes. "And now you have Charlie." Ham's crimson cheeks caused Russ to grin, but his voice remained sad. "Don't screw that one up."

"Where are you, Russ? Why this maudlin feeling all of a sudden? Is it this circus you're engulfed in?"

Russ regarded Ham as though he must have cheated his way through the third grade. "It's just age, Ham. What I see around me that I can't fix. Like you."

Ham's jaw dropped and he sputtered, "I don't understand. What do you mean 'like me'?"

"You have a son, yes?"

Ham felt the stab to his heart, a bitter regret that he seldom acknowledged. "I take it Drew told you."

"And he's how old?"

"He's about to turn sixteen. On the twelfth of next month."

Ham felt his eyes burn under the intensity of Russ' stare. "And now the big one. When was the last time you saw him?"

"That's not fair," Ham flushed. "His mother turned him against me." Ham paused, honesty overtaking pride. "Or at least, I hope that's it."

"When was the last time?" Russ insisted.

"He was eleven," Ham admitted, cheeks flushing with his shame.

"Is he a Truckee River fan?"

Ham shrugged, his discomfort growing impossibly large, like a boulder in the room.

"Try it. Invite him to come to Tahoe for a couple of weeks to stay at the great Russ Porter's house."

Anybody else who'd interfered or laid claim to that type of power would have set Ham off on a rant. With Russ, though, he knew it was just truth. "I don't want to try to buy him."

"Why not?" Russ challenged. "Wouldn't it be worth the cost?"

When Ham didn't reply, Russ began to tinker with the keys but his words continued, words that could be taken as accusatory but were clearly not intended to be so. "That's what troubles me about you, Ham. You've got this shell, a hardwood exterior that you rarely peel back. And it only hurts you, the more so over time."

Ham's discomfort came less from anger than understanding, but he couldn't fully admit the truth, not even to himself. Instead, he meekly countered. "That's not entirely true. There's Drew."

Russ' look was one of pity rather than agreement. "She's the exception that proves the rule. Take Charlie, for instance."

"What about her?" Ham bristled.

"I see you, how you look at her, how you act around her. You obviously are swept up, you want her, I'd even call it adoration. But as soon as she gets close, you pull back, show that fear of yours."

"I'm not afraid," Ham protested.

Russ's gentle grin showed he was not fooled. "Of course you are. But of what? Rejection? Anticipation of future loss? Or of winning? You expect to lose so you refuse to win, is that it?"

Ham's mouth opened to reply with challenging words his spinning mind refused to form. He flapped his lips a few times.

"Back to your son. You don't want to buy him; and again I say, why not? You don't want to show him you love him unless you know he loves you? That's the most selfish thing I've ever heard, and it makes me ashamed to be your friend."

Ham ducked the hurt and rebuke, focusing only on the proffered apple. "I'm your friend?"

Russ smiled indulgently, but his words were harsh. "Of course you are, Ham. But then, that's the point, isn't it? You hear that and ignore the obvious. What you're doing with your son, what you're doing with everybody but Drew, is you demand that they demonstrate acceptance of you before you'll return the love. And that, my friend, is a wasted life."

Ham threw up his hands in supplication. "Russ, you are miles beyond me. I don't have your brain and I don't have your gift for words. What is it you're saying?"

"I saw you in my room, looking over the awards of my life. Guess what? That's not life, that's only living."

Ham pursed his lips, perplexed and a bit angry and embarrassed at his lack of understanding. "From one genius, you; to an idiot, me; please use simpler words."

Russ laughed heartily and said, "You underestimate yourself. But all I'm saying is, don't wait for affection so you can return affection. You give, unconditionally and absolutely. John Lennon said it best: all you need is love. All you need to do is to give love. If you haven't loved unconditionally, at least once, you've lived in vain."

Ham nodded, almost ashamed of his own life, hearing it summed up so easily and simply. Yet he protested. "Well, again, I point to Drew. That's unconditional."

"There is Drew," Russ admitted. "Is she as important as your own child? As a woman you share your journey with? Or is she just the fallback because there's nowhere else to go?"

Ham raised hand to lips, looking for wisdom in the bourbon that was not there. He'd left it upstairs, much to his regret. If his head was going to pound, he'd rather have a pleasant reason for it.

Unable to formulate anything articulate with which to answer Russ' spot-on accusation, he deflected. "I really liked what you were playing. What is it?"

Russ might not have heard the question. Or maybe he had and his answer was a riddle.

"I haven't done much since Blake passed, you know? I mean, we weren't like Lennon and McCartney, who broke up the band and went their separate ways. Not even like Jagger and Richards, who came and went in later years, doing solo work and all that. Blake and I didn't work separately. I mean, sometimes for a lark one or the other of us would appear with somebody else, or sit and jam on somebody else's records, but we were a team. We were a *band*, man, and that was our strength. We relied on each other, brought out the best in the other." He paused, staring at nothing on the wall before turning still sad eyes back on Ham. "But your friend, our little spitfire of a woman, she inspires me, brings back an old fire I thought was dead." He shook his head, sorrow his companion. "Yet I can't help but wonder if Blake would be okay with me carrying on. Maybe I should quit."

"Look," Ham replied, his voice gentle and soothing. "I don't pretend I knew Blake anywhere near as well as you, or as Charlie, for that matter. But I can tell you this. Blake was the kindest, most giving, caring and loving man I've ever met. If he had an egotistic or jealous bone in his body, I never saw it. I can't believe that he'd want anything other than for you to carry on, not just for you, but for his sake. I think he'd be pleased and happy for you."

Russ might not have heard, for he continued on as before. "Blake was the soul of the band, and in that sense the leader. I always admired him, looked up to him, loved him. I remember once, I lost my temper, told our drummer and bass player they could either do it my way or Blake and I would go out on our own, kind of a Jan and Dean." Russ laughed softly at the memory, shaking his head. "I actually said that, that we'd be like Jan and Dean. Where I remembered that from I can't even guess. Anyway, the thing is that Blake didn't even blink. He simply stared them down."

Russ' eyes dimmed and his grief became palpable. Ham, touched and not quite sure what to do, laid a hand on the great man's shoulder and left it there, a silent partner to his pain.

"Sometimes I feel like memories are all I've got. That's why I get such a wonderful relief with Drew. She won't let me go there. She says life is now and there's nothing else. Pretty wise, your friend and partner."

Ham, though intimidated by the company he found himself keeping, pressed forward with a concern that had haunted him for the past couple of days. Something he needed to know. "I have to ask, because she is the best friend I've ever had, the one person I've been closest to in life. Are you playing with her?"

Russ' muffled laughter complemented his soft eyes. "I'm going to paraphrase you here. I don't pretend to know Drew anywhere near as well as you, but here's what I do know. I sincerely doubt that she would let anybody, including me, play her. She is definitely nobody's fool."

"That doesn't really answer the question."

"I think it does, Ham. But if you need it spelled out, I'm not playing here. She's sparked something in me that I'd long since forgotten was there. And I like it."

"I guess part of my discomfort is that I can't believe it, that I know you, knew Blake, that we're, well, that we're kind of friends. It's just so mind boggling."

There was not the slightest trace of smugness or ego in Russ' voice when he responded. "I know. I've dealt with that almost my entire life. But you get used to it. You will get used to it. I promise. You'll realize I'm just a man."

Russ, maybe as embarrassed as Ham, turned his attention back to the keyboard and began to play that soft haunting melody that had drawn Ham to this studio in the first place. Only this time, he crooned the words.

Dressed in black and colored blue,
  I'm uncertain and afraid.
In a fog, my mind's a blank, a lonely masquerade —
Pretending I can cope with this, living out that lie.
Nothing left, emptiness, black and blue inside

Russ didn't explain, but Ham knew. It was a tribute, the ache at the loss of his partner, band mate and best friend; a soul companion, a bond that death could not break.

Ham ignored the tears streaming down his face. He'd wipe them off tomorrow.

If at all.

CHAPTER THIRTEEN

PARTNERS AT THE CROSSROADS

Ham woke early, though not as early as Charlie, apparently. He sat up, peered around the room and listened, but nothing moved, no sounds emerged. He rubbed tired red eyes, yawned deeply and pulled himself out of the comfort of the king-sized bed. He padded to the bathroom and began his morning ritual.

Showered, shaved and dressed for the day, he descended the stairs and turned toward the kitchen, where voices could be heard. The household did indeed had a jump on him.

Aromas made his mouth water before he even pushed open the door and gained entry. At the table off to one corner of the spacious kitchen sat Charlie, Russ and Gary. Gardner, apron neatly applied, manned the stove, providing food to order. Ham rubbed eager hands together and asked hopefully, "I'm not too late?"

"Not at all," Gardner assured him. "The kitchen's open all day. What'll it be?"

"A little of everything," Ham replied. "It all smells so good. But I'll settle for eggs, coffee and orange juice, if I may."

As Gardner turned to his task, Ham grabbed a chair and plopped down beside the others. "I don't know how you do it, Russ. You were still up when I went to bed and now look at you: refreshed and alert, while I drag my exhausted ass to the table."

Charlie patted the singer's shoulder affectionately. "He's just naturally healthy, as well as alert, wise and wealthy, ain't ya, Uncle Russ?"

"Where's Drew? Still asleep?" At Russ' nod, Ham continued, "What about you, Gary? What time did you get in? Did it take that long to process Damon?"

Gary finished a mouthful of pancake and delicately wiped his mouth. "Got in about ten last night. And no, it didn't take that long. I went out on a bender afterwards."

Ham's surprise registered on his face. "You? That's pretty out of character, isn't it?"

Gary scowled around his next mouthful. "That was one of the most miserable performances I've had to witness in a long while. Your Mr. Damon does not have much in the way of stoicism."

"And that means?"

"That means he peed his pants and began to sob when they placed the cuffs on him and led him down the long hallway toward a cell. It was embarrassing to watch, it was humiliating for him, and it was an exhibition of raw terror for the entire world to see. I was so horrified that I ran out of there, didn't slow until I got to my car, then broke every speed law on the books in my rush to that bar up the street. Where," he concluded, "my car still is, since at least I had sense enough not to drive it back here."

Drew appeared just in time to catch the end of Gary's story. "You got drunk and you didn't invite me? Not nice, Gary, not nice at all."

"Morning, Drew, come sit down," Russ invited. "Gardner's making some of his justly famous recipes."

"Whatever you'd like," Gardner affirmed.

"Thank you. Ham, eggs, bacon, hash browns, coffee and tomato juice if you have it." Turning to Gary, she asked, "What happened to push you over the edge?"

After he repeated what he'd told them of his experience at the jail, Drew nodded. "Yeah, I've seen that a couple of times. Did they strip search him, put him in jail clothes?" Gary nodded grimly and Drew added, "That's when it'll happen if it's going to. Older guys mostly, those without any experience with the penal system. They go through that indignity and it hits home. This is really happening. Then they lose it. What about bail?

"Arraignment and bail hearing at four this afternoon. The charges right now include murder of the John Doe in the harbor—they haven't been able to identify him yet—kidnapping and mutilation of a corpse."

Drew and Ham gave soft whistles. "They're not screwing around, are they?"

"That they are not," Gary affirmed. "But it's bullshit. There isn't the slighted hint of evidence for kidnapping. They just threw that in there to up the ante and scare the shit out of Ronny. Which, of course, worked. Same for mutilation. I expect that'll be dropped today, since they can't accuse Damon of conspiracy with the shark. And as for murder," he summed up, "like they say in the movies, 'You ain't got nothin' on me, Copper.'"

"You think he'll get bail?" Ham asked. "On a murder charge?"

"It happens. Not often, I grant you, but when the case is as weak as this one, I'm guessing yeah, I can bail him out. As long as he's got the money. It's going to be a hefty amount.

The judge will do that just to appease the prosecutor. Flaming judges," he grumbled.

Russ laughed along with the others. "You're not a fan, I take it."

"Only once or twice in my career have I been up against a judge that had more than half a brain in his or her head. The rest are filled with ignorance and fluff."

"How about D.A.s," Charlie teased. "I don't suppose you're real keen on their existence either."

"They all ought to be in prison," he huffed. "They tromp all over everybody's rights, they violate *Brady* all the time, and in my experience a large majority of them have no problem with suborning perjury. Bunch of little rat fink twerps."

"By golly," Charlie grinned, "it looks like I may have been right."

"Forgive my ignorance," Russ laughed. "I got the gist of your complaints, but I'm lost on whatever Brady is."

"Sorry," Gary sighed. "I get worked up over having to deal with these bozos, like your D.A. here in Santa Cruz." He paused for a sip of coffee before explaining, "The Brady Rule states that prosecutors must turn over exculpatory evidence to the defense. Which means any, every and all evidence favorable to the accused. But they pretend that, for instance, an eye witness statement that the defendant was seen a thousand miles away at the time of the crime isn't really *Brady* material because it's hearsay. Or irrelevant, even. So they roll it up into a ball and stick in the back of some musty drawer somewhere. Goddam pricks."

Gary helped himself to a mouthful of bacon.

"Won't that idiot D.A.—what's his name again?" Charlie asked.

"Robert Turner."

"Robert Turner, right. Won't he fight to keep Ronny in jail? Wouldn't that give him more media exposure?"

"Yes, on both counts," Gary affirmed. "But that's not a major challenge. I'll have a little chat with him before court is called to order. Remind him of the discussion we had earlier out here on the lawn. And I will sweeten the deal with an offer to let him save face. If he wants, he can rant and rage, even demand as large a bail as Ronny can front, but I won't tolerate a petition for no bail at all. I'll out the son of a bitch right there in court if he tries to pull that crap on me."

Russ regarded the attorney with a mixture of curiosity and amusement. "I'm beginning to understand why Drew and Ham insist you're the best. I'm glad you're on my side, bro. I don't think I'd like to go up against you."

"Now that," Gary said with gusto, "is the greatest compliment I have ever had." To Russ, he sweetly drawled, "Does that also mean you will override Drew and Ham and insist on raising my salary above the pittance they pay me? For instance, to a superstar level?"

"Quit whining, Gary," Ham answered. "It doesn't become you."

"I already offered," Russ added. "Drew slapped my wrist. I'm not gonna try it again. You're on your own."

Leaning over to get right in Ham's face, Gary confided, "Fine with all that, then. But I'm here to say I am definitely entitled to whine, and as much as I want, when I'm facing penury. You freaking piker, you."

"Moving on," Ham sighed. "What do you think, Drew? Go back and pin Barbara Bessel down on her secret activities, or talk to our other presumed target?"

"You mean Bodie Briggs?" At Ham's nod, she turned to Russ. "Anything you can tell us that we might need to know?"

Russ paused, as if brushing off a dusty memory, before he finally shook his head. "Not a thing comes to mind. If I've ever heard of him, it's all gone into the musical netherworld."

"Well, let's go see what's what with Mr. Briggs," Drew suggested. "After we stop at the jail to see how Ronny is faring, now that's he's spent a night in a cell."

"Want me to come along?" Gary offered. "It can't be any worse than yesterday. At least I don't think it can."

"No need," Ham replied, "though I appreciate the thought. I'd feel better if you stayed close to Charlie and Russ for the time being. We'll meet up with you this afternoon at the courthouse. Ready, Drew?"

"Let me grab my things and we're set to go."

Ham whispered his goodbyes to Charlie and rose to meet Drew at the door. No sooner had they left the porch than Lost bounded toward them, leapt into Drew's arms and busied himself with licking all over her face. "Where the hell did he come from?" Ham demanded.

"I let him out for exercise and to do his business. And it's what business of yours?"

"None," Ham shrugged. "I'm just surprised the little ankle biter didn't run off."

He finished with a silent, *Wish he had, the goddam cur.*

Drew carried the mutt with her as she approached the driver's side of the car. Grinning at Ham, she wondered, "Suppose he'd like to see the jail? Introduce him to Pete?"

Ham smirked evilly. "As much as I'd pay to see that, I'd say we probably shouldn't. Besides, what would you do with him while we visit Bodie? Or while we're in court, for that matter."

"I guess you're right," Drew conceded. "Here, you hold him while I put my things in the car, then I'll take him back inside."

As she held Lost out to Ham, the little dog began to snarl, growl, snap and bare his fangs. Ham stumbled back a good two or three feet and turned ashen as fear coursed through his veins. "Oh, for heaven's sake," Drew sighed. "Okay, you load the car, I'll hold him. God," she muttered as she headed towards the house, "what do you think, Lost? A grown man afraid of a little bitty harmless dog."

I'm going to shoot that dog. Then I'm going to shoot Drew.

While Drew tended to the killer pooch, Ham fed the address into the GPS. He had just completed the task when Drew slipped in next to him, started the car and backed out the drive. She drove less than a mile before she asked, "Your SUV, the one that went after you in the alley. It was black?"

"Yeah. Cadillac. I saw it again at Barbara's house, remember?"

"Well, I'm seeing it now. Don't turn around. Look through your side mirror, you should be able to spot it two cars back. It pulled out from the curb as we exited the driveway. Not exactly subtle."

Ham did as instructed, located the vehicle in question and nodded his head. "There are probably dozens like it in this town, but it sure as hell looks like the one. If it is, then as for subtle, maybe it's not intended to be."

"True, though I don't see the purpose. It's not like we're going to be scared off."

Ham considered, shrugged in agreement. "Maybe just to let us know they know everything we do."

"Again, to what avail?"

"To no avail," he grimly replied. "But just for kicks and grins, and to let them know we're onto them, go ahead and do some evasive maneuvers."

Drew tossed him a conspiratorial grin, hit the accelerator and performed an illegal pass of the car ahead. As she nearly sideswiped the target, Ham screeched, "Jeez, Drew, for heaven's sake, you're supposed to be scaring them, not me!"

"Dogs and cars, huh? What next, little kids and kittens?"

"Just be careful, there's...uh oh. We may have been a bit rash."

"I see it," Drew replied.

The black SUV, now revealed to be an unmarked police car, hit the siren and let the scream accompany the lights flashing from the grill. With a sigh of resignation, she pulled off the road and onto the curb. "Well, crap," was her only comment.

Much to Ham's surprise, and amusement, he recognized Pete strutting up from the rear. "Oh, this should be cute."

Drew kept her hands on the steering wheel, the preferred place for any approaching cop with a hair trigger. "Hello, Pete," she sweetly drawled when he leaned down to peer in the open window. "How's your day going? They put you on traffic patrol now? My, my. Val must've been some kind of pissed."

Pete's look ice but his voice remained neutral. "Actually, I wanted to catch you before you do any more interviews, and I wanted to do it away from the house. I don't need my ass bitten off again for embarrassing your famous patron. There's a coffee shop about three-quarters of a mile on your left. Meet me there. We'll talk."

Drew did as instructed and pulled into a parking space near the entrance. They did not have long to wait; a little more than two minutes after they claimed a booth Pete strolled in and joined them. "Did you order me coffee?"

In answer, the waitress returned with three cups, a carafe of brew, and various packets of additives. Pete put his hands around one cup as if to warm them—or to stake his claim. He scowled at them and announced, "I told you that Barbara Bessler left her home after you guys departed and after I talked with her, and drove straight to Barry Braxton's place. What I didn't know at the time was that Steve was there."

Ham's mouth fought to remain closed, lost the battle. "What the hell are you talking about? And why the secrecy? Didn't you just ask Steve why he was there? I mean, if he was, it was probably part of his investigation."

Pete stirred cream into his coffee, appearing so rapt that he momentarily lost interest in his own conversation. "I did ask him," he finally replied.

When he didn't elaborate, a clearly exasperated Drew prodded, "And?"

"And he flashed me wide innocent eyes and swore he hadn't been."

Ham drummed fingers on the table and peered intently at Pete, trying to take the size of the man. Finally, he shook his head and sighed. "Forgive me, but I don't know if I buy what I think you want to sell me. How do you know it was Steve? Did you go in and see him?"

"No," Pete admitted, "I recognized his car. He'd parked it in Barry's yard, on the lawn. I couldn't help but notice, nor could anybody else; which means he'd been in a hurry, or he would have been a bit more discrete."

"Well, crap," Drew laughed. "Doesn't that suggest that it was somebody else's car? Steve doesn't drive a unique make, does he?"

Pete sneered. "Yes, Ms. Big City, Used To Be A Detective But Is Now Just A Lowly Private Eye. He does." A "so there" look appeared on his face, so much so that Ham expected him to stick his tongue out and say, "Nyah, nyah, nyah."

Ham waited, impatient but determined. If Pete wanted to play games while Santa Cruz burned, let him. He'd give the cop no pleasure in watching him squirm with anticipation. Officious prick.

Pete made a show of stirring additional cream into his cup and taking a slow and dainty sip of the brew. "They make the best coffee in town," he announced, as though there was nothing else of import to discuss.

"Okay," Drew sighed. "You have our attention but good. We admit to eagerness for details. So please quit with the pretense and tell us, quickly and tersely, exactly what you have in mind."

Pete's smiled smug self-congratulation as he proceeded to clue them in. "Steve has a tear on the driver's side fender, a crack actually, quite noticeable. Val has told him time and again to go ahead and get it fixed but he just hasn't bothered. Says it's a badge of honor from a run-in with a perp he took down. So, whatever, we all just ignore it. But yesterday I couldn't ignore it. He didn't tell me he was going to interview Barry. He also never told me Barbara Bessler arrived. See what I'm driving at here?"

"That you and Steve aren't close?" Drew guessed. "You don't share your girlish secrets?"

"Listen, you bi—"

Ham sprang to his feet, knocking the table and rattling cups, fists clenched. "Finish that sentence and I'll take you outside and cause you to rue the day and hour you ever learned that word."

Pete reddened and waved surrender. "Sorry. That temper thing again. I really do have to work on it before it gets me killed. Or worse." Turning to Drew, he added, "Please accept my genuine apology. I was way out of line." He forced a weak grin. "Next time feel free to shoot."

She nodded as Ham, mollified, resumed his seat. "Let's all remember our boundaries here." He nodded at his partner. "That means you, too."

"Touché," she conceded. "Apologies, Pete. Please do continue."

Pete gestured to the waitress for a refill and waited until she'd accomplished her task and moved on before resuming. "Steve's a straight guy, or at least that's what I've always thought. But lately he's been on the, how do I put this, the more cunning side, I guess." At their questioning looks, he explained, "A lot more secretive, even with me, his partner. And just, I don't know, more thoughtful, more quiet, I guess is what I mean. He's always been talkative, good natured and open, and now he's like the anti-Steve. Secretive, on the sad side, and almost always off in his own world, someplace the rest of us aren't invited. So this latest thing has thrown me, and I mean a lot."

"Well, where is Steve now? Why isn't he with you?"

"I don't know, Drew. As far as I know he's at the station. At least he was last time I spoke with him, which was about an hour ago. As for why I'm alone, I told him I had personal errands to run that might take me most of the morning."

"And he believed that?"

"Sure," he nodded. "It's happened before, to both of us. We cover for each other. I mean," he shrugged, "sometimes things pile up and we nip a little official time for personal use. You guys never did that?" Their smiles were admissions of guilt and he grinned in return. "I really wanted to fill you guys in before you end up tripping over my toes, if you know what I mean."

"Yeah," Drew replied, "we know. What you mean is if Steve's up to something maybe he doesn't want publicly known, you'd prefer we don't tip him off to any suspicious behavior. Am I close here?"

"Yeah. Look, I'm not accusing him. But I am worried. Really worried. This just isn't like him and I'm hoping he hasn't gotten himself into something that will burn him in the end. If he has, I'd like to help him get out of it. And I would consider it a personal favor if you two wouldn't interfere with that."

"You mean," Ham grunted, "that if we find him dirty we should just ignore it? Is that what you're trying not to say in so many words?"

"Yes, it is," Drew answered for him. "That's why he's here instead of telling his story to Val. The chief of police won't play ball on that, not even for one of her own. Right, little man?"

Pete's cheeks turned scarlet but he refused the bait. "I don't want my partner burned. And I know you understand that feeling. If he's done something, yeah, you bet I'll cover it up and get him out of it if there's any possible way. I make no apologies for that. He'd do the same for me. And don't look at me like that. You were cops, you know the code."

Ham shivered his eyelid in a subtle wink at Drew and shrugged for Pete's benefit. "Let's suppose we do. What's in it for us?"

Pete nodded, obviously pleased with the question. He dropped his voice and replied, "I might be able to get some evidence lost in the Damon case."

Ham and Drew both leaned back, appearing thoughtful, if not eager. "That's worth my license," Drew replied softly, "not to mention worth a long stretch in the penitentiary. Nope," she decided, "I don't think Ronny's worth it. Keep your evidence and we'll see you in court."

Pete rose, threw a couple of dollars on the table and snapped, "Have it your own way. I could have helped you, you don't want it, then go screw yourselves. And while you do it, be looking over your shoulders. I'll be there." And with that he stomped out as fast as his short legs could propel him.

Once he cleared the door, they both broke into laughter. "We should have given him a standing ovation," Drew suggested. "I mean, that was one great performance."

"Wasn't it, though."

"You don't really think Steve was there, do you?"

"No, Drew, I don't. What I'm not sure about is whether Steve is part of this act Pete put on. If he is, we don't want him anywhere around Vegas, period, end of story."

"How stupid do they think we are, offering a bribe in order to catch us dirty? He was probably wired." She sighed and threw her hands wide. "I hope to god it is just Pete. If Steve's playing us, we really missed our guess about him. I'd hate to think we've lost that much edge. I'd hate to think we have to lower our rates that much."

"I agree, I don't think Steve's so stupid as to think we're that gullible, ignorant or needy. Let's proceed on the assumption that our instincts are still sound and continue to act accordingly."

"Right, then," she agreed. "On to the station house. Where we may or may not find Steve awaiting our arrival."

They wove their way through early afternoon traffic, encountered few delays, and reached the precinct within fifteen minutes of settling the check at the coffee house. Only a few cars littered the lot, meaning they wouldn't have to navigate many obstacles in order to see their client. That, Ham knew, was a bit of an advantage in an otherwise loaded for bear day.

Drew led them to the reception desk and smiled sweetly at the officer seated there. "Good afternoon. I'm Drew Thornton and this is my partner, Ham McCalister. We're here to see our client, Ronny Damon. And by the way, is Steve Cassel in?"

"Steve's here, yeah," the sergeant nodded. "Did you want to see him too?" At her nod, he said, "Have a seat. I'll locate Steve and I'll find out if you can meet with your client. I won't be but a moment."

"Cooperative fellow," Ham said approvingly, when the officer disappeared around the partition. "You can't possibly think we were expected, can you?"

"Oh my word, no," Drew agreed. "We're just a couple of out of state, out of our level private eyes. How would we know the world of big time California cops?"

Steve emerged from the bullpen, a smile gracing his features. "Hey, guys. What's up? What can I do for you?"

"First we'd like to see Ronny," Ham replied. "Then we'd like to go somewhere for a private conversation. Is Pete here?"

Steve's eyes clouded and his voice turned curt. "No, he's not. I have yet to see him today, though I talked to him on the phone. He's got some things to attend to. Why?"

Ham shrugged elaborately. "No reason," he replied. "Just asking. Anyway, can we see Ronny?" At Steve's nod, he added, "How's he doing?"

"About what you'd expect. He's a wreck. Let's get your guns checked and then I'll take you to an interview room where you can talk to him privately."

After seeing to the proper forms and storage of their weapons, Steve spun on his heels, turned toward the hall branching left from the check-in desk and called back over his shoulder, "Follow me. It's down here."

They ended up in the familiar confines of an interrogation room which, like all others around the country, held a single table and three chairs. The only other adornment consisted of a handcuff ring, used to hold the prisoner immobile. "I'll be back with your client. How about some coffee? Or a soda?"

"Coffee," they replied in unison. When Steve left, Ham leaned across the table and silently mouthed, "Bugged?"

Drew's nod indicated a belief that they were not to have a confidential conversation as per their right.

Ham sat back. "We'll let them know how we feel about that."

They fell silent until the door opened and Steve escorted in a disheveled and embarrassed looking Ronny Damon. The three paper cups he cradled in his hands he placed in the middle of the table. From his shirt pocket he pulled packets of cream and sugar, along with one spoon. He stopped at the door when Ronny pleaded, "Can't these things come off? I mean, come on, where am I going to run?"

"Sorry, Damon. The cuffs stay on. Policy." With that he exited, closing the door softly behind him.

Ronny opened his mouth to impart something but Ham and Drew held up restraining hands. "Let's go over the situation here, Ronny," Drew stated. "First off, Ham and I no longer represent you in any investigation." When Ronny began to object, she quickly forestalled him. "No, no, we're not leaving you high and dry. But now we work for Gary, who *does* represent you in this and all other tangential cases. It's at Gary's instructions that we're here to talk to you."

"What this means," Ham interjected, "is that anything you tell us becomes attorney work product, which is strictly confidential and protected by attorney-client privilege. If, on the other hand, we were working directly for you such privilege can be challenged."

"And," Drew continued, "the reason for telling you this before we begin is to firmly protect confidentiality, make damn sure it cannot be challenged or questioned. If we resigned after interviewing you, we're subject to discovery. There would be no attorney-client privilege or attorney work product. Understand?"

"They can't make you tell? Or Gary?"

"Nope," Drew confirmed. "Nor, for instance, are they allowed to overhear our conversation, either, say, through wiretapping or eavesdropping. That's a no-no. It constitutes police misconduct and sets the officers involved, and the department as a whole, up for penalties both civil and criminal. And that is one messy shit full load of grief. They definitely do not want to let themselves in for those kinds of penalties, especially since cops don't do so well in prison. Not real liked, if you know what I mean."

"You understand all this, Ronny? That check you gave us was payment in full for services rendered prior to now. Any further remuneration you owe will be owed to Gary."

"Yeah, I get it. Now maybe you can tell me what your, or rather, what Gary's plans are to get me the hell out of here and get these damned charges dropped. I can prove—"

"Wait," Drew interrupted. To Ham, she inquired, "Did you get it all?"

Ham smiled, held up his cell phone and affirmed, "Yep. Recorded, complete with video. Dated and time stamped for all the world to see."

"Right," Drew said. "That will do it. They'll have shut it off." Turning back to their former client, she nodded. "Go ahead, Ronny. Tell us a story."

CHAPTER FOURTEEN

CONFUSION IS A SPLENDID STATE OF MIND

Drew and Ham retrieved their weapons, signed the forms and walked out into the mild heat and cooling gusts of ocean breeze. They said not a word but turned their attention to the mechanical guide directing them to their next destination.

Drew kept a watchful eye on the rear view mirror as she made her way through and around fairly light midday traffic. Ham, too, spent considerable time studying images in his side view mirror.

After the interview with Damon, Steve's embarrassment all but admitted that somebody had listened to, and probably illegally recorded, the conversation. That is, until Ham and Drew played out that cautionary farce.

Ham figured Val had probably been the one to pull the plug. Steve would most have called her in to listen rather than unilaterally making that decision. Moreover, the chief likely had been the one to dream up the scheme in the first place. No cop would take it upon himself to violate rights that way. Or at least, he lamented, no decent cop. But if that were that to be the case, Val was not exactly a by the book, straight arrow leader.

Drew startled him out of his reverie with an abrupt question. "How much of that do you believe?"

"From Ronny? Hell, I don't know. All of it. None of it. He's scared enough for me to think that he might be telling the truth, if for no other reason than to make sure we have what we need to save his sorry ass. On the other hand," Ham shrugged, "he's unctuous enough that I'm not sure he's capable of not telling a lie."

Drew pulled the car to a stop in front of the apartment house they sought. She checked her notebook and nodded. "Apartment 424. Think there's an elevator?"

"I'm not even sure there's reliable stairs. How come we keep running across filth and squalor? Damn and double damn, just for a change I'd like to feel clean when I go home at night."

They entered a dilapidated lobby featuring ripped carpets, dim lighting of chandeliers from better days, and furniture adornments from somebody's grandmother's mother's house.

At the back of the room an open elevator rested, door agape. As they made their way toward it, a voice from a dim recess brought them to a halt. "Excuse me," a man's voice shrilled. "Where do you think you're going?"

Ham turned toward the sound of the voice and for the first time noticed a small reception desk. Behind it stood a man, middle-aged, but with an impressive head of hair, graying and waving its way near to the shoulders. "Can I help you?"

"We're just on our way to see somebody. Is that a problem?"

"No, sir," the man assured him. "But if you don't live here —and I know you don't, I know everybody who does—you have to sign in. For security reasons. You know."

"Yes," Ham replied politely, and peering at the name tag, added, "yes, I do know, Mr. Costa. I'm a former cop, myself. So is she," he added, pointing at Drew.

Costa's raised eyebrows indicated he was impressed. "Well, we don't get a lot of officers or other officials through here. Not that we need to, of course."

"Of course. Where do we sign?"

The receptionist pulled a book from below and opened it to the appropriate page. "Right there. Name, and who you're visiting."

Ham signed for both of them and pushed the book back to Costa. "There you go. Now, do we have leave to proceed?"

Costa examined the signings and shrugged. "If you want. But Bodie's not here."

Ham and Drew exchanged skeptical glances and Ham wearily responded. "And how, may I ask, do you happen to know that?"

Costa's amusement appeared genuine as he half answered, half mocked in return, "I happen to know because I saw him leave not half an hour ago. You can't miss Bodie and you can't miss his car. A beautiful brand new Dodge Challenger, white with black stripes on the top."

"Did you talk to him? Did he say where he was going?"

Now Costa's eyes reflected a certain wariness. "Look, I like Bodie. He's a good guy. Very pleasant, always has good words of greetings, and thanks me when I do favors, like signing deliveries for him. If he's in any kind of trouble, I'm not your man. Do your own work, Detective."

Ham put on his best manners. "Mr. Costa, as I said, I'm a former detective. Now my partner and I are private investigators. We wish to speak with him, yes, but not because he's in any trouble. On the contrary, we want to help the man. He may be in danger."

Again the raised eyebrows. "No kidding. Well, I did talk to him, but he gave no hint as to where he was headed. Should I give him a message if he returns?"

"By all means," Drew answered. "Here's my card. You tell him exactly what we told you and tell him it's very important to call me. Will you do that?"

"Of course, of course, by all means."

Once they were back in the car, Drew said, "That is one funny little old man. He strikes me as the town gossip. I would dearly love to hear what he actually tells Bodie when he sees him. He'll pounce all over him, drooling excitement. And, oh, the tales he can tell his compatriots."

Ham chuckled agreement even as he punched in Barbara Bessler's home address. "Okay, let's see what she has to say about hosting Ronny. And why she went rushing to Barry Braxton's place after we left. And why her SUV matches the one that tried to run me over. And then, just for the hell of it, let's try to get her to tell us the truth about Steve. Or Pete, now that I think about it."

"What do you mean? Why Pete?" Drew sounded surprised. "You think she may know something Pete's hiding from us? Like what?"

"Well, suppose it wasn't Steve at Barbara's house. Suppose it was Pete, that he went in himself. And then claimed Steve did it. That way, if she said a cop was by and harassed her, we'd assume it was Steve she was talking about."

"Interesting. I see your point, it's a good one, and it's the scenario I'd prefer. But we shall see what we shall see."

The ride lasted less than twenty minutes. As they pulled into the drive to Barbara's house, Ham found himself as awed as the day he first explored the grounds. Until he saw it what was parked there.

"A beautiful brand new Dodge Challenger, white with black stripes on the top, that's what Costa said, remember? Well, now, thar she be. How the hell about that? Coincidence? I think not."

Drew pulled to a stop behind Bodie's car, effectively blocking him in. "If he wants to leave behind the wheels of his very nice new car, as opposed to running on his two legs, he'll answer my questions first."

They strode determinedly forward. Ham had nearly reached the welcome porch when the door flew open and an impeccably dressed Barbara emerged. As before, her hair appeared to have been freshly styled and the demure dress reeked of cash. "To what, may I inquire, do I owe this unexpected and not all together welcome interruption of my business?"

"And what business would that be, Barbara?" Drew offered her most innocent smile. "Hiding suspects? Suborning perjury? Perhaps accessory before and after the facts?"

"My business is none of yours. I'm going to ask you to leave. And I will call my good friend, the mayor, if you don't. I'm sure he'll have the police here in force." Her icy voice belied the gentle smile she affected.

"Boy, you do get around don't you, Barbara? The mayor. Ronny. Steve. Barry's house. Bodie in your home even as we speak."

Her smile wavered, but beyond that she gave away nothing. "Following me, stalking me, or any other attempt to intimidate is a waste of your time. It would be better served at home playing with your boyfriend, the infamous Russ Porter, don't you think?"

Drew appeared to chew the bait and spit it right back. "Jealous, Barbara, dear? Don't be. That's a waste of your time. You're not his type."

She ostentatiously eyed Drew up and down, then up again. "And why is that do you suppose? Too old?"

"Too flat-chested."

Ham nearly spit out a lungful of breath before he stepped in to end it. "Barbara, we still believe you're potentially in danger. We know for a fact that Ronny is. And I'm betting my fee the cops are going to want some explanations very damn soon. I'd like to know what kind of dirt they're going to get on Ronny before they bleed you dry and button you up." As she began her response, he waved her off. "Assuming you have some interest, personal or professional or both, you're probably not happy about Ronny facing murder charges." When she merely folded her arms across her chest, the light dawned. "Or maybe you are. But then the question becomes a big huge flaming why, doesn't it? So, you tell me if you want to in any way help him, or you can tell the cops and let them smear Ronny into a guilty verdict, if that's your wish."

Bodie emerged from the shadowed hallway, gently pulled Barbara back, took her place in the doorway and looked daggers at Ham. "I'm acting as her attorney. You want to talk to somebody, you talk to me, not to her." Turning to look over his shoulder, he gently said, "Barb, would you be so kind as to go fix us some tea? I'll be there before you can properly steep it." She withdrew and he stepped onto the porch, pulling the heavy door behind him.

"Questions?"

Ham regarded him curiously, noting how different he looked from the publicity stills Ham had stored in his files. He looked several years older than those pictures, though clearly younger than his claimed client by at least fifteen years. Instead of that longish red hair Ham was familiar with, Bodie sported black hair so short that it barely touched the tips of his ears. An old man's cut. And instead of the habitual jeans, biker boots, short sleeve tee and leather vest that adorned said stills, he stood erect and impeccably dressed as if ready for court.

With sudden inspiration, he got it. That was exactly why Bodie had outfitted himself in such a manner. "What's this about you being an attorney? I found nothing to suggest that in your background."

"I didn't say I am an attorney, I said I am acting in that capacity for Barbara. Be that as it may, however, the fact remains that I am indeed a member of the California bar."

Drew shook the wonder from her mind and got herself to ask, "I have several questions, but let's start with this one. You're an attorney."

"That's not a question," he replied, his smile cold and confident.

"And that's not funny," she rejoined. "The question, Mr. Smart Ass, is if you're a member of the bar, why do you live at Poverty South Personified?"

He swung his arm at his car, the one neatly pinned in by Drew. "Doesn't that suggest to you an answer?"

"Yeah," she nodded. "It suggests you are hiding something, a lot of something, and it further suggests that I will do a background on you that makes a top secret clearance look like a casual query."

He smiled tenderly, as if to a confused but trying child. "No, Detective, that's not it. It suggests I keep a very low profile office."

Ham's eyes widened even as he nodded understanding. "You don't live there? It's an office? What the hell kind of practice do you run?"

Now, when he answered, Bodie's smile took on a menacing edge. "Confidential," he replied, "that's the hell of a kind I run. Now," he continued as he opened the door, reentered the house and turned back to face them, "I do believe we have come full circle, so let me repeat Barb's demand. Get the hell off this property, stay off this property, and if you come back I will have you arrested for trespassing." He slammed the door with a firm and sarcastic, "Have a nice day."

They exchanged chagrinned looks, silently considering options. Finally, Drew sighed and said, "I guess we're done here. Let's go."

They jumped in the car and gunned the engine to life. Ham knew that symptom and placed a reassuring hand on her arm. "I understand you're pissed and I know you'd love to squeal tires and burn rubber backing out of here just to let them know it, too. But this time, in this case, I think it's to our advantage to keep that display of displeasure between ourselves, rather than make a public admission of how they trumped us." Shaking his head, he went on, "Let them think they bested us without giving them the satisfaction of acknowledging that they won, they completely turned us upside down. That way, when we've investigated them three sides from Sunday and we thrash into them like a hurricane hitting the Florida coast, it'll be a lot more gratifying. We can watch them fall apart. And that," he assured her, "is the best revenge of all."

If a smile can be sweetly evil, he thought, Drew displayed it. While she made no verbal response, she answered Ham by backing slowly out the drive, giving a couple of soft toots of the horn by way of ta-ta, and leisurely proceeded down the lane and away from Barbara's sanctuary.

Ham returned Drew's evil-sweet grin and dialed up Gary's number. "Hey, I got something for you," he explained when Gary picked up, "a member of the bar I need you to look up for me. California bar, that's which one. His name is Bodie Briggs. Yeah, that one. But I'm thinking that's a stage name of some sort. That's where Russ comes in. You may have to get him to call in a few favors in order to run down the chatter on Briggs." He listened a minute the added, "Good, call me as soon as you get anything. Oh, and Gary, once you find out his real name, whether it's Bodie Briggs or not, get a complete background on his legal standing. School, current workload, past cases, anything you can." Ham cut the connection and nodded to Drew. "Right, that's in the works. What do you say we try to find our bright and exceptional friend, Barry Braxton? We can ask him if he's found any new brain cells to play with." Ham snorted.

"Hold on," Drew admonished him. "Barbara claimed that Barry is one of the brightest people she knows. Either she's aware of something we aren't or she lied to us."

"You don't trust her and neither do I. I vote for the latter."

"I'm not so sure," Drew shrugged. "At the time, she didn't view us a threat. Or at least I don't think she did," Drew frowned. "Oh, hell, get your cop friend, the one with the California State Police, to background him for us. He stills owes you, doesn't he?"

"Danny Sanchez. And yeah, he still does. And always will." Ham relished the memory. "I had to prop him up, keep him from falling over when I brought him up to the lake to meet Russ. It was great," Ham chortled as he dialed. "He stammered all the way home. Couldn't thank me enough, will owe me always, etcetera, etcetera." For Drew's benefit, Ham set the phone on speaker.

"Danny," he all but shouted when Captain Sanchez answered. "It's me, Ham. How you doing, buddy?"

Sanchez's words feigned a gruffness that was belied by the good humor in his voice. "I'm groaning inside, that's how I'm doing."

"Oh?" Ham inquired innocently. "What is the reason for that, I wonder?"

"Of course you wonder," Danny snorted. "Okay, what do you want this time? Remembering that if it's personal, and I do it and get caught, my ass is in an unemployed sling."

"Why, Danny, old pal, what makes you think I want anything?" At the pointed silence from Sanchez' end of the line, Ham laughed. "Okay, yes, I need a favor. I need a complete background on one Barry Braxton, of Santa Cruz. He's recorded, written and released songs under that name, but it could be a stage designation. There's a group here and it looks like several may have played that musical ploy."

"Played that musical ploy? What, you get that phraseology from your buddy Russ? You sure as hell didn't coin it yourself."

"Speaking of Russ, this is really more a favor for him than for me."

An astonished silence followed that statement. "Well, why the hell didn't you say so?" Danny demanded, in an excited voice. "It means another trip, though."

"That's a promise. As long..."

"Oh crap," Danny sighed. "Here it comes. As long as what?"

"As long as you get this done before the day in over. Preferably by evening."

"Danny Sanchez, your man for the impossible. Okay, Ham On Rye, I'll give it what I've got. But it means memorabilia signed by The Great One, not just room and board."

"I think that can be arranged. Anything else?"

Danny's voice dripped lust when he replied, "Yeah, that hottie partner of yours. Man, I hadn't seen her since our college days. She wasn't quite so put together back then, if you know what I mean."

Ham glanced over, noted Drew's cheeks burning and managed not to laugh. "Yeah, what about her?"

"Can you arrange for her to be there? I'd love to get to know her a bit. More than a bit, if you catch my drift."

Ham wouldn't swear to it but it sure sounded like Danny had drooled his way through that drift. "Well, the fact is—"

He cut himself off at Drew's desperate shake of the head. "Sorry," he mouthed to Drew. To Danny, he answered with a simple, "I'll have to get back to you on that."

They said goodbyes and Ham pocketed his phone. "Hopefully, we'll get the dope on the dope and see where it leads. I get the feeling we're running out of time."

Drew's eyes, when she turned to Ham for a quick glance, reflected unusual trepidation. "Yeah, I've got the jitters myself right now. Too many people playing too many games. And us without a scorecard or a rules list. It's got my attention alright. My confused attention."

Ham glanced at his watch. "We'd better grab a quick bite then beat it over to the courthouse. I want to talk to Gary before the hearing starts."

She nodded but otherwise made no response, merely pulled into a parking space in front of a tiny hole-in-the-wall café with a faded sign that read "Eats". Ham followed her inside, as lost in his own thoughts as she was in hers, and they followed a young petite surfer girl to a table in a darkened corner. A ripped and faded red tablecloth was consistent with the tired ambience.

The waitress silently handed them menus covered in torn plastic and speckled with dried condiments but Ham disregarded the mess as of no consequence. Just a few bites to nourish the soul, then onward to battle. It was ever thus, from the day first born.

He harrumphed, looked over the menu, spotted the least objectionable item—grilled cheese, how badly could they screw that one up?—and ordered that along with coffee. Drew nodded agreement and the waitress set off upon her task.

When she was out of earshot, Ham focused on his partner, surprised and alarmed by her demeanor. She had begun to wring her hands, worry etched her brow and her lips were pressed tight.

From long, affectionate experience he diagnosed the symptoms. Her worry was for somebody else. Not for herself; she had no fear for self. On the contrary, she was brave sometimes to the point of foolhardiness. Who, then? Himself? Nah. Ronny was even less likely. Surely not Barbara, Barry or Bodie. Maybe Val, there was some kind of connection there. Possibly Steve, though both of them now had their suspicions, so no, probably not. Definitely not Pete, the bozo of Santa Cruz. Which meant Russ.

Which meant she was worried over a fact that he himself had missed.

"Okay, Drew, tell me about it. What am I missing?"

She toyed with her napkin; picked up, peered at and put aside a dirty glass of water; and, as per habit when deeply troubled, drummed her fists on the table.

"Go ahead," he gently prodded. "Get it off your chest."

She turned troubled eyes toward him and almost begged, "Don't laugh, don't snap and don't make light."

Ham's surprise leapt to his eyes but he merely shrugged. "Okay, I promise."

"It's Russ. They're after him." At Ham's questioning look she nodded firmly. "Yes, him. And I mean physically. I think they may be intending to kill him."

Now Ham's astonishment could not be contained. "I promised I wouldn't laugh or make fun, and I won't and I'm not. But," he asked, hands held apart in supplication, "is it possible this is a, you know, physical thing between the two of you?"

Her eyes burned and she snapped, "Because we have sex, so I'm worried about not getting laid tonight? What the hell is wrong with you?"

"That's not what I meant at all," Ham backpedaled, knowing he meant exactly that. "What I artlessly tried to convey was that you might be unduly concerned that Russ is getting pulled into this thing. You're worried it will result in embarrassment to him, perhaps even tarnish a legacy he's spent a lifetime developing. See what I mean? It's just like you to care that much."

Drew shook her head "Nope, it's not that. It's because every damn time we turn around, every new step we take, involves somebody trying to push Russ into the middle. That's the key to this whole thing, the entire case."

Ham considered, nodding solemnly as the waitress returned with sandwiches and coffee. Pushing the sandwich away, he took a deep gulp of the bitter, lukewarm brew and leaned back in his chair, a man in search of a thought. He mostly stared at nothing in the corner, though occasionally he noticed Drew pick up the grilled cheese, take a small bite and again push it away in favor of more coffee.

"Consider," she sighed, "how this started. Russ and I walk into some lounge singer's act. Ronny uses that to lure me here, hoping, no doubt, that Russ will follow. His boat is used in the harbor, irresistible bait to the cops and to the

D.A., which gives them the excuse to come make a show at Russ' place. Further, the musical scale itself is bait to hook Russ. Now you tell me, what could be the purpose of all that except to lure Russ out into the open?"

Ham rubbed his chin and sighed. "I'm sorry, I don't see the point. You mean kill him to gain international notoriety? That sickness again?"

She shook her head, quick and firm. "No, though I wouldn't completely rule it out. But it's too elaborate for a simple assassination. They're after him for money. Massive amounts, I'm guessing they're thinking."

Ham's face drained of all color as memories came flooding back. "You mean like Blake?" He immediately countered with a furious, "That makes absolutely no sense. You don't kill according to some musical theory just to draw him out and...." He trailed off, the words unspoken.

"Precisely," she whispered.

"No," he finally announced, "and for one very good reason. He's not that hard to get to that they'd have to go to elaborate lengths. I mean, he doesn't go around protected by a mob of muscle or anything like that."

"I know," she agreed, "and it may not be that. It may be an attempt to steal his assets."

Ham regarded her thoughtfully, stood, threw a twenty next to his uneaten sandwich and nodded toward the door. "I'll drive." In answer, she tossed him the keys.

They drove through downtown, weaving in and out, a touch dangerous, Ham knew, and more than a touch illegal, but he deemed it worth the risk. Especially since he feared that if he dawdled Drew might well jump out and take it on the run.

He slowed to a crawl along Russ' driveway, remembering the sudden drop to the ocean. At that Drew did precisely what he'd seen in his mind's eye earlier. She jumped out and outraced the car to the picturesque dwelling and its patron therein.

CHAPTER FIFTEEN

DISORDER IN THE COURT

Concerned that Drew's well developed and infamous radar now pinged for a purpose, Ham slammed the brakes and halted the vehicle midway up the drive before he himself jumped out and half ran, half loped the remaining distance to the door. When he burst through he knew. Drew, damn her clairvoyant ass, was right again, before his lesser sensitivity even registered the question.

He found Gardner sprawled on the couch, hand to head, wearing a rag stained with blood. Since he was alone, Ham figured Drew had raced to Russ' side, an assumption confirmed by the muddled Man Friday. Nodding toward the stairs, he mumbled, "Up there, with Russ."

Ham took a moment to ask, though he, too, felt the anxiety of dread and the need to rush those very stairs. "What happened here?"

"Two men," Gardner grunted. "Entered through the veranda, caught me unaware, bashed my head half to death. By the time I came around they were gone and Drew was storming through the door." His eyes watered as he pleaded, "I never saw them. They were so silent, so quiet. I didn't know. I'm so sorry."

Ham patted the man's shoulder. "You can't blame yourself, Gardner. No way. Even had you seen them enter, I doubt you'd have been able to stop them." At the handyman's offended look, he hastened to add, "No doubt they came prepared to overcome resistance. That's what I mean." Gardner's sigh conceded the point. "What about Charlie? And Russ? Do you know anything?"

"Nothing at all. I heard a scream when Drew went upstairs, but what it was I don't know." Struggling to hold his focus, he waved toward the stairs. "Go."

Ham needed no further prodding. He flew up the stairs, complaints from his hip be damned. His first goal was to find Charlie.

As he turned to check his own room to see if she was there, his eyes caught movement from down and to the left. He whipped out his pistol, but before he took aim Drew stepped into full view. "I've called an ambulance," she whispered hoarsely. "Gardner's been hit, which I guess you saw. Russ is unconscious, clubbed over the head. I haven't seen Charlie or Gary yet."

Ham silently, slowly, pushed the door of his room open, crouching low as he did. It was an old habit formed from the knowledge that if an intruder intended an attack, he'd come at him high, aiming for heart or head.

Muffled sounds of struggle caused him to raise his weapon and sweep the room. Behind him, he knew, Drew did the same but higher up. Nothing, nobody. Just muted cries.

Ham tossed caution aside. He rushed the corner blind. If peril threatened Charlie, if that was the source of the sounds, he'd beat that son of a bitch to a death beyond horror. Or die trying and let Drew take the bastard out afterward. Either way, no way would he allow Charlie to suffer.

When he barged in, there was a writhing Charlie, legs bound, hands tied to the bedpost. Her wild eyes flashed murder.

Ham rushed to her, ripped the tape from her mouth—which earned him a screech, more of pain than gratitude—then used his pocket knife to start cutting her bonds. His face grim, his voice quaking, he demanded, "Who did this?"

If he expected weeping or fear, his mistake lay in underestimating Charlie. Instead of weeping, she peered over his shoulder to address Drew and snarled, "Where is he? You didn't hurt him, did you? I want to kill him!" To Ham, she snapped, "Give me your gun."

"Charlie, I—"

"I'm going to kill the bastard! Now give me your gun."

"Whoa," Ham said. Part of his brain wanted to laugh with relief that Charlie was okay and wanting to spit bullets, but first things first. "Slow down a bit, Charlie, and let me catch up. Russ is hurt, but he's alive, and an ambulance is on the way. Now tell us what happened."

She nodded, exhaled a few calming sighs, and then explained. "Russ and I were in the solarium. We heard footsteps approach. Before we understood what the hell was going on, two masked men, ski masks, I think, stepped into view. One turned and motioned us toward the stairs. Silently, like words were his enemy. Russ, being Russ, refused and began cursing them and their ancestry. The other one walked up behind Russ and knocked him out with a gun barrel to the back of the head. When I screamed at them, one held my arms, the other muzzled me with that damn tape, and they both joined in to carry me up the stairs, where they unceremoniously tossed me on the bed and trussed me like a Thanksgiving turkey. Beyond that," she spat, 'I have no idea. The bastards. Give me your gun."

Ham shrugged an unhappy reply and shifted his gaze to the floor. "You're in a frenzy, Charlie, and I understand that. Please, you need to calm yourself. We'll take care of this."

"Damn you, Ham! I am not a child. And look at me when you're talking to me, not at the stinking carpet!"

The sudden arrival of screaming sirens and pounding feet saved him from reply. With a horrified glance at Drew and a warning wave to Charlie, Ham leapt for the door and pounded down the stairs. He'd nearly made it to the bottom when Drew shoved him aside and swept into the room. "The end of the hall," she shouted. "Last I saw he was unconscious."

Drew stood aside as the ambulance personnel moved past her, lugging a stretcher and a tool box full of whatever. And though she did step aside, she wasted not a second before dogging their tails all the way to Russ.

"I'm going to have them check you, as well," Ham informed Charlie.

"You will do nothing of the sort," she snapped. "Uncle Russ needs attention and I'm not going to delay them just so they can examine my headache."

He sighed defeat but tried again. "Will you at least let them take you so you can be checked out at the hospital? That won't interfere with anything."

Her sudden smile preceded the warm and thoroughly unexpected lingering kiss. "You are a dear," she sighed, affectionately patting his cheek. "Just so very slow."

Before a puzzled Ham could demand clarification, the medics rushed by, transporting Russ. Ham had just enough time to realize that they'd stabilized Russ' neck with a brace before he left them to their work. He tried to ask a thoroughly hassled and harried Drew for explanations but she, too, blew by him. She did, however, yell back over her shoulder, "You go to court, cover us. I'm going with Russ," before he lost sight of her as well.

It was only then that he saw Gardner, still on the sofa, still holding his hand to his head, and a rag to the blood. "Charlie, run out and tell them to hold on a second. Gardner's going, too."

She spun on her heels and raced to keep them from premature departure. As she did, Ham helped Gardner rise and gently ushered him to the door and down the steps. By the time the ambulance came into view a member of the rescue crew reached them and asked, "This the other victim?"

Ham nodded and watched the EMT tenderly help the elderly man along. Only then did it hit him. Where the hell was Gary?

Ham rapidly punched up the number, got an answer on the first ring. He shouted into the phone, trying to be heard over the screaming siren of the departing ambulance. "Where are you? We've had an incident." Quickly, Ham described what had happened.

"My rates just doubled," Gary informed him. And FYI, I'm at the courthouse waiting to talk to Ronny. They should bring him in within a few minutes. Are you going to be able to make the hearing?"

"Yeah. Drew's going to the hospital but I'll be there. I'll fill you in on what Ronny, the maestro of this farce, tried to slide by me."

"By time you get here I'll have talked to him. We can compare stories. If he's lying he's dying. I'll see to that. And I'll demand my fee up front."

"You do that," Ham said. "See you soon." With that he broke the connection and headed towards the stairs. He'd almost begun the climb when he detected a soft sound, a rustling perhaps, some whisper on the wind. Just enough to trigger a pause. To cause wonder.

For the hairs on his neck to rise.

It came from behind. Or maybe below. Maybe both? He snapped his fingers in inspiration. The studio.

He crept cautiously to the door, noticed it stood ajar and pulled it wide enough to slip through. He descended the carpeted stairs silently, guarded, gun leading the way. Only one small shaft of light danced across the walls as he moved into inky darkness.

There. Again. That soft rustling, like papers being shuffled. From the sound of it, somebody was snooping through Russ' work. Or his records, his finances or whatever. At that moment, the searcher concerned him. Not the purpose. That was for later.

As he reached the bottom, he stopped short and waited, listening, ears attuned to the slightest vibration. Nothing, not even soft breathing. Maybe, he thought, his imagination toyed with him. It would not be the first time a stressful situation triggered false perception.

Ham crouched and slowly rounded the corner into the main area in which the recording equipment sat. He caught the slightest outline of shadow before the perp extinguished the light. Then nothing.

No friendly person would plunge a room into darkness.

So. He'd somehow given himself away. How mattered not, though he'd ponder it later, if only to learn from the mistake. The type of mistake that could get him killed.

Like now, maybe.

Ham waited, squatting low. His leg muscles burned with the effort and began to cramp. He figured he would be forced to stand or suffer the indignity and peril of collapsing to the floor.

Just as he stood tall, damning the telltale creak from his knee, he felt—or maybe intuited—a fleeting motion, the merest tremble of air. He froze, all senses heightened, anticipating attack, ready to fight it off by gun or by hand, it was all the same to him.

Bring it on, asshole. Let's do it.

Nothing. No attack, not even discernible movement. No noise. Zilch.

His mind tempted him with the thought that he'd only imagined the flicker of air, that and nothing more. But he knew better. His instincts, honed to razor sharpness from years on the force, could not be so easily deceived. Some damn somebody was there.

The tackle that knocked him back into the wall left him sprawling , and the perp stepped on his foot as he rushed past Ham and on up the stairs. He reached the door before Ham could stop him and dashed on through. Ham feared that the intruder might close and jam the door shut but the perp never slowed, just continued on to and out the front door.

By the time Ham made it to the porch, the invader had neared a house half way down the block, where a black SUV sat awaiting. The intruder jumped in and the car roared to life. Ham let loose three rounds, two of which hit the passenger door, though apparently not the driver, as he stomped on the accelerator.

But his run would be difficult, for the third shot found its target. The right rear tire was going flat even as the SUV roared away.

The SUV that tried to run him down. Bet on it.

Ham ran to his own auto, gunned it to life and screeched out and onto the road, headed in the same direction as the perp. Though the street continued straight on for about a half a mile, he saw no one. No cars, no people, just a sleepy little lane devoid of action.

He pulled up to the end of the road, a "T" intersection from which he could opt for north or south. He examined the stretch ahead on both sides and though he noticed activity none of it involved his wanted vehicle.

With a disgusted sigh, he returned to the house and proceeded to the studio. Even as he hit the stairs, he connected with Steve's cell phone.

"Steve, this is Ham. It's happened again. That black SUV. Yeah, the same one. Only this time the guy decided to help himself to a tour of Russ' studio. I got the plate. Are you ready?" After citing the license plate, he added, "Oh and by the way, you might want to add to your BOLO the fact that there are two bullet holes in the passenger side door, and they should be looking for a flat right rear tire. Though the way he was going, it may be just rim. Most of the rubber is probably already stripped."

Ham heard a pen scratching over paper before Steve addressed him. "Okay, got all that. I'll put a 'be on the lookout' for the car and will let you know the moment we get a hit. See you in court, yes?"

When Ham rang off, after assurances he wouldn't miss the hearing, he entered the studio proper and flipped the lights to action. Sure enough, a safe stood ajar, papers covered the desk and files littered the chair.

He rifled through the safe, noted money and other valuables that had not been disturbed, a detail which confirmed his suspicion. This had not been a botched burglary. Glancing at papers strewn about the desk, he noted most dealt with old contracts, recording and performing, as well as BMI songwriting paperwork and copyright notices.

Ham shook his head, the one which he was in over. Russ would have to sort this out. He'd be the only one who could.

He glanced at his watch, noted the time and sped back to his room. Thanks to Mr. Unwanted Visitor, Ham's arrival at the courthouse would be untimely at best. Another reason to go hunt down that miserable prick.

Before the guy with the SUV fetish comes hunting me again.

He changed in a flash, only taking time on knotting his tie. His less than nimble fingers fumbled their way through that task, even as Ham cursed and cajoled them.

Ready at last for the formality of a courtroom, he jumped in the car and headed out. Since he'd been there several times now, there had been no need for the GPS. As it was, he would be lucky to arrive before the hearing ended.

He risked ticket, life and limb in his haste to reach the hall of justice, where parking was at a premium, and not even available. It took more than five minutes driving up and down the lot before he caught a break. Just before he passed a Camaro on the left, he observed white reverse lights come to life. He stomped on the brakes and impatiently waved an invite for the driver to exit. After a couple of minutes spent tending to his hair in the rearview mirror, the driver condescended to do exactly that.

Ham waved him goodbye with a finger, pulled into the spot and trotted most of the several hundred yards to the entrance. To his dismay, the line for the metal detector looked to be a couple of dozen people deep. But he had no choice.

He had inched up the line for two, perhaps three minutes before the thought hit. His damn gun. No way would he get through and there was no storage area to leave it. He had no option but to jog back to the car, stow the weapon and trot back to the line. As he gasped and sweated, drawing unwanted attention from the people who guarded the entryway, he at least had the satisfaction of noting the line had been reduced by half. It wouldn't be long now.

Finally, after what felt like many more moments than had in fact elapsed, he walked through the detector and raced off to a board where the case list offered up the specific courtrooms where hearings would be held.

He ran upstairs to the room just in time to see Gary approaching his seat. Ham pushed his way past irritated spectators and bulled down the aisle to catch the attorney's sleeve before he entered the bar, but Gary had not time for last minute promptings. "Can't now, Ham. The judge will be here any moment."

"Sorry, Gary, I got delayed by a burglar." At Gary's puzzled look, Ham shook his head. "Never mind. What's going on? I thought you were going to blackmail the district attorney into resigning and relinquishing his law license. How comes he's at the prosecution table?"

Gary's smile was evil in its beauty. "Patience, Ham. There's nobody I'd rather go up against than Robert Turner. If I get him out now they might put somebody who's actually competent in that chair. No," he said, "I'm content to wait."

"Okay, but did you get what you need from Ronny? He told me that—"

"All rise," the bailiff interrupted. Gary shooed Ham away and took his place at the defense table while Ham squirmed into a seat on the crowded front bench.

The presiding judge solemnly sat and thoughtfully pulled papers off the bench in order to read the indictment. "This is the case of the State of California v. Ronny Patrick Damon," she intoned before she smacked a gavel for silence. "Mr. Prosecutor, you may proceed."

BRENT KROETCH

The District Attorney had apparently decided he would personally work the high profile case rather than assign it to one of his underlings. He stood, stiff as his rounded back and protruding belly allowed, pulling himself to full height. "Thank you, Your Honor. This is a hearing to show probable cause, following which the defense will request bail. We intend to show there is cause to believe Mr. Damon committed the crime of murder for which he is charged, as well as kidnapping, and mutilation of a corpse. We will further argue that if bail is to be granted, it should be in an amount sufficient to guarantee the defendant's presence at trial."

The judge addressed Gary and inquired, "Does the defense intend to put on a case?"

"No, your honor, we do not believe that will be necessary. The prosecution has no evidence to support the charges at hand."

The judge shrugged..

The D.A. spent the better part of an hour presenting no witnesses and no actual evidence, merely a long, rambling supposition as to what may have happened. There was nothing conclusive or even persuasive to indicate that there had been a kidnapping—hell, even the D.A. had used the word 'presumed'—let alone mutilation. As for murder, at least the corpse had finally been identified as a long time beach resident with a list of petty criminal offenses. An individual, the D.A. emphasized, who had a physical resemblance to Mr. Damon. He speculated Ronny had chosen this victim in order to lead police to think him dead, which indeed had worked for a time. Therefore, proof was not needed, since the "pudding is in the plan."

Ham nearly lost it at that. He managed to control himself only by feigning a deep cough. The judge raised her gavel and presumably was about to pound for silence and for Ham to remove himself from her courtroom. Ham quickly sobered and nodded his apology. Nevertheless, she intoned, "Consider yourself warned."

Gary took less than five minutes to poke more holes in the prosecution's case than could be found in a truckload of newly processed Swiss cheese. Once again, Ham deemed Gary not just the best, but unbeatable. He half expected the judge herself to escort Ronny to the door and out the building.

But ... when Gary finished, the judge motioned the D.A. to sit down, a clear indication that rebuttal would be not only unnecessary but unwelcome. "I think I've got enough to go on here. Mr. Damon is hereby ordered remanded to the sheriff's department pending a plea for bail. The charge is murder in the first degree. While the substantiation is weak, there's at least enough prima facie evidence to deem it worthy of a jury making the decision." She held up a hand for emphasis as she concluded, "The charge of mutilation is summarily dismissed, as is kidnapping. Now then, Mr. Prosecutor, are you going to be objecting to bail, and if so, why?"

"We do not entirely object, Your Honor. But may I remind the court, this is a case of first degree murder, with special circumstances. That makes the defendant eligible for the death penalty and would therefore give him great cause to run. Any bail would have to be levied with that in mind." With a smug smile of satisfaction, he sat down.

"I see. And just what are the special circumstances, which you have neither filed nor mentioned?"

Robert Turner seemed confused for a moment, then brightened. "Lying in wait. Yeah, that's it, lying in wait."

"And your proof of this," the judge audibly sighed, "is what?"

Turner at least had the sense to redden briefly before he answered, "We're still investigating that, Your Honor. We expect new evidence to emerge before trial."

"Fine," she snapped. "When you get it, present it. Until then, we'll go by the law. Special circumstances are not warranted at this time and, as I said before, the case is weak. Bail will be granted; we just need to agree on the terms."

Turning to the defense table, she addressed Ronny directly. "How old are you, Mr. Damon?"

"Fifty-two, Your Honor."

"And you were born where?"

"San Diego."

"How long have you lived here in Santa Cruz?"

"Almost thirty years."

"Are you employed?"

"Self-employed, Your Honor. I own a recording studio and a publishing firm."

As she continued her questioning, Ham's attention wandered, knowing the outcome. There would be bail, probably in the hundreds of thousands range, maybe a million or two. It almost made him feel bad for his erstwhile client, though not too bad. The vision of seeing Ronny for the first time, his hair combed over in an attempt to hide the baldness apparent there, and his unctuousness saved Ham from deep pity. Then the judge caught Ham's attention when she solemnly intoned, "And most of your hair is in your ears, I see."

Ham couldn't stop himself. He burst out laughing, sides shaking, and didn't stop until the harsh rap of the gavel broke through his hysteria and riveted his attention.

"What is so funny that you disrupt my court?" a clearly livid judge demanded. "You'd better have one very good explanation if you don't want to spend the night in jail for contempt. I already warned you once."

Ham wiped streaming eyes, swiveled his head back and forth, and saw nothing but bewildered faces all around. Not a single person laughed, smiled or in any way acted amused.

Forcing calmness, he replied, "Why, what you just said."

"What, that this is indeed a very serious charge?"

Oh, my dear God, Ham thought. *Oh no. No, no, no, no, no.* Could it be that a memory from their first meeting had superimposed itself on the present? That remark about Ronny's appearance, that his hair is all in his ears? Had it merely been in his head that he'd projected onto the judge, not her pronouncement? It had to be, he realized, just as he understood explanations were useless. Instead, he lowered bewildered eyes to the ground and mumbled, "Um, no. I guess I misunderstood."

"Misunderstood," a dangerously irate judge echoed. Then, before Ham could offer further excuse or explanation, she pounded her gavel. "Enough," she snapped. "I'm giving you a night in jail to think about court decorum. Bailiff, take him away."

CHAPTER SIXTEEN

GOING OFF SCALE

Ham walked from the jail, released at precisely 8:47 a.m., and found Drew waiting, car idling and set to go. Sweaty, dirty and reeking of the smell from the broken-down toilet in his cell, his mood was as foul as his stench.

"You need a bath," was all Drew said as he crawled into the passenger seat.

"Yeah. That and that bastard judge in a dark alley. I swear to God, I'm going to get that son of a bitch if it's the last thing I do."

"Well," Drew teased, "you can't get that son of a bitch, given that she's a woman. Maybe you can get that bitch of a bitch. What about that?"

"Shut the hell up and drive," Ham growled. "I am not in the mood. Just leave it alone, how about for once."

Drew piloted their vehicle through the sleepy morning traffic, a far cry from their normal morning commute, her stick sheathed, not poking the bear any further. Much to Ham's relief.

They continued in black silence until Drew finally asked, "I heard the story. What the hell got into you? I've never seen you do anything so completely unprofessional before. I mean, wow."

"Never mind. Just get me home."

"Speaking of which, Charlie's gone back to Tahoe. Russ sent her in his plane. She fought him but he refused to take no for an answer. And even Charlie will defer to Russ when he gets bullheaded like that." She shrugged. "I think he's concerned that she' really will kill the guy that tied her up and gagged her. Should we ever find him."

"Probably a good idea," Ham agreed. "I'll give her a call when we get to the house."

They lapsed into silence as Drew unerringly navigated them back to Russ' place, now so familiar with the route that the GPS was superfluous, as had been the case for Ham on his way to the courthouse. He'd not needed it on his way from there to the jail, either, since Pete had been only too thrilled to escort him.

"Pete did the strip search personally." He paused for effect before he half shouted, half whimpered, "He took pictures!"

Drew refused to take the bait and he sighed, a cause lost. "How's Russ?" he asked instead.

"He'll be fine. They'll be releasing him tomorrow they think. He's got a concussion, so they want to watch him a bit more. But forget all that for now. We'll talk after you get cleaned up and get some decent food in you. You're going to need it."

"And that is because?"

Drew clamped her lips tight, a sign Ham recognized. With a sigh, he accepted that she would discuss nothing more until she'd finished mothering him to distraction. Or smothering.

Lighten up, Ham. You got yourself into it, nobody else. Except that judge, the one he was going to hunt down like a rabid animal and then—

Drew's laughter brought him back to reality and the moment. "What?" he demanded.

"Ham, you are such an open book it's amazing that Charlie keeps reading."

He sighed and shook his head in resignation. "Am I supposed to know what that means?" He might have added more, but his cell buzzed its insistent demand for attention. "It's Danny Sanchez," he informed Drew. "Yeah, what's up?"

"I heard about your little adventure," Danny chuckled. "Man, would I have loved to get a picture of that booking."

"Is that why you called? Just to bust my nuts with piss poor hilarity? If so, I'm busy. And I would have thought a captain with the state police would be, too. Don't you have anything better to do?"

"Okay," Sanchez snickered, "don't get your shorts in a knot. I actually have some background for you on your Mr. Barry Braxton. Also known as Larry Bessler."

Ham's gasp arrested Drew's attention. In response to her raised brows, he set the phone on loudspeaker. "Would you repeat that, Danny?"

"What, you taping me? Well, no matter, your client, or suspect or whatever, stage name Barry Braxton. His real name is Larry Bessler. Well, Lawrence, formally. He graduated from the University of California with a degree in mathematics. Got a master of science degree in math from Stanford. Dropped off the face of science and earth following that particular achievement. I'm guessing that's because he did his music thing under his new name, never let on about his background."

"Well, Barbara sure knew. She could have saved a bunch of lives if she'd have been of a mind to do so."

"What was that?" Danny inquired. "I didn't catch it."

"Nothing, just Drew grumbling about a new suspect we are going to pull in."

"Yeah? How are you going to do that? You have no arrest powers, not even in Nevada anymore and—" Light must have dawned because he stopped short and said, "Oh crap."

"Only in an emergency and as a last resort," Ham assured him.

"Don't you have any friends to play with in Santa Cruz who can back your play and effect an arrest? Why me?"

"Danny, I'll be straight with you. We just don't know who we can trust. And I don't want to make a mistake here."

"I'll be straight with you, too. I want that invite and some souvenirs, and I'm going to want all that in a timely fashion."

"I'll see to it," Ham assured him. "Thanks, Danny. I owe you. Again."

Drew spoke up when he cut the connection. "We know what we're going to be doing today, by God."

Ham nodded and stored the phone in its holster just as Drew pulled up the drive. Much to their surprise, Russ stood on the porch awaiting them. They were even more startled when he strode up to the car. Drew parked and jumped out, concern coloring her eyes. "What's up?"

"Val called."

"She called you? Why didn't she get in touch with us? Or was it not about the investigation?"

"Oh, it was about the investigation alright. There's been another murder. They found the body a little while ago. They're still working the scene."

"That doesn't answer my question. Why call you unless you're somehow connected?"

Russ' expression was grim and his eyes narrowed in anger. "Oh yeah, I'm connected alright. I'm connected because I'm an idiot. It's a harmonic," he whispered. "A goddam harmonic."

Ham and Drew exchanged anxious glances. "Does this make any sense to you?" Ham wondered.

Drew shook her head. Russ looked up to the heavens, eyes shut tight, looking to block out the self-directed anger. He remained so for nearly a minute before he opened his eyes and and looked from Drew to Ham. "It's a C minor harmonic scale rather than a natural C minor. So instead of Bb its B C. He's completed the scale. Meaning that unless he starts a new one, that's the end of it. He's done his thing." He sighed, a sound of repressed pain. "I should have anticipated this, it makes more sense. God, I am such an idiot."

Drew's voice and eyes expressed a tenderness Ham had rarely seen from his partner as she smoothed the hair off Russ' forehead and declared, "Then you're the most brilliant, talented idiot I've ever met."

Better get sized for the tux, Ham thought to himself. Russ may not know it yet, but he was hooked and being reeled in by the world's finest fisherman.

"Who's the victim?" she asked. "Anybody you know?"

Russ nodded emphatically. "It's Beau Clarke and, yes, that's his real name. I've known him for a number of years. He was a fine man and a good musician. And," he added grimly, "he had no connection to Ronny Damon."

Ham's brows rose. "Are you sure? Never mind, of course you're sure. But now it makes no sense."

"Back to this scale thing," Drew directed. "Tell me why he's completed it."

"Okay," Russ sighed, "I was working on a C minor scale. The next victim would have been somebody whose initials are B B. The scale would be complete when he killed a one-name singer whose name starts with C." He paused to let them catch up before he began again. "But there's also a C minor harmonic scale. The only difference is that there's not a B flat note. It's a B. Therefore, the scale finishes with B and C. Beau Clarke. So that's it. He's murdered his way through the C minor harmonic scale." He paused, perhaps for emphasis, maybe in despair. "It's over. And I could maybe have saved him if I'd gotten it right."

Drew wrapped an arm around him, the cop comforting the legend. Ham could only shake his head.

He left them to their moment until Russ looked up and caught his eye. "Val left the address, said for you to come as soon as possible."

"He needs a shower and food first," Drew insisted.

"It can wait," Ham replied. "We'd better get moving."

"I guess you didn't take the hint. I'm not getting in the vehicle with you. Not until you shower and put on clean clothes. Speaking of which, I'd better air the car out."

"You spend the night in a cell with a backed up commode," Ham retorted, "then you can rag on me about smells. But okay, I get your point. Even I can't stand me anymore. You get the address from Russ and program it in, I'll jump in the shower. We'll be out of here before you know it." With that he trotted off to effect the needed transformation.

As he rushed past the kitchen on his way to the stairs, the aroma emanating from within brought him up short. He popped his head in, saw Gardner wrapping leftovers. "Can I get a couple of whatever smells so good?"

Gardner smiled at him over his shoulder. "Sticky buns. How many would you like?"

"How many you got? No, just kidding. Can you put a couple on a plate for me to take with me? I'll eat as I change."

While Gardner prepared the snack, Ham walked to the table and patted Gary on the shoulder. He looked up from the newspaper he'd been absorbed in and smiled. "Well, well, the prodigal, laughable son. Welcome back."

"Thanks for springing me, Gary," he purred sarcastically. "Nice job, great effort. Boy, yeah, I really owe you one."

"Easy, Ham," Gary said. "There wasn't anything I could do. That judge wasn't about to reconsider her order and an emergency appeal would have been useless since you would have been released before I could schedule a hearing."

Ham harrumphed, grabbed the plate and a couple of napkins and ran all the way up the stairs.

After shaving, tending to his teeth and taking a quick shower, he wolfed down two sticky buns and dressed in casual street clothes. He took a minute to inspect himself in the mirror, nodded with satisfaction—or at least resignation—and hurried down the stairs, outside and to the car, where Drew and Russ still stood.

As he approached, he slowed and glanced back and forth between them, taking in their expressions. "Oh, hell. What now?"

Drew stared at her shoes as she announced, "We just heard from Val that Barbara Bessler's dead. Killed with a bullet to the head. B and b carved into her cheeks."

"Son of a bitch," Ham moaned. "What the hell is going on?" Turning to Russ, he demanded, "I thought you said it was some kind of harmonic thingy, that he'd finished it, that it's over. So what does this mean? Can you explain it?"

Russ spread arms wide, as if appealing to heaven. "God knows! I wish I did. I don't know, and I can't guess what's next. Like I said, he's finished the harmonic, but killing

Barbara may mean he's working on the C minor rather than the harmonic. Which means you need to be prepared for another murder, because we're back to the one named singer with a name beginning with C."

"But then Beau Clarke must be an outlier," Ham guessed. "Could it even be a completely separate deal? Maybe it's not part of the music scale murders."

Russ rubbed at his lips, obviously pondering a new hypothesis. "It's possible," he finally announced, "that's he's doing both scales. Remember, the scales don't diverge until the final two notes. In the C minor scale, it's B flat followed by C. In the harmonic version, it's B followed by C. Therefore, the first four murders apply to both scales. Maybe he's finishing what he began, which is both of them."

Drew's eyes lit with inspiration. "By god," she mumbled, "that may just be it." She tenderly tapped Russ on the cheek. "Don't ever again tell me again that you're an idiot."

"Where did they find Barbara?" Ham asked.

"Well, here's one more coincidence for us," Drew drawled. "They found her at her house. Where they found Beau Clarke."

"What? They've been out at Barb's? Why didn't you tell us that in the first place, Russ?"

"Because, Russ doesn't know where Barbara lives," Drew answered for him. He just had an address, not a name."

"I don't understand," Ham said, and looking it. "How come they didn't see Barbara's body when they found Beau Clarke?"

"She'd been left in a storage shed out back. Clarke was in the kitchen."

"Did Clarke have his initials carved in his cheeks?"

"Yeah, and Val is really upset. There's no way to keep the lid on a serial killer story like this."

"Who do we have for our presumed next victim? Assuming," Ham amended, "that our perp is going to complete the other scale as well. The regular C minor one."

"I'd have to check the file. None I can remember off hand. Russ? Anything?"

Russ pulled at his lip, apparently deep in thought. "There's one I just remembered," he finally said. "There may be others, of course, probably are, but there's one that I'm familiar with. And guess what," he frowned, "her biggest hit was 'Modesto In The Morning', which is in C minor. She's known as Chloe. You ever hear of her?" When they both shook their heads, he nodded understanding. "Well, it was some years ago."

"Is she associated with Ronny?" Drew asked.

"No. But then, neither was Beau Clarke. So I throw that one in your investigative lap. As for me, I'm gonna get me some heat over here and hunker down until this thing is over. I'm still not sure but what I'm some kind of target here myself. Though damned if I know why."

"That may be best, Russ," Drew said slowly, "at least until we find out how and why you keep getting roped in to this. But I got a better way. You join Charlie up at Tahoe, keep her company and watch over her until we've packed this away."

Russ regarded Drew, questions written in his eyes. "I don't know. I think I'd feel like I was abandoning you in time of need, running away, too scared to stay. I may be a legend but I am still a man, and a man's got to do what a manly man's got to do," he added with a wry grin.

"I'll be safe, don't worry. Val won't let Ham shoot me. Although, now that I think of it, Pete might allow me to shoot Ham."

Ham's eyes narrowed and his face darkened. "That little prick. If he ever so much as lays a hand on me again, I'm going to stick that self-same hand right up his ass."

Drew's eyes danced as she demurely informed Russ, "Pete and Ham spent quality time together. Ham happened to be nude at the time."

Russ coughed his way through a snort of laughter. "I see. Some personal issue, perhaps."

Ham was about to retort when from the corner of his eye he noticed Lost come bounding through the door and straight at him. He screeched in terror, pulled open the car door and jumped in just before the little mutt lunged, probably for his throat, Ham fumed. Flaming mongrel.

He looked up to find Drew and Russ doubled over, hooting and whooping at his discomfiture. Flipping them off, he pulled his gun and ostentatiously waved it back and forth. "Some day," he mouthed.

Drew picked her pooch up, cooing softly while petting him into a state of bliss. She handed him off to Russ, who handled the dog with as much tenderness as Drew, much to Ham's disgust.

Until an idea hit with a flash of intuition and shoved other concerns from his mind.

Irritation overwhelmed him as he realized he'd almost missed it. In frustration, he slapped himself upside the head, punishment for the ultimate halfwit. And that might be giving himself too much credit, he thought as he emerged from the car as rapidly as he'd gotten in.

For once, he ignored Lost's snarls and barks. Didn't even look at him. Instead, he marched up to Russ and asked, "You got a car I can borrow? Like right now?"

"Sure," he shrugged. "Take the Jeep from the garage. Ask Gardner to get you the key."

"What's going on?" Drew demanded. "You going somewhere without me?" As he nodded absently, she added, "What are you thinking? Loop your partner in, Ham. I mean, you do understand this partner thing, right?"

"There's something I want to check out, and it needs to be done immediately. But we also need to know what they're unearthing out at Barbara's. You go there, let me take care of what I need to tend to, and we'll meet up and compare notes. Good enough?"

"Okay," she shrugged. "I guess it'll have to do."

Ham raced up the porch and into the kitchen. No Gardner. Dammit! He retraced his steps to the foyer, turned and headed for the veranda, where Gardner and Gary sat drinking coffee and chatting like old buddies. "Gardner," he called out, "Russ has offered me the use of the Jeep. He said you could provide the keys."

Gardner's eyebrows raised, but he stood, nodded and waved Ham to follow. Near the front door, from a small basket hidden under a shelf on the adorning entry table, Gardner produced a single key attached to a dangling keyring. "Thanks," Ham said. He took the key and ran down the steps.

Whereupon he spotted Lost, sprinting in his best imitation of a speeding cheetah, aiming straight for Ham's unprotected body. "Drew," he shrieked. "Stop him!"

She whistled sharply and the little nipper skidded to a stop, sat on his haunches and calmly watched Ham sidestep around him.

Satisfied his life would be spared, Ham grinned thanks at Drew and gave a wave of gratitude to Russ. He continued on to the garage, where the doors stood open, and jumped into the Jeep. He roared the engine to life, backed out and drove a mite faster than he thought normally appropriate, turned onto the street and gunned the engine. Only when he reached the dead-end did he remember he hadn't a GPS to set.

He idled the car as he rifled the glove compartment. Finding nothing there, he searched the middle console and discovered the GPS and power cord. Ham plugged in, flipped open his notebook to retrieve the address, punched it up, and waited until the unit found the satellite and provided instruction.

He hurried to the directed address, the junkie pad Barry Braxton maintained for whatever purpose his devious and mathematical mind might have entertained. As he screeched to a halt, he saw what he was unsurprised to find. Barbara's black SUV, the very one that attempted to run him over in the alley during his morning jog, sat parked one door down from Mr. Druggie's flophouse.

Ham shook his head in disgust. The mathematical, musical genius, so enamored of his own virtuoso brilliance that he disdained all others as far inferior, and then behaved like an imbecile himself.

Parking the stolen car one door away. Yeah, boy, that would hoodwink any investigator.

Sure it would, Barry. Or should I say, "Larry"?

Ham pulled his weapon from its holster and used it to rap at Barry's door. Nothing and nobody responded on the other side, which he had expected. Undeterred, he moved to the large front window, rapped again with his gun. The glass shattered inward. *That should get his attention,* Ham reflected.

Did it ever. Barry appeared suddenly at the door, a weapon of his own held up and ready, his eyes boring into Ham's. When Ham just grinned, Barry slowly lowered his gun and nodded. "I guess you know."

"I guess I do, Larry. Shall we talk?"

Barry waved Ham into the filth of his abode. "Have a seat. I won't bother to offer you refreshments."

"First question, Barry. Why this false front, this hippie pad that would have been a bad scene even back in the day?"

When Barry shrugged and pretentiously stifled a yawn, Ham thrilled inside. Got him, he thought. His ingrained superiority lent itself to intemperate arrogance, and therefore to underestimating of his enemies. Of which Ham was categorically one.

"It's for when the police come to see you," Ham guessed.

Barry's brows rose, but he merely shrugged as he deadpanned, "Don't know what you mean, bro."

"What I mean, bro, is that you're a little less clever than your Stanford degree would indicate."

Barry regarded him long seconds before he nodded. "So you do know. I take it you know more than that, yes?"

Ham's eyes narrowed as Barry idly toyed with his gun, waving it around the room, though pointedly not directly at Ham. Still, he caught the warning. Nevertheless, he persisted as if he were unconcerned, unthreatened. "Yeah, I know more than that. For instance, I know—"

His cell phone sprang to life, showing Drew's caller identification. "Excuse me a second, Barry. I gotta take this." Completing the connection, he greeted her with a simple, "Yeah."

"I'm out here at Barbara's. Val's been filling me in. It's pretty hideous. I saw Beau Clarke's broken body. He was badly beaten and tortured in ways that I don't even want to name. It's one sick mother loving jerkoff who did him, I'm telling you."

"Yeah, I know. I'm sitting with him now."

Silence met his statement until, finally, came a sigh of understanding. "Alright, you can't talk, you're light years ahead of me and the cops, and you'll spend the next forty years gloating and patting yourself on the back. Congratulations." Turning more serious, she added, "Be careful. I've seen this psycho's work. You want me to get you backup?"

"Thanks, no, but I appreciate it. I'll be leaving here before long and I'll see you then." He disconnected, holstered the phone and raised his eyes to Barry. He stared at him for several long seconds, saying nothing and hearing nothing in return. But he did detect veiled anxiety in the man's eyes.

Ham's smile signaled danger ahead. For Barry. "I'm your foreboding come to life, Barry. I am the walking, talking embodiment of the totality of all you dread."

Barry's face contorted, then just as quickly returned to normal. "I'm sure I have no idea what you are saying, other than some empty threat designed to do I don't know what."

"They told me you were clever, Barry. I'm not seeing it."

At that Barry's eyes grew narrow and his face flushed scarlet. "That's because you don't live on my level."

"Meaning, I take it, that I'm not as smart as you."

"Your words," Barry retorted.

"My words," Ham agreed. "And make no mistake, I do not fool myself thinking I'm in your mental class. I could not have attained any type of degree at Stanford, let alone a Master of Science degree in mathematics. But," Ham sighed, waving a finger to indicate he had yet to make his point, "I am much better at this game than you are or could ever hope to become. You're playing out of your domain and in mine now. If you're as clever as you think you are, you'll understand this. My guess is that you're not."

Again Barry's face flamed resentment, anger and, unexpectedly, some degree of understanding. Maybe his arrogance wasn't so all consuming as Ham had supposed.

"What is it you want?" Barry finally asked.

"I want you, Barry. I want your ass in the sling it belongs in."

Barry regarded him intently for several long seconds, and then burst into strained laughter. "Okay, I get it. You think I'm the music man killer?" He shook his head in disgust and added, "If so, you're even dumber than I surmised."

"No, Barry, I think you're too stupid to set up and pull off such a perfect scenario, this series of painstakingly well-planned crimes. Nope," he summed up, "you're just a one-off, routine, run of the mill murderer. And that's all you'll ever be."

"I should've killed you," he retorted. "I sure could have if I'd had a mind to."

"No, you couldn't even do that. Your attempt to run me over with your sister's car was an injudicious notion. You were good enough to keep my attention off the plate number, I'll give you that if it makes you feel better about yourself. But the foolishness of using your sister's car is beyond ridiculous. You were asking to be caught. Not to mention dragging your sister into it as well. Which it did, right?"

Barry abruptly stood and began to pace the small confines of the room, a task made more difficult by the necessity of dodging piles of trash. Waving his pistol threateningly toward Ham, he warned, "You leave Barbara out of this. She wasn't—" He stopped abruptly.

"I notice you have enough sense of self-preservation not to complete that statement," Ham replied softly, "but it's too late. You already admitted you know she's dead. You killed Beau Clarke. How did you get out there, is my question. I haven't heard that your car is there, yet you took your sister's car when you left. Which, by the way, again, was incomprehensibly reckless. It announced your presence there, and it proclaimed your return to your hovel. God, man," Ham sighed with exasperation, "were you trying to get caught?" A sudden thought, a realization, whacked Ham upside the head and whipped it back again. "Jeezus," he breathed, "that's exactly it, isn't it? You set yourself up to be caught."

Barry froze in mid-step, shoulders slumped. "I was trying to protect her," he whispered into the void.

"How would killing me protect her? Especially you using her car to do it? That just—Ham slapped his forehead in understanding. "She was involved in the music scale murders, wasn't she?" Barry nodded, sadness coloring his face and Ham continued, "So you thought by drawing suspicion on yourself, with, I'm guessing, unshakeable alibis for the actual crimes, you'd stymie the investigation and keep Barbara out of the sphere of allegation. They'd spend so much time on you they'd never think to look at your sister." Ham nodded, understanding the reason, if not the act. "You may as well tell me the rest."

Barry returned to the dirty and worn couch, took a seat and held his weapon in place. Looking at the floor rather than Ham, he admitted, "Bodie Briggs put all this together. I mean, people have always told me I'm brilliant, but, man, Bodie, he's the real deal."

"How was Barbara involved?"

"I'm not going to discuss that."

"How were you involved?"

"I wasn't entirely. More on the sidelines. I was a background player."

"About the murders?" a skeptical Ham challenged.

Barry turned mournful eyes on Ham as he admitted, "I didn't do the murders but I knew about them. We all did, and we were all running a little scared. I mean, it was all so close to home, you know?" He sank down further into the sofa. "The idea of it nearly killed me. I wished it had killed me. Instead," he added, tears touching the corner of his eyes, "it ended up killing Barbara."

"Let me guess," Ham tried. "You murdered her killer."

"Beau killed Barbara," he admitted. "I killed Beau." With a snarl of rage, he added, "She was my sister. What would you have done if you were in my place?"

"You tortured him," Ham accused.

"You damn right I did. The son of a bitch had it coming. Barbara was no angel but she treated people well, at least for the most part. She treated Beau well, for God's sake. And she was my sister. The bastard took my sister away from me. He paid for that. Simple and done." Raising the weapon, staring Ham in the eyes, he announced, "You know I can't let you go. They'd send me to prison, even though the bastard had it coming, deserved it. I'm not going to face that. I can't."

"You know you can't stop me," Ham replied softly, danger coloring his voice. "Barry, you tortured a man. You're one badass killer. But I make you look like a whimpering sissy. So go ahead and try me if you wish. But don't expect to walk away."

Barry turned sad eyes on Ham, eyes in which Ham read resignation. His voice gentle, his hand steady, he raised his weapon. "I don't expect to," he replied.

Barry pointed his weapon at Ham's chest. As Ham raised his own gun to fighting stance, Barry abruptly turned the pistol sideways and jammed it against his head. He smiled once at Ham.

And blew his brains all over the wall.

WHEN THE MUSIC FADES

CHAPTER SEVENTEEN

TOEING THE LINE

Ham walked outside, leaving the gruesome evidence of Barry's guilt behind. He punched Drew's number and got her on the line after one ring. "Yeah, what's up?" she asked breathlessly. "Are you okay?"

"Yeah, fine," he said, sorrow tinging the words. "It's Barry. He killed Beau Clarke after Clarke killed Barbara. Barry was part of a cabal running the music scale murders. Barbara, too, I'm guessing."

Silence met him from the other end until Drew asked, "Cabal? How many are there? And who else?"

"That," Ham assured her, "we will know before this day is done. Unless somebody offs Bodie Briggs first. He's the key to everything."

"Is that a fact," Drew replied, pure delight in her voice.

Ham understood her far too well to bite. The delight arose from inside knowledge. And she would use it to pay him back for his enigmatic rush to Barry's place. He waited, knowing it would irritate, and he grinned when she exploded, "Well? Don't you want me to tell you?"

"Of course I do. Whenever you're ready."

She sighed her disappointment. "The police disagree with you, Ham. They believe Beau Clarke might have been the one behind the murders. He's—wait, hang on, there's a call from Steve."

Ham lingered on hold, expecting to hear of a new find, perhaps at Beau's place. What he was not prepared for was her breathless explanation. "Security tape shows Ronny leaving Barbara's house shortly before they found Beau's body. They put a warrant out on him."

"Shit. Okay. Look, when are you going to finish up over there? We need to get to Bodie before the cops do. He's Ronny's out, if I'm reading this right."

"Where are you? I'll come pick you up."

Ham shook his head, a futile gesture over the phone. "No, I've got Russ' jeep, remember? Let's meet at Bodie's address, the flophouse apartment he claims as his office. First one there hangs back. And look for his car. It wasn't at Barbara's, was it?"

"Not when the cops arrived, no."

"But he had been there at some point," Ham reminded. "So was Ronny. Maybe we should share with them what he told us at the station."

"I'll tell Val on my way out. She's still here processing. So is Pete, if you want to say hello."

"Oh, I'll say hello, alright. I'll hello him to death. But that will have to wait. Business before fun."

"Right, give me five minutes to talk to Val and I'll be on my way." She hung up without further word and Ham holstered his phone before entering the car.

He brought the Jeep to life and slowly drove away before he thought to inform Drew, Steve, Val, or anybody else about Barry. He pulled to the side of the road and punched up Drew's number again. "Listen," he said when she answered, "are you with Val? Good. Here's another bit. Tell her Barry put a bullet through his head a few minutes ago, right after he admitted he killed Beau. Who he says killed his sister, Barbara." With that, he clicked off in order to return to his immediate task. Further explanation would have to wait.

He arrived at the apartment that housed Bodie's office and smiled grimly when he spotted the guy's distinct car in the lot. Ham parked further down, a bit out of sight but close enough to watch the auto in case his target chose to run.

Only minutes later, Drew arrived and parked in a space a few down from his own. She nodded as she approached the Jeep and continued her march toward the entrance. Ham ran up alongside her just before she reached the doorway and grabbed her arm, forcing her to halt. "Remember the attendant, the guy who watches the comings and goings and insists visitors sign in? He's a bit of a gossip." At her impatient expression, he hurried his point. "Let me talk to him on our behalf. I don't want him to warn Bodie we're on our way up."

They entered and let their eyes adjust from the blinding afternoon sun to the dim and dank interior. Once acclimated, Ham went over to the manager behind his welcome desk, staring curiously at the both of them.

This time the man was not sporting his name tag, which forced Ham to search his memory. When it hit, he mentally snapped his fingers and nodded a gracious hello to the host. "Hello, Mr. Costa. Remember me?"

"Of course, yes. Good to see you again."

"Remember my partner, Drew Thornton? We're here to see Bodie Briggs. I noticed his car is outside."

"He's in," Costa agreed, "been here for the past few hours, I'd say. I'll announce you if you'd like."

Ham shook his head in firm denial. "That is precisely what I do not wish you to do," he informed the greeter.

Costa eyed him suspiciously and slowly declared, "I could get fired for that. Sorry, no way."

"Ever hear of Russ Porter?" Drew interjected.

The man's eyes flew wide and he nodded eagerly. "Truckee River. Sure. Why?"

"How would you like to come over to his beach house, meet him, have a little dinner, a couple of drinks, maybe even take a dip in the pool?"

Costa's eyes grew to even larger, impossibly sized saucers. Ham reached out to steady him, afraid the older man would faint.

"You can arrange that? How do I know you really can? I've always heard he's a recluse."

"Because," Drew preened, "he's my boyfriend. And if he wants to get any more, he'll grant me this small request."

Costa turned inquiring eyes on Ham, who nodded. "Okay, then," he shrugged, "I'll let you pass unannounced. If I get caught, you'll back me up that I didn't see you?"

"Of course. You must have been in the bathroom. No surveillance tapes, I take it."

The manager shook his head. "Does it look like the kind of place that would spend money on technology?" he said as he scribbled down his name and number on a card for Drew. "Call me when you set it up. In the meantime, remember, keep me out of this."

They rode the shaky elevator to Bodie's floor, found his apartment and knocked, not hard, not soft, just routine business. Within seconds Bodie threw the door wide and exclaimed, "It's about time. I was getting worried. Where have you—He stopped abruptly, his eyes narrowed, and he announced, "I'm not taking new clients at this time. My calendar is full."

"It's about to get a damn sight fuller," Drew snapped as she barged her way in and past a startled Bodie.

Ham gently pushed Briggs back into his office apartment and closed the door behind him.

Briggs glared back and forth between the two and with clenched jaw demanded, "What the hell is this? I know who you are; my client Barbara Bessler told me about you two clowns. What are you doing here? You'd best be careful. I'm an attorney at law. I'll sue your asses off, including your pretty butt, little lady."

"Oh, Bodie," Drew sighed. "You can't win cases when you're sitting on death row. It's hard to get a jury to care."

Bodie studied them for several long seconds before shrugging his shoulders. He ushered his uninvited guests to two chairs placed before his desk and waved them to sit. "Well, tell me what's on your mind. But do make it quick," he said as he pointedly studied his watch. "I have another appointment and he's overdue."

"He's not coming, Bodie," Ham replied.

Briggs blinked and waited. When Ham offered no further comment, Bodie sat back and attempted nonchalance. "I'm sure I don't know what you're talking about. But it's your dime, so go right ahead."

"Barry—or Larry, if you prefer—is permanently delayed. In fact, he's dead."

"So is Beau Clarke, and so is Barbara Bessler. But then, I expect you already knew about those two," Drew said accusingly.

Bodie stood to his full six-and-a-half-foot height and pointed at the door. "Get out. Now, before I call the police here to eject and arrest you for trespassing."

"Great," Ham agreed mildly. "By all means, call the police. We're patient, and these chairs are not so uncomfortable that we'll mind waiting for them."

"Fine," Briggs snarled. "You stay. I'll leave." As he rounded the desk his face collided with Ham's well placed fist, followed by a blow from Drew's palm precisely to his solar plexus.

"I don't think so," Ham declared, while Drew ordered, "Sit your ass back down in that chair and don't move until you have my permission."

First he had to pick himself up off the floor, where he was doubled over, half squatting, half sitting. From the looks of it, the struggle to rise might take the better part of the afternoon, so Ham reached down, grabbed the man under both arms and dragged him back to his chair. "Like she said, sit."

Bodie struggled for breath for several wheezing minutes before he regained control and, though still in raspy voice, said, "As you correctly surmised—though how, I don't know, unless from Frank Costa, that gossipy old fart—I am in fact expecting Barry. It's on a confidential matter, so don't ask. But why do you say Barry is dead? Do you know something I don't?"

"It's pretty much the other way around," Drew informed him. "Hence, our visit. It's true that we have no police power, neither here nor in Nevada, but you should understand," she announced, tone firm and fierce, "we don't particularly give a damn. If we want to take you down, we'll just up and do it. Got it?"

"Barry and I had a nice conversation before he put a bullet through his head." At Bodie's shocked expression, Ham nodded. "Yep, shot himself. Died instantly, he did. But like I said, not before we had a far-ranging and friendly chat.

Okay," he amended, "maybe not so friendly, but you catch the gist, don't you?"

Still rubbing his chest, Bodie semi-whispered, "What do expect me to do? Confess all my darkest secrets? Why would I do that?"

"Because," Drew snapped, "I will personally beat the crap out of you if you don't."

Ham chuckled, with amusement and for emphasis. "Don't think for a second she won't, or can't. Hell, it won't be me who tries to get you to talk; I don't have to. She's a lot meaner that I am and a big sight more lethal."

Bodie's eyes narrowed, whether in anger or contemplation, Ham didn't know. That is, until he spoke up with a harsh, "I want an attorney. Which means, Mister Smart Ass, anything I say now cannot—repeat cannot—be used in a court of law. So what's the point?"

"I don't care about that," Ham shrugged. "I just want to understand the why. And all the whos."

Though he continued to rub the pained area, Bodie's voice relaxed to normal. "If you talked to Barry, like you claim, why ask me? Didn't you say he gave you information?"

"That he did," Ham confirmed. "He gave you up. Pointed to you as the brains behind the music scale murders."

Bodie grinned savagely. "Did he now? How very interesting. I wonder why he would say something like that."

Without acknowledging the question, Ham continued. "What he didn't understand was why you had Barbara killed. Weren't you aware Barry would turn on you for that?"

Bodie shrugged it off. "My, my. What curious things you two discussed. I would have loved to have been a fly on the wall. Or a hornet with a hyperactive stinger." He smiled, smug and superior. "Yes, I quite like that image."

Drew jumped up, strode to Bodie's side, grabbed a handful of hair and pulled his head back, forcing his eyes to hers. "You get one more, hear me? Your act is tiresome. And so are you. Now answer the man's questions or you and I are going to go a couple of rounds." With that, she slammed his forehead into the hard wood of his desk.

When Bodie looked up, Ham read a mixture of fear, anger and cunning emerge in his eyes. He pulled a handkerchief from a drawer and dabbed at his forehead. Since there was no blood, Ham figured it for a stalling tactic. If so, it lasted only a short time before Bodie returned the cloth to the drawer and nodded gravely. "Fine, we'll play it as you wish. Remember nothing can be used against me. First off, I've requested a lawyer. Second, this is under threat of torture. Any judge, in any court in this country, would throw out any testimony so gained and cite you for contempt in the process."

"Been there, done that," Ham mumbled. "Let's start over. What was your thinking in all this? Why the music scale, in particular."

Bodie sighed and in a voice only slightly above inaudible began to explain. "Ronny hired me to take down Russ Porter."

Drew's head snapped up and a gasp escaped her lips. "That bastard," she snarled. "Is that why you sent the assassins to Russ' house? Who were they? I'd like to have a chat with them."

Briggs laughed, shaking his head at her lesser intellect. "Beau and Barry. And they weren't there as assassins. It was just intended to scare Porter and give the cops something else to think about. And of course," he shrugged, "we had it nicely pinned on Ronny. As was the break-in at the studio. It was going to cost him."

"God," Drew exploded, "is this for real? Are you for real?"

"Yeah, it's for real and so am I," Bodie assured her. "It's not something I'm making up or using for cover. It's plain fact. Porter turned Ronny down years ago on a project Ronny wanted to do for him, and it cost Ronny millions in lost support. The way he viewed it, Porter's backing would have punched his ticket to the dance. He even convinced me to invest everything I had, all my inheritance, with the promise of a fifty-fifty partnership."

Bodie rose and helped himself to a beer from the fridge. "Anybody?" he asked, holding the can aloft. When he got no takers, he returned to his seat, popped the top and took a long hit from the can. Satisfied, he continued, "He assured me, he had me convinced, that Porter was in. He even showed me a letter from him stating so. The letter, I found out later, was a forgery."

"How could you let yourself get suckered in by a scam?" Ham wondered. "Barry told me you're even more intelligent than he. If true, I'm thinking Barry must not have had much going on upstairs."

Bodie scowled, regret tingeing his voice. "Not at all true, but I do see your point. But I was star struck. Star struck and greedy. I thought I'd be on that big stage. Ronnie said I'd get to be the opening act for Porter's concerts." He spread his hands. "I was young, or at least younger. And not nearly so wise."

"Okay," Ham replied, "we get it. Ronny took you for everything you had. You wanted revenge. But *killing* people?"

Bodie sneered. "Ronny lost my money trying to set himself up as a player. But Porter turned him down, said he wouldn't work with a sleaze, and when word of that got out it cost Ronny his reputation and much of his livelihood. He's hated the air Porter breathes ever since. He's the one who wanted revenge, but he couldn't do it alone. He didn't have the balls or the brains."

He took another long swallow from the can, wiped a sleeve across his lips and added, "You remember the old saw that revenge is a dish best served cold. Well, I served mine on ice. I played Ronny over the years, made him believe I agreed it was all Russ' fault. So when the time came, he turned to me. And I used his greed against him."

"What was his intent?" Drew demanded. "Did he want Russ killed?"

Bodie laughed bitterly. "No, no, nothing like that. He wanted Porter set up, framed. Ronny planned to provide an alibi proving Porter's innocence in return for money, access and managing power."

"Is that why his canoe was placed with the body in the harbor?" Ham inquired.

Bodie nodded, drank and continued "When he came to me, I agreed to help. Only I did it my way, which included taking down Ronny's stable and his income. The stupid bastard was convinced I'd let bygones be bygones if he paid me a paltry sum as recompense for screwing me out of a five million dollar investment. It was everything I had, and I've spent my life trying to recoup what I lost to that son of a bitch. Which is why," he sighed as he swung his arms, "I'm stuck in this shithole. I tell everybody it's my office, but it's also where I'm forced to live."

"What was the point of doing the music scale?" Ham probed. "Why the names, why etch the initials on their cheeks, and, most especially, why people with their best songs in C minor?"

Bodie shook his head, a look of disgust on his face. "Are you really that thick, then? Come on, man, think," he urged. "It was a *game*. I was *toying* with Ronny, and there was not thing one he could do about it. I was depriving him of his source of income the way we deprived me of mine. Check and mate, pecker."

"Why didn't you just get yourself a good law practice? You could have made millions from that," Drew pointed out, repulsed by the man's callousness.

Bodie's laugh was mocking. "Screw that! I never wanted to practice law. I never wanted to be a lawyer. It's boring. Anybody can do it. I only got the degree because there was nothing else to do. I took and passed the bar just for the hell of it. But now," he added bitterly, "it's my income and my agony."

"So because you're bored and lazy you plot revenge that gets innocent people killed? That's pretty sick. But why did Barry join you in this criminal scheme? I don't get it."

Bodie's grin was casual as he replied, "You are so far off. No surprise there; you don't need any brain cells to be a cop. Beau was Barry's first and only homicide."

"But why didn't Ronny just tell the police that it was you?" Drew challenged. "It would have gotten him off the hook."

"Are you kidding me? God, you're as slow as your partner," Bodie sneered. "I have him on tape telling me about his plan to hit Russ Porter up in exchange for proving the guy's innocence. The figure twenty-million came up, also on tape." He held up a finger to forestall comment, "I know what you're going to say. That extortion is better than a murder charge. Except," he grinned, "Ronny, once he knew the score, became an accessory after the fact. On all counts. He couldn't turn me in without taking himself down with me. I had him roped, tied and hung."

"I assume you intended to extort Ronny in turn?"

Bodie smirked. "It was almost too easy. Damon's a simpleton."

"What was Beau's part, then?"

"He was my gofer," he told Ham. "It was he, for instance, who broke into the studio, which you interrupted."

"What was the purpose?"

"We were looking to uncover any unreleased product Porter might have stored. We intended to stash it in Ronny's office and help the cops via a tip about the theft. One way or another, Ronnie was going down."

"What about Barry?" Drew inquired. "How was he involved?"

"Huh!" Bodie snorted. "Barry was the group pacifist. He wanted no details and no foreknowledge. He watched Ronny for us, followed you guys, and agreed to throw the fear of God into you in that alley. Beyond that, not a lot of action on his part."

"And Barbara?"

"She was an unintended consequence. After Amber Bailey, Barry was overcome by remorse." Bodie shook his head, regret in his eyes. "That was my biggest mistake, my only one, really. I should never have gotten Barry involved. The man was just too soft. There was no steel in there at all."

He stared off, lost in his own world, for several long seconds before he shook his head, as though shaking away the regret. "Anyway, he confessed to his sister who, not surprisingly, pretty much flipped out. She ran over here and confronted me with a threat. If I didn't put an immediate end to this—to everything, including bringing Ronny down— she'd personally go to the cops and lay it out for them, even if it meant taking down her brother."

"Let me guess. You told Beau."

"I told Beau," Bodie agreed. "He did the predictable thing, and Barry did the same."

"So you get rid of Barbara and Beau, and you come out of this with your skirts clean, is that it?" Bodie's only response was to spread his hands in acknowledgement, looking as though he awaited due applause.

A disgusted Ham plunged ahead. "Except for one thing: you, personally, murdered those people."

"Oh, that's such an ugly word. Let's just say I helped them see the light."

Ham just stood, rooted to the spot, shaking his head in bewilderment. "You are the most heartless monster I have ever run across."

Bodie's cackle offered no apology. "You don't get it, man. But I'm not surprised. Look, here's the deal. The music fades, the singer dies. That's the way it goes." He smirked at Ham's glare and turned it back on him. "I am a genius, pure, simple and certified, IQ off the charts. My brain is not wired like the ordinary witless people that populate the earth. Rules don't apply to those few of us who are supermen, the best and brightest, like they do to the rest of you."

Ham shook his head, less in negation than sorrow. "Do you ever listen to yourself, Bodie? You're just parroting an interpretation of Nietzsche. There's nothing original here, it's been done before. To wit, Leopold and Loeb: Chicago, 1924. IQs also off the charts, higher than those of us who are mere mortals can possibly comprehend, just like you said. To prove their interpretation of Nietzsche's superman and the lack of moral or legal boundaries for them and their ilk, they killed a boy as a demonstration of how such people as themselves—what few there were—could easily pull off the perfect crime. I'm assuming that there's no need to explain that, since I'm citing their case as a prime example, it didn't work out the way they intended. They each got life plus ninety-nine years. And guess what? You're next."

The killer looked momentarily wary, but pressed on. "I came up with a beautiful and complicated plan, and yes, diabolical, I'll give you that. But that sometimes is a necessary component, the means to an end."

"You think the ends justify the means?" Drew snapped. "Even Malcolm X disowned that philosophy."

Ham rolled his eyes. "And again with the Nietzsche fetish," he taunted.

Bodie looked genuinely disappointed. He sighed deeply and said, softly, almost pityingly, "Machiavelli. Open a book, why don't you."

"Whatever, Your Assholiness."

"I don't expect you to follow any of what I'm saying. The ends do indeed justify the means when people on my plane are societal controllers."

"Again, whatever, Your Tedious Jackoffness," an irritated and fed up Ham snapped. "You, Beau, Barry and Barbara formed a cabal to bring down Ronny, and in the process of multiple murder, you did just that. Happy now?"

Sounding totally unconcerned and unashamed, he agreed as though they were discussing the latest twist in El Nino. "Yeah. Me. Beau. Barry. Barbara, though later. Ronny, though unwittingly and as a stooge. No one else. Didn't need anyone else. I did it all myself."

Ham felt a sudden rage driven need to reach over and slap the idiocy out of the genius. Would have, if Drew hadn't interrupted.

"Barbara unceremoniously tossed us from her house when she learned Ronny was not the dead man in the ocean, and the reason was because she had work to do to cover Barry's ass. Is that it?" she guessed.

"That right," Bodie replied. "Though I don't know what she intended to do with or to you." As he finished his statement he casually reached into the drawer, muttering as he did. "Didn't I put that handkerchief in here? It's got to be somewhere."

He had barely finished the sentence when a roar shattered the stillness of the undersized room: a boom from Drew's weapon, an expelled bullet that missed Bodie's nose by a few centimeters and flew on into the wall behind. "Don't move a muscle," she ordered as she pulled the drawer wide and extracted the pistol Bodie had hidden there.

She glanced at Ham, who nodded. Standing up, he yanked out his cell, but before he dialed, his glance shifted to Bodie. "If he moves," he intoned for the man's benefit, "shoot off a toe. That should discourage him from stirring again."

He punched the number and gained connection with Steve, and was explaining the situation when he heard gunshot followed by an agonized scream. Without turning around, he shouted over his shoulder, "Nine left, Bodie. I wouldn't try it again." Into the phone, Ham instructed, "Steve, you might want to bring medics with you. Bodie's had an accident."

Less than ten minutes elapsed before sirens screamed to a halt in front of the building. Almost as soon as they faded into silence, the door swung open and two EMTs burst through, with Steve on their heels.

He said nothing before he moved over to examine the medics' work but when he did, he turned inquiring eyes upon Drew and Ham. "He went for my gun," Drew informed him. "In the struggle, he pulled the trigger and hit himself in the foot. Looks like he blew off a toe."

"That's not what happened," Bodie screamed, voice angry and pained. "She shot me. The bitch shot me!"

Steve looked to Ham. "Well?"

"I saw what Drew saw."

"Liar," Bodie screeched. "Liar, liar, liar!"

"Good enough," Steve agreed. "My report will state that the suspect shot himself trying to steal your weapon."

"Incompetent idiot," Drew snarled. "Three shots on a dime in his victims, and now he can't even manage to miss his own ass."

"Did you get Ronny?"

"Pete's gone to pick him up," the detective told her. "Hopefully—" His cell phone's ring interrupted and when he answered he turned his back to them and spoke softly. Finally, he stored the phone and turned to face them.

"Pete got him. He was speeding out of his residence when Pete pulled in. He gave chase and caught up to him on the outskirts of Los Gatos, were Ronny took a curve at high speed and the predictable occurred. Pete's taking him to the hospital, says Ronny's not badly hurt and can be questioned unless the doctors claim otherwise. He's going to sit by Ronny's side during the examination to make damn sure Damon doesn't get cute and somehow convince the doctors he should be released."

"Good enough," Ham nodded. "Can we interview him?" At Steve's nod, Ham said, "This time I don't care if you record it.'

When the EMTs hastened their charge from the room, Ham, Drew and Steve hurried behind. With sirens blaring and lights flashing, they wove through traffic for the seven-mile ride to their destination. With no lights or sirens of their own, Drew held back, navigating with care lest they become victims of their haste. By time they arrived, the sirens and lights were done and gone, and when they reached the room where Ronny was being held, they found Pete by his side. His handcuffed side.

"Well, well," Pete greeted, showing them a friendly face for the first time, "our heroes. What would we town cops do without big city pee-eyes to bail us out?" Though the words sounded harsh, his wide grin seemed genuine.

Not that Ham would let that deter him from his revenge. But that was for later, he reminded himself, just as he reminded himself of Bodie's serving up revenge on ice.

He smiled at the shorter detective and offered his hand. "Glad to pinch hit, Pete. But you're the starter. Where's Steve?"

"He's with Bodie." Pete actually giggled. "I hear he shot himself. What a darn shame. Poor guy." Pete eyed Ham curiously. "By the way, Steve wanted me to pass on a message. What you guys talked about in Porter's room? He says never mind, all is well. What's that supposed to mean?"

"He didn't say?" Pete shook his head and Ham added, "Nothing, really. Take him out for a drink, get him to open up. It's all good."

"We want a few words with Ronny," Drew informed him, "if that's okay with you."

Pete nodded toward the bed. "Be my guest. I'll wait outside."

"Good lord," Drew whispered. "What's got into him, I wonder."

"I don't know," Ham replied, equally softly. "Maybe there is a decent bone somewhere in that body. Maybe he's actually grateful."

"And maybe he just wants to be on the winning side."

Ham's sigh acknowledged the point. Turning to face Ronny, he inquired, "Looks like your career is off its rails, doesn't it?"

"You've got to help me," Ronny pleaded. "I'm in a real jam here, one not of my making, either. It's all Bodie. I assure you, he's the one."

"You told us at the station that your primary purpose in hiring us was because you found out Russ and Drew were involved with each other, and that was a great way to get to Russ. Well, now we know why you wanted us, don't we? You figured a fee of $240,000 was dirt cheap compared to the twenty million you intended to collect from Russ."

"You've got to help me," a desperate Ronny begged. "I'm your client, you have a duty to me. And I've got confidentiality so you can't repeat anything you know. Look," he offered, "I'll throw in an additional hundred thousand dollars."

Ham sighed, like a father disappointed with his wayward ward. "Ronny, you just don't get it, do you? Gary is our client, not you. He hired us to investigate the case, not to protect you per se. His main interest, I believe, was to serve Russ' interests, and in that I judge that Drew and I functioned very, very well. As for you personally, our duty to you has been discharged. Originally, you hired us to find out who the murderer is when the planted evidence pointed to you. We did that, so in that sense we succeeded. If your claim now is that what you really meant was you wanted us to protect you from murder charges, well, let's just say we failed and let it go at that."

"This is a waste of time," Drew announced. "Can I shoot him?"

Ronny's eyes grew wide with horror as Ham thoughtfully rubbed his chin, considering Drew's request as if it were a serious one, not the dry joke he knew it for. "I don't know," he finally replied. "Let me ask Pete." Poking his head out the door he waved Pete over and into the room. He pointed at

Ronny and explained, "Drew wants to know, can she shoot him? Personally, I think it's a fine idea."

"Hmm," he sighed as he, too, rubbed a thoughtful chin. "You know, if you pulled your gun to, say, inspect it, he might lunge for it and accidentally blow off a toe. It's been known to happen." He pulled on his lip, apparently still considering. Finally, his mind made up, he nodded. "What the hell, let's try it and see."

CHAPTER EIGHTEEN

AND SO IT BEGINS

Ham glanced at the boy in the passenger seat, riding silently but nervously beside him. Not yet a full day since they'd returned to Tahoe from Santa Cruz, and here he was, a boy who now looked every bit the young man. An inch taller than his dad, with black curly hair Ham could only wish for, and a build that Ham hadn't known since his own teen years, the lad could have whipped the old man, both physically and in the dapper department. Smiling to himself, Ham vowed to keep on the kid's good side in order to avoid the humiliation of age getting thrashed by youth.

Whether the boy's nervousness was a reflection of the imminent meeting with a Rock God or due to his proximity to a long estranged father, Ham couldn't know. He suspected a combination of both.

The boy broke the silence with an intake of breath and a louder expulsion. "I can't believe you know Russ Porter. Mom is wrong about you."

Don't ask.

"I can match that, Dylan. I can't believe you even know who Russ Porter is," Ham laughed. "He's old enough to be your grandfather."

"Oh, come on, Dad. I know everything about Truckee River. I've watched all the tracks on You Tube, Googled a lot about them, even read the bio books! Heck, everybody my age knows every song ever written and recorded by those guys," the boy assured him. "They're so retro they're the new cool."

"All right," Ham smiled. "Whatever that means. Does it also mean your old man's cool?"

The boy laughed, and the sound, while joyous, triggered pangs of memory. His son's chuckle was a perfect imitation of Blake Garrett.

"I guess it does, doesn't it?" Dylan's chest puffed with pride as he added breathlessly, "Just wait 'til I tell the guys."

I should have met somebody famous a lot sooner. Russ was absolutely right. It was hard advice to follow, but it was the best thing I ever could have done. An easy and brilliant way to connect with my son. Thank you, Russ. Thank you.

"How was your flight here to Reno?"

"Oh my gosh," the boy gushed. "I am so stoked I can't wait to get home and put this up on social media. I took a bunch of pictures. Have you ever flown on his plane?"

Ham nodded, added casually, knowing he was about to score a few more goals, "A couple of times."

"I just can't believe I got to do that. God, I ate everything on the plane, I think. Did you talk him into sending it for me?"

"No," Ham laughed. "I wouldn't be that presumptuous. He offered. It was his idea."

"How long will it take us to drive to his house at Tahoe?"

"About an hour, a little more."

Ham glanced over, saw his son's eyes imitating saucers. "Nobody will believe this. *I* don't believe this." He all but jumped up and down in his seat, heedless of the constraints of the seatbelt. "You must be really, really good friends."

"You remember Drew?"

Dylan's voice rang with confusion, as he admitted, "Barely. Why do you ask?"

"Well, in addition to being my partner in the business and my closest friend, she's also Russ Porter's sweetheart."

The boy turned burning eyes upon his dad. He shook his head sadly as he admitted, "I don't know anything about the real you, do I? Only the stuff Mom's told me."

Don't ask!

"She was pissed, you know, about my coming."

Oh, crap, here we go.

"Was she?"

"She says you're trying to buy me."

Like Russ says, the price is cheap.

"I'm trying to be your dad. Is that okay?"

"Dad, it is for me. I'm just telling you all this because I want to get to know you. I want to be your son."

Ham turned tender eyes to the boy and patted his shoulder. "You will always be my son. We'll consider this a new beginning. I'm not going to let you avoid me for any amount of time ever again," he promised.

With a wide grin, Dylan responded, "Don't want to."

They pulled into Russ' palatial Tahoe home, only to be greeted by an outsized sign, in large red letters: BEWARE OF TEENY TINY LITTLE FRIENDLY TAIL-WAGGING DOG.

Ham blushed the color of a ruby as he attempted to avoid his son's eyes as the boy asked, "What does that mean?"

He inhaled deeply, a calming breath to keep from snapping his reply. "You'll have to ask Drew," he said evasively. "That would be her handiwork." *Maybe he'll forget.*

They pulled to the side parking area and Ham grabbed his son's luggage. "Let's go meet The Great One," he said.

Charlie threw the door wide just as they approached and, in true Charlie fashion, swept the boy up in a bear hug. She actually managed to shift him upwards a couple of inches so that he stood on tiptoe. "Dylan, my name is Charlie. I have been so looking forward to meeting you! Welcome to Uncle Russ' home. Soon to be Drew's too, I'm guessing."

Before Drew could respond, Charlie turned to Ham and enthused, "He's beautiful. "My god, Hamster, how come you don't look like that?"

Dylan blushed furiously, but his smile was genuine. Apparently inheriting his father's instincts, he inquired, "Are you Dad's girlfriend?"

Charlie's laughter was light and merry. "I suppose that's a question you should address to your dad."

He turned inquiring brows to Ham, who simply grinned foolishly. "Wow," Dylan uttered to nobody in particular. "She's drop dead."

The unspoken part Ham got: the "How'd you ever get her?" part.

More Mom defamation? Don't ask.

Drew stepped forward and offered up a hug. "Hey, Dylan. It's wonderful to see you again. It's been, what, ten years?"

"You must be Drew," the lad replied. "Dad's partner." At her nod, he nodded satisfaction. "The memories are dim but they're there."

And then he fell silent, a stunned, disoriented stillness. For there, emerging from the doorway was the superstar he'd loved and revered since his interest in music got tweaked by the girls at school, as he had explained to Ham on the phone when he'd accepted the invite.

Ham remembered his first introductions to Blake and Russ. Nothing had ever intimidated him as much as being in the presence of those two masters of the arts. Nor did he expect anything ever would again.

Charlie nudged Dylan with her elbow. "Close your mouth. He's just a man. Like your dad."

Dylan broke into laughter, sobered and corrected her. "My dad's not a world heavyweight. According to my mother he's just—"

"Okay," Ham harrumphed. "Obviously, this is Russ. Russ, this is my son, Dylan McCalister."

Dylan offered his hand, a hand that Russ refused. "A handshake won't do." Whereupon he reached out and enveloped the boy in a hug, finishing by tussling his hair. "You are indeed a better looking version of your dad. Welcome."

Dylan's eyes shone with wonder and delight as he stared at this legend in the flesh. "I can't believe you're a friend of my dad's."

Russ smiled gently and informed him, "Oh, it's much more than that. Your father is one of my closest confidants, my protector and my comrade. He's a good man, and you should be proud to claim him as your own." Turning to Ham, he asked, "I hate to take him away from you, but would you mind if I show him around?" Looking at Dylan, he said, "Maybe you'd like to see the studio and some of my memorabilia from the days?"

The boy, stars in his eyes, could only nod agreement to the star.

"Before you go, Russ, dear, I have to tell you something," Drew disclosed. "I used your name to get a favor we needed for the investigation. I'm afraid I put you on the hook."

Russ' good natured grin impressed Ham. This was a man, he thought, that truly allowed Drew to be herself. As much as he loved and admired the man, his esteem took an even greater leap as a result of the open affection for his partner. "What did you do?"

Drew's attempt to look contrite failed utterly in Ham's opinion. Still, she attempted an apologetic explanation. "I had to promise a guest greeter at an apartment house that you would have him over to your Santa Cruz house for drinks, also for dinner, and maybe a swim. I need to live up to my promise. So. When do you want him to come?"

Russ shrugged, suggesting it was no problem. "Why don't you ask him if he wants to come up here this weekend instead? I'll send the plane down to Santa Cruz to pick him up." He turned to Dylan, his eyes glinting with mischief. "What do you think? You think he'd like that?"

"Mr. Porter," the kid replied, "if he doesn't, he's a fool; and you shouldn't waste your time."

Russ' booming laughter echoed around the room. When he sobered, he clamped Dylan on the shoulder. "Dylan, you are a wise man. A chip off your dad's block. And by the way, call me Russ. We're all family here."

His son paled so rapidly Ham thought he might faint. A not abnormal reaction to Russ calling you his family, Ham recognized. He watched, face alight with pride, as Russ led his son from the room and on to an adventure few would ever experience.

As Drew called Costa's number to extend the invite, Ham's phone whined its insistent demand for attention. He answered on the first ring, since the caller ID read Danny Sanchez, his buddy at the California Highway Patrol. "Yeah, Danny, what you got?"

Ham listened intently for near a minute then burst into uncontrollable laughter. He struggled to control himself, fought harder to breathe and finally gave up and simply let himself guffaw. Barely able to talk, he mumbled, "Thanks, Danny. And I will pay my debt. Come on up this weekend. You can meet my son. Yeah, Dylan. He's here and taking the tour." He nodded uselessly into the phone and clicked off with a final, "Good enough, see you then."

"Oh, this is too good," he chuckled to Charlie and Drew. "Charlie, you remember Pete?" At her hard jaw and curt nod, he laughed again and continued. "Then you should enjoy this; and Drew, I'm damn sure you will as well." Wringing his hands with glee, he announced, "I got my revenge. And it was served on ice."

Charlie and Drew exchanged puzzled glances. "Alright, Hamster, I can see you're inordinately pleased," Charlie pointed out, "but what exactly does that mean?"

"It means I got him!" he exulted. "And by the way," he informed Drew, "I'm going to have to admit to Russ that, just like you did, I used his name to secure a favor, but it means I got Pete."

The quirk of Drew's mouth indicated that their using Russ may be getting out of hand, maybe a little too casual, so he rushed to assure her, "No, I won't make a habit of it."

"So what is, dearest?" Charlie prompted. "Your audience awaits."

"The point," Ham announced, "is that I won. Pete lost, I won. God, I love it. I won, I won, I won."

"Ham," Drew sighed, "if you will quit gloating and out with it?"

"Sorry," he chortled, "I can't help myself. But okay, here's the story. It seems Danny, my cop friend at the California Highway Patrol," he added for Charlie's benefit, "has a sergeant buddy in the CHP station near Santa Cruz. At Danny's behest, his buddy did a little background on the sly and he found out that Pete makes frequent stops at a particular bar in town." Ham stood with a beatific expression on his face, eyes dancing as he looked at his audience.

"Out with it, Ham, before your 'audience' deserts you," Drew threatened.

"She has a point," Charlie agreed.

He sighed, disappointment evident. He'd hoped for a bit more heightened anticipation. But what the hell, he thought, the story's the thing.

"Okay, well, Danny's friend managed to 'bump' into Pete one night at the bar. They introduced themselves and began to celebrate a new brother cop friendship. They imbibed a series of vodka shooters; only, unknown to Pete, Danny's buddy had arranged with the bartender in advance and via a one-hundred-dollar bill to put only water in his glass and vodka in Pete's. When they exited, the friend watched Pete stumble to his car and back out of the parking space he occupied. In doing so, Pete tapped the bumper of the car behind him and continued on. This made it technically a hit and run."

Their dawning grins revealed that they were now anticipating him and he nodded his delight. "That's right," he affirmed. "Danny's friend jumped in his unmarked, hit siren and lights and pulled Pete over. And here's where it gets good," he all but squealed as he vigorously rubbed his hands together in pure glee. "He arrested Pete, booked him and... are you ready for this? He had him strip searched." Over Drew's gales of laughter, he shouted, "And naturally he took pictures, copies of which he gave to Pete upon release."

Charlie, still chortling, nevertheless challenged him. "That's horrible. Won't this get Danny and his friend in trouble?"

"It would," Drew answered for him, "if Pete could stand the public humiliation caused by the pictures being released, with, of course, copies provided directly to Val."

"I see your point," Charlie smiled. "I just hate to see somebody lose their job over a practical and," staring directly at Ham, "childish prank."

"Won't work, Charlie," Ham grinned. "Nothing can shame me on this one. It's just too perfect."

Russ and Dylan approached and, apparently overhearing, Russ asked, "What's so perfect?"

Ham turned, saw his son and decided to move on to less inappropriate behavior. "Just cop stuff," he responded. To his son, he inquired, "You got the tour? Impressive, isn't it?"

"That's putting it mildly. I'm still trying to, like, take all this in."

Russ waved them all to the bar set up near the family room, where he poured wine for himself and Drew, soda for Charlie and Dylan, and a beer for Ham. "Here's to family," he toasted.

"Speaking of which," he added. "It's been a long day. We should finish this up and all of us get a good night's sleep. We want to be well rested, because we're going into Reno tomorrow where we can celebrate Dylan's arrival in style."

Ham smiled at the boy's popping eyes and pleased blush. It would be a day the kid would never forget, he knew, out partying with a member of Truckee River.

"And," Russ added, then hesitated a moment before continuing, "well, and then, as long as we're there we're going to have a wedding. Drew and I are getting married tomorrow at the chapel in the Ringers Casino Resort." Turning to Dylan, he placed a hand on the boy's shoulder. "I would be honored, young sir, if you would act as my best man."

Dylan raised astonished and inquiring eyebrows, both aimed at his dad. Ham, in return, responded with a proud grin and a thumbs up to indicate "Go for it."

"You'll act as my maid of honor?" Drew asked a beaming Charlie who, in turn, nodded delightedly as she enveloped Drew in a hug. "And you, Ham, will walk me down the aisle."

Ham beamed at his son and was rewarded with the stars shining in his eyes. "Welcome to your new world, Dylan. This is what it is."

"And the house is always open to you," Russ added. "Absolutely any and every time you please." Laughing at Ham, he added, "If that's okay with your dad."

As he beamed at his boy, he recognized the truth in Russ' words. Ham may in fact be buying his son. But at least he'd earned the favor by doing his best to help Russ out, and in the end it was okay. Buying his son was part of paying for his mistakes. A payment damn sure worth the cost, and a whole lot more. He had his boy back, and this time he'd never walk away. "As God is my witness," he whispered, "I will not need a third chance."

THE END

BRENT KROETCH

Brent Kroetch holds a doctorate in economics and is the author of numerous books and articles, both academic and fiction. He taught college courses, following which he served in government and private industry. He is a long time resident of Virginia, where he lives with his wife and dog, visited often by his married daughter and son and their wonderful soul mates.

Though now writing fiction only, specifically mysteries, he previously wrote and released music under the stage name of Brett Williams. He also wrote songs released by other artists, including Jessica Rogers, Red Hawk and Eric Kurtz, and is the recipient of two Telly Awards for music videos.

Due to his interest and experience in the music industry, Brent turned his attention to that field in his latest mystery.

When The Music Fades To Murder The Singer Must Die is one in a series that features private detective Ham McCalister and his "walking weapon in heels" partner, Ms. Drew Thornton.

bkroetch@aol.com

571-309-6838

If You Enjoyed This Book

Please write a review.

This is important to the author and helps to get

the word out to others

Visit

PENMORE PRESS

www.penmorepress.com

All Penmore Press books are available directly through our website, amazon.com, Barnes and Noble and Nook, Sony Reader, Apple iTunes, Kobo books and via leading bookshops across the United States, Canada, the UK, Australia and Europe.

ÆGIR'S CURSE

BY
LEAH DEVLIN

A thousand years ago, the Viking colony of Vinland was ravaged by a swift-moving plague ... a curse inflicted by the sea god Ægir. The last surviving Norseman set the encampment and his longboat ablaze to ensure that the disease would die with him and his brethren.

In present-day Norway, a distinguished professor is found murdered, his priceless map of Vinland missing. The ensuing investigation leads to the reclusive world of Lindsey Nolan, a scientist and recovering alcoholic who has been sober for five years. Lindsey reluctantly agrees to help the detective who's hunting the murderer, but she has a bigger problem on her hands: a mysterious disease that's spreading like wildfire through the population of Woods Hole. As she races against a rising body count to discover the source of the plague, disturbing events threaten her hard-won sobriety—and her life. Will Lindsey be the next victim of Ægir's curse?

Leah Devlin is rapidly establishing herself as a writer of modern day mystery-thrillers. This story is as tight as a piano wire. Life at a seaside town in New England is full of treacherous undercurrents and peril, as residents are threatened by a menace from a thousand years ago. Murder, romance and deceit are a potent mix in this gripping novel, which I didn't want to put down.—James Boschert, author of the Talon Series and *Force 12 in German Bight*

PENMORE PRESS
www.penmorepress.com

Force 12 in German Bight

by
James Boschert

Considering that oil and gas have been flowing from under the North Sea for the best part of half a century, it is perhaps surprising that more writers have not taken the uncompromising conditions that are experienced in this area – which extends from the north of Scotland to the coasts of Norway and Germany – for the setting of a novel. James Boschert's latest redresses the balance.

The book takes its title from the name of an area regularly referred to in the legendary BBC Shipping Forecast, one which experiences some of the worst weather conditions around the British Isles. It is a fast-paced story which smacks of authenticity in every line. A world of hard men, hard liquor, hard drugs and cold-blooded murder. The reality of the setting and the characters, ex-military men from both sides of the Atlantic, crooked wheeler-dealers, and Danish detectives, male and female, are all in on the action.

This is not story telling akin to a latter day Bulldog Drummond, nor a James Bond, but simply a snortingly good yarn which will jangle the nerve ends, fill your nose with the smell of salt and diesel oil, your ears with the deafening sound of machinery aboard a monster pipe-dredging ship and, above all, make you remember never to underestimate the power of the sea.

–Roger Paine, former Commander, Royal Navy .

PENMORE PRESS
www.penmorepress.com

No Accident
by
Robert Crouch

Kent Fisher is an environmental health officer with more baggage than an airport carousel. When he's summoned to the Tombstone Adventure Park to investigate what appears to be a fatal work accident, Kent quickly discovers that the details don't add up. What was Sydney Collins doing at the park so early in the morning? Why would he wear a shirt and tie while operating a tractor? And who removed the guard to the power takeoff shaft that killed him?

Despite his supervisor's insistence on closing the case, Kent's curiosity—fueled by his contentious history with the dead man's employer, wealthy playboy Miles Birchill- soon raises questions about the death and the complex deception behind it. But as Kent digs deeper, he sets his personal and professional lives on a collision course that could ultimately destroy the people closest to him. Sydney Collins had secrets, and someone in the village will do whatever it takes to keep them buried.

Set in the Sussex countryside, No Accident is the first book in Robert Crouch's Kent Fisher Mysteries series.

PENMORE PRESS
www.penmorepress.com

THE MAN IN THE SPIDER WEB COAT
BY
PHILIP ACKMAN

Titus Buchanan, a professor who runs a think tank at Williams College, believes he's figured out how to stage a successful revolution. When the United Nations adopts a historic vote spelling the end of colonialism, Buchanan seizes the opportunity to test his theory. His laboratory will be the Splendid Islands, a collection of palm-fringed cays scattered across three quarters of a million square miles of the South Pacific. Its inhabitants will be his lab rats.

But complications arise. The Splendids belong to New Zealand, and New Zealand has no intention of giving them up. The United States has its own secret "space age" agenda for the islands. The Queen of England is bound to support New Zealand, but she doesn't want Britain to fall out with the Americans, who favor independence. Meanwhile, the islanders, gripped with revolutionary fever, have ideas about self-rule. Reverend Geoffrey Brown, originally recruited by Buchanan to run the revolution, joins forces with an unlikely crew of locals and sets out to match wits with powerful opponents.

PENMORE PRESS
www.penmorepress.com

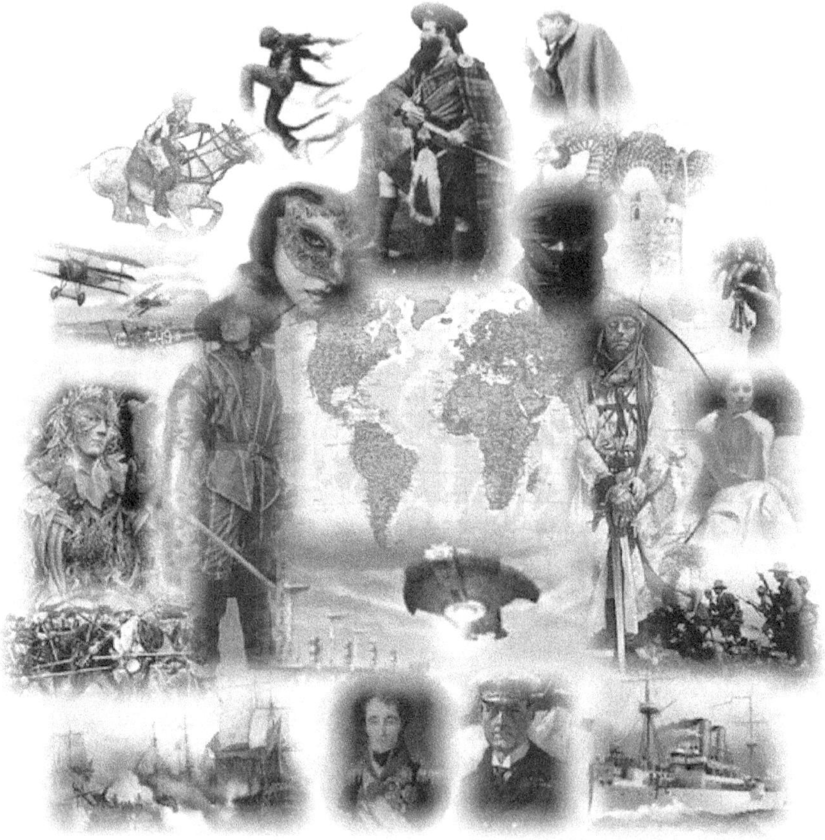

Penmore Press

Challenging, Intriguing, Adventurous, Historical and Imaginative

www.penmorepress.com